Fire Spells Between Friends

Fire Spells Between Friends

A Queer Historical
Romance

Fae & Human
Relations
Book 2

Sarah Wallace & S.O. Callahan

For those seeking magic, may this story serve as a gentle reminder to look within yourself.

CONTENTS

CONTENT WARNING

Breeze Spells and Bridegrooms is a cozy historical fantasy set in a queer normative world. As such, we hope our readers will find it a soft and light read.

But please note that this book will contain some on-page sex scenes and prejudice between human and fae communities.

CONTENT WARNING

Fire Spells Between Friends is a cozy historical fantasy set in a queernormative world. As such, we hope our readers will find it a soft and light read.

But please note that this book will contain some on-page sex scenes and prejudice between human and fae communities, as well as one Main Character experiencing some bigotry first-hand.

CHAPTER 1

EMRYS

UNDER NORMAL CIRCUMSTANCES, Emrys Wrenwhistle would not have been so heedless in his jaunt across town in the middle of a heavy, late-night storm. Rain was rarely enough to scare London's society back inside. Keen eyes were always watching a man of his status, even on an evening as dark and dreary as this. His younger brother Wyndham's wedding a few weeks prior would do him no favors on that front either, to be certain.

How will it look, his mother had tutted, *with both your brothers married and settled into their new lives before you've even given a hint of carrying on the family name?*

The eldest of the four Wrenwhistle siblings, Auberon, had been recently married as well, sparking what had quickly become their mother's singular focus: seeing all of her children thrust into matrimonial bliss.

It was society's expectation, of course, but Emrys' duty went beyond simply *carrying on the family name*. He was heir to all that the Wrenwhistle family worked for generations to build, entwining with human society and making a place for themselves in one of the largest cities in the world. The results of his Scurius Exam had proven him to be the most magically powerful, thus the one set to inherit, while his siblings were free to do as they wished.

After a quiet courtship, Auberon had narrowly finished reciting his vows before he'd swept his bride away to their new home in the countryside and the simple life awaiting them there.

Wyndham, on the contrary, had made a spectacle of himself. Not only had he used the project he'd been assigned by the Council for Fae & Human Magical Relations to flaunt his magic in a way Emrys rarely had the opportunity for, he'd gone and captivated the entire city by very publicly falling in love with his partner in the matter. For months, the only Wrenwhistle anyone cared to talk about was him, and there was seemingly no end in sight.

How was Emrys to maintain his position in the family when Wyndham had all but dedicated his life to outshining him? It was a rivalry born the day Emrys was named as heir, and he would sooner consume an entire bouquet of foxglove than see his youngest sibling win.

The sting of resentment burned its way up his throat as he turned onto a familiar street. Fortunately, the shops and businesses that lined both sides of the narrow alley sat dark and quiet, empty until morning. The same could not be said for the rooms above; several of the windows were dimly lit, though all of them had the curtains drawn, much to his relief.

With his focus aimed skyward, Emrys failed to notice himself walking dangerously close to the center of the street, which had become overrun with the sludge of horse waste and mud thanks to the frightful weather. He charged directly into the standing water, splashing it up both legs of his trousers and soaking his stockings through.

He cursed under his breath, sidestepping away from the large puddle. There was no time for him to pause and inspect the damage to his clothes, even if he could've seen it in the low light. Emrys broke into a bounding stride with nothing left to lose in the situation.

When he reached the weathered door that he'd searched for countless times in the dark, he braced one hand against the frame and dug into the pocket of his greatcoat with the other. When he found it empty, he tried the other side. His brows furrowed as he tried the pockets of his trousers, his coat, and finally his breast pocket, all equally unfruitful.

"Damn it all," he hissed, reaching for the handle to test it.

Locked, of course.

Emrys cupped his hands around his face against the storefront window to his left. The glass was so clouded that it was impossible to see anything inside. Emrys stepped close to the door again, taking a quick glance over one shoulder, then the other. He gripped the doorknob and sighed heavily, closing his eyes. Why did it have to be iron?

After waiting for a flash of lightning to flicker across the sky, Emrys timed his next move with the rumble of thunder that masked the heel of his shoe crashing against the lock. Emrys stepped out of the rain into the musty room that always smelled of paper dust and ink. He took the time to hang up his hat and greatcoat before he shut the door as well as he could. He grimaced at the way the latch barely caught. He'd have to remedy that in the morning.

As he made his way to the set of rickety steps in the far corner, Emrys felt himself drawn back to the very first time he'd walked through the room nearly five years earlier. He'd been decidedly more intoxicated at the time. The memory lit up in his mind as he reached the staircase.

"YOU WOULDN'T REALLY," Keelan Cricket said, scandalized. Emrys gave his best friend one of his mischievous smirks and turned to look at the person leaning so far over the edge of a ladder that they were a gust of wind away from toppling over. At least, that was Emrys' estimation. He had bet his friends on being correct. A simple breeze spell ought to do the trick.

"Watch me," Emrys challenged with a flourish, striding boldly away from the group. They'd been stumbling from one public house to the next on a streak of revelry that would've sent his mother into an absolute fit if she'd known.

Emrys crossed his arms over his chest and sidled up next to the ladder.

"Whatever are you doing there, friend?" he asked, even though it was quite obvious what they were trying to accomplish.

"I'm trying to hang my sign."

Emrys tilted his head a bit and squinted at the handmade banner, not quite sure if it was the lettering or his vision that was blurry.

"Pimpernel-Smith Press," Emrys read slowly, before turning his attention back to the newcomer so he could inspect them more closely. They were slender, even a bit gangly, with a head full of wild, dark curls. "Are you the apprentice?"

"Owner," they responded plainly. This took Emrys by surprise.

"Aren't you a bit young to be the owner of…anything?" he asked.

"Aren't you a bit old to be making a loud, drunken fool of yourself in public?"

Emrys scoffed and prepared to offer a hateful reply, but his retort died on his tongue as the stranger turned on the ladder to give him the most dashing smile he'd ever seen.

They stared at each other for a moment, and then Pimpernel-Smith chuckled in a way that made Emrys shiver wantonly.

"If you're just going to stand there, the least you can do is help me."

Emrys felt compelled to oblige and held the sign up for Pimpernel-Smith to take after they had moved the ladder over. Emrys caught a glimpse of his friends who were still standing at the end of the alley, indicating that they'd appreciate him hurrying up with the original plan so they could get back to drinking. He offered them a rude gesture and turned his focus back to the stranger.

Pimpernel-Smith. Why did that sound so familiar?

After the sign was secure, it seemed Emrys had run out of good reasons to be there. He'd missed his opportunity to play his prank. He'd also somehow been charmed into offering his assistance on a task he would have never agreed to under normal circumstances. Who did they think they were, asking him to labor like a commoner?

But then, who was he to agree to it so easily? Just because they'd been bold and were markedly attractive, he was ready to help them without hesitation?

Maybe he'd had more to drink than he realized.

Pimpernel-Smith collected the ladder and gave Emrys a once-over, eyes lingering in all the right places as they trailed slowly back up from his boots. The coquettish grin on their mouth grew and Emrys felt himself lose all interest in rejoining his companions.

Desire must've been painted all over his face, because Pimpernel-Smith quirked an eyebrow, turned to the entryway of the new press shop, and maneuvered themself and the ladder inside, leaving the door wide open. Emrys had always been the type to ask forgiveness rather than permission, so he'd followed them inside and up to the room on the second floor.

EMRYS KEPT his hand away from the handrail to save himself from getting a splinter in his palm. He hopped up the steps two at a time, expertly avoiding the one near the middle that groaned like an old mule when stepped upon. At the top, he used his arm to brush aside the ragged curtain, a wash of candlelight spilling out to greet him. His focus landed on the figure hunched over in the chair near the small writing desk, one leg flung haphazardly over the armrest as they pressed quill pen to paper against their thigh. They didn't look up before they spoke.

"You broke the lock," Torquil said mildly.

"I've misplaced my key," Emrys explained as he stepped into the cramped space. Torquil finally lifted their head, offering a small, crooked grin.

"Again?" they asked as their attention fell back to the paper. Emrys noted that they looked as tired as he felt.

"Why are you still awake?" Emrys asked, changing the subject as he crossed his arms and propped his shoulder against the thick, knotted post that stood in the middle of the room. Without question, it was the sturdiest of all his surroundings. The desk, the half-empty wardrobe on the far wall, and the sorry excuse for a bed had all seen better days. Even the diminutive stove hardly served its purpose on cold nights.

Torquil sat up more fully then, setting their things on the desk before they stretched their arms high over their head until a soft groan escaped them. With a sigh, they let their arms fall to their lap. "Work."

"Ugh," Emrys sneered. "Such a waste of your time."

Torquil laughed quietly at that. They pulled their leg from over the armrest and slowly got to their feet. Emrys couldn't help but notice the way their shirt was untucked from their trousers and already unbuttoned halfway down their chest. "What do you suggest I do with my time instead?"

"Oh, I could name a great number of things," Emrys assured them, watching as they stepped closer with bare feet.

"Tell me one," Torquil teased, closing the distance between them. They reached up to slide their ink-stained fingertips along the stubble on Emrys' jaw. "Perhaps I'll give you a shave? I daresay you need it."

He'd only arrived home from his family's extended post-wedding stay at the country estate a few hours earlier. There had been no time to take care of such things.

Emrys gave Torquil a critical look. "You think I would trust you with a razor at the moment? You can scarcely keep your eyes open."

Torquil hummed softly. "You'd like for me to do something that requires less focus, then?" Their gaze fell to Emrys' lips. "Something a bit more relaxing?"

Emrys caught Torquil's wrist and nuzzled his rough cheek against their open palm before placing a gentle kiss there, then another.

"How I missed you, my precocious wordsmith," he murmured before pulling Torquil close for a proper kiss.

§

EMRYS TRACED a delicate fingertip along the faint point of Torquil's ear, savoring the way their body draped over his own. He was certain that they were matched not only in the rate of their breathing, but in the beating of their hearts. His magic swirled languidly in his chest, satisfied after brushing against the whisper of Torquil's own magic. He could only feel it in the moments when they were distracted enough to let it free.

It was like nothing he had ever experienced before. There were times that he was sure he could almost feel the sensation of their magics touching on his skin. It was not entirely unlike the warm sweep of summer sunshine on his face or the tickle of a down feather against his arm.

Emrys thought of the grand display of combined magic he had witnessed at the wedding ceremony. Wyndham and his new husband Roger had performed what was quite possibly the most impressive wedding spell anyone had ever seen. The mix of fae and human magic had been downright mesmerizing.

Had the two of them felt something similar to what Emrys felt?

Could Torquil feel it, too?

Emrys' expression soured as he thought of something his brother had mentioned on their ride out to the estate before the ceremony.

At least I had someone to sneak out for, Wyndham had said with the most self-assured smile on his face. *Isn't it odd that, even as the Wrenwhistle heir, nobody can seem to stand you? Come to think of it, your name hardly even comes up in the* Tribune. *I daresay that's quite an accomplishment, all things considered.*

Emrys moved his fingers from Torquil's ear to trace lazily up and down the curve of their spine. He pressed his lips to their temple. Torquil drew in a slow breath, stirring from a light sleep.

"What is it?" they asked, tucking in closer. "Must you leave already?"

"We've a bit of a problem," Emrys said quietly.

Torquil let out a small moan. "I suppose I can go one more round, but you'll have to be more gentle this time." They started to sit up, but Emrys pulled them back against his chest.

"No, not *that*. It's something Wyndham said."

"Oh. Go on, then."

"He's always been too clever for his own good. It seems that he's noticed something amiss with your papers."

Torquil forced their way out of Emrys' grip with a huff, blanket pooling as they sat back, straddling Emrys' hips. "Impossible."

"*My name*," Emrys clarified. "You never mention me anymore."

Torquil's eyebrows went up, before their lips curled into a lopsided smirk.

"And to think of all the things I could write if I really wanted to," they purred, sliding their hands from Emrys' shoulders down to his navel and back again. "Greetings fortunate folk and hopeful humans," they began playfully. "This writer is pleased to bring forth some delightfully interesting information about the elusive Mr. Emrys Wrenwhistle, heir to the family name and last remaining bachelor of the Wrenwhistle brothers."

Emrys rolled his eyes, but grinned despite himself.

"Let it be known that Mr. Wrenwhistle is absolutely fantastic in bed.

While his conversational skills can sometimes leave much to be desired—"

"I beg pardon!" Emrys laughed.

"—he makes up for it entirely by being the most attentive and thorough of lovers. One could not ask for a better experience in the bedroom. Though it should be noted that his performance can be heavily impacted by an overindulgence of drink, so keep this in mind when offering him refreshments if you intend to seduce him at any point in the evening."

"That was *one* time," Emrys complained.

Torquil gave him a knowing look.

"Oh, all right," Emrys relented. He reached up and took Torquil by the back of the neck, pulling them down for a slow kiss. "But I always make up for it, do I not?"

Torquil chuckled. "Always."

"In all seriousness," Emrys said, holding Torquil's gaze in the candlelight. "I know I've said a million times that we must be careful, but Wyndham will never let this go now that he's picked up on it. He and Roger will return from their honeymoon any day now, and when they do I'd like to have one less reason for his smug arse to tout his success over mine."

"What success is that?"

"Being married before me." Emrys looked away. "Making history with said marriage." The union of two prominent families—one fae and one human—had been a major step in the efforts to join both sides of society in a way that had rarely been done before. Torquil knew better than anyone, of course. Their parents had been at the forefront of this particular crusade, before they'd escaped the prejudice of London twenty-five years earlier to welcome a baby with softly-pointed ears, dark curls, and a true gift with words, though Emrys supposed that last detail wasn't properly discovered until later.

Torquil brought their hand to Emrys' cheek so that their eyes met again.

"History is made every day," they said gently. "Just because someone else has done something remarkable does not mean you've lost your chance to do the same." Torquil grinned and pressed their lips to Emrys' forehead. "Go home. Get some rest."

"I'll send the locksmith to fix your door first thing," Emrys promised.

Torquil snorted out a laugh. "You'd better. I've half a mind to report seeing a man of your build sneaking about in the dark. I would hate to have your first reappearance in the *Tribune* be a piece on your arrest."

CHAPTER 2
TORQUIL

TORQUIL SAT on the edge of the bed, listening to the sound of Emrys making his way back downstairs and out the door. Once they heard the door shut, they slid back into the chair in front of the writing desk. Nearly a month after the wedding in the country, there still wasn't much to report yet. London society was still chattering about the event, the spell, and the couple. Torquil had enjoyed their own participation in that arena, but they were ready to turn their attention to different matters, mend different problems.

They picked up their quill and twirled it between their fingers. Emrys had asked to be mentioned. The truth was, Torquil had avoided doing so, not only because Emrys had begged for caution, but because writing was too honest. They prided themself on being somewhat mysterious. It was a well-honed art to smile enigmatically and make people guess. But when it came to writing, Torquil could not help the truth from spilling onto the page. Sarcasm came through in speckles of the ink, irritation shone around the curves of the letters, and admiration wove its way into the punctuation.

Torquil was quite certain any mention of Emrys would be too telling. The man was objectively attractive, with his golden brown hair always styled in the most fashionable way, his fae-green eyes, and his average yet still notable figure that indicated he was always up for sport the way wealthy gentlemen like himself often were. Though Torquil had never shied away from admiring people of any gender in their column —not only for the sake of a neutral level of admiration, but also because they were attracted to people of multiple genders—they had long worried that any attention of Emrys would be too pointed. However, if Wyndham Wrenwhistle was noticing the omission, it may not take long for others to notice too.

They curled one leg under their body, hitched their other heel on the rung of the chair, and bent over the desk. Dipping the quill in the inkwell, Torquil took a breath, and began to write.

Critics had accused them of writing without thought. But the truth was, Torquil poured thought into every line. Every rumor was written with a mind to the impact. Every coupling reported was done so with consideration of the longevity of the relationship. Torquil had single-handedly brought dozens of couples together over the years, forged alliances between families, and built up businesses. They had also destroyed double that number of couples and ruined reputations. There was balance to these things. Some relationships weren't meant to last. Some people deserved to be taken down a notch.

Although Torquil had followed in their father's professional footsteps as a printer, they had started their path out of a sense of justice. They had an isolated sort of upbringing in the country because the Pimper-nels had expelled their only daughter. Torquil's childhood had been a rather lonely one, with parents who had cheerfully shut out the rest of the world and taken a lackadaisical approach to parenting. While Torquil's parents had been content to let the world pass them by, Torquil was not. They wanted to challenge the harm their grandparents had caused, to fight back, to prove that they were worthy. They had been determined to create change. They wanted to *fix* things. With that intention, they had moved to London and started the *Tribune*. Their dreams had been the driving force behind every installment of the gossip column.

Torquil's recent project had been something of a personal triumph. They had joined together two confirmed bachelors, Roger Barnes and Wyndham Wrenwhistle, a human and a fae, and brought about a significant change in society. It was a single ripple, but Torquil intended to make it a wave. They had already noticed some added changes: they had been offered a seat on the Council for Fae & Human Magical Relations, they'd received letters from readers admitting their own love affairs between humans and fae, letters filled with relief that those affairs could now turn into properly recognized marriages. Things were *finally* changing.

Torquil wrote in silence. The only sound in the room was the scratching of pen against paper. Their drafts were always messy, with crossed out words and scribbled-in notes. They dated it when they were done and got up slowly. They were overdue for a refill of the water in the basin by their bed, but they scrubbed themself down, shivering from the cold water, and began to dress. Unlike their aristocratic friend, they did not have the luxury of sleeping late into the morning. The mornings were when Torquil did the bulk of their work. Sleep would have to wait.

They took their paper downstairs and laid it on the press, giving the ruined lock a weary look. They knew Emrys would keep his word and send a locksmith as soon as he awoke. "First thing" really meant sometime around noon, if Torquil had a guess. They also knew Emrys would probably take the opportunity to replace the whole damn door. If it weren't for the man's frequent absentmindedness, Torquil might have suspected the broken lock had been intentional, solely to give Emrys an opportunity to fix something. Emrys was forever trying to offer them assistance. *You should have a nicer bed. This curtain is a rag; let me buy you a new one. Are you sure you don't want a new coat?* And, worst of all, *why do you insist on living in this dreadful little building? I could buy you your own flat.* Torquil always turned down each offer, big and small.

They gave the lock another long look and then went to a tiny cupboard in the corner of the room. The broken lock meant that much less safety. While Torquil did their best not to be *too* damaging in their reporting of gossip, they were no stranger to harassment. The protection spell was probably overdue for a refresh anyway. Torquil gathered the necessary supplies and trudged outside, shivering in the early morning chill.

Torquil's parents had attempted to teach them magic. But try as they might, Torquil could never master their mother's exquisite manipulation of nature, or even their father's sturdy spellcasting. Instead, their magic came out like a sauce with too much spice: overwhelming and never quite what anyone wanted. Performing it felt like an itch under their skin. Their parents insisted that its uniqueness was a good thing. But after being rejected from both fae and human institutions, Torquil had learned early on that their magic was just too strange for others. Before long, its strangeness was too unpalatable even for Torquil.

So they had stopped performing magic unless absolutely necessary. They repressed the urge to feel magic as their mother had taught them, they intentionally reduced their ingredients to what would fit in a tiny cabinet, and they lived their life as magic-free as possible.

However, in the matter of safety, they had accepted that magic was just a bit necessary. So they had accepted their parents' offer to set up a protection spell around the press building, and Torquil would refresh the spell every few months. After years of neglect, trying to sense the magic was a strain, so they didn't bother. They simply refreshed the spell in patches and hoped for the best. They went through the routine quickly, too tired to do more than the bare minimum.

Then they went inside and the real work began. They typeset for their next edition, using their messy copy as a guide. They printed the usual amount of *Tribune* copies, enough for the faithful subscribers, the rare out-of-town requests, and the day-of rush.

Just as the ink began to dry, a knock came at the door. Three loud knocks followed by two softer ones. Torquil smiled and opened the door.

A short and pudgy adolescent with dark blond hair and bright blue eyes stepped inside. "You know your lock's ruined."

"I know," Torquil said.

Sal shrugged, unbothered. "Morning distribution today or afternoon?"

"Morning," Torquil said. "I just finished."

Sal nodded. "I'll spread the word."

She left and Torquil closed the door behind her. They began sorting the papers into piles. Almost an hour later, Sal returned. Torquil handed her a small stack. "You can charge the usual price."

"You really should raise it."

"I know."

Sal snorted and turned back to the door, nearly colliding with a scullery maid who scooted into the building. Her cheeks were rosy from exertion. She held her hands out. "I'm here for the Berkeley Square lot."

Torquil handed over a stack.

After the maid came a stablehand. The upper class runners always arrived earliest, eager to give their employers the news first. The boot boy who arrived next handed Torquil a slip of paper, which they pocketed before passing over a coin and another stack of columns. The stream of people continued, from domestic staff to urchins looking for a little extra pay. They came to Torquil because they always gave the delivery people a decent cut. The cut was even bigger if the delivery was picked up or came back with a bit of gossip.

By the time the papers had run out, Torquil was exhausted. They went to their bedroom, pulled out an iron lockbox, and carried it downstairs. Then they collapsed onto a rickety chair beside the press, setting the heavy box on their lap. Leaning back, they hitched their foot onto the edge of the press and pulled out the small collection in their pocket. They grinned. Servants always had the best gossip. Sometimes Torquil's sources were from the upper crust, letters sent to sully names or announce celebrations. But most of the time, their sources were the domestic staff.

The rosy-cheeked maid returned first, handing back two slightly crumpled copies and a small purse of collected coins. "They were out of town," she said apologetically.

Torquil nodded and unlocked the box. They dumped the contents of the purse into the box and then counted out a few coins to give her. The morning continued to drag on as people trickled back in to hand over payment for the copies. Just when Torquil thought they might be done, the locksmith arrived.

"Here for a door," the locksmith said, giving the door in question a critical look. Then he handed over a small bag. "Was also paid to bring the resident a hot cross bun."

Torquil snorted and took the bag. "Thank you." They resumed their seat and watched the locksmith work. The bread inside smelled too good to resist, so Torquil ate as they watched, contemplating how strange it was to be finishing their day's work just as Emrys was waking up. Torquil sighed as they finished their meal and then crumpled the bag. They missed Emrys and rather wished the gentleman had brought the food himself. They could've eaten it together, with Torquil in Emrys' lap or with their legs stretched over Emrys'. They sucked crumbs off their fingertips. Such a silly fantasy.

The locksmith finished up his work and, as Torquil had predicted, refused payment, saying he'd been promised a good tip if he didn't accept money from the resident. He handed over a pair of keys and left.

Torquil palmed the keys, feeling the weight of them. Emrys had ordered a lock with a different metal. He always seemed to find ways to slip into Torquil's space. Torquil didn't *mind*, exactly. They just wished Emrys could slip in their space in a different way, like going to bed with them—and staying the night. With that thought, Torquil cleaned up the press, locked the door, and went back to bed.

TORQUIL'S TRIBUNE

MONDAY 22 NOVEMBER, 1813

Greetings fortunate folk and hopeful humans,

After such a thrilling beginning to the Season, it is understandable that things have been slow as of late. This writer does not have a great deal of news as of yet, but we hope readers will be forgiving of that. As an offering, here is a small list of unmarried hopefuls that we hope will find love soon.

Mr. Benedict Brooks has been seen on the arm of several gentlemen but is as yet unattached. Who will he end up with? We are eager to find out.

Mr. Keelan Cricket is good-humored and companionable and has no shortage of friends, but is love around the corner?

Mx. Fern Hillcrest has dazzled sitting rooms and ballrooms alike with their effervescent wit and ready smile. Will love dazzle them this Season?

Mr. Gerald Irving is sophisticated and droll. Perhaps this Season he will find a match for his intellect and his heart?

Lady Cynthia Proust is accomplished on the pianoforte and sings divinely. Will her sirensong win over anyone in London?

Mr. Sage Ravenwing graced these pages frequently last

month. Will he continue to break hearts or will he finally give away his own?

Miss Lydia Stanton makes her debut this Season and is sure to be a social triumph as she comes into her own.

Miss Harriet Thackeray has a jolly disposition and always brightens up a party. Anyone who marries her is sure to never be bored.

Mr. Cyril Thompson has excellent taste in fashion and has been known to be an enjoyable conversation partner. Though many have thought his heart was elsewhere, the gentleman remains unmarried and could possibly be open to romance.

Miss Aveline Wrenwhistle is lovely and charming and will surely catch someone's eye soon.

And last, but certainly not least, Mr. Emrys Wrenwhistle. As heir to the Wrenwhistle fortune and heir to the same beauty of his siblings, Mr. Wrenwhistle might well be the most eligible bachelor in London. Who shall win his heart?

We omitted a few unattached gentlefolk as their names have been linked with others. As ever, this writer is eager to hear any news, admiration, or observations.

Your esteemed editor,
Torquil Pimpernel-Smith

CHAPTER 3

EMRYS

EMRYS GRINNED behind his cup of tea as he read the words of that morning's *Tribune* for the third time, allowing them to seep in and settle with no sense of urgency. The birds outside the open window to his right chirped and chattered brightly after the previous night's storm, likely celebrating their success at not being drowned in their nests or blown away in the wind altogether.

He'd known that he could trust Torquil to play the situation just right. The flattery was enough to get society talking without raising any suspicions that Emrys had been the one to request his own name being put in the paper. The only thing that could have made it better would've been seeing Wyndham's reaction as he read the words, but alas, he was left to imagine the moment instead.

Aveline sighed wistfully from her chair nearby, drawing Emrys' attention.

"Torquil always has such kind words to say about me, but they seem to be the only person in all of London to believe them," she said with a pout.

Her fingertips brushed gently over the cluster of bright red berries she'd just added to the spray of holly and pine leaves neatly embroidered on one corner of a crisp linen handkerchief. The large workbag open across her lap revealed two others that were identical to the one she was holding. Emrys felt certain he would be in possession of one of them within a fortnight.

As the third Wrenwhistle sibling and a hopeless romantic, Aveline was taken with a bout of melancholy after Wyndham's wedding. Emrys understood her frustration after watching their youngest brother get married before either of them, and in such a consequential way. With the help of the *Tribune*, both sides of society had become enraptured with Wyndham and Roger's whirlwind affair of the heart. Gossip abound, there were even some who placed bets on just how long it would take before the two seemingly oblivious parties would succumb to their emotions. Emrys would never admit how much money he'd lost in the endeavor.

"You try too hard, sister." He drained his cup of tea and set it down with the saucer on the side table. "The thing you search for endlessly will surely remain elusive. If it's meant to be, it will find you when you least expect it."

"Nonsense," Aveline protested airily as she resumed her needle-point. "All I ever do is wait around for my beloved to come and find me. You see I am still sitting here, alone."

Emrys chuckled. "Perhaps you should work on improving your many talents while you wait." He lifted his copy of the *Tribune* and waved it in her direction. "Lady Proust is ready to sing and play her way into an engagement this Season, it seems, and even that wild Harriet Thackeray has a sense of humor on her side."

"And what, exactly, do you have to offer *your* future spouse?" Aveline asked. "Snide commentary and endless arrogance?"

Emrys grinned and gestured casually to the room at large.

Aveline sneered at him and collected her work into her bag rather hastily. As she excused herself from the room, their mother bustled in with a wide smile.

"What a mention you've had in the *Tribune* this morning!" Mrs. Wrenwhistle smoothed her skirts after sitting next to Emrys on the sofa, impressively energetic after traveling the previous day. The way she practically lunged for the cup the servant handed to her suggested it was a result of copious amounts of strong tea.

Emrys offered her a charming look. "Yes, now that Wyndham has successfully bedded his bespectacled beau, I suppose there's no choice but for everyone to return their focus to the most important Wrenwhistle sibling."

Mrs. Wrenwhistle pressed her lips together in a disapproving way, but the expression quickly faded. There was little room for her to deny it.

"I believe such a proclamation is one we should not let go to waste," she said after taking a swallow of her tea.

"There's no need to worry ourselves with convincing everyone I am beautiful, Mother. They already know."

"Emrys," Mrs. Wrenwhistle chided on a sigh. "I am referring to you being the most eligible bachelor in London, of course. Everyone who's anyone has read the words this morning. I predict that we will have a tray overflowing with calling cards by the end of the week, if not sooner."

Emrys felt the weight of the rest of her words before she said them.

He had known this was coming since Wyndham's magical testing had been completed all those years ago, the results naming seventeen-year-old Emrys as the most powerful sibling and, as such, the Wrenwhistle heir.

His mother's hand came to rest on his forearm, and he met her gaze.

"It's time to stop playing your childish games," she said sternly. "I will be taking control of your social engagements for the rest of the Season. I'll sort out your callers, we can make visits for tea, I can arrange for ideal partners at all of the dinner parties. Just leave everything to me. We will have you matched with your someone special in no time at all." Mrs. Wrenwhistle's smile returned as she patted his sleeve affectionately. "Doesn't that sound lovely?"

For a long time, Emrys' response would've been a resounding *yes*.

It had been nothing short of intoxicating, knowing his future was set with any comforts he might ever wish for. He never had to wonder what career he would pursue if he did not choose to have one. He never had to lift more than a finger to get what he wanted. Emrys was one charismatic smile away from anything and everything his heart desired.

Well, *almost* everything.

Emrys had long since accepted that matters of his heart would never truly be his own to manage. His mother had said it plainly enough: he was to be matched.

His future spouse would need to be someone of a respectable background, likely with a name as important as his own. They would need to be cultured and well-versed in the ways of society, ready to handle the execution of social events as well as his mother did.

Of course, there was also the expectation of carrying on the Wrenwhistle name. Emrys had given little thought to being a father. His own father was rarely present thanks to his work overseeing the various businesses he'd invested in. While Emrys had never felt particularly upset about it, he could admit that he hadn't the first idea about how to set a good example for his own future children.

"Emrys?" his mother said, pulling him back to their conversation.

"Yes, Mother," Emrys agreed finally. "Lovely." He offered her a mild grin that didn't quite reach his eyes, but Mrs. Wrenwhistle didn't seem to notice.

"Do remember that we have a party to attend this evening," his mother said as she got to her feet. Emrys watched her leave and then settled his focus on the copy of the *Tribune* he was still holding.

"Who shall win his heart, indeed," he murmured.

CHAPTER 4

TORQUIL

Torquil awoke with a dreadful start at the sound of banging on their door. Grumbling, they kicked off their blanket and hurried downstairs. They unlocked the door and opened it to reveal a harried person in an old-fashioned livery-esque uniform. Torquil didn't recognize the uniform and their curiosity was instantly piqued.

"Are you Pimpernel-Smith?"

"Yes?"

"I'm Lex. I'm an aide for the Council for Fae & Human Magical Relations and I've been assigned to you. You're late for the Council meeting. I was sent to fetch you."

Torquil felt as if they'd been plunged in icy water. "I'm sorry," they stammered. "I didn't realize I was expected today. I'll get dressed. Will you wait here for a moment?"

Lex nodded.

Torquil closed the door and ran back upstairs. They sorted through their clothes with shaking hands. There wasn't time to debate on the best outfit. They had hoped to make a good impression on their first day on the Council, but that opportunity was well and truly gone. They picked out the least wrinkled suit they owned and scrambled into it, combed fingers through their curly hair, put on their shoes, grabbed the new key, and went back down to meet Lex. They locked the door, irritated with how strange that now felt with the new lock.

Lex wasted no time in leading them down the street.

Torquil had never had a reason to go to the Council chambers in person. Quite honestly, they avoided high society at large, preferring to write observations of it rather than engage with it directly. It always seemed so much safer that way. But when they'd been approached at the wedding and offered a position on the Council for Fae & Human Magical Relations, they knew better than to refuse. Torquil was filled with ideas for how things *should* be and what needed to be changed, fixed, and updated, so it made sense to accept the opportunity. But it also meant they had to leave the safety of their building and interact with the very people who had looked down on them their whole life. Torquil had spent the past month trying not to dwell on that aspect. And now they were late on their first day.

The crisp morning air didn't seem to make it inside the building, which was stuffy and warm. Poor Lex was sweating noticeably by the time she opened a tall door and whispered, "In here!"

Torquil walked into a large room with a long table. The councilmembers sat on one side, as if they were posing for a painting of *The Last Supper*. Torquil thought it was a thoroughly impractical arrangement, but now was certainly not the time to say so. They felt everyone's eyes on them as they made their way through the room.

"I'm sorry I'm late," they said as they approached the table. "I didn't realize I was to start today."

"An oversight on our part, I'm sure," Councilmember Wrenwhistle said warmly. She was fae, tall and thin, with pale skin. Her white hair was pinned up fashionably. She managed to exude elegance without having to lift a finger. Torquil could see that Emrys had inherited some of his grandmother's looks. "Your aide will provide you with a schedule before you leave."

Torquil nodded and took the empty seat at the end of the table. "It was a *Tribune* day," they explained, before realizing they didn't know why they were saying it.

"Shall we continue with business?" one of the human members said irritably.

"Perhaps," Councilmember Barnes said, "we ought to do a round of introductions. Councilmember Pimpernel-Smith has never met any of us officially. It would probably be wise to ensure they know who we all are." He gave Torquil a friendly smile. Torquil could see decided similarities between the gentleman and his son, Roger Barnes. They were both attractive people with light brown skin, dark eyes, dark curly hair, round faces, and fat figures. Like his son, Councilmember Barnes seemed to convey a gentleness of spirit that helped to put Torquil at ease.

"Thank you," Torquil said. "I would appreciate that."

"Excellent suggestion, Norman," Wrenwhistle said. "I am Iris Wrenwhistle. I'm the head of the fae half of the Council. Which means I am responsible for appointing fae members and I handle any issues with our side of things. If there is a debate, the heads of Council normally make the final decision." She paused. "However, your addition to our number may reduce the need for that last duty. It was young Roger's suggestion that we have an odd number so as to make split votes less of an issue. I think eventually we would like to add even more fae-human members. In the meantime, you can report to me with any questions or issues."

Torquil nodded their understanding, relieved. Wrenwhistle was an intimidating woman, but Torquil knew enough about her to know she was very intelligent and kind underneath her regal bearing.

"Cricket," said a short lady, next in line. She had brown hair and a sour expression on her pale pink face.

"Applewood," said the third fae councilmember, a woman seated next to Torquil. Applewood was of medium height and build, with dark brown skin, black hair, and a warm voice.

"I am Councilmember Williams." Torquil turned back to the center of the table at the older gentleman with a ruddy face and beady eyes. "I am the head of the human side of the Council. This is Gibbs and Barnes." He gestured down the line, each councilmember nodding in response to their introduction. Gibbs was short and pale, with thin blond hair and a fussy expression. "Now," Williams continued, "can we continue with our order of business?"

Wrenwhistle raised an eyebrow. "Certainly." She turned her gaze back to Torquil. "We were discussing the new rubric proposed by my grandson and his husband."

"Ah," Torquil said, attempting to regain footing. "The Barnes-Wrenwhistle Method."

Gibbs gave a snort. "Is that what you're calling it?"

"I received many letters supporting that name. I quite like it."

"Very apt," Barnes said, looking amused.

"However," Williams said loudly. "We still need to determine a number of logistics first. There are certified examiners all over the country. We shall have to see to it that they are all aware of the new rubrics and can test accordingly."

Gibbs stood and put a set of papers, a quill, and an inkwell in front of Torquil. "Why don't you take notes?"

Torquil blinked at him, nonplussed.

Wrenwhistle turned to Gibbs as he sat back down. "Tired of note-taking duties, are you?"

Gibbs looked affronted. "Well, as the newest member of the Council, it only seems—"

"Besides," Cricket piped up, "writing seems like a very appropriate responsibility, considering."

"I don't mind," Torquil said, dipping the quill into the ink. "But you should know that my handwriting is dreadful." They attempted a winning smile.

Barnes chuckled. "So is my Roger's. If we're continuing the idea that the newest member of the Council play at secretary, we will not be pleased when the newlyweds join. I'm quite sure the papers Roger gave us last month were written extremely slowly. His handwriting is usually undecipherable."

"Perhaps you'll want my grandson to take over," Wrenwhistle went on, giving Gibbs an arch look. "His handwriting is quite nice."

Gibbs' face reddened. "I'm not suggesting we pass the responsibility around like some sort of rubber ball," he sputtered. "I only think—"

"Yes, it is quite clear what you were thinking," Wrenwhistle said, her voice colder than before.

Torquil twirled the quill uneasily between their thumb and forefinger. They weren't entirely surprised they were being treated like a secretary or another aide. They'd been treated less than by fae and humans alike all of their life. Still, they'd hoped the recent wedding would start changing these sorts of attitudes, especially on the Council. At least Wrenwhistle and Barnes seemed to be championing them. Torquil supposed, dully, that those two had the largest stake in ensuring the offspring of fae-human marriages were treated well. Or perhaps they were simply the kindest councilmembers. It was frightfully hard to tell. Torquil bent over the paper and wrote out the date and scribbled *Pimpernel-Smith to take over note duties for the time being*, before looking up expectantly.

Wrenwhistle sighed. "Thank you, Pimpernel-Smith. We will discuss this in my office later."

Torquil nodded.

The conversation turned out to be rather boring, as the councilmembers debated how to get the rubric to the different examiners, whether the examiners would need to be trained, and at what point the new rubric would take effect. Torquil was a little surprised this hadn't been discussed before the rubric was approved.

There was also a strong concern that they dearly wanted to bring up, but they weren't sure if they ought to. However, when the conversation reached a small lag, they decided their concern was the very reason they were on the Council in the first place, so they took a deep breath and said, "And what about fae-human children? Which rubric will they be expected to use?"

Everyone's gaze swiveled to Torquil. They focused on tilting their chin up and poising the quill as if they were waiting for a brilliant response.

"I beg pardon?" Cricket said.

"Children like me," Torquil clarified. "What rubric will they be held to?"

Silence greeted the question.

"You see, I was never tested," they went on. "My parents tried, but it seemed no examiners were willing to test a half-fae-half-human. So I have no magical score. It puts me at a great disadvantage, for no one would hire someone without a score. And marriage prospects are nonexistent. It seems to me this is an excellent opportunity to correct that particular problem."

"What?" Williams said. "So you think we should create a third rubric especially for your kind?"

Torquil took pride in not flinching at the word choice. "Not at all," they said.

"If you had a choice," Barnes said in a gentler tone, "would one rubric suit you and your magic better?"

Torquil was grateful for the question. They considered their answer carefully. "In my limited experience, when a child has two parents of different magical upbringings, they're taught both, or a portion of both. I think if I had been given the choice, I would have felt more comfortable with the Hastings Exam when I was that age, since human spells tend to come a little easier for me. But others might choose differently. Would it be possible to provide the option?"

Again, the Council was silent in response. At least this time it was a thoughtful sort of silence.

"I think that sounds reasonable," Applewood said. "We can add a note that children who are familiar with both systems might choose the one they're most comfortable with."

Torquil nodded and wrote that down. Feeling bold, they added, "Of course, it wouldn't be a bad idea to have a third rubric. And, from what I understand, the Wrenwhistles discovered a new way of doing magic that combined both systems in a fluid manner. It might be worth bringing that into the equation as well."

"An intriguing point," Barnes said.

"How would you propose we do that?" Cricket said, her voice a mixture of confusion and curiosity.

Torquil shrugged and gave a little smile. "I'm afraid I'm not enough of an expert on either rubric, or either magic system, to have that answer readily for you. But I believe Mr. Roger Wrenwhistle first proposed his suggestion for amending the rubric in order to be more comprehensive. Perhaps we ought to explore all of our new learnings before we take action. It will prevent us from having to redo our work later."

"It seems to me," Gibbs said, "that it's a little early for you to be making such suggestions."

"Ah," Torquil said. They twiddled the quill again. "So you were thinking this position to be more along the lines of secretary than councilmember? My mistake."

Gibbs jumped to his feet angrily.

"Sit down," Wrenwhistle said. "They are perfectly correct. If you cannot keep a civil tongue then you will be dismissed from the discussion."

Torquil turned back to the paper in order to avoid looking too smug. But just as they reached their quill into the inkwell, it tipped over and ink spilled across the table. Torquil jumped up to try and—well they weren't sure what they'd planned to do. But before they could so much as right the inkwell, the ink began pooling back into the well. Then the well tipped back to its rightful position. Applewood rubbed out the ink stain on the table with her handkerchief.

"There," Wrenwhistle said, "no harm done."

She gave them a warm smile again, but Torquil felt as though they had lost all of the meager footing they had managed to gain. What the hell were they doing here? They couldn't control their own magic half so well. Were they really properly equipped to determine the future of magic for the country? They quietly murmured their thanks and pulled the inkwell closer, annoyed that their hand was shaking.

"Well," Barnes said in a bright voice, "I rather think Pimpernel-Smith has brought up a very good point. Perhaps we ought to consider the matter further before making any decisions? Besides, it is altogether possible that the architects of this rubric had some plans for launching it. It doesn't seem practical to make decisions without them."

"But they aren't even back in London yet," Cricket said. "Do you really expect us to wait for them?"

"Young Barnes—well, Wrenwhistle now," Williams said, "may well have considered the matter. Goodness knows that young man has an endless stream of ideas."

Some chuckles met this remark.

"Indeed," Wrenwhistle said. "All things considered, perhaps we ought to delay this matter until then. It is not ideal, as I know we are all eager to launch the rubric. But better to be thorough than hasty. Besides, it's Pimpernel-Smith's first day and I should like to show them around before the day is over. I propose we return to our offices and adjourn until the entire Council is present."

Williams nodded. "Agreed. I should like to talk to my side for a bit before you all go to your offices."

The fae councilmembers all stood and began filing out. Torquil hastened to follow.

Wrenwhistle waited for them at the door. "Let's go to my office first."

Torquil had never gone to a university, but they felt very much as if they were sitting in a dean's office as they took their seat across the desk.

Wrenwhistle sat down, folded her hands on top of her desk, and let out a long breath. "I'm very sorry about all of that."

"I'm so sorry I was late," Torquil blurted.

She gave a small smile. "It wasn't your fault. Williams sent your aide to fetch you without telling me. I hadn't planned for you to come in today at all. I know it's a *Tribune* day and I expected you to be busy. I was honestly surprised you made it."

"Lex didn't let up on knocking until I was awake," Torquil said. "Which is probably a good trait, to be honest."

She chuckled. "Yes, I thought Lex would be a good fit for you. She's very eager to do well." She reached into her desk and pulled out a piece of paper. "But we'll be sure it doesn't happen again. Most days, we don't even meet together. We're usually conducting work in our offices, or doing projects together."

Torquil was secretly relieved to hear this.

She took a moment to pencil out a schedule and then handed the paper over. "The schedule changes weekly, depending on what is on our agenda. But here is what this week will look like."

Torquil glanced over the schedule and then folded it and put it in their pocket. "Thank you."

She folded her hands on the desk again. "Your ideas were sound. You deserve to be here."

Torquil clasped their hands in their lap. "Thank you," they whispered.

"I'll speak to Gibbs privately. He shouldn't have put you in that position."

Torquil shrugged. "I am a writer."

"Hm. And he made sure you knew it."

Torquil met her gaze. "I didn't expect to be welcomed with open arms. I knew it was unlikely for public opinion to change overnight, from just one wedding."

She raised an eyebrow. "That is very gracious of you, but I haven't quite forgiven my colleagues for treating you poorly when they were so encouraging of the wedding in question."

Torquil tilted their head in acknowledgement. "Their opinion of the wedding is a good sign, in any case. It's exactly what I'd hoped for."

Her mouth twitched. "And I imagine you were particularly strategic in picking out the couple to carry that hope through."

Torquil didn't dare react to that statement.

She laughed. "I've always liked you, you know. You're the kind of person who's always five steps ahead of everyone else. You weren't the only one attempting to pair the two up. If I hadn't liked your strategy, I would have intervened."

Torquil grinned. Apparently Iris Wrenwhistle was also the kind of person who was always five steps ahead. "I'm glad you aren't displeased."

She waved a dismissive hand. "Wyndham told me from the beginning that the engagement announcement was a mistake. It didn't take much to determine what had happened. Your column had been quite focused on the pair of them, even before the announcement. And I haven't forgotten that you managed to get Lord Ashleigh to marry the son of his political rival two years ago. That little scheme kept Parliament from raising the taxes on eggs." She picked up a neat pile of papers and straightened them unnecessarily. "You are exactly the sort of person I'd like to have on this Council. It just might take some time to get everyone else to recognize your value."

"Barnes doesn't seem to hate me."

She chuckled. "That dear man doesn't hate anyone. Neither does his son, actually. I think things will go much more smoothly once my grandson and his husband return to London. Applewood is another you can rely on. She's quiet but she's a good sort. I've seen to it that your office is next to hers." She paused. "Ordinarily, we like to pair newer councilmembers with more senior ones in a sort of mentorship capacity. However, we've decided to put Wyndham and Roger in an office together, considering how well they work as a team."

Torquil smirked. "Are you sure work will get done in that office?"

She returned the smile. "It will, because you'll be sharing it with them." Before Torquil could register that information, she said, "You look dead on your feet, poor thing. Why don't you go home early? You can meet me here in the morning; I'll go over your duties and show you to your office."

Torquil left and trudged back home, feeling weary down to their bones. They placed the schedule on their writing desk and carefully peeled off their clothes, trying to keep them as unwrinkled as possible. Then they crawled into bed. As they drifted off to sleep, they wished Emrys was there. Emrys would let them snuggle into his chest and would make them feel safe and valued. They deeply hoped accepting the Council's offer hadn't been the biggest mistake they'd ever made.

CHAPTER 5

EMRYS

MRS. WRENWHISTLE WASTED ABSOLUTELY no time making good on her promise. After a long night of indulgence at the dinner party, Emrys woke to a dull headache and a flurry of activity.

His mother urged him out of bed, thrust a glass of water into his hand, and went about instructing the servants on how to dress him for the day. He was set to receive a number of calls, the first of which would be arriving any moment.

"How can I be expected to make a good impression when I've only just woken up?" Emrys ambled to the dressing mirrors and managed a small sip of water before it and his night clothes were whisked away by adept hands.

"You said it yourself," Mrs. Wrenwhistle called cheerily from the other side of the screens separating them. "Everyone already knows all about you. This is your chance to learn more about *them*. To find someone who will suit you and your needs."

Emrys stared blearily at his reflection, allowing himself to be dressed and groomed to his mother's high expectations. He assessed his appearance as layer after layer of fine clothing was added to his outfit; satin waistcoat the color of his favorite breakfast jam embossed with roses, silk cravat of the palest yellow. He did not particularly care for the coat, but he had been described as *handsomely built* whilst wearing it on more than one occasion, so he relented.

By the time his dark golden hair was appropriately styled and his cravat tied and decorated with a bejeweled pin, he was awake enough to collect his thoughts and mentally ready himself for the task ahead. He'd been preparing for this for nearly twenty years so he knew what was expected. Emrys tugged on the lapels of his light gray coat and gave himself a curt nod in the mirror before he turned and followed his mother downstairs.

As irony would have it, Lady Cynthia Proust was the first to be announced and welcomed into the sitting room a short time later. Emrys thought back to his conversation with Aveline as he stood and welcomed the lady and her chaperone, bowing his head politely as he offered them both a seat.

"Lady Proust," Emrys began with a trained smile. "I was only just speaking with my sister about your mention in the *Tribune* yesterday, and how eager I am to hear your many musical talents."

Lady Proust blushed in an exaggerated way, hiding a delicate laugh behind a gloved hand as her eyelashes fluttered. "Mr. Wrenwhistle, you flatter me."

Emrys found himself hoping what Torquil had printed about her aptitudes was not an exaggeration, lest he be forced to overstate his praise when the time came. He decided to remain hopeful. If nothing else, he could return to the city's *esteemed editor* and seek consolation for their falsehoods.

"My older brother Auberon was captivated by his own wife's skill on the piano early on in their courtship. Perhaps this trait runs in our family."

Under his mother's watchful presence from her conspicuously-placed chair, the two of them chatted easily about nothing of consequence for a quarter of an hour, almost as if they had each been offered the same list of approved conversation topics to read over just before they had entered the room. Emrys was relieved that Lady Proust was nice enough to speak with, just as she had been during the few occasions their paths had crossed at social events over the years. She was no great beauty, but her large blue eyes and shapely figure were appealing in their own right.

He learned she was as accomplished as her title would imply. She did not enjoy drawing or fancy needlework, though she held great interest in making simple ruffled collars for her four Pomeranian dogs to wear. "They are all the same soft cream color," she explained, "so it is otherwise impossible to tell them apart!" Emrys found this highly amusing at first, but then realized it was actually a rather good idea. If he was to meet them in the near future, he would hate to be introduced to them by name and then immediately forget them.

When she asked about his preferred forms of leisure, he was quick to provide that he was skilled at riding, rowing, and fencing, although he would never turn down an invitation for sport of any kind, especially if it allowed him to be out of doors. He'd always found fresh air enriching regardless of the circumstance, unlike the rest of his siblings who seemed happiest in nature only when they were far from London.

Before long, the conversation shifted to less of a back-and-forth and more of an interrogation, thanks to his mother's heavy questioning from her seat nearby. How did Lady Proust plan to run her household? Was she comfortable giving orders to the servants? What was her experience with planning social events? Managing a budget? How many children did she desire?

To her credit, Lady Proust answered each question with finesse. She had clearly been preparing for this as long as Emrys had, probably under even more scrutiny. She was ready with an answer to each inquiry before Mrs. Wrenwhistle could finish asking it. Each response was given with a poised smile.

As glad as Emrys was to see that his mother was pleased with how the meeting was going, he couldn't help but wonder if the answers Lady Proust was giving were anything close to the truth. Did she honestly enjoy the thought of hosting dinner parties every week? Was she truly interested in giving Emrys 'as many children as he saw fit' to carry on the family name?

Something curled uneasily in Emrys' stomach as he considered it all.

"Perhaps we can hear you play now," Emrys said, cutting his mother off mid-sentence. She directed a harsh look at him, before turning a polite smile at their guests.

"Of course! Come and play for us, dear," Mrs. Wrenwhistle encouraged, herding all of them into the connecting room where the piano sat waiting.

Lady Proust made a bit of a show out of settling herself onto the bench seat, smiling all the while. She did not ask what any of them wanted to hear. Instead, she readied her fingers and started in on a melody that was familiar, though Emrys couldn't name it. Her performance was technically quite lovely, but it seemed to lack any sort of emotion behind it. Another practiced answer to a question she knew she would be asked.

When Lady Proust and her chaperone eventually departed, Emrys blew out a huff of a sigh, rubbing at his eyes with a finger and thumb. It was decided that he would *not* be choosing someone based on their musical talents alone. While he was quickly learning which questions he did not particularly care to hear answers to, such as the proper etiquette of sending out invitations, Emrys wondered what he *did* want to know about his future spouse. Was there truly nothing more to a strong, society-driven marriage than disposition and propriety?

"Tea," Emrys barked, which he instantly regretted as one of the servants slipped out of the room. The stress of the morning affected him more than he'd realized. He was not one to treat the staff so poorly.

There was hardly enough time to sit down before the next caller was announced. Emrys stood and clasped his hands behind his back, a dignified smile returning to his features.

CHAPTER 6

TORQUIL

O<small>N DAYS</small> when the *Tribune* did not go out, Torquil kept themself busy by obtaining content for the paper. So early the next morning, they emerged from the press building and strode into the city.

They had developed something of a circuit, although the exact stops on the route changed each day. There was always at least one shop owner to visit. Torquil had a favorite modiste who routinely supplied them with a wealth of information. That morning, her assistant greeted them on the steps of the shop and passed Torquil several sheets of small note paper. Torquil gave them a handful of coins in return before pocketing the notes.

As they continued toward Mayfair, the owner of a teashop hailed them from the doorway. They greeted him, pleased. They were even more pleased when the shop owner handed over a crumpled paper covered in names of patrons who had entered his shop and, more importantly, what had been overheard. They duly thanked him and gave him some money in return.

Once in Mayfair, the route got more involved. There were a few domestic servants that regularly provided something of note. They did not disappoint as Torquil rapped gently on the service entrances and sidled down narrow alleyways that led to the side entrances of the elegant townhouses. Sometimes they received notes, sometimes it was simply hushed conversations. Torquil had a small notebook and pencil for the latter. Either way, coins exchanged hands and Torquil's purse grew lighter while the pocket holding notes grew fuller.

Occasionally the exchange went in the opposite direction. A footman paused in the act of collecting the morning papers to beckon Torquil over. He reached into his liveried coat to pull out a small bundle of tallow candles. "Her ladyship wished to express her gratitude for your discretion," he said in a low voice.

Torquil smiled and took the candles. "Tell her she's quite welcome and that her token of gratitude is most appreciated."

The footman gave them a knowing nod and scuttled back into the townhouse.

By the time Torquil was through Mayfair, it was late enough in the day that the wealthy and fashionable were beginning to trickle out of their homes to promenade. Torquil made their way to Hyde Park and eased their gait to a slower stroll.

With the candles and the nearly empty purse in one pocket, and the wad of notes bulging in the other pocket, Torquil felt satisfied with their morning's work. They clasped their hands behind their back and wandered through the park, keeping an eye out for interesting pairings and suspicious goings on.

Sal found them as they were observing a family near the duck pond.

"You look tired," she remarked.

"Thank you."

"At least you're in a good mood."

They glanced at her. "Should I not be?"

She shrugged. "Your new lock is…an interesting choice."

They turned from the pond and continued down the path. Sal joined them. "It is. It was not my choice though. It was paid for by a friend."

"Hmph. That's trusting of you."

"He's worthy of my trust."

"Is the rest of London?"

"No."

She was silent as they rounded a bend. Torquil watched a couple passing them, noting how one lady blushed at her companion's comments. The couple ignored Torquil and Sal, but Torquil was quite sure they had not escaped the pair's attention.

"Are you being careful?" Sal asked at last.

"As careful as I can be," they replied. "I enhanced my protection spell yesterday."

"Good."

They crooked a smile at her. "Worried?"

"Should I not be? This new job of yours puts an even bigger target on your back."

They shrugged. "I wouldn't worry too much about that. At least not yet. The Council doesn't have enough power to be truly effective. All they really do is handle magical testing and occasionally offer funding for magical research."

"And provide the facade of improved fae and human relations," she added.

"And that," they agreed.

"But you wouldn't have accepted the position if that was all you expected the Council to ever be."

They looked at her in some surprise.

"So it stands to reason," she continued, "that you anticipate the Council's role to expand in some way. People may not like that."

"That...is an interesting observation," they said cautiously.

She laughed. "You think I stuck with you all these years without picking up some of your tricks?"

They huffed in amusement. "Fair enough."

Sal had been one of the first people they met in London, the first person to express an interest in helping distribute the gossip column, and one of the first people to return to their door after the initial introduction. Emrys had been another noteworthy return visitor, but Torquil quickly pushed the thought of their lover away.

"I'll be careful," they assured her.

She grunted. "Good. And before I forget..." She reached into her pocket and passed over a handful of notes. "You can add this to your stack."

CHAPTER 7

EMRYS

Two FULL DAYS of listening to his mother interrogate potential marriage partners left Emrys on the brink of madness. She was ruthless, using each person as an opportunity to test out new questions, each more brutal than the last. One of the suitors that morning had left holding back tears. When Emrys demanded to know why she was acting in such a way, she had simply patted his cheek lovingly and said that she only wanted the best for him.

After surviving all of that, Emrys felt he had well earned his trip across town once the sun had set. He needed to check on the new lock he'd paid for, among other things.

When he arrived at the press building, he grabbed the handle and gave it a turn. It was secure and much sturdier than what had been there before, just as he'd asked. With a firm grip, Emrys called to his magic and felt as the air swirled around his hand and the new mechanism until there was a soft *click*. He turned the handle again and the door gave, allowing him inside.

At the top of the steps, Emrys burst dramatically through the curtain with a groan of frustration. He knew this was the one place he could show the feelings he'd been repressing around his mother and all of the other fine members of society that had been paraded around before him like prized racehorses.

"Something the matter?" Torquil asked from where they were stretched out on the floor on their back, ankles crossed and propped up on the seat of their chair. They closed the book they were reading and set it aside, hands coming to rest on their stomach as they peered up at him.

"As it turns out," Emrys said crisply, "your latest column did not even scrape the *surface* of eligible people in London!" He ran a hand through his hair and sat heavily on the edge of the unmade bed, but stood up almost immediately after to continue pacing around the tight space. "Ask me how I know."

"How do you know?" Torquil asked obediently, amusement in their tone.

"Because I've had at least a dozen of them in my house since yesterday morning," he fussed. Emrys used a single hand to tug at one end of his cravat, whipping the length of fabric away from his neck as it unraveled. There was a tiny clattering noise, and he realized absently that he'd forgotten the pin.

As Emrys balled up the silk and tossed it to the ground, Torquil moved their feet from the chair and sat up, leaning over to collect the cravat pin from where it had landed on the worn wooden slats that formed the floor of the second story, which was more of a glorified loft than anything.

"Is that not what you were hoping for?" Torquil asked as they stood easily, frowning at the trail of clothes that formed behind Emrys as he stomped around.

"I was *hoping* to force Wyndham to swallow his words." Emrys whirled around to where Torquil was bent at the waist, picking up his coat. "I did not realize the only one who would face repercussions in this situation was me."

Torquil chuckled and tossed the discarded clothes onto the chair. Emrys' jaw worked irritably as he looked down at Torquil's slender fingers working the top button of his waistcoat free.

"I apologize for any part I've played in your suffering." The sultry tone of their voice immediately caused a shift in Emrys' attitude. "It seems we've both had a trying couple of days." Two more buttons were undone before Torquil gazed up at Emrys through thick lashes. He felt the first sparks of lust within him.

"How fortunate that I have you to help me forget," Emrys said, a sly grin forming on his mouth.

The excitement Emrys found in keeping multiple lovers had become a thing of the past. He couldn't say for certain when the change happened, but the thrill of spontaneity and the uncertainty of what to expect with someone new had lost its appeal almost entirely. Emrys had never admitted it to Torquil—or anyone else—but he had slowly whittled his intimate partners down to one. Torquil knew what he liked, Emrys knew what Torquil liked, and at some point Emrys had decided that was more enticing than any random romp could ever hope to be.

When the last of his waistcoat buttons had been unfastened, Torquil slid the garment from his shoulders and sent it to land with the rest of his things in the chair. Emrys swallowed thickly and searched Torquil's eyes as their purposeful touch found the front of his trousers.

"I hope you're pleased with the new lock," Emrys said, grasping at the tail of their faltering conversation. Torquil teased him endlessly about his desire for them to talk during their meetings. He knew it wasn't the done thing, but he was of the opinion that they'd become more than bedroom partners. They were friends.

Torquil's playful eye roll was expected as their grin grew.

"It's not iron."

Emrys made quick work of unbuttoning his shirt far enough to pull it off over his head. "Now I won't have to worry about forgetting my key," he said, proud of himself. "And you won't have to worry about me kicking the door in."

"Do you know who else will benefit from the new lock?"

Emrys' brows pinched together as he considered the question. Torquil worked alone, as far as he knew.

Before he could think of an answer, or even a good guess, Torquil sank to their knees and leaned forward to press their lips to Emrys' stomach. Their fingers tucked into the waistband of his trousers at each hip and began working them down as they continued their trail of slow kisses.

Emrys let his eyes slide shut as his head tilted back, one hand finding its way into Torquil's hair. "You?" he managed.

Torquil snorted out a laugh and wrapped their hand around Emrys' length, working him slowly. "Every other fae in London," they said cheekily before taking him in their mouth.

Emrys let out a slow groan as he picked his head back up, returning his focus to Torquil. "You let every other fae in London come inside? No wonder you're always so exhausted," he teased.

Torquil resumed work with their hand to allow for a reply.

"I do not, but you've certainly opened the invitation thanks to the change in metal. You realize you're not the only fae who will be pleased to find a lock that is not made of iron, don't you?"

Emrys made a face of discredit at Torquil's accusation. Everyone knew that even the strongest fae magic was useless against iron. What kind of visitors to the press would be concerned with such things? Emrys' confusion must've been evident.

"I know it's not something you have to worry about, but this isn't exactly the safest street," Torquil explained. "I've too many nosy and needy neighbors. Too many people who take offense to the words I publish. Too many opinions about who I am on both sides of society to be losing any of my security."

Emrys' mouth snapped open to respond, realization of what he'd done finally registering, but Torquil stopped him with a deft turn of their wrist.

"May I continue now?" they asked pointedly before wrapping their lips around Emrys again.

His reaction was hot and ready, bolstered by a defensiveness that he hadn't been expecting. Of course he knew Torquil lived in one of the worst parts of town. Of course he understood how important it was for both Torquil and the press to be guarded. The entire building was coated with human protection spells and fae magic for that very reason. How could he have been so thoughtless?

As badly as Emrys wanted to fix his mistake, his focus was starting to fade. The tight slide of Torquil's lips was exactly what he'd been wanting to help wash away the stress. Any ambition he'd had dissolved as Torquil palmed the base of his erection the way he liked, and the last coherent thought he had, made fuzzy by Torquil's soft hum around him, was that he would use his own magic to fortify the building when he left, just as he'd done so many times before.

TORQUIL'S TRIBUNE

Greetings, fatigued folk and harangued humans,

There is much rejoicing throughout the land as the newly wed Wyndham and Roger Wrenwhistle return to London. Many have complained that the couple's absence has created a void of interesting gossip. Hopefully now these complainers will stop sending their letters to this writer.

In accordance with fae tradition, there will be a lavish party at the Wrenwhistle townhouse, heralding the end of the wedding celebrations. As this marriage was between a fae and a human, however, this party will depart from the typical ones of its kind and include human guests.

Lest readers think this column will revert to its obsession over the newly married Wrenwhistles, we can report that the guest list will include many of the unattached hopefuls in our last issue. So there will be much to report on next week.

In other news, the Council for Fae & Human Magical Relations has paused in their launch of the new Barnes-Wrenwhistle rubrics. It was decided that it would be prudent to wait until the couple returned and could contribute to the discussion. Here's hoping they reach a plan soon.

Your esteemed editor,
Torquil Pimpernel-Smith

CHAPTER 8

TORQUIL

COUNCILMEMBER WRENWHISTLE GAVE Torquil the day off in order to publish the *Tribune*. "I will not be able to do so every time," she explained, "but all of the projects I have in mind for you will be best explained when Wyndham and Roger return. Get some rest before the work begins."

After they released the paper and paid all of their delivery people, they collapsed into bed. They wondered idly as they fell asleep if Emrys realized how much gossip he provided them in his visits. Emrys had complained about how his mother was in a rare mood, what with her matchmaking efforts for him and her preparation for the party. He also seemed on edge at the prospect of his younger brother returning to town. Considering the man's lack of forethought, it was unlikely he realized his complaints contained the details Torquil needed for the paper. They smiled to themself, thinking about cravat pins clinking to the ground and the way Emrys held Torquil particularly tight on his most recent visit. They were sure he found entertainment elsewhere; most fae did. But it was so comforting being in Emrys' orbit, however irregularly.

When they returned to the Council chambers the following day, Lex greeted them and announced that Councilmember Iris Wrenwhistle wanted to see them. Torquil put their things on their desk and trooped down the hall to the woman's office.

She smiled at them and gestured to a chair. As soon as they were seated, she slid a paper across the desk. One glance told them it was the most recent copy of the *Tribune*.

They grinned. "Would you like me to sign it for you?"

Her smile widened and she slid another piece of paper across the desk.

Torquil picked it up. It was made of thick, high-quality paper. The elegant script provided the details for the newly wed Wrenwhistles' upcoming party.

Torquil glanced at Wrenwhistle. "Did I misprint any details?"

"That's an invitation."

"Yes."

"For you."

They stared at her.

"I'd like you to attend the party. This is your official invitation."

Torquil skimmed a finger along the edge of the paper. "Am I attending this party in my official capacity as a writer?"

"No," she said, folding her hands on the desk and leaning forward slightly. "You are attending this party in your social capacity as a councilmember."

"I don't think—"

She held up a hand to forestall Torquil's arguments. "I know you have avoided society for years. I understand why. But you cannot create the change you seek merely by playing other people like pawns in a chess game. You are a member of this Council. Change happens in the Council chambers *and* in dinner parties, ballrooms, and sitting rooms."

Torquil swallowed. "I'm not at all sure I will accomplish the change I seek by attending personally. I'm *here* personally, and none of the other councilmembers have adapted their opinions."

She raised an eyebrow.

Torquil had never spoken to any of their own grandparents—their father's parents were dead and their mother's parents...well, the Pimpernels had wanted nothing to do with Torquil—but Torquil felt as though Iris Wrenwhistle was looking at them like a disappointed grandmother. They huffed out a sigh. "Change doesn't happen overnight," they muttered.

She smiled. "Exactly. We will ease you into things. This party will be a good start."

"Are you entirely sure a large-scale party is easing me into things?"

"Would you prefer I invite you to tea? Everyone will be delighted to focus all of their attention on you."

"Oh."

She chuckled. "I know what I'm doing, Torquil. Trust me. I'll introduce you to people as well as I'm able. If you're really uncomfortable, find a seat in a corner and just observe."

They nodded, giving up the battle.

She reached into her desk and pulled out a small purse that she placed in front of them. "I'd like you to get yourself fitted for an appropriate suit. I'll write down the name of a tailor I trust and provide you with a referral, in case they give you any trouble."

Torquil didn't move. "I can't accept your money, Councilmember Wrenwhistle."

"Call me Iris. And consider it an advance. You get paid for your work on the Council." She jotted down a note on a piece of paper and placed it next to the purse. "That is your project for the day."

Glumly, Torquil picked up the purse and the note and returned to their office to collect their things. Then they trudged to the tailor Iris had recommended.

They were unsurprised to be met with distrust upon entering the shop.

"May I help you?" one assistant asked in a spun-sugar tone.

Torquil handed the note over. "I'm here on the recommendation of Iris Wrenwhistle."

The assistant's demeanor immediately changed and they hurried in search of the tailor. Soon, Torquil was being measured and draped. When they explained that they needed an outfit for the 28th, the tailor offered a rack of ready-made clothes. As it turned out, the ready-made suits were significantly less expensive. Torquil bought three: two for evening wear and one for day wear, allowing the tailor to provide suggestions on which to pick. If Iris was going to follow through on her threat to introduce them to society, they would need to be prepared.

As their items were being wrapped in parcels, they wandered the shop. A selection of jewelry caught their eye and they picked up a cravat pin, twiddling it between their fingers. They had always admired elegant things, but it was one thing to admire them and another thing to buy them. They were already uncomfortable with spending so much on clothes as it was. They put the cravat pin back before anyone could persuade them to buy it, collected their parcels, and left.

Stepping out onto the street, they debated whether or not to go home. Finally, they returned to the Council chambers and Iris' office. Without preamble, they unwrapped each parcel and held up the suits for her inspection.

She beamed and reached a hand out to slide her fingers down the material. "Excellent choices," she said. She tugged on the sleeve of one of the coats. "Wear this one to the party."

They nodded and folded the clothes over their arm. "Anything else?"

"No," she said, returning to her work. "I'll see you at the party, Torquil."

Torquil stood and headed for the door, pausing with one hand on the doorknob. "Iris?" they said quietly.

"Yes?"

They swallowed. "My grandparents won't be there, will they?"

The thought of coming face-to-face with the people who had caused so much grief and pain was horrifying. Torquil had no idea what they would even say to them. *Am I such an abomination? Why did you abandon us? Abandon me?* It was one thing to live in the same city as the people who hated them, and to become famous and successful despite them. It was another thing entirely to actually interact with such people.

Iris looked up in surprise and then her expression quickly changed to one of sympathy. "No," she said, her tone gentle. "I would never do that to you." She hesitated. "Your grandmother is in mourning for her husband currently. I believe she means to stay abroad until the mourning period is over."

Torquil was not aware their grandfather had died, although they couldn't drum up any sort of emotion in response. "Thank you," they said.

They returned home and carefully hung up their new clothes. They stared at them for a long time. Then they placed the invitation on their writing desk and collapsed back into bed.

CHAPTER 9

EMRYS

EMRYS HAD NEVER BEEN MORE glad to see one of his siblings than when Wyndham stepped out of the carriage that morning. He'd emerged with an air of rejuvenation to face the crowd gathered to greet them. This was only topped by the enormous smile Roger wore as he was helped down.

Their arrival marked the shift of Mrs. Wrenwhistle's attention from one brother to the next, and Emrys could finally breathe a sigh of relief over the pause in his endless stream of suitors, if only for a little while. He was more than happy to hand all of that focus right back to the couple everyone had been losing their minds over for the past several months.

Hours later, after the excitement had settled and he'd finally been able to slip away from the house unnoticed, Emrys couldn't help but laugh to himself as he used his magic to unlock the worn wooden door separating him from one of his favorite places of respite.

"Well," he began, unable to mask his delight. "Everyone's favorite twosome has finally returned."

Emrys found Torquil lying across the bed on their stomach, knees bent and ankles crossed in the air. They didn't look up from what they were writing on a stack of papers. Emrys grabbed the back of Torquil's chair and pulled it away from the desk so he could sling a leg over the seat and sit backwards, crossing his forearms on the backrest.

"Pleased, are you?" Torquil asked, grinning down at the words they were still writing. Emrys watched them for a moment, taking advantage of the rare opportunity to let his focus on them linger.

"Both are looking fresh-faced and thoroughly fucked," Emrys assured them. He reached into the pocket of his coat and pulled out a bundle of parchment, the contents long since cooled but still fragrant. "I dare you to put *that* in the *Tribune*."

Torquil laughed at that, finally lifting their attention away from their work.

"I'd rather not be a participant in your malevolence toward them," Torquil said, setting their quill in the pot tucked carefully into the bunched blanket. Emrys grinned at them, not entirely sure what the word meant. It was another he would have to look up later on. He held out the treat he'd brought along instead, changing the subject. Torquil narrowed their eyes in suspicion.

"It's only sugared almonds." Emrys unfolded the parchment and held it out again, taking one for himself to pop into his mouth.

"Where are they from?" Torquil asked, sitting up carefully to avoid spilling their ink. Emrys sighed loudly, putting on an annoyed look that held no weight.

"From the cart you prefer," he promised blandly.

Torquil's eyes lit up. Emrys had discovered over the years that food was the only generosity Torquil would accept without putting up some kind of a fight. Torquil collected the ink and papers and hurried off the bed to set it all on the desk. Emrys stood from the little chair and turned to sit on it the correct way in just enough time to catch Torquil around the waist, pulling them onto his lap. Torquil leaned into him, settling against his chest with no effort at all as they dug around in the parchment with their fingertips. Emrys knew they were searching for the ones with the most sugar that always settled at the bottom.

"At Mother's insistence, Wyndham and Roger will be staying with us while their new townhouse is renovated. I'm not sure if I'm more glad that they'll be suffering as newlyweds under our roof or that it'll continue to distract from the other important task at hand."

Torquil chuckled as they chewed. "Can it not be both?"

"Yes, I suppose so." Emrys used his free hand to trace his neatly groomed fingernails along Torquil's exposed thigh. It was another treat to have found them lounging in a shirt and nothing else; a fae trait if there ever was one, and certainly one that Emrys appreciated. "They had hardly been home a quarter of an hour before Wyndham looked as though he was ready to shove Roger back into the carriage and leave."

Torquil gave Emrys a sideways glance. "And did you have anything to do with that?"

Emrys could do nothing to hide his mischievous expression. "Perhaps."

Torquil grinned and shook their head as they ate a few more almonds. They sat together in companionable silence for a while, Emrys taking everything he needed—and wanted, truthfully—from his visit.

When the parchment was empty, save for the loose sugar left behind, Torquil turned their attention on Emrys. They made slow work of removing the sugar from their fingertips in a painfully suggestive way that Emrys could feel all the way to his core. Torquil shifted on Emrys' lap as they slid their arms around his shoulders and neck. Their kiss was gentle, easy to lean into.

Emrys brought his hands together behind Torquil's back to crumple up the parchment. He'd made the mistake one too many times of throwing things carelessly onto the bestrewn writing desk and completely ruining Torquil's work, so he broke their kiss to look for a safe spot to set it down instead.

A small, obnoxiously decorative paper caught his attention. He could recognize his mother's work anywhere.

"Planning on crashing Wyndham's party, then?" Emrys asked, sliding his hands from Torquil's hips to their shoulders and back down again as their lips met. "You must really be desperate for something to write about."

The silence that followed was telling. Emrys pulled away again to look up into Torquil's eyes.

"Iris invited me," they finally admitted. "Or rather, she informed me that I would be attending."

Emrys laughed. "That sounds like her."

"I'm to start going to more social events now that I'm on the Council."

"That's wonderful," Emrys said, rubbing his thumbs against the thin fabric covering their hips.

"Is it?" Torquil grimaced, leaning to rest their forehead on Emrys' shoulder. "It feels like punishment." Emrys laughed again, quieter this time, and wrapped his arms around Torquil, hugging them close. "I've been trying to think of an excuse for why I cannot go."

Emrys gasped sharply. "You would deny my grandmother?"

Torquil made a miserable whimper against the crook of Emrys' shoulder, and Emrys grinned.

"Don't fret," he said gently. "Just remember, no matter how much you hate it, Wyndham will be having a worse time than you. That's what always helps me."

🔥

THE PARTY HAD BEEN GOING for nearly three hours by the time Emrys gave up on looking for Torquil in the crowd of guests ambling about.

It had been a similar experience at the Wrenwhistle estate: Torquil appeared at the wedding reception just long enough to say they had shown up, before vanishing again. Emrys knew how much Torquil disliked being in the public eye. For someone who knew so much about everyone else's business, they were shockingly elusive, but it was hard to deny the reasoning behind it.

He thought back to the few occasions Torquil had opened up to him about feeling like they did not have a place in society. Humans and fae alike had their reasons for why Torquil did not belong to either side, and the only place left was stuck in the middle. Torquil had decided it was safest to belong to nobody but themself. Emrys thought that was incredibly brave, but quite obviously very lonely, as well. Not that Torquil would ever admit it.

The thought of being invisible in a room full of people was something Emrys could not even begin to imagine. He made a point of using every last bit of etiquette training he'd been given whenever possible, approaching everyone he knew and requesting introductions to those he did not. None could feign interest in topics others enjoyed better than he could. It was the easiest way to please his mother, first and foremost, but he could not deny that he also quite enjoyed being the center of attention.

With a drink in his hand, Emrys strode to where Wyndham and Roger had planted themselves on one of the sofas that had been repositioned along the wall and helped himself to a seat on a chair nearby. He offered them a smug look.

"Glad to be back yet?" Emrys goaded, reclining a bit in his seat to further accentuate the way they were sitting so stiffly next to one another.

"Yes, it's very nice to be back in London," Roger offered politely, patting his hand atop the ones he and Wyndham already had clasped together on Roger's thigh. He had always been a fidgety sort of person. "Though we will not soon forget the pleasure we found in the country over the past weeks, to be sure."

Emrys had to bite back his smirk. The man really made it too easy. Wyndham gave Emrys a look of warning that he would've been smart to mind, but he'd missed this too much to let it go.

"I couldn't help but overhear last evening that you seem to have brought that pleasure home with you," Emrys said with a wink. It was a bold lie on his part, but the look on Roger's face said there must've been some truth to it. "If you would be so kind as to keep your amorous commotion to a minimum while we all share the house, I know the rest of us would greatly appreciate it."

Roger stuttered as he attempted to respond, but Wyndham got there first.

"Haven't you got anyone else to bother?" his brother asked mildly.

Emrys arched an eyebrow at him. He'd been expecting anything other than such a calm, collected response.

"On second thought," Emrys said as he stood from the chair, heeding his brother's request, "if this is what a copious amount of copulation does for Wyndham's horrid temper, then I say well done, Roger." He offered them a nod and turned back to join the rest of the party.

It took no time at all for him to find his grandmother speaking with a few of the other councilmembers. Emrys got her attention with a gentle touch on the back of her shoulder before he bent to kiss her cheek.

Iris gave him a bright smile. "Are you having a nice evening, darling?"

"I cannot recall the last time I did not enjoy myself at a party," he told her honestly.

She laughed in her sweet way and nodded as she made a quick assessment of the adjoined rooms. Emrys did not have to guess who she was looking for, though he couldn't tell her he knew who she was expecting to see.

"I suppose everyone is not so lucky," his grandmother said, a hint of disappointment in her tone.

Emrys sipped his wine and took another glance of his own around the crowded space.

He had often wondered what it would be like to attend a social event with someone on his arm. He was endlessly curious about how it must feel to enjoy an evening full of food and dance and good company knowing that, at the end of it, someone would be waiting to curl up with him in bed and laugh about the night's happenings together.

Emrys knew that he was probably closer to that reality than ever before. Several of the callers he'd welcomed earlier in the week were at the party as well, sending all of their most endearing glances his way. Only a few had been so bold as to approach him. He had to commend them for that.

"No, I suppose not," Emrys finally responded.

Just as he moved to tip his wine glass back so he could drain the rest of it, his grandmother's attention sharpened on something behind him. Her pleased expression caused Emrys to forget himself, and he spun around to see Torquil standing in the wide doorway. A rousing mix of emotions swirled with his magic in his chest as a grin broke across his features.

"Luckily for us, there is always room for growth," Iris said.

CHAPTER 10
TORQUIL

TORQUIL HAD AGONIZED for hours over whether to arrive early, on time, late, or not at all. They fussed over their hair, wishing for once that it was less unruly. Then they had fussed over their cravat, irritated that they did not know how to tie it nicely. Their father hadn't known anything other than a simple knot, and their mother had always been dismissive of the very idea of society. So Torquil had never learned much by way of fancy attire or social graces. With no schooling on small talk, an extreme discomfort with attention, and acute anxiety in crowds, they now felt entirely unprepared for the evening. It was hard to imagine Iris' scheme being successful to any degree.

Finally they walked to the other side of town, but had been too nervous to enter the house. Instead, they wandered around the block and into the park until they finally got up the nerve to attend the party. As soon as they walked through the door, they regretted it. They ought to have arrived early. A bit of painful small talk, a few awkward smiles, and then they could have scooted out, obligation complete.

Now the house was full of guests. Several turned at Torquil's entrance, not bothering to hide their expressions of shock, disapproval, or outright contempt. Mrs. Wrenwhistle bustled over to them.

"Mx. Pimpernel-Smith!" she said. "Or should I call you Councilmember now? Are you here to write about the party for your column?"

They pasted on a smile. "I answer to both, ma'am." They paused and then added, "Iris invited me."

She gave them a tight smile that seemed to match their own. "Of course." She looked around the room and then said, "Ah, good. There she is now."

Iris came forward and took both of Torquil's hands in her own. "I'm so glad you made it."

Mrs. Wrenwhistle hurried off, clearly relieved to be absolved of her hostessing duties where Torquil was concerned.

Torquil winced. "I'm sorry I'm late."

Iris squeezed their hands. "It's fashionable to be late. Would you like some wine?" Without waiting for an answer, she tucked their hand around her arm and led them through the room. She grabbed a glass of wine off a passing tray and handed it over. Before Torquil could take their first sip, they were being introduced to people.

Some of them, like Councilmember Barnes' wife and Councilmember Applewood's wife, were pleased to meet them. Most, however, gave them the same tight smiles Mrs. Wrenwhistle had offered. Torquil couldn't be sure if it was their fae-human status or their gossip column that people took most issue with. As they followed Iris through the room, they recognized face after face that they had written about, secret after secret that they knew. How could they make small talk with these people? *Good evening. How is your mistress? Nice to see you. Did you have a good elopement? Feeling better after last year's scandal?*

At one point, they were even introduced to Emrys. The moment was fraught with the relief of seeing a friendly face and the agony of not being able to curl into Emrys' arms. They exchanged polite nods and neutral pleasantries, until Torquil's tour continued into the next room.

Iris guided them to a refreshment table and said, "You've made it through the worst of it. Have a bite if you'd like, take a seat if you need to, but I'd like to see you talking to someone this evening." She considered. "I'll even give you leave to find a single person and latch onto them for the night. I'd offer but I'm very social and I'm not sure you'd like that."

They chuckled. "Probably not. Thank you." She gave their shoulder a pat and walked off.

Torquil drained their glass and filled a plate with some tiny sandwiches. They glanced around the room, noting the newlyweds sitting to the side. They debated joining the couple. They weren't entirely sure how well they were liked by Wyndham and Roger Wrenwhistle. So they were surprised when Wyndham gave them a friendly nod.

Torquil strode over. "The men of the hour," they greeted with a grin. "Welcome back to London."

Wyndham smirked. "Why don't you join us? Considering the way you downed that glass of wine, it looks like you could use a moment."

Feeling a little embarrassed for the brief show of nerves, Torquil took a seat opposite the sofa.

"Are you all right?" Roger said.

Torquil raised an eyebrow. "Do I look that bad, Mr. Wrenwhistle?"

Roger shook his head slightly. "I didn't mean that—"

"Actually," Wyndham cut in, "that suit is the nicest thing I've ever seen you wear."

Roger sighed and gave his husband a reproving glance. "You look a little...er..."

"Miserable," Wyndham supplied.

Torquil took a deep breath and let it out slowly. "I'm afraid social niceties are not my strongest suit. But as a councilmember, socializing is...apparently an expectation now."

"Oh," Roger said, looking sympathetic. He hesitated for a moment and then said, "Wyn doesn't like parties either."

Wyndham clicked his tongue, but didn't argue the point. Torquil found themself smiling. They remembered what Emrys had said the night prior: *Just remember, no matter how much you hate it, Wyndham will be having a worse time than you.* Oddly enough, it hadn't occurred to them to seek refuge with the couple the party was being held for.

Wyndham waved a hand at Torquil's plate. "Eat, Pimpernel-Smith. You don't have to talk if you don't want to. Goodness knows I'm not one for idle chatter."

Relief filled Torquil's chest at the words. They ate one of the sandwiches as the three of them sat in silence. Finally, they said, "I'd ask you how married life is treating you, but I imagine you're sick to death of answering that question."

Roger chuckled. "Oh, our answer is practically rote by now. We're very happy. We love the country. Our home is beautiful. Wyn spoils me. We have a kitten."

"Mother hates her," Wyndham put in.

Torquil coughed around a bite of sandwich. "You brought the kitten with you?"

Roger blinked in surprise. "Of course. You wouldn't expect us to leave the poor thing, would you?"

Torquil shrugged. "Most people do, I expect. What's her name?"

Roger's expression softened. "Peony."

Torquil grinned. "How sweet. What's she like?"

"Oh, she's a right little hellion," Wyndham said easily.

Roger batted at his husband without rancor. "Nonsense. She's perfect. Just a little playful."

Wyndham snorted.

"Are you looking forward to working on the Council?" Torquil said, unable to think of any more kitten-related questions.

Roger sat up. "Oh, yes. We have a great many ideas. I'd show you my notes but they're upstairs."

"How are *you* liking work on the Council?" Wyndham asked, raising an eyebrow.

Torquil shifted in their seat. "It's been interesting."

"*Interesting*," Wyndham parroted.

"Your grandmother and your father have been very kind and welcoming," they said.

Wyndham rolled his eyes. "Ah. So everyone else has been horrid."

Roger wrung his hands. "Oh, dear. Have they really? I know they can be dreadfully intimidating."

"I'm sure you won't have any trouble," Torquil said as soothingly as they could. "They're just…not quite sure what to make of me yet. That's all."

Wyndham narrowed his eyes. "Because of your parentage or because of your paper?"

Torquil shrugged. "Both?"

recently. Whoever wins the heart of one of the most eligible gentlemen in London will need to be an extraordinary catch indeed. People are already wondering what the gentleman is looking for: charm, beauty, elegance, breeding, poise, wit?

Miss Aveline has not received the same marked attention as her brother in terms of suitors. However, this humble writer suggests that only a fool would be unaware of the young lady's charms.

Other notable guests of the party include the entire Council and almost every titled and wealthy fae within a fifty mile radius.

This writer waits with bated breath for the next big event.

Your esteemed editor,
Torquil Pimpernel-Smith

CHAPTER 11

EMRYS

EVEN WITH THE help of powerful cleaning spells performed by two of their servants who were skilled with human magic, the townhouse was in no shape to welcome callers the next morning. After Wyndham and Roger had taken their leave, the party had spilled over into the early hours, and evidently into other parts of the house that had not been designated for guests.

Emrys couldn't help but laugh to himself over his mother's frantic rushing about as she ranted over the disrespect and disregard for etiquette that some people had. He wanted to tell her it was likely because she had sent out too many invitations. Their home was reasonably sized for hosting, but with everyone clamoring to be included in a party celebrating the couple who had demonstrated the most fascinating show of magic anyone had seen in some time, it should have been expected that every last invitation would be accepted and that others without one would sneak in, as well. Emrys knew better than to voice his thoughts on the subject, however.

"I've already sent out letters to this morning's callers, instructing them to meet us in the Park instead," Mrs. Wrenwhistle informed him briskly, swiping a hand over her neatly-styled hair to tuck away a strand that had fallen loose near her temple.

Emrys' high spirits dimmed with this information. He'd secretly hoped his mother's frustration would distract her from the rest of their plans. But she had never been one to miss an appointment, especially if it was one that would bring light to how well their family looked in society.

"Mother, may I please come with you?" Aveline was always ready for a chance to be seen, as well.

Mrs. Wrenwhistle turned to where she was sitting and appraised her with a quick glance. "Yes, we'll all go. Someone hurry up and inform Wyndham and Roger. We're leaving at half ten."

Aveline gasped with delight and picked up her skirts as she pranced toward the stairs. Emrys smirked, knowing that Wyndham would be furious over such a demand so early in the morning. Perhaps their time in the Park would be fun, after all.

When they arrived, Emrys helped his mother and sister from the carriage, leaving Wyndham to see after his husband. A hint of curiosity drew his attention to the people he could already see promenading along the main stretch where they were being dropped off.

The air was cold, and most were thoroughly bundled in their heavy coats and scarves. Mrs. Wrenwhistle had donned a thick shawl and her hideously oversized fur muff. It was one of the first gifts their father had given her in their marriage and she treated it like a prized possession. Emrys also liked to think it was a bit romantic that her hands were kept warm by the accessory even in his absence, as was often the case.

Emrys grinned with an exhale, the air clouding in front of his face.

"Nothing says *finding love* like freezing your bollocks off."

"Emrys," Mrs. Wrenwhistle scolded under her breath. "Your potential suitor should be here any moment. Do not let them hear you speaking this way."

Wyndham scoffed. "They'd be better off getting used to it now."

Emrys cut him a challenging look. "Yes, we're all still shocked that Roger was unaffected by your atrocious disposition enough to agree to a lifetime of it. Perhaps it is best to show your true colors from the start."

Roger put a hand on Wyndham's chest, restraining him before he could respond. Emrys got a thrill from the way his brother's jaw tightened.

"What I would give to have children who behaved themselves in public," Mrs. Wrenwhistle muttered tightly through gritted teeth. She pushed her way between her sons and used her bundled hands to urge Emrys along. He relented, turning so he could start down the gravel path with the rest of them close behind.

"The *Tribune* may as well have been called *The Wrenwhistles* this morning," Aveline said with a smile, pulling her long wrap tighter around her shoulders. "We should invite Torquil to all of our parties from now on so they can keep describing us in such a lovely manner, don't you think?"

"It was nice to sit and chat with them for once," Roger agreed earnestly.

Mrs. Wrenwhistle was notably silent on the subject.

Emrys thought back to the previous night. Even after his initial excitement over seeing that Torquil actually accepted the invitation had worn off, he really had not expected how invigorating it was to share a room with them that did not contain a familiar little writing desk and creaky old bed.

He'd found that he could not keep himself from looking in Torquil's direction every few minutes, checking to make sure they were...safe? That notion seemed foolish. How could they have been unsafe inside what had arguably been the most magic-filled space in the whole city at the time?

A grin tugged at the corners of Emrys' lips as he thought of the moment his grandmother had dragged Torquil in his direction.

"Darling, I am unsure if you've ever been properly introduced to the newest member of the Council," Iris had said to him in her tone that meant she wanted him to be serious for once. "Torquil Pimpernel-Smith. Torquil, this is one of my other grandsons, Emrys."

Barely able to contain his amusement, Emrys had bowed his head slightly before putting on his most endearing smile. Torquil's expression had been one of pure distress, though Emrys thought he could see a hint of something more.

"A pleasure to have a formal introduction," Emrys said. He decided to play along, hopeful that it would put Torquil more at ease. On a couple of occasions, they

had done something similar in the bedroom, using pretend scenarios to build up the tension between them.

After a short pause, Emrys felt a wash of relief—and arousal—when Torquil offered their quirky half-grin in response.

"The pleasure is all mine, I assure you," they said with an answering bow.

Emrys swallowed, remembering suddenly that his grandmother was still standing there. "Your column has done wonders for my family," he started, attempting a recovery. "I should think I owe you my gratitude, as well."

"Not at all," Torquil reassured him. "I write to inform. I should be the one thanking you and your siblings for all of the easy material."

Emrys chuckled at that. "I will accept that on everyone's behalf, although I'm not sure Wyndham has always felt very appreciative of your exposing words."

Torquil shrugged. "As I said, I share facts. I stir thoughts. I entertain minds. What others decide to do is not my problem."

IT HAD BEEN fortunate for Emrys that his grandmother pulled Torquil off for more introductions at that point, or else he was certain he would've needed to excuse himself instead.

His distraction had continued throughout the rest of the evening as he mingled with Keelan and his other friends and worked to maintain the relationships he knew would be important for his future. For him, that was what parties were usually all about. It was his preferred version of being seen by all of the right people. Not that a promenade in the Park wasn't effective, but it was far easier to talk to boring people with a drink in his hand.

"Ah!" Mrs. Wrenwhistle exclaimed with a bright smile and what Emrys thought sounded like a hint of relief. "There they are."

He followed his mother's gaze down the leaf-littered path that connected to the one they were on. When he realized who she was referring to, his stomach dropped.

"Mrs. Wrenwhistle," the older of the two called back in greeting. "What a splendid idea it was to move this rendezvous to the Park." Their bright red nose and chattering teeth said otherwise, but Emrys knew as well as anyone that it was a bad look to deny his mother of anything.

"Yes, a perfect excuse to get out and enjoy this...*fine* weather," Mrs. Wrenwhistle agreed, forcing pleasantries of her own. She gestured toward the two people they had been waiting on, making the introductions since no one else was there to announce them. "Mx. Hortense Irving and Mr. Gerald Irving," she said, giving Emrys a pleased look.

He put on a smile, recognizing that unnecessary introductions were becoming a bit of a pattern in his life. He had known Gerald Irving for years; they belonged to the same social club. The man was a superior fencer—his swordplay was something to be admired—though, unfortunately, this compliment could not be extended to the bedroom. Emrys had learned that lesson the hard way.

"Mx. Irving, Mr. Irving," he greeted as the three of them bowed in unison.

"I say," Mr. Irving began almost immediately in monotone, "what a fashionable coat you've got there. I simply could not decide which of mine to wear this morning. Dashed cold, is it not?"

Emrys somehow managed to hide his grimace, nodding instead as he offered the man his arm. "I suppose we must be grateful for one so that we may enjoy the other," he said with a small shrug.

"Or we can complain about both," Mr. Irving offered with an upturned nose.

Emrys' eyes went wide as he turned his focus on the path ahead, wondering with a newfound sense of embarrassment how he *ever* could have been so drunk as to sleep with the man walking beside him.

He was handsome enough, but it had taken a great many glasses of wine to make his droll way of speaking and generally negative attitude fade into something that Emrys had found palatable enough to take to bed one night when they were much younger and, at least on his own part, much more foolish.

As Irving carried the conversation, Emrys supplied sounds of acknowledgement whenever it seemed appropriate, listening but not absorbing anything he was saying.

Emrys knew he would be wise to pay attention. Despite how he felt, there was a very real chance that someone like Gerald Irving was his most ideal match. The Irvings were another prominent human family in society. They were also quite wealthy, and despite not being the most magically powerful of his five siblings by a longshot, Gerald had still shown up on the same list as Emrys in the *Tribune*.

That morning's gossip paper was tucked into his breast pocket, protected from the chilly air underneath his layers of clothing.

Emrys' thoughts tumbled over what Torquil had written about him.

Whoever wins the heart of one of the most eligible gentlemen in London will need to be an extraordinary catch indeed. People are already wondering what the gentleman is looking for.

What *was* Emrys looking for? His brow furrowed as he realized he truly did not know. He had always known that he would be expected to marry someday. His family's name and legacy depended on it.

Emrys peered over his shoulder at the rest of the party trailing behind them. His mother noticed and offered him an encouraging grin, nodding her approval.

Perhaps it wasn't that Emrys did not know what he wanted. He simply understood that what he wanted would make little difference when it came to picking a spouse. It was less about what he desired and more about which desirable traits someone possessed. It did not matter if he found someone attractive, or entertaining, or interesting. Instead, they needed to be an equal, both in social status as well as magical aptitude. That was what his mother had always told him.

Resigned, Emrys forced himself to try and catch up with whatever Irving had been going on about at his side, though he couldn't quite muster the energy to bring back his hollow smile.

CHAPTER 12

TORQUIL

GOING to a party one evening and then publishing the *Tribune* early the next morning was not ideal. Reporting to the Council chambers almost as soon as the papers had been distributed made it all even worse, but Torquil couldn't bring themself to be too irritated, considering how understanding Iris had been the past week in letting them leave early and take extra days off.

Despite fatigue, they found themself almost looking forward to work. It was a meeting day, according to the calendar Iris had provided. Wyndham and Roger were reporting for their first day and Torquil hoped the gentlemen's presence would mark a change in the dynamic. As such, they arrived in the chambers early.

They walked in amidst a flurry of activity. Roger was moving chairs around the long table, assisted by two nervous-looking aides. Wyndham was leaning against the corner of the table, watching his husband with an expression of equal parts amusement and fondness.

Roger saw Torquil first and greeted them with a cheery "Good morning!"

Wyndham twisted around to nod at Torquil.

"Good morning," Torquil replied, walking to the front of the room.

"What's all this?" Cricket said, entering through a side door.

Roger gave an annoyed sort of huff. "I had no idea the Council sat like this even when there wasn't an audience."

"Bit premature for you to be making changes like this, isn't it?" Gibbs said, entering the room as well.

Councilmembers trickled into the room, most of them offering a remark of surprise, irritation, or confusion. Barnes walked in and chuckled before giving his son a kiss on the cheek and shaking Wyndham's hand in greeting. Applewood didn't comment at all, but merely gave a small smile before sedately taking a seat. Williams was particularly perturbed and was in the midst of lecturing Roger that such goingson needed prior approval when Iris strode in.

"Ah," she said, looking at the tableau. "I see you're ready to work already, Mr. Wrenwhistle." Roger beamed. Wyndham gave his grandmother a kiss on the cheek in greeting. She turned her cheek for him and then gave Williams an arch look. "Is there a problem?"

"He can't just come in here and start changing things," Gibbs said.

"Can't he?" Barnes replied in a mild tone as he took his seat.

"How you've gotten any work done when you're all sitting on one side of the table is beyond me," Roger said, taking a seat as well.

"We checked the calendar," Wyndham added as he sat next to Roger. "There aren't any audiences today. This seemed more conducive to productive conversation. Unless, of course, there's a meeting room I'm unaware of?" He said this with a charming smile, seemingly oblivious to the fact that taking his seat next to his husband had quickly upset the careful seating arrangements dividing fae and humans. Torquil suspected Wyndham either didn't care that he was causing an upset or was intentionally being provocative.

Torquil decided to throw their lot in with the couple and took their seat on Roger's other side, adding to the disarray. They couldn't help a small vindictive pleasure in seeing Cricket gasp and Gibbs glare. They glanced at Iris, who gave them an approving nod before sitting next to her grandson.

"This is absurd," Gibbs complained. "None of you are following protocol at all."

"Exactly." Williams said, stubbornly taking his old seat. "These sorts of changes require approval."

"I can't imagine a small change in seating is such an issue," Roger said.

"I give my approval," Iris said coolly.

"And mine," Wyndham said with a grin.

Barnes raised his hand to add his own approval, surprising nobody.

"I wasn't too fond of the old arrangement, to be honest," Apple-wood said.

"Nor I," Torquil said.

Gibbs narrowed his eyes at them.

"As Councilmember Roger Wrenwhistle pointed out," Torquil added, "this arrangement is much better suited to conversation."

Cricket sighed. "They do have a point," she muttered and took her seat.

"We appointed three young people to this Council to add fresh ideas," Iris said. "What is the point of doing so if we're going to balk at every change they suggest? I'm not saying every idea will be perfect," she went on, "but this one is quite minor and has merit. Let's not quibble about the details. We have work to do."

The rest of the Council sat down, grumbling quietly. Roger smiled. "Thank you, Councilmember Wrenwhistle—goodness, we will need to determine a good way to tell the three of us apart when we talk, won't we? Such a mouthful. Did we miss anything of import while we were out of town? I did have a list of ideas I wanted to share, but I don't want to get ahead of myself."

Torquil was impressed. The gentleman spoke with uncharacteristic confidence. They looked over at Roger, noting the way the man's chin was tilted up slightly. Marriage, it seemed, was very good for him. Then Torquil noticed that Wyndham's hand was reaching over into Roger's lap to clasp his hand tightly, and they noticed the blush on Roger's cheeks. Ah. So the confidence was an act. Still, they thought as they hid a smile, marriage looked very good on him.

Iris chuckled a little. "In truth, we decided to wait until your return before starting any big projects," she said. "We'd like to launch the new rubric but it was determined that it would be better to wait for you before doing so, as you might have some ideas for how that would look."

"And," Barnes put in, "young Councilmember Pimpernel-Smith

made an excellent observation that fae-human children ought to be considered before we take any action."

Roger looked delighted. "I *do* have some ideas for how we should launch the rubric. But I agree that we ought to have everything figured out first." He turned to Torquil. "You made a very good point," he said. "Did you have any particular ideas for which rubric would work best?"

Torquil couldn't help the smile at Roger's compliment, as well as the question that had been asked without a trace of sarcasm. "A few," they said. "My first idea—which I offered to the Council—was to give these particular children the choice of rubric they would like to be held to. Many may have a preference in magic system. However..." Roger nodded encouragingly. "I don't think it would be amiss to have a separate rubric altogether. I was trained by both of my parents. I'm not sure I would ever score well on either the fae or human rubric, even if the newer ones had been available when I was a child. That is, if an examiner had been willing to see me," they added.

Roger frowned at this. "Do you mean to say they *refused* to test you?"

Torquil nodded.

Roger huffed. "Well, we'll certainly have to change *that.*"

"I should like that very much," Torquil said earnestly. "I understand a third rubric may be asking a bit much but—"

"Why would you say that?" Wyndham said. "If you are skilled in both magic systems but not fully a master of either, that is essentially a third magic system in its own right. I'm sure I couldn't manage Roger's spells. And though Roger has gained impressive proficiency in feeling magic, he cannot manipulate fae magic the way I can. For a person to be able to do both, even partially, is...extraordinary."

Torquil felt something twist in their chest that they couldn't quite name. To have their magic validated so immediately—not only validated, but complimented—was unlike anything they had ever experienced.

"Well, if you're so keen to do a third rubric," Williams said testily, "perhaps that's what you ought to work on."

"I quite agree," Iris said, so swiftly that Torquil suspected she'd planned to make that suggestion herself. "I think the three of you will work together very well. We already know Wyndham and Roger make a good team when it comes to building rubrics. I'm sure Torquil will be a match for your creativity." She turned to the rest of the room. "And perhaps we ought to shelve the rest of the rubric project until the third one is complete."

Cricket scoffed. "Well, since the *Tribune* so conveniently wrote about the rubrics, the public is clamoring for them to take effect."

"Not very far-sighted of you," Gibbs sneered.

Torquil shrugged. "Thankfully, the writer of the *Tribune* is present and will be more than happy to explain the delay."

"Besides," Applewood said softly, "we didn't expect there to be a delay either. Just last week we were prepared to launch it. If there's any shortsightedness to be had, it's on the Council's side for providing the *Tribune* with that bit of news in the first place."

"Quite so," Iris said. "Thank you, Councilmember Applewood. I propose we all continue with our other projects in the meantime. Williams, perhaps you'd like a report of current state?"

Williams grumbled that he would. Torquil sat back as the councilmembers gave a report on each of their projects: Gibbs shared some of the updated statistics of passing rates for the human magical test, the Hastings Exam, and the fae magical test, the Sciurus Exam; Barnes and Applewood described some improvements to the process for examiner applications; and Cricket provided a budget report. Finally, the Council was dismissed.

"Torquil, would you show the Wrenwhistles to your shared office?" Iris said.

Torquil nodded and led the two gentlemen out of the room and to the end of the hall to their office. Wyndham was the last one into the room and he closed the door and leaned against it.

"Stars above," he grumbled.

Roger gave Torquil a concerned glance. "I see what you meant about them acting horrid."

Torquil chuckled. "That was probably one of the more enjoyable conversations I've experienced here."

Wyndham scoffed. "Of course it was. Fools."

"Well, I'm glad we were grouped together," Roger said. "I cannot wait to witness your magic, Torquil. I'm sure it must be extraordinary."

Torquil grimaced. "It's certainly something. To be honest, I barely use it if I can help it."

Roger's mouth dropped open. "Whyever not?"

Torquil shrugged. "My magic is not very comfortable for me."

"What do you mean? Is it painful?"

Torquil sank into one of the chairs. "Not...painful." They scrubbed a hand through their hair. "It just never feels right. Doing magic makes me feel like my skin is too tight or—I don't know—like the room is filled with too much incense. I don't even bother to feel my magic when I cast anymore."

"That's awful," Roger said, taking a chair opposite. "So you never do magic?"

"I do it as little as possible."

Roger and Wyndham shared a look. Then Wyndham said, "How much of your dislike of your magic is based on your own personal feeling, and how much is based on how others react to it?"

Torquil opened their mouth to respond and then quickly closed it again. "I'm not sure," they finally admitted.

Wyndham nodded as if this was what he expected to hear. "Fae magic is still considered somewhat taboo," he said. "For most humans, fae magic is wild and terrifying. We were all taught at very young ages to never perform magic in front of humans unless it was absolutely necessary. I've always felt most comfortable in the country because of it. My magic can roam freely there." He paused. "But if you've had people criticize your magic for a long time, I can see how it might not feel safe to use it."

Torquil almost replied that they'd never said they didn't feel safe. But Wyndham had hit on a truth that Torquil had tried not to admit to themself for years.

Roger leaned forward in his seat and said softly, "Do you think you'll feel safe enough to use your magic in front of us?"

"I'm quite rusty."

"Don't worry about that," Roger said quickly. "Wyn gets very excited when he starts new projects—even if he won't admit it. He'll demand spell after spell from you, if I know him."

Wyndham rolled his eyes. "You're one to talk. This one," he said, coming forward to lean his hip against the back of Roger's chair and wrap his arm around his husband's shoulders, "is like a dog after a bone when magic is involved."

Roger tsked. "I'm nothing of the sort."

Torquil laughed, ignoring the small pang in their chest at the thought that they shared a similar familiarity with Emrys. "Very well. I'll comply for the sake of science. But please don't say I didn't warn you," they cautioned. "I've been told my magic is——"

Roger held up a hand. "If anyone knows what it's like to be judged incorrectly for their magic, it's us. We've both experienced our own slights and discriminations due to our magical abilities. We won't judge you."

"Well," Wyndham drawled. "We might judge you, but we won't be asses about it."

"Fair enough," Torquil said with a grin.

"Do we have to meet here, do you think?" Roger said. "I'm wondering because I know Wyn does much better when we're in private —" Wyndham snorted. Roger blushed. "I mean Wyn performs his magic much more comfortably when there aren't as many people near-by," he amended, shooting an irritated glance at his husband. "So perhaps you will too."

"We might need to ask Iris first," Torquil said. "But I imagine she won't care where we work as long as we give her updates."

Roger nodded. "Would you like to practice at your home or ours? We're staying with the Wrenwhistles while our home is being renovated. But I'm sure we could take over one of the sitting rooms."

"My home makes this office look luxurious," Torquil said. "I think it would be more comfortable anywhere else."

Wyndham nodded. "I'll go tell my grandmother then. And we'll inform my mother when we go home." He left the room without waiting for their response.

Roger gave Torquil a gentle smile. "When we've moved into our own home, it will be even better. Mrs. Wrenwhistle is very nice but… er…well, I suppose I've gotten spoiled living without parental supervision for the past month."

Torquil chuckled. "I can imagine."

Roger turned to the desk he was closest to and rooted through the drawers for some paper, an ink well, a blotter, and a quill. "Are you familiar with the other rubrics we've put together?"

"Yes, but the reports I received were not detailed enough for me to be an expert on the subject."

Roger nodded as if he expected that answer. "My handwriting is not the neatest, so you'll have to forgive that, but I think it will be best if you have an idea of what we've already put together so we can use that as a model."

"That sounds reasonable."

"I'll write it out in more detail, but essentially, we're testing children on five primary criteria: power, focus, control, understanding, and intuition. The two rubrics handle the criteria slightly differently, but they are as comparable as we could manage." Roger started jotting down notes on his paper. "You know," he said in a musing tone, "I would have been worried about being grouped with someone else on our first project here. But you are astonishingly easy to work with already."

Torquil blinked in surprise. "How do you figure that?"

"I'm very accustomed to presenting ideas to the Council," Roger said, his tone turning serious. "I know what it's like to have suggestions shot down, to be laughed out of a room, to be talked over." He paused in his writing to give Torquil a steady glance. "For a group of people tasked with unity between communities, they are shockingly bad at being a unified community themselves." He turned back to the paper to continue writing. "You aren't comfortable performing magic, but you're willing to do it anyway if it means helping others. You proclaimed a lack of proficiency in both magic systems, but you're unafraid to learn more." He sighed as he put the quill away and moved the paper to the other side of the desk to dry. "If this Council was filled with more people like you, I would be a lot more optimistic about our future."

Torquil smiled warmly at him. "That's very kind of you to say. The feeling's mutual."

Roger's expression brightened. "Thank you!"

Wyndham returned. "My grandmother has given approval for us to work outside the chambers. But, as you predicted," he said with a glance at Torquil, "she would like to be updated on our progress. Why don't you come by our house tomorrow around one? You can even stay for dinner, if you'd like. Roger and I tend to work long hours when we're doing this sort of thing."

"One will work," Torquil said. "We'll see about dinner. But thank you."

"Are we leaving already?" Roger said.

"Don't see why not," Wyndham replied.

Roger shrugged and followed his husband out the door, after giving Torquil a friendly wave goodbye.

Torquil sat in the empty office for a long moment. They felt a mix of emotions. They felt hope for the first time since they'd started with the Council. They felt anxious about the prospect of performing their magic in front of an audience. They flexed their hand briefly, noting the ink stains on their fingertips, and wondered if the magic would still come as it used to.

They strode to the desk Roger had used, sliding the paper closer to read over it. Roger and Wyndham believed in them. They were both eager to see Torquil's magic, even with the threat of unpleasantness. Torquil's chest warmed at the memory of Wyndham's words in the Council chamber. They could do this.

CHAPTER 13
EMRYS

"Have you no sympathy at all for your closest friend?" Emrys cast a sullen look at Keelan, their horses moving at a walk as they followed a path along the lake in Hyde Park. The early afternoon hour meant they had plenty of company to occasionally nod at and exchange pleasantries with.

"Of course I do," Keelan said, though there was more amusement in his tone than commiseration. "But you cannot deny that if our situations were reversed, you would also find at least a hint of joy in my misery."

Emrys gave a heavy sigh, unable to argue the point. Even if he wanted to try and deny it for the sake of a friendly argument, his verve was in tatters. Emrys had lost count of the number of callers he had entertained under his mother's watchful eye, participating in more meaningless conversations than he'd ever thought possible. Details of each interaction had already started to blur together, leaving names and talents and attributes a horrible jumble in his head.

"It's all just so...so very..." Emrys struggled to find the word.

"Absurd?" Keelan offered.

"Put on," Emrys decided. "It seems that being oneself has no place in finding a spouse. At least not in a situation like mine." He frowned down at the narrow leather straps in his hands, watching the dark bay neck of his borrowed mount bobbing in rhythm with her steps.

"Such is the price for being the most outstanding sibling in a prominent family," Keelan said matter-of-factly.

"Why should I be the one to suffer? Would it not make more sense that I be rewarded for my magical aptitude by having the freedom to marry for love rather than duty?" His brothers had been allowed such privilege, as would Aveline when she finally settled down.

Keelan made a thin hum of uncertainty. "Your reward is inheritance. Knowing your future is secure. In turn, you find an equally powerful partner to ensure that your children and grandchildren are guaranteed the same."

"Yes, I know the reason for it," Emrys retorted. "I am simply saying that it all feels very unfair."

Keelan chuckled, finally offering the look of pity Emrys had been seeking all along. "Have you really not been introduced to a single person who might provide you with everything you are looking for?"

Emrys huffed out a weak, anguished laugh of his own. "Even the most palatable of them have left me feeling hopeless."

"I find that hard to believe," Keelan said dismissively.

"This morning I had tea with *Lydia Stanton*."

The grin Keelan had been sporting faded instantly, his eyes widening. "Lydia Stanton? She's—"

"Eighteen," Emrys finished for him. "And only just." He shook his head. "I've got waistcoats older than that, Keelan."

Both men nodded politely as they rode past a group of ladies walking together at a rather brisk pace, arms pumping. Emrys watched as Keelan allowed his attention to linger on them even after they'd passed by, a roguish yet somewhat longing expression on his face.

"If it makes you feel any better," Keelan began absently, before turning his focus back to their conversation, "if I did not find so much pleasure in those with a more delicate countenance and character than your own, I would offer myself."

Emrys rolled his eyes. The two of them had long since discovered they were better off as friends. "It doesn't."

Keelan scoffed, reaching across the distance between them to smack the back of his hand against Emrys' upper arm. "You ass," he said light-heartedly. "I'm going to make a fine husband someday."

"I'm not sure a marriage of last resort is better than one of convenience." Emrys cut him a look. "At any rate, if my mother thought you would make a good match for me, I'm certain she would've already tried to set something more official up between us."

"I'll be sure to remember that when you've turned down every other eligible person in London," Keelan said dryly.

Melancholy washed through Emrys at the thought.

"It will never go that far," he said. "If I cannot choose someone myself, then I know they will be picked for me. Mother has made it perfectly clear that this whole process is really for her benefit, not mine."

"How so?"

"It's the questions she asks. I shudder to even say it aloud, but it's almost as though she's...looking for her replacement." The thought of spending the rest of his life with someone exactly like his mother made him feel sick. The sound of distress that came from Keelan reassured him that he was not alone in that.

"You've got to pick someone then, and quickly." Keelan had a true urgency in his voice. "If it's love you're after, I'm certain it will develop over time with the right person. For now, you must simply decide what it is that you think could give those feelings a foundation to grow on." He paused, making a thoughtful face. "Close your eyes."

"I'm on a horse," Emrys complained.

Keelan huffed out an impatient sigh and reached to take his reins. "Close your eyes," he repeated, and Emrys did. "Now think of your ideal morning. What are you doing? Are you still in bed? Taking breakfast in your room?" Emrys tried to visualize it. As of late, his mornings had been a rushed affair, leaving little time to enjoy such pleasures as a slow breakfast.

"I cannot say," Emrys said with a shrug. "My mornings always look different, depending on my obligations."

"What about on days when you've nothing planned until the afternoon?"

"I suppose I would like to be awake early enough to hear the birds singing, but not be out of bed until it's necessary."

"So you'll want someone who can be flexible, up with the sun if needed, but not always. What about mealtime? Do you prefer a chat, or would you rather eat without being disturbed?"

"You know the answer to that as well as I do," Emrys grumbled, feeling ridiculous over this little game. Anyone who had ever met him knew well enough that he preferred conversation over silence.

"Fine. Last one. Imagine yourself falling into bed after a long, tiring day. You've no interest in doing anything aside from letting sleep take you."

"Yes, all right," Emrys said, urging him to get to the point.

"Now look at the person beside you. Which of your potential suitors do you see?"

Emrys' eyes flew open, his magic twisting tightly in his chest at the face he had seen there, sharing a pillow with a mess of dark, unruly curls and a familiar grin waiting for him.

Emrys yanked his reins back from Keelan hard enough that his horse took it as instruction for her to turn. He steered her back in the right direction, giving his friend an annoyed look.

"And what do you know about love?" he demanded.

Keelan grinned ruefully. "Nothing at all. But if I'm going to spend the rest of my life with someone, at the very least I'm going to enjoy our quiet moments together."

Emrys looked ahead, brows pinching together as he considered this. Against his better judgment, he allowed the trickle of thoughts Keelan's questions had started to become a steady stream. Quiet moments. Existing in the same space with no expectations other than enjoying the company of one another. Familiarity.

Certainly that was one reason fae often kept lovers, even after they got married. To maintain those connections for respite and pleasure without the demands of a joint existence weighing on them. It was what Emrys had always told himself he wanted from all of his previous bedroom partners, Torquil included.

If that were truly the case, however, why was it so easy for him to imagine Torquil in each of the scenarios Keelan spoke of? What would it be like to share a meal with them, rather than just another cheap street snack? How would it feel to allow Torquil to fall asleep in his arms, and for once not have to wake them so he could sneak out before the sun came up?

He thought of seeing Torquil at the party. What would their reaction have been if he had offered his arm? Reached for their hand to kiss their knuckles? Walked them around the rooms and introduced them to everyone he knew, rather than pretending they had never met?

A pang of guilt nearly made him wince. He'd treated that fake introduction like it was something to laugh about later on, and Torquil had played along beautifully. Emrys realized only in hindsight how cruel it had been to act in such a way simply because of everyone else's expectations. Torquil was not someone Emrys would've ever interacted with socially before earning their place on the Council. Even his own grandmother had known this and acted accordingly.

Something like sunshine spread throughout Emrys' chest as his thoughts settled. They had been formally introduced. By his grandmother, of all people. They were no longer strangers in the eyes of others. He could spend as much time as he wished speaking with Torquil now, and not only in the confines of the little room above the press. Their friendship needn't remain a secret any longer.

A private grin tilted the corners of his lips as Emrys slowly realized that everything, *everything*, was about to change.

CHAPTER 14

TORQUIL

Torquil stared at their cabinet of magical ingredients for a long time. They had spent the whole morning debating whether or not to practice before going to the Wrenwhistle residence. They kept cycling through the same thought process: *It's silly to practice something you've known since you were eight*, and then, *but you will look like such a fool if you attempt to cast and come up blank*. Now they were staring at their meager resources, trying to determine if they ought to bring anything with them. Surely Roger would have plenty of supplies.

They had read over Roger's notes late into the night and then again in the morning, trying desperately to come up with ways to apply the rubric to their own strange magic. They hated the idea of letting everyone down before they'd even begun.

They closed the cabinet when they realized there were only supplies for the protection spell anyway.

They left early, taking the long walk to Mayfair, pulling their coat close. As much as they had put up a fuss when Iris had insisted they buy more clothes, they were admittedly grateful now for her insistence. They would have hated to go under Mrs. Wrenwhistle's critical gaze in their old worn clothing.

On their way, they took their usual route for non-*Tribune* days. For the most part, it was a perfectly normal walk, except now everyone seemed intrigued by their new clothes. The haberdasher complimented their outfit before reciting a string of gossip. One of the footmen handed Torquil a note and then fretfully dusted off the front of their lapel as if he couldn't help himself. A maid teased them for the outfit, asking if they were going to see a lover and another asked if the outfit had been a gift *from* a lover. Torquil might have been worried except both comments had been delivered with a wink and a promise not to spread *that* tale. A bootboy gawked openly at the suit.

When one of Torquil's favorite housekeepers opened the door and arched an eyebrow in surprise, they finally felt compelled to say something. "It's just a new suit," they complained.

She laughed and passed over a folded paper. "New clothes are never *just* anything," she remarked.

"It's for my work on the Council. Everyone keeps thinking it's something more."

She shrugged and gave their cravat a tweak. "And if it was, do you think we'd mind? After the way you exposed his lordship's abuse of the maids last year, you earned the trust of this entire street of domestics." She gave them a buttered roll and sent them on their way.

Torquil ate the roll as they headed to the Wrenwhistles' townhouse, thinking about what the housekeeper had said. It felt wrong to mingle with the upper crust and then take gossip from their servants. Then again, they considered as they dusted crumbs off their hands, the upper crust likely assumed they were collecting gossip anyway, and the servants didn't seem to mind, so why should they?

The Wrenwhistles' butler greeted them stoically and led the way to a richly furnished sitting room. Roger was already sitting in front of a porcelain tea set, hands clasped in his lap. Torquil felt immediate relief at seeing the man waiting for them. When Roger looked up and grinned, Torquil returned the smile. Roger ushered Torquil to a seat near the fire.

"Wyn isn't up yet," he said. "That is to say, he's awake. But he's taking his breakfast upstairs."

"London hours," Torquil said.

Roger rolled his eyes good-naturedly. "Yes, but it's something of a way of life with him." He chuckled. "I expected to align with his schedule after we were married, but I simply could not. Imagine laying about in bed all morning! Would you like some tea?"

"I couldn't do it. And tea would be lovely, thank you."

"How do you like it?"

"I'm not particular," Torquil said, looking around the room with interest.

"Not particular?" Roger echoed.

Torquil shrugged. "I rarely have tea. It can get expensive, you know. I've learned to do without."

Roger's mouth dropped open and he paled considerably. "Heavens," he murmured. He poured Torquil a cup and then put a splash of milk and a lump of sugar in it. "Do tell me if you'd like more of anything," he said, handing it over.

"I'm sure this will do nicely," they assured him, taking a sip.

"Did you have a chance to look over the notes?" Roger asked.

Torquil put the cup down gently. "Yes. But…er…I'm afraid I don't have any ideas as to how to apply your rubric to my magic."

Roger shook his head before Torquil had finished speaking. "We were at it for weeks. I didn't expect you to come up with something in a single day. That's what this project is for."

Torquil breathed out slowly. "Oh, good. Thank you."

"Did you have any questions about the rubric?"

"Not exactly. As I've said, I never gained true proficiency in either magic system. At least, not completely. So I keep trying to imagine where I would fall if I were to be tested and—" They grimaced. "—I don't think I'd do very well. I could probably do well on some aspects in each though."

Roger frowned. "I ought to be taking notes," he muttered. He stood up and went to a desk in the corner of the room. Torquil hadn't paid it much mind when they walked in, but now they saw it was covered with ingredients and tools. To one side, a mountain of books was piled so high as to reach the top of the desk.

"Is this your office?"

"For the time being," Roger said, pulling a piece of paper out of the desk and grabbing a quill and ink before scuttling back to the sofa.

"Mrs. Wrenwhistle is not fond of my mess, I'm afraid. So I'll be glad when we have our own space and I'm not bothering her. I've been informed this is one of the lesser sitting rooms," he explained in a low voice. "Apparently, the light is the least flattering to the wallpaper in here, so she rarely uses it. Wyn used all of his wiles to nab it for our use."

Torquil laughed. "Who knew there was a hierarchy of sitting rooms?"

Roger laughed and then covered his mouth with his fingers.

Wyndham walked in at that moment. He arched an eyebrow and then closed the doors. "Having fun without me, are you?"

"Just discussing the mysterious hierarchy of sitting rooms," Roger said. "I haven't sent for your tea yet."

Wyndham leaned over the back of the sofa to kiss his husband's cheek. "The hierarchy is a mystery to everyone but my mother, I assure you. I'll ring for it."

As he rang for a servant and asked for another pot of tea to be brought in, Roger leaned forward and explained, "Wyn is very particular about his tea. It takes some getting used to, so I didn't want to assume you'd like it."

Torquil gave him a grateful smile. "That was very considerate of you."

Wyndham propped his hip on the arm of the sofa. "So, how do we wish to go about this project?"

"Well," Roger said, looking energized by the change in topic, "I thought it might be best if Torquil could show us a spell or two. Perhaps we can start with human magic before moving on to fae magic. Then we can determine how we want to proceed. Will that be all right?"

Torquil nodded, trying not to let on how nervous they were. "Of course."

"I put some ingredients on the desk," Roger said. He stood up and strode back over to it, gesturing for Torquil to follow. "I got the most practical sorts of things that are used in human magic. I also got some raw ingredients in case you'd prefer that. And I had my valet go out this morning and fetch some potted plants in case you could use those for the fae side of things." He tapped his lips, looking thoughtful. "What else? Oh, you mentioned that you were rusty so I had some books brought down for you. These are some of my favorites."

"Some?" Torquil said, looking at the tottering pile.

Wyndham snorted. "You should see our library in the country."

Roger's expression went decidedly dreamy. "It's lovely." He seemed to shake himself mentally and then plucked a book off the top of the pile. "I've been trying to find books that discuss fae-human magic but none of them do. I even asked my father for advice and he sent me this one. But it only mentions the matter once and even then it's only incidental. Listen." He opened the book and flipped through the pages until he found what he was looking for. "'Little research has been done for children born from one human parent and one fae parent. Studies have shown that those children cannot fully perform either fae magic or human magic. From this little knowledge, many assume it is inadvisable for mixed-race couples to have children of their own in order to avoid this magical handicap.'" Roger's face wrinkled in disgust. "It's just dreadful. Imagine suggesting people not have children because they don't fit into our preconceived notions of how magic should look."

Torquil hummed thoughtfully. "And yet, it is a frightfully popular opinion."

Roger closed the book with a snap. "Well, we're going to fix all of that. What spell would you like to start with?"

Torquil looked over the ingredients. "I'm not sure," they said slowly.

"All right," Roger said in a cheerful tone. "Let's see…" He peered over the ingredients next to Torquil. "Can you do a fire spell?"

"Yes," Torquil said. *At least I used to*.

"Why don't we do a simple one-ingredient fire spell then?" Roger said, snatching up a bottle filled with powder. "It won't be as strong as some of the spells with more ingredients, but it will be something to start with." Torquil nodded as Roger picked up a small piece of spell-paper and a pencil. He rotated the pencil in his fingers and tapped the point with one fingertip. "Sharp enough," he said and added with a sigh, "I really was getting terribly spoiled at home."

Roger bustled over to the fireplace and knelt in front of it. Torquil took up position beside him.

"Wyn, would you—" A breeze flew through the window and into

the fireplace, extinguishing the flame before Roger could finish his question. He chuckled. "Thank you."

Torquil glanced over their shoulder at Wyndham, who was looking smug. He set his teacup on the table and came to crouch on Torquil's other side, looking every bit as eager as his husband.

Torquil took a deep breath then accepted the paper and pencil from Roger. They scribbled down a simple sigil and set the paper into the fireplace. Then they took the bottle, opened it, and gently sprinkled some powder on top of the paper. With an embarrassingly shaking hand, they cast the spell.

As usual, nothing seemed to happen immediately. Torquil breathed out and called upon senses they hadn't used in years. First they felt the spell. The magic was active but oh, so faint. Torquil reached out for a breeze and gently coaxed it toward their spell. It just needed a small trickle of air. The spell caught and came to life, bright and merry. It was small, of course; all of Torquil's spells were small. But it was a fire, exactly as requested.

They sat back on their heels and glanced at their companions, who both looked thoughtful in the most infuriatingly inscrutable way. Torquil rubbed their hands on their trousers. "Well?" they prompted, hoping they didn't sound too anxious.

Roger blinked and looked up at them. "I'm afraid I'm still learning my way around feeling magic. I think I missed all of what you did—at least, I missed what I couldn't see. I'm so sorry. Is there…" He paused, apparently trying to find the right words. "…always a delay before the magic takes hold?"

"Er…"

"There wasn't a delay," Wyndham said. "Not really." He gave Torquil a long look. "Do you always use fae magic to help along your human spells?"

Torquil bit their lip and nodded. "It's a bit of a cheat," they admitted. "My spells have always lacked power. I learned early on that the best way to give them a boost was to…er…call on the magic that was already around."

"That's fascinating," Wyndham said.

"Why am I not taking notes?" Roger exclaimed, jumping to his feet and getting his paper and pen. He bent over the table and scribbled some things down. Then he leaned back and looked over what he had written. "Did you say it was a cheat? I don't think I'd characterize it in that way."

"Nor would I," Wyndham said. "Let's do another. How about a wind spell this time?"

Roger finished what he was writing then gathered the supplies for a wind spell. Wyndham took out an embroidered handkerchief and laid in front of them.

"See if you can pick that up with it."

The wind spell was easier. It was still faint at first, but calling upon the wind to add to the wind spell was a much easier integration. Once again, Torquil coaxed the fae magic into their spell and encouraged it to pick up the handkerchief. It fluttered in a little circuit around them and then drifted to the ground. A small spell, as usual.

"I felt it that time," Roger said, eager. "It's...well, it's faint, but I felt it."

Wyndham gave a hum in apparent agreement. "Definitely not a cheat," he said at last. Then he picked up a fresh sheet of paper and the ingredients Torquil had already used and placed them in front of them. "Do it again."

They spent hours casting spells for Roger and Wyndham. They were glad Roger had given a small warning about the long hours Wyndham worked on such projects. As they worked, they started to lose some of their self-conscious anxiety. Neither of the men seemed perturbed by Torquil's magic. They didn't even seem judgmental, despite Wyndham's joking the day before. But it was exhausting putting out spell after spell, after years of letting the skill go dormant. Torquil was relieved when Roger finally called for a brief respite and sent for more tea.

They collapsed on the chair they had occupied earlier while the two men took the sofa. When the tea was brought in and poured out, Torquil finally had the courage to say, "I've been told that my magic is too...well, unsavory, I guess, for the more refined palate."

Wyndham gave a snort. "Who told you that?"

"A fae shopkeeper back home," Torquil said. "One of my friends growing up. A fae tutor who didn't accept the job of teaching me. Everyone who can sense magic, really. Except my mother," they added.

"And how did she describe your magic?"

"She said that it was…pungent, I suppose? But not in a bad way." They shrugged. "Then again, she was biased."

"It *is* pungent," Wyndham said. "But not in a bad way. It's different. There's a unique *flavor* to it. I've never felt anything like it before. Well, aside from your building. I assume you're putting some sort of spell up there."

"Yes. My parents set it up when I first settled there. I've been patching it over time. Not very well, probably. I don't like trying to feel my magic so I just put it together where I think it needs to go."

Wyndham frowned. "Perhaps that's why it felt so strange when we went there after our engagement announcement."

Torquil didn't bother inquiring further. Wyndham describing their protection spell as strange was one of the kinder descriptions of their magic. "I still don't have any idea how we shall put that into a rubric. I don't even know if other fae-human children perform their magic the same way."

"Definitely something we can look into," Roger said. "But I think we have enough to go on for now."

"Do we?" Torquil said. "What have you gathered so far?"

"It's interesting," Roger said. "I've been thinking about that stupid text I read to you earlier. And at first I thought your magic was very… oh, I don't know…faint, I suppose? Not weak or anything," he added quickly. "Just that all of the spells you've done have been on the smaller side. And I thought it was because you're out of practice. But it's clearly just how your magic is. Both of you are characterizing the magic as being strong, pungent. I'm still trying to reconcile those two seemingly opposite traits. How can magic be both quiet and loud? Gentle and pungent?" He shook his head and a smile took over his face. "It's such a delightful mystery."

Torquil gave a surprised laugh. "Happy to oblige."

"Are you?" Roger said. "Because I have some ideas of how we can —but then again, perhaps I ought to do some research—"

"Perhaps we ought to pause here for the night so you can do some research first?" Wyndham suggested.

Roger brightened. "Excellent notion! I'll do that and make a list of spells to work through. And I think Wyn will need to compile a list of his own—"

"I will?"

"—and then tomorrow, we can have you go through the list. Specifically, I want to know what your magic is like when you're performing spells that are new to you. How are you at learning spells? Does your magic look the same? Does your magic change at all when you use raw ingredients instead of prepared ones? And we've been focusing on human spells but I'd very much like to see you cast a fae spell."

Torquil winced. "I've never been particularly good at casting fae spells."

"Nonsense," Wyndham said brusquely. "You did it consistently today."

"But those were human spells and I just used fae magic to boost them. I can't start with a fae spell. I always need a human spell to start with."

Roger's eyes widened. He grabbed up his notes and leafed through them. "And you said that when you use human spells, they never start off very strong so you need fae magic to make them stronger."

"That's right."

A laugh bubbled out of Roger before he clapped a hand over his mouth. "That's remarkable."

"What is?" Torquil said.

"I think we've been looking at your magic all wrong. It's not a matter of you being unable to master human magic or fae magic. Your magic is a blend of both. It's impossible to separate them. Your human magic depends on your fae magic for strength and your fae magic depends on the human magic for structure."

Torquil sat back. When Roger put it like that, it all made so much sense. "Oh," they said quietly.

"That answers the question of whether we really need a third rubric," Roger said, bending over his paper to write more notes. "We decidedly *do*. It is positively criminal that your magic has been ignored by academic research for so long."

"I think we should also add to our list of possibilities," Wyndham said, "I'd like to see how you sense our spells."

"You would?" Torquil asked.

Wyndham shrugged. "A hunch." He shared a look with Roger that Torquil could not entirely decipher. Then he turned to Torquil. "Is that agreeable with you?"

"Of course," Torquil said. "I'm game."

"Good," Roger said. "Then we have our work cut out for us. We will compile a list of spells to try. With our new discovery in mind, we'll make sure the list is compatible with both kinds of magic." He looked up at his husband. "We may need to go back to starting earlier, you know. We have events to attend."

Wyndham made a disgusted face. "If I must."

Torquil laughed. "I'm up before the sun most days so that won't bother me."

Wyndham turned his disgusted expression upon Torquil. "Bizarre magic I can understand. But *up before the sun*? *Most* days? Are you mad?"

"I have a paper to print," Torquil said. "I won't expect either of you to be up at that time. Especially since you have so many social events."

"Well, you were at the party the other night," Roger said. "Didn't you say it was an expectation now that you're a councilmember? I expect you'll have a number of social events as well."

"Damn," Torquil said. "I keep forgetting that. I honestly keep hoping your grandmother will forget too."

Wyndham chuckled. "She won't," he said in a cheerful tone. "But you can always pretend urgent Council business with us. I can't stand most of the people we meet in society. But you're not a bad sort." He paused. "That is, you're not a bad sort when you aren't inaccurately posting engagement news."

"Let's call it premature engagement news," Torquil said with a wry smile. "You would have gotten there eventually. You just needed a push."

"You smile now," Wyndham said with a cocky expression. "But if my grandmother is taking you under her wing—and it looks very much like she is—you will be at the center of society in no time."

Torquil felt as if they couldn't breathe for a moment. "Not really?" they said quietly.

Roger reached forward to place a hand on Torquil's arm. "It will be all right. Don't listen to him. We'll be there as well. And as Wyn said, you can always pretend you have business to discuss with us." He looked pensive. "But in all seriousness, Torquil, I think what we're discovering about your magic is quite *momentous*. People have been talking about fae-humans as less than for years. When we announce that your magic system is entirely unique, a blend of two systems, I think it will make quite an impact." He squeezed their arm. "I think we'll be able to change the way people see your community."

It was remarkable, really, how a single word could change the tone of a sentence. Roger hadn't said "your kind" or "you people." Torquil was so accustomed to seeing themself as alone that imagining themself in the context of a community was a massive shift in perspective.

"In other words," Wyndham said, "you might need to start changing the way you see yourself in terms of society."

Torquil tore their brain from their current thought process. "What do you mean?"

"I mean that you're accustomed to people being unkind to you. Which is undoubtedly why you dislike society so much. But what if you were, in fact, at the center of society? Not as an object of ridicule or disdain, but as an equal?"

"I think a lot would have to change before that happened," Torquil said softly.

"I suspect my grandmother is already working on some of that," Wyndham said.

"As are we," Roger hastened to add.

Torquil gave a small smile. "Five steps ahead of everyone else," they muttered.

CHAPTER 15

EMRYS

AFTER BEING HELPED from his greatcoat and hat, Emrys hastened toward the stairs, pulling his thin leather gloves off before he grasped the banister. His ride in the Park had taken longer than planned and he was left with precious little time to dress for dinner. Once he reached the top, he took the sharp turn down the hallway in the direction of his bedroom, the heels of his riding boots clacking loudly.

Voices coming from behind the closed door of the sitting room caught his attention. The timbre of one in particular was all the excuse he needed to push the door open, allowing himself inside.

Collectively, Wyndham, Roger, and Torquil turned to look at him from where they were all sitting rather close together near the fireplace. Emrys felt the tug of his magic in his chest at the wild mix of company before him. He couldn't decide which urge was stronger: the one to make a snide comment directed at his brother over the seemingly private situation, or the one to say anything he could to get a smile out of Torquil.

Perhaps it could be one in the same?

"Well," Emrys began haughtily, slapping his gloves in the palm of his hand as he directed a smirk at Roger. "Is Wyndham boring you so badly in the bedroom that you've had to seek additional participants already?"

Roger's jaw went slack in surprise as Wyndham's expression darkened.

"N-no!" Roger yelped, pulling his hand from where it had been resting on Torquil's arm.

Emrys chuckled, his gaze shifting to catch Torquil's reaction. What he found instead was even more pleasing.

Torquil's full attention was on him, specifically on his lower half. Emrys peered down at the tight riding breeches he was wearing that left nothing to the imagination. It was an outfit he'd never worn around Torquil before, but with a reaction such as that, he decided it was something he would be changing immediately. Emrys let his smirk turn sly as he looked up at Torquil again.

"I'm just coming in from a very enlightening ride in the Park. There's nothing quite like fresh air and a chat with a dear friend to clear the mind," Emrys told the group at large.

"We've had a productive afternoon, as well," Roger countered as he adjusted his spectacles.

"Busy plotting another grand announcement in the *Tribune*?" Emrys asked, his tone lightly mocking. "What'll it be this time, I wonder?"

Wyndham got to his feet then, with Roger close behind.

"Certainly the readers of the *Tribune* will be happy to consume anything other than another description of the way you epitomize being the most eligible *and* the most undesirable man in the city," Wyndham said, before looking at Torquil. "No offense meant toward you, of course."

Torquil nodded once before turning back to Emrys with a smirk of their own. "None taken. I simply write what everyone else is already thinking, which is often a hard truth for those I've written about."

Emrys narrowed his eyes at them, catching the inside of his lip between his teeth to keep from smiling bigger than he already was.

"*Whoever wins the heart of one of the most eligible gentlemen in London will need to be an extraordinary catch indeed. People are already wondering what the gentleman is looking for: charm, beauty, elegance, breeding, poise, wit?*" Emrys recited. "You cannot deny that I am keeping a great deal of mystery alive in your column."

Wyndham clicked his tongue. "He's gone and memorized it. How sad." He arched a brow at Torquil. "You know he carries the most recent copy of the *Tribune* around like a pocket-sized religious text, referencing it multiple times a day when he's got nothing better to do."

That shook Emrys a bit, heat flashing to the skin beneath his cravat.

Roger chuckled, the weasel. "It's true."

"In fact, I'm certain there's one in his breast pocket at this very moment."

Emrys crossed his arms over his chest as he scrambled to devise a plan on how to best defend himself. The copy was there, as Wyndham had said. He swallowed, trying to come up with a reasonable explanation.

"I like to be prepared," he tried, tilting his chin up with forced confidence. "I never know who I'm going to encounter, and it's important to always have a little gossip at hand to spark an interesting conversation. I know that's nothing either of you would care about. You'd much rather hide away from society altogether, just as I've found you doing here."

As the words came out, he realized they applied to Torquil just as easily as they did Wyndham and Roger. Perhaps the three of them really would make a great team, all equally uninterested in leaving the confines of their quiet rooms and safe spaces. Certainly having no desire to attend parties and other social events left plenty of time to come up with solutions to any number of problems. The rest of the Council was never known to skip an event.

"We've been *working*," Roger argued with restraint.

"Indeed," Emrys said with a thickly suggestive tone. "I'm sure you have."

Wyndham made a disgusted noise in the back of his throat and reached to take Roger's hand, their fingers intertwining. "I've had enough of this," he said coolly. "We're going to dress for dinner."

"Torquil," Roger sputtered as Wyndham pulled him toward the door. "The invitation still stands for you to join us this evening!"

Emrys turned a curious look on Torquil as they stood up out of their chair, offering the rest of them a one-shouldered shrug and a half grin.

"I think I've taken up enough of your time for one day. If I'm honest, I'm feeling rather fatigued after using my magic."

A streak of raw jealousy shot through Emrys at the confession. Wyndham and Roger had spent less than a week working with Torquil and they'd already managed to see them *willingly* perform magic?

"Of course," Roger called over his shoulder with genuine understanding. "Perhaps another time soon, then."

With that, the two of them slipped out of the room and out of sight, leaving Emrys and Torquil alone in the small space. The crackling fire in the hearth was the only sound as a weighted silence stretched between them. Torquil was the first to break it as they took a few steps closer, arms crossing to mirror the way Emrys was still standing.

"Let's see it, then," they said boldly with a twinkle in their eye.

Emrys breathed in deeply, giving Torquil a hard look as he sighed out his exhale. Wyndham would pay for this. Emrys uncrossed his arms, shifting his gloves to his left hand so he could reach into the breast pocket of his waistcoat. He pulled his copy of the *Tribune* out, holding the folded paper up between his index and middle finger.

Torquil looked entirely too smug as they plucked it out of his grasp, unfolding it at an excruciatingly slow pace before scanning the printed words as though they didn't already know exactly what they said.

Emrys started to say something, but stopped, realizing he hadn't the first idea of which thought to give a voice to. There were so many swirling around in his head.

Torquil met and held his gaze as they folded the paper back up exactly the way Emrys had it. Emrys tried to reach for it, but Torquil stuffed it into their own pocket instead with a wink.

"I want that back," Emrys challenged.

"You can come and get it," Torquil said as they stepped around him toward the door that had been left open.

"Tonight?" Emrys asked, perhaps a bit too eager, as he turned to watch them go.

Torquil paused at his question, resting their hand on the frame of the doorway. The radiance of the fire at his back was nothing compared to the heat Emrys felt as Torquil's gaze raked over him, once again lingering on his figure-hugging breeches. Emrys swallowed thickly when

Torquil finally looked at him again with an unmistakably covetous gleam in their eyes.

"Perhaps another time soon," they said, echoing Roger's words in a hushed tone. "I'm too tired to be any good right now." Torquil sent a final glance at Emrys' legs. "But whenever you find me again, you'd better be wearing those."

Emrys waited in the sitting room long enough to regain his composure before he rushed to his bedroom to change.

CHAPTER 16

TORQUIL

TORQUIL WOULD HAVE VERY MUCH LIKED to go to bed. Hours of performing magic after years of stifling it was exhausting in every way. They felt raw and stretched too thin. But the *Tribune* was coming out in two days and they hadn't a clue what to write. So instead of crawling under their blanket, they sank onto their chair. They picked up a blank paper, dipped their pen in ink, blotted it, and then hitched their foot on the edge of the desk in order to scoot down in the seat, using their thigh as a desk. They dated the paper for the publication date and then stared at the page.

What to write about? Were they inadvertently causing damage by focusing on certain people? They knew Wyndham and Emrys were often at odds. That hadn't been difficult to glean after years of knowing Emrys and hearing him complain about his baby brother. But seeing their mutual dislike in person had been…interesting. Torquil thought back to what Wyndham had said: *He's gone and memorized it. How sad.* They thought of the way Emrys' chin had gone up and his arms had crossed over his chest, defensive. They carefully dropped the pen back in its holder and pulled out the copy Emrys had kept folded in his pocket. They unfolded it and read over the words, wondering a bit about why Emrys had chosen *that* column to hold onto. Was it merely because it was the most recent? Because it had a whole little paragraph about him? It wasn't even the most complimentary.

When Emrys was alone with Torquil, he dropped his defenses. He was open and gentle. He teased, yes, but Torquil had always liked that, and there was never any malice to the teasing. But with his brother, it was as if Emrys attacked before he could be attacked in return. Wyndham clearly did the same. Torquil had practically seen the other man's hackles raising at Emrys' snide insinuations.

Torquil had no siblings, and their childhood friendships had been infrequent and inconsistent, so they had little ground for comparison. But Torquil didn't like how the two brothers interacted, shifting into something meaner and harsher in the other's presence. Perhaps something could be done about it.

They ran a thumb over the column again, allowing a small smile at the idea of Emrys holding any token of theirs close. Then they dropped their foot from the desk and swung it under their body to sit on. They leveraged themself forward over the desk, placed the column aside, and pulled forward the scraps of paper they had accumulated. Gossip. News. They picked up the pen and twiddled it between their fingers. Perhaps it was time to leave Wyndham and Emrys out of the paper, at least temporarily. Much as they hated to leave Emrys without something to hold onto, they disliked having their words used as fodder to widen the gap between the two.

For a brief, fleeting moment, they wished they could write Emrys a letter. Write what they truly wanted. Give him something worth holding close and memorizing. But that would be far too risky. The last thing either of them needed was a scandal. They sighed, casting away the thought as quickly as it had appeared.

Then they plucked out a random scrap and read over it. *S. Ravenwing drunk at Cricket dinner party.* Hm. Not entirely surprising, considering how openly the man was in love with Wyndham. He'd been noticeably heartbroken when the fae's engagement to Roger had been announced. Something to work on. But not yet. Ravenwing needed to heal a bit more first. They set the scrap aside and reached for another. *Lady Fitzhugh called on the St. Clair residence for tea.* Also not surprising, but certainly more promising. Torquil jotted it down. Mr. Brooks had been spotted with another fae gentleman. Torquil added it to the list. They kept working until they had a small collection of newsworthy items. Then they tweaked each piece, adding words, polishing others. An observation here, a joke to the reader there.

When they reached the end of the list, they deliberated for a long moment, twiddling the pen again. Aveline was not caught up in her brothers' fight, at least as far as Torquil could determine. They really wanted to see the woman married by the end of the Season. She was far too sweet and pretty and, from what they had observed, of too romantic a disposition to be single. They smiled and added a bit about the Wren-whistle sister. That would certainly get the two brothers talking, but hopefully not at each other's throats.

They started to drop the pen back into the holder, content with the draft, but paused. Unbidden, Roger's words from earlier came to mind: *I think we'll be able to change the way people see your community.* Roger saw the fae-human populace as a community. But despite that identity, Torquil had yet to meet others like them. Did other fae-humans perform magic in the same way? Was Torquil truly unique in the way they manipulated their spells, or had others learned similar methods?

Slowly, they dipped the pen into the ink, blotted it, and then hovered the pen tip over the page. It was risky, of course. The Council might object to Torquil writing something like this without their consent. Then again, if Torquil was truly a valued member of the Council, their suggestions would be taken with more respect. With their tongue between their teeth, they wrote, struggling to determine how honest or vulnerable to be. It took twice as long to write the one short paragraph than it had taken to write the rest of the column. But when they were done, they sat back, kicked their foot out to land on the desk again, and held the paper up, reading over it. This was personal, more personal than anything they'd ever written in the *Tribune*. And they desperately wanted it to work.

Finally, they set the paper down, put away the pen, and stripped out of their clothes. It was a chilly night so Torquil wrapped themself in their blanket and curled up on their side. For the first time in a long time, they felt eager about the work ahead.

❧

THE NEXT DAY, Torquil made the same journey to Mayfair, no longer surprised when the modiste's assistants cooed over their clothes or the way one of the butlers tsked and fixed their cravat.

"If you're going out into society, you must look the part," the man said. "You'll get better intel that way."

As had happened the day before, their new outfit did not impact the amount of gossip they received from others and they felt a sense of accomplishment when they arrived at the Wrenwhistle home. They entered the house with less anxiety than the previous day. They were brought to the same sitting room where Roger was waiting. He was drinking tea and reading through a stack of papers. He looked up with a smile when Torquil walked in.

"Good morning," he said brightly.

"Good morning."

"I'm afraid I started without you," Roger said. "Very bad manners. I do apologize. Barely slept a wink last night. I was so excited about the project."

Torquil grinned. "You don't need to stand on ceremony with me, I assure you. I take it you have a plan for today's work?"

Roger poured Torquil a cup of tea, added milk and sugar, and then handed it over before reaching for his papers again. "Yes, I do. Yesterday we had you perform spells you already knew. Today I'd like to watch you perform spells you don't know. I'll teach you," he added. "But I'd like to see if your use of fae magic is a practiced skill or if it's more…instinctual."

"That makes sense."

"That might keep us busy all day. But after that, I'd like to see how you feel about using raw ingredients."

"Ah," Torquil said. "Your other experiment."

Roger and Wyndham had stunned society with their wedding spell, using an untreated willow branch instead of the powdered leaves and bark typical of human magic.

"Y-yes," Roger said, hesitantly. "But Wyn and I have discussed it and we think the raw materials might react favorably to your fae magic."

Torquil considered. "It's certainly worth trying. My magic has never been particularly strong so I don't think it would be all that risky."

"Well, we'll try to enact some safeguards all the same. And then as Wyn suggested yesterday, we'd like to have you watch *us* perform magic."

As if summoned, Wyndham strode into the room. "It is decidedly too early to be working on anything," he griped before flopping onto the sofa beside Roger.

Roger patted Wyndham's knee. "I was just telling Torquil about our plans for today."

Wyndham poured himself a cup of tea and grunted in response.

Roger chuckled. "Torquil's barely finished their tea, so you have some time to wake up."

Wyndham rolled his eyes. "I'd prefer to have several more hours."

"I did warn you."

He sighed and glanced at Torquil. "I promise I won't be disagreeable for the rest of the project."

They arched an eyebrow.

"All right, I promise I'll be less disagreeable."

Torquil laughed and finished their tea.

Roger clapped his hands together. "Shall we begin?" He picked up a book that had been placed on the table and opened it to a marked page. "Have you ever performed a cleaning spell?"

They shook their head.

"Good. It's a bit more complicated and not something children are too keen to learn, as a rule." Roger held the book out to Torquil. "How do you prefer to learn? Would you like to do the spell yourself with me walking you through it or would you prefer to watch me do it first?"

Torquil glanced over the spell. "I think the first will suffice."

"Excellent." Roger fetched some spellpaper and a pencil, along with the necessary ingredients, which included his recently used teacup. "It's rather difficult to acquire dirty things in this house," he said with an apologetic smile. "Mrs. Wrenwhistle takes her reputation of elegance very seriously. So she would not hear of me asking one of the servants to bring me a dirty plate to practice on. I had to ask for a plate of biscuits first so I could dirty the plate myself."

Wyndham hummed in agreement. "A great deal of sacrifice went into that experiment."

The cleaning spell turned out to be a combination of a wet spell and a dry spell. It was *very* fiddly. At first, Torquil tried to get the human magic portion *just* right. But after a few failed attempts, they gave up, used the human spellwork to start the process, and let their fae magic take over. After that, they were able to clean the teacup every time Roger splashed tea or milk into it.

They were just about to try again when the door burst open and Mrs. Wrenwhistle strutted in, holding a squirming ginger kitten at arm's length. "Wyndham, this creature has *destroyed* my velvet *chaise longue*. Can you not keep it under control?"

Roger hustled forward and scooped the kitten into his arms and then cradled it against his chest. "I'm so sorry, Mrs. Wrenwhistle! I thought she was in our room."

She patted her hairdo. "She was in your room. But the servants have begun moving your things to the other townhouse and she escaped."

"They have?" Wyndham said.

"Yes! I told you it would be ready soon. Oh, Mx. Pimpernel-Smith. You're here." She gave them a brief and rather unconvincing smile. "The servants have been working for nearly two hours. I'm surprised you didn't hear them."

"Perhaps we'd better pack up our belongings," Roger said, glancing at his husband.

Wyndham looked perturbed. "I don't see why you couldn't have given us better warning."

"Well, you're so *busy*, Wynnie. Whenever was I supposed to tell you? They're perfectly capable. That valet of yours, Roger, has made quite sure of that."

Both men seemed to relax at those words. "All the same," Roger said, "perhaps we ought to start packing our things in here."

She gave a glance around the room, lips pursing at the sight of the tower of books and the mess they had made from their work. "Yes, perhaps you should."

"I'm sorry to interrupt our project, Torquil," Roger said, trying to hold onto the kitten as she attempted to squirm out of his grasp.

"Mother, you might want to close the door," Wyndham said.

She hurried out, closing the door behind her with a snap.

The cat dropped to the ground and began sniffing the furniture, Torquil's shoes, and the ingredients that were still on the ground. Torquil bent down to scratch behind the kitten's ears. She flopped to her side and rubbed her cheek against their foot.

"She likes you," Roger said, sounding pleased.

"I've always liked cats," Torquil said, rubbing her cheek with their thumb. "Would you like any help with packing up?"

"That's really very kind of you, but you needn't bother."

"I helped make the mess—"

"Don't be ridiculous," Wyndham said, brushing past them and putting all the items on the desk into an orderly pile.

Roger pulled spellpaper and ingredients out of the orderly pile Wyndham had just started. "You're welcome to stay and keep us company, if you'd like. And perhaps for dinner?"

"Please don't be put off by my mother's current state," Wyndham said. "Or, for that matter, by my brother's behavior yesterday."

Torquil couldn't help but chuckle. "I don't mind your brother," they said honestly. "I do not think your mother cares for me, though. Perhaps it would be best if I took up your generous offer after you've moved."

"Won't be getting in that socializing practice," Wyndham said in a singsong voice.

"I might just wait for Iris to prompt me before I do more of that. Are you sure I can't help you?"

Roger performed a shrinking spell on the stack of books. "Quite sure. We've moved multiple times in the past six months. We're practically old hat at it."

Torquil glanced back down at Peony, who was busy rubbing her head against their ankle. She rolled off their foot in an inelegant flop, shook herself, and then trotted across the room to investigate what her owners were up to. Since they were clearly not needed for packing duty or kitten entertainment duty, Torquil left.

CHAPTER 17

EMRYS

THE CLATTERING and bumping coming from Wyndham's bedroom made it difficult for Emrys to enjoy his late breakfast. He had needed an extra two spoonfuls of sugar, besides his usual generous helping, purely for mental sustenance. He glowered at the wall that separated their rooms as he took a long pull of his tea, listening as one voice spoke over the others, giving directions that seemed easy enough to follow without the need for so much unnecessary noise.

Despite the disruption in his morning, Emrys was grateful for the distraction keeping his mother busy. The family had an event to attend that evening, but otherwise his afternoon was blissfully free of any obligations, including appointments with callers.

After giving it more thought, the string of questions Keelan had asked in the Park felt even heavier. The faces of everyone his mother had set him up with began to swirl in his head as he gave real consideration to each of them in the various scenarios: waking up together, sharing meals, falling into bed, attending the opera, picking out their wedding flowers.

Emrys felt his stomach sour so quickly over the topic that he nearly had to spit out the bite of scone he'd taken for fear of losing the rest of his breakfast altogether. He took a steadying breath, pressing his lips together.

He could already envision their country estate decorated for another lavish wedding. It would be far bigger than his older brother Auberon's humble ceremony had been over the past summer, and even the massive crowd that had assembled for Wyndham's celebration would not match the number of guests who would want to attend the one with his own name attached.

"Emrys Wrenwhistle," he muttered under his breath with forced swagger. "The heir to his family's fortune and arguably the most sought after bachelor this Season is finally ready to announce the lucky person with whom he will be sharing the rest of his days."

He mocked himself with a fanfare sound, sticking his hands out as if to present said lucky person to an invisible throng of Londoners waiting with bated breath to hear who it was. However, when he tried to force a name out of his mouth, nothing came. He sighed and let his hands fall back to his lap.

Emrys tried Keelan's trick again next. He shut his eyes tight and forced himself to look out at the imagined swarm of people at his future wedding. There were his parents, his grandmother, his siblings and their respective spouses. Behind them were more faces he had known his entire life; his friends and their families, members of the Council. In his mind, all of them wore smiles of approval and encouragement. Even Wyndham seemed impressed with his decision. Not that he cared what Wyndham thought.

He tried desperately to decide which of his mother's hand-picked suitors would make them all look so proud.

When Auberon met his wife Rose, they had found an immediate connection. They shared so many traits and embodied being two halves of the same whole, what with their gentle personalities and love of simplicity that had pulled them to live in the countryside year-round.

A loud bang from the next room shifted his thoughts to his youngest sibling's new marriage. Wyndham and Roger had existed in many of the same social circles since childhood, but it wasn't until they'd been forced to work closely together on their projects for the Council that they had discovered their feelings for one another. Emrys was still adjusting to seeing the two of them so connected, always holding hands and sharing private looks.

Emrys felt the scratch of indignation. His magical talent and future inheritance should've been enticing enough to make him the first of his siblings to get married, second at the very least, but Wyndham had gone and ruined that with the chaos he and Roger created with their surprise engagement and swift wedding.

With gritted teeth, Emrys squeezed his eyes shut even tighter. Why was he the last of his brothers to find love? Was he destined to be the only one of his siblings to marry out of obligation and nothing more? Was he truly as undesirable as Wyndham so frequently implied? He needed answers.

Emrys huffed and opened his eyes, jaw set.

Torquil would tell him the truth. Who else knew more about the first sparks of romance or what served as the foundation for a successful marriage than the one person who made a profit from writing about those exact topics every week? And when it came right down to it, Torquil knew him better than anyone else. They had shared plenty of personal conversations over the years. Perhaps Torquil could even offer some helpful advice on the matter. He certainly wasn't getting it from anyone else.

With a newfound sense of hope, Emrys finished his last sip of tea and left his room with a grin, curious to see how flustered Wyndham was over the disorder that was sure to be unfolding on their unanticipated moving day.

&

EMRYS LET himself into the sitting room where Wyndham and Roger were busy stowing away all of the things they'd only just finished unpacking a few days prior. Roger's head snapped up, a look of concern on his face.

"Shut the door behind you!" he warned in a panicked tone.

Emrys arched a brow, but did as he was asked. Shut doors usually held a heavier meaning where Wyndham was concerned. "If you're planning on doing something lewd, please let me know so I can leave," he said flatly, wandering closer to where they were working. The faintest hint of a familiar presence caused his magic to stir, and he spoke before he could consider the words. "Was Torquil here again this morning?"

"Torquil was here for a couple of hours, yes," Roger said from where he was handing items to Wyndham to put into a crate. "We had to stop working when your mother announced that our townhouse was ready. She made it very plain that we should make haste and clear out."

Emrys chuckled. "Sounds about right." He settled on the arm of the sofa to watch as Wyndham and Roger worked together.

The pair of them seemed so different upon first glance. Not only in appearance, or in that Wyndham was fae and Roger was human, but also in their personalities and the way they carried themselves. Somehow, though, they suited each other perfectly.

"Was there something you wanted?" Wyndham gave him a dismissive glance. "Or are we here to serve as your entertainment?"

"I'd be delighted to see something entertaining." Emrys crossed his arms casually, his smile growing. "What are you offering? A rousing show of magic? A skit about life as newlyweds? Although, as I said, you can spare me the explicit material. I've overheard my fill of that since you arrived."

"Done entirely for your misery, I can assure you," Wyndham retorted.

Just as another cutting response formed on Emrys' tongue, he felt two sets of needles pierce the fine wool of his trousers and dig into both sides of his ankle. He hissed through his teeth and pulled his foot forward, dragging the small creature that was still attached to him from under the sofa.

"Dratted beast," he cursed under his breath, reaching between his legs to pry the kitten's claws from his skin. She let go before he could touch her and disappeared back into the depths of her clever hiding spot.

Wyndham's laughter broke the silence. Emrys looked up to see him pulling a horrified Roger to his side, planting a kiss on the top of his head.

"Well done, Peony," his brother called out with what sounded like a hint of pride.

Emrys stood up and stepped away from the sofa, hoping to avoid any more unbidden attacks. "You ought to warn people when that thing is on the prowl."

"It's so much more enjoyable when we don't," Wyndham said, returning to his task. "You did ask for entertainment, and I am most *certainly* entertained."

Emrys decided to leave the pair to their packing. Provoking his siblings was only entertaining when they allowed themselves to become annoyed, and it seemed that Wyndham was in a particularly unmovable mood. He shut the door on his way out, if for no other reason than to make sure the little cat did not find him again.

Freshly determined to make the most of his free afternoon, Emrys returned to his room and attempted to tackle the stack of letters on his writing desk. Keeping up with correspondence had never been one of his strengths. After managing one short missive to a distant cousin and another to a friend he had not seen in years, he gave up in favor of reading, which was also quickly abandoned. By the time he realized he should've gone out instead of trying to entertain his distracted mind at home, the sun was setting.

When his mother found him, he was on his balcony, lost in thought.

"Emrys," she snapped, her skirts rustling as she came up behind him. "Why aren't you dressed? We have to leave for the party soon."

Emrys turned to look at her as he straightened from where he'd had his forearms crossed on the railing. Even after such a busy day, she'd collected herself into an elegant, high-waisted evening dress with a sparkling garnet necklace to match, not a single curl of hair out of place.

He offered an apologetic grin. "I must've lost track of time."

"It appears that way," she said, giving him a critical look. "I'll send an extra servant to help you dress. Lady Proust and Miss Stanton will both be in attendance tonight and I expect your name to be on each of their dance cards at least once."

The implication in her words remained long after she left him to get ready. If his mother expected him to dance with either of them more than once, it meant that both ladies had successfully worked their way into her favor, which was no easy task. But what about them had left his mother with such positive opinions?

Emrys pondered the question as he dressed. Both Lady Proust and Miss Stanton were poised and elegant, each pretty in their own way. The similarities lessened from there. Lady Proust was much more practiced in her ways of courtship, as she was closer to Emrys in age. What Lydia Stanton lacked in experience, however, she made up for in bounds with her youthful energy and excitement for what the future held.

Emrys obeyed his mother's wishes and shared a dance with each of them that night. He tried to give both a fair opportunity at showing who they really were without his mother hovering over his shoulder, and he found that he did enjoy their company.

Lady Proust was quite witty and had a confidence about her that he found endearing. He could near imagine what life might be like with her running their home so effortlessly. Miss Stanton was almost unbearably sweet, and though it felt genuine, there was something about the way she batted her lashes that gave him the impression she had some fire to her, as well. He had always been attracted to a person who was unafraid to be authentically themself no matter the situation.

It wasn't until Emrys finally crawled into bed in the early hours of the following morning that he realized why he still felt unfulfilled by each of these perfectly nice women. He stared up at nothing, thoughts sloshing a bit with the wine he'd had.

"There's your answer, Torquil," he whispered to himself as his eyes slid shut. "Smart, bold, cheeky. Someone who can make me laugh. Someone...who will care about me, and allow me to look after them in return." Emrys tucked his hand beneath the pillow behind his head and sighed slowly. "Find me someone like that, and they will have my heart forever."

TORQUIL'S TRIBUNE

ᚦHURSDAY 2 ᚦECEMBER, 1813

Greetings, fabulous folk and honorable humans,

As December creeps into our fair city, gossip creeps into this humble writer's hands.

Sources say Lady Fitzhugh called on the St. Clair residence for tea recently. Tongues have been wagging for months that Lady Fitzhugh and the lovely Miss St. Clair might be wandering down the path towards love. We certainly hope it is true. The two ladies would, by all accounts, be very well matched.

Mr. Brooks was seen in the Park on the arm of a gentleman. The name of this gentleman is a mystery, although this potential suitor was of the fae variety, and was not Mr. Marigold or Mr. Ravenwing. Mr. Brooks is certainly making his way through the fae population this Season.

Mr. Thompson was seated next to Mx. Hillcrest at a dinner party the other night. Sources say the pair hit it off beautifully. Many are wondering what this means for Miss Thackeray, although this writer suggests a little more creativity on the part of the populace would be much appreciated.

Miss Wrenwhistle received several callers for tea this week.

None of them were particularly noteworthy, but it *is* noteworthy that London is finally recognizing the young lady's charms.

Mr. Irving has been with ladies and gentlemen alike recently. Sources suggest that sparks did not fly in any of these encounters. This writer humbly suggests that Mr. Irving cast his eye elsewhere: the library, perhaps? Hatchard's Bookshop? People of Mr. Irving's serious disposition are unlikely to find love in ballrooms or amidst bites of teacake.

One final note: the Council for Fae & Human Magical Relations is turning their focus to the matter of fae-human magic. Some might say it's about time. As the matter is of particular importance to this writer, we are soliciting information from you, dear readers. If any readers are of the fae-human variety, we would appreciate information regarding your magical casting style. Please spare no detail. We would like to know if you use both human and fae magic interchangeably, if you use one and not the other, or if you use a combination of both—and, if so, how that manifests. Added description of strength of magic is also most welcome. Personally, this writer has discovered that human spells come more easily initially, while fae magic is necessary for added power. No anecdotes will be too strange, no descriptions will be too long, and no magic will be too unusual. We want to hear everything. Responses can be directed to the Pimpernel-Smith Press. We are grateful in advance for any information we receive.

Your esteemed editor,
Torquil Pimpernel-Smith

CHAPTER 18

TORQUIL

AFTER RELEASING THE *TRIBUNE*, Torquil had received a note from Roger with profuse apologies, a new address, and a request that the work be continued the following day due to the upset of the move. They had been extremely relieved to strip out of everything but their shirt, return to bed, and sleep through the day.

They were awoken by gentle fingers combing through their hair. They blinked up at Emrys, perched on the edge of their bed and smiling down at them.

"I almost didn't wake you," he admitted. "You looked so sweet. I can't remember the last time I saw you sleep."

They chuckled. "It's probably just as well that you did wake me. What time is it?"

Emrys pulled out a pocket watch. "A little after midnight."

Torquil yawned. "Well, I've been asleep since around noon so I'd say it's about time I woke up."

"You slept for twelve hours? You must have been tired."

"All the better to see you, my dear," Torquil said with a toothy grin.

Emrys rolled his eyes good-naturedly. "If anything, I rather think I'm the wolf in this scenario."

Torquil cocked an eyebrow. "Are you indeed? Not sure your mother would agree with that. I daresay she'd think I'm luring you off the respectable path."

They slid one bare leg out from under the covers and over Emrys' lap to illustrate their point.

Emrys gave a thoughtful hum as he ran a hand up Torquil's thigh. "It's been a while since I've been lured. How would you do it?"

Torquil grabbed Emrys' lapel and pulled him down for a kiss. When their lips met, Torquil realized with a pang just how much they'd missed these late night visits. As soon as they broke off the kiss, Torquil began making quick work of Emrys' clothes. Emrys sat passively for a minute, watching the buttons coming undone under nimble fingers.

"You know," he said in a musing tone. "Perhaps you're right after all."

Torquil pressed soft kisses down Emrys' neck. The hollow of his throat had always been delightfully sensitive. Emrys groaned, cast off his waistcoat and shirt, slid an arm around Torquil's back, and deftly maneuvered them both until he was lying on the bed with Torquil straddling his waist.

Torquil laughed and resumed kissing down to Emrys' shoulder. "All the better to eat you with," they murmured. They sat back up and began to unbutton Emrys' trousers, arching an eyebrow at him. "I believe I gave very specific instructions for the next time you visited."

"My apologies," Emrys said in mock contrition. "I obviously wasn't thinking clearly. My head was too filled with how much I missed a certain cheeky writer. I will not pretend sadness that my brother and his little husband have moved out. But it does mean I no longer have the unexpected pleasure of finding you in the house."

Torquil paused. "You saw me only a couple of days ago."

Emrys huffed. "Not the same. That encounter was spoiled by Wyndham's—" He waved a hand expressively.

Torquil tilted their head. "Wyndham's...?"

Emrys heaved a sigh. "Must we discuss my brother right now?"

"You brought him up."

"He's just so...so...ugh. You know perfectly well you were full of criticism about him before he and Roger began their so-called project—"

"It *was* a project," Torquil said with a laugh. "And I never said he was perfect. He has plenty of faults."

"*Thank* you! Be so kind as to mention that the next time you write about him."

"Hmm. Perhaps that ought to be my new angle. Pointing out the faults of everyone I write about."

Emrys' eyes lit up.

"Dear foolish folk and harrowing humans. Sources say that Mr. Emrys Wrenwhistle discards his clothes in a most unseemly manner—"

"Can you blame me?" Emrys said, gesturing to his clothes on the floor.

"—and he enjoys making lewd jokes to adorably flustered innocents."

Emrys blew a raspberry. "I would hardly call Roger an innocent. Not with Wyndham in his orbit. I'm certain the man lost his innocence well before their marriage. Put *that* in your paper."

"Hardly newsworthy, I'm afraid."

"More's the pity." He seemed to consider for a moment while his fingers idly stroked over Torquil's hip. "You didn't mention me this morning. Or Wyndham and Roger, for that matter."

"Oh, is that what prompted this visit?"

"Of course not! I came to visit you and, frankly, this conversation is going far longer than I expected. My mother was quite put out though."

"I can imagine." Torquil lowered themself down and brushed a kiss over Emrys' mouth. "As much as I pride myself on the sharpness of my writing, I don't like my words being hurled like daggers between you and your brother." They nipped his lip lightly with their teeth. "If you would like the readers of the *Tribune* to speculate on your mysterious future spouse, you might consider a bit more civility."

Emrys groaned. "With Wyndham? You must be joking."

Torquil's grin was sly.

"I shall *consider* it. Did you tell him this as well? It is impossible to be civil to that little beast sometimes."

"I haven't seen him yet. Roger asked me to visit tomorrow instead. They are still settling in."

"I'll just bet they are."

"But if the topic comes up then, yes, I will tell him the same thing. Although I can't imagine it will. I don't think your brother cares if he's mentioned in my paper."

Emrys grunted in response. "All right," he said in the tone of the much put-upon. "I shall *attempt* civility. But no promises."

Torquil answered with a sweet kiss, deepening it just the way Emrys liked. Predictably, the man moaned beneath them, his grip around Torquil's waist tightened, and the conversation was effectively put to an end.

◈

TORQUIL WAS grateful the next morning that Emrys had decided to visit. He had stayed for several hours, even indulging in a rare doze that Torquil secretly adored. There were a number of moments over the course of the evening, when they caught emotions in Emrys' eye—at some points wistfulness, at others unmistakable fondness—that they didn't quite know what to do with. By the time Emrys gathered his now very wrinkled clothes and gave Torquil a long and lingering kiss good-bye, it was around the hour that Torquil would have woken up anyway.

They sorted through the gossip they had received from their various delivery people, putting the papers into piles of useful and less than useful information. Then they got dressed and left to take a longer route on their way to Wyndham and Roger's new home.

They walked through Hyde Park first, greeting some of their sources in the lower-classes, and noting with interest which members of the *ton* were already out and about. Then they went to the shops, pleased when a baker handed them a chicken pasty along with the news that Mrs. Featherstonhaugh had ordered a large and elaborate cake for what was supposedly a quiet and unassuming dinner party with the Mayhew family. Her son had been seen quite frequently with Captain Mayhew. Torquil wondered if the expensive cake would result in a marriage proposal.

They meandered through the neighborhood, catching servants as they were going about their morning work, greeting them like old friends, and collecting notes and tidbits as they went.

When they arrived at the address Roger had provided, they were led into a study that was still very much in disarray post-move. It was, however, decidedly more comfortable. Mrs. Wrenwhistle had left her mark on the decor and the furnishings, but the mess felt more at home in the study than it had in the sitting room with unfavorable light. Torquil rather liked it. The room was unoccupied but Torquil had only just begun perusing the disorganized bookshelf when Roger bustled in.

"Terribly sorry!"

"No need to apologize," Torquil said. "I only arrived a few moments ago. Your new home is lovely."

Roger smiled. "Thank you. It is *such* a relief to be on our own again. I had gotten dreadfully spoiled during our honeymoon." He looked stricken suddenly. "Not that I mean any sort of insult to the Wrenwhistles, of course—"

Torquil chuckled and held up a hand to forestall Roger's panic. "I've been living on my own for years. Trust me. I understand completely."

Roger relaxed visibly. "Oh. Good. I lived on my own too for a bit. The study Wyn ordered for me in the country makes my bachelor rooms pale in comparison. But it was nice to make a mess and not worry about upsetting anyone."

Torquil glanced around the room. "I can imagine."

Roger laughed and moved to a sofa. "Wyn is pristine. Rather like his mother in that way, actually. Only don't tell him that. He likes things to be just so. But we've reached a happy accord in which the study is allowed to be a mess—and it is arranged to facilitate the least amount of mess—as long as the rest of the house is tidy."

"Does it work?" Torquil said, laughing, as they sat down opposite Roger.

Roger gave a sheepish smile. "Mostly."

"The joys of married life," Torquil said.

"That's quite a topic to walk into," Wyndham said as he breezed through the door. He glanced at the empty table. "Why isn't the tea out yet?"

"You got here before the tea did," Roger replied.

"That was a mistake," Wyndham muttered, pulling on the bell rope before sitting next to his husband. "Why are we discussing the joys of married life? Gathering fodder for your paper or idle chatter between friends? And while we're on the subject, why aren't you relishing the joys of married life, Torquil?"

Torquil blinked at the barrage of questions and tried to squash the brief feeling of joy that flitted through them at Wyndham's casual mention of friends. "You seem to be under some misapprehensions about my social status," they said. "I am not exactly eligible."

Wyndham snorted. "Don't be ridiculous. Which reminds me, why haven't I seen you at any events lately?"

"I haven't been invited—or should I say, *instructed*—to attend any recently."

"Hm."

They arched an eyebrow.

Wyndham donned an innocent look. "I'm only wondering. My grandmother's interest in your social calendar has piqued my curiosity, that's all."

Torquil was spared any further inquisition when the tea arrived. Wyndham all but pounced on the teapot, which gained him mild criticism from his husband, who quickly saw to it that Torquil was served next. All three of them sipped their tea in silence for a moment.

Finally, Torquil said, "Are we continuing with the cleaning spell today?"

Wyndham's expression suggested he had not, in fact, tired of the previous topic and was amused by the subject change. But Roger, bless him, brightened. "Yes! I thought that might be good since we were cut off rather abruptly last time. I would like to experiment with raw materials too, but I think it might be best to wait until the room is fully unpacked."

"Why bother?" Wyndham said dryly. "We might as well start with catastrophe since it will most certainly end up that way."

Roger tsked at him and got everything ready for the cleaning spell.

The three of them worked steadily for hours. Torquil was beginning to regret waking up in the middle of the night when a footman strode into the room and announced the arrival of Mr. Emrys Wrenwhistle.

CHAPTER 19

EMRYS

IT TOOK little effort for Emrys to cast a critical gaze around the study as he stepped into the disarranged space. The rest of the rooms he had passed and peeked into seemed entirely put together already, which was unsurprising. His mother had perfected the process of designing fresh, fashionable living spaces. Her touch, it seemed, had been left out of the study entirely.

Emrys purposefully avoided the eyes of everyone else in the room as he started to wander with his hands clasped behind his back, a grin playing across his features as he pretended to inspect a stack of books, then a half-empty box of glass jars. His eyebrows went up enough to feign interest as he came to the mess of items and papers scattered across the desk they had been working at. The residual magic was thick in the air.

"Are you lost?" Wyndham asked, breaking the silence.

Emrys chuckled, looking up at him. "I've come to check on you, of course. What sort of brother would I be without ensuring my siblings are safe and well situated?"

"I'm certain you did not offer such a line to Auberon when he and Rose moved into their new home," Wyndham countered with mild annoyance.

Emrys' nose wrinkled at the thought. Their brother and his wife shared a modest country house that could hardly be described as easily accessible. The rest of the family had visited once since they'd taken up residence there, and the only things Emrys could recall were the uneven road leading up to it and being entirely unimpressed with the location. He had little interest in calling on them again without proper motive.

"They live so very far away," Emrys said with distaste before his half-grin returned. "But you and your dearest are within walking distance. Such a treat for all of us, wouldn't you agree?"

"It will make it much easier to accommodate the frequent last-minute plans that seem to be custom in your family," Roger reasoned. Wyndham gave him a hard look, and Roger shrugged apologetically.

With the two men distracted, Emrys finally allowed himself to turn his attention to Torquil. Their time together the previous night was still fresh in his mind, causing his magic to whirl in his chest at the sight of them. The excitement dipped sharply when he noticed the faint shadows under their eyes and the grim set of their mouth. Emrys' smirk vanished.

"Oh, confound it," he cursed under his breath, only just catching himself before he stepped around the desk to guide Torquil to a seat. Emrys could feel it now: the tug of fatigue in the air masked by the spells they'd been casting. "Have you no empathy?"

Roger and Wyndham startled out of their private interaction, both giving Emrys a look of confusion before directing it at Torquil, who took a small retreating step.

"Oh dear," Roger said with a frown. "I-I did not even stop to consider—"

"I'm fine," Torquil promised quickly, a small, wavering grin tugging at the corner of their lips. Emrys recognized it as the one they used when they were most certainly *not* fine, but trying to avoid the subject.

"We've been working away since morning," Roger went on, growing steadily more distressed. "Wyn and I have become so accustomed to it over the last several months." He pressed a hand to his forehead. Wyndham reached out to put a hand on his husband's back. "Please forgive us for being so inconsiderate."

"Truly, I am fine," Torquil said. They darted a glance at Emrys before briefly scrutinizing their shoes. "I've been awake since the middle of the night, that's all."

"Allow us to send you home with a tincture," Wyndham offered.

Emrys wanted so badly to argue that Torquil's exhaustion had nothing to do with a lack of sleep and everything to do with how they had clearly been overworked by the two of them. Torquil was far too forbearing when it came to looking after their own health and wellbeing.

Though he never mentioned it, Emrys had become increasingly aware of the way Torquil's bones pressed against him in their intimate moments, and how the thick curls of their dark hair had seemed to grow dull. It was not his place to express concerns on the matter. Instead, he had continued to do what little he was permitted, sending food on occasion and providing their favorite indulgences like the sugared almonds as often as he could without raising suspicion.

"I prefer not using such things if I can help it, but I do appreciate the offer." Torquil took another slow step toward the door. "Perhaps I should take my leave now."

"*No*," Emrys said, surprising even himself. He cleared his throat, forming an explanation in the time it took for all of the attention in the room to land on him once again. He put on his practiced smile and gestured to the space around them. "My reason for calling unannounced was to extend an invitation. To celebrate."

"Oh," Roger said cautiously. "What...er...what are we celebrating?"

Emrys tried mightily to avoid sounding tart. "Your new home. Your new Council positions. Your marriage. You've barely been out since your return to London. I know everyone is desperate to see you both."

"Out?" Roger asked.

"Mother has organized for me to attend the opera this evening with Miss Stanton. It would be remiss of me not to offer for you to join us."

Wyndham let out a long sigh directed toward the ceiling before he looked down at Roger.

"Would you like to go?" he asked softly.

The grin Roger gave was telling. "I do love the opera," he hedged.

"Very well," Wyndham accepted, albeit begrudgingly. He looked at the clock. "We will meet you there. We've just enough time to dress."

"Shall I assume that you will be out too late to expect me at the same time tomorrow?" Torquil asked. Somehow Emrys had missed them edging closer toward the door.

"It will be a late start for all of us," Emrys said pointedly as he turned to face Torquil. "The invitation is for you, as well." It was the only way Emrys could fulfill his self-imposed obligation and keep Torquil close for the rest of the night to make sure their weariness was not something more serious. He silently pleaded for Torquil not to argue, just this once.

"I haven't got time to change," Torquil said after a pause.

They both looked down at Torquil's outfit. The clothes were admittedly quite plain for an evening at the opera house.

"Perhaps you can borrow a tailcoat from Wyndham? You're both —" Emrys bit back his words before he could say something rude. "I would guess that you're nearly the same size."

"Wyndham is significantly taller than I am," Torquil said, brows pinching. It was true. Wyndham hardly ever encountered someone who matched his height. The dramatic coiffure of his hair only added to the spectacle.

Emrys waited, knowing that his brother would be unable to resist an opportunity to speak about his wardrobe.

"I do keep a few coats that are fitted in a shorter style," came Wyndham's response, slow and thoughtful. "I would be happy for you to try them on, at the very least. And I'll tie your cravat into a more fashionable knot. Come along," he instructed, leaving no room for argument.

Torquil flashed a glare at Emrys, but the only thing Emrys noticed was the delightful blush that had appeared on their face. With a smirk, he offered Torquil a private wink and left the three of them to figure out how to fit Torquil into the plans, bringing them one step further into his life outside of the tiny room above the press.

THE OPERA HOUSE was teeming with fae and humans alike. The weather had turned wet and dreadfully cold, and the warmth of the atmosphere inside the grand building was tempting to all. Lively chatter echoed off the walls and high ceiling despite the magic coating them to prevent it from happening.

Emrys sent someone ahead to check if anyone had already been escorted to the Wrenwhistle box. It came as no surprise that he was the first of their party to arrive. If he had not been waiting for Miss Stanton, he would have proceeded to his seat, but he knew his mother would scold him for it. Instead, he found a place to stand and offered polite greetings to everyone he knew as they passed by, his focus never straying too far from the main doors.

Miss Stanton arrived with her mother soon after. Emrys could not help but notice the way she took in her surroundings with a youthful wonder, gaze cast upward before her mother subtly corrected her. He grinned at the exchange between them. Emrys had been much the same at her age, excited to experience new things and be a part of society's most extravagant happenings.

As the two women approached, Emrys gave a slight bow.

"Mrs. Stanton, Miss Stanton. Thank you for braving the weather to join me. I understand it is less than preferable to be out in such conditions." Their noses were pink from the chill outside. Emrys found it endearing.

"Mr. Wrenwhistle," Mrs. Stanton greeted with a polite smile. "We could not pass up such a generous invitation."

"I assure you, the pleasure is mine." Emrys felt his magic moving in his chest with curiosity as he offered his arm to Miss Stanton. Without hesitation, she slid her gloved hand into place. "Shall we?" Emrys asked as he gave a final glance at the doors before turning toward the nearest staircase.

With her mother settled in a chair behind them to play chaperone, Emrys watched with mild amusement as Miss Stanton seemed unable to decide what she wanted to look at first. From their perspective, the entire theater was visible, save for the boxes directly above and below. Her hands gripped the top of the wall in front of them as she peered down with a look of delight on her face.

"I take it this is your first time?" Emrys asked sedately.

She sat back in her chair with a shy smile.

"Is it so obvious?" she asked. Emrys laughed quietly and nodded.

"It's all just so very beautiful," Miss Stanton went on, leaning forward again, this time keeping her hands tucked neatly together on her lap. "I feel as though I've stumbled into one of the paintings hanging in our sitting room. It's a theater very similar to this one, full of rich colors with a golden frame. I've admired it since I was a girl."

Emrys stuck the tip of his tongue out to wet his lips, a feeble attempt at restraining his words. It was her first Season out, yes, but Miss Stanton was still only a girl. If it was not evident enough in her behavior, then certainly it could be noted in the way she spoke so romantically of everything she encountered. The opera was *beautiful*, just as their dance they shared had been *magnificent*.

Perhaps he had become too jaded. The things he found wondrous in his own youth had not changed. Nature still came back to life every spring without being commanded. People still came together to celebrate important events with enough joy and well-wishes to last a lifetime. Even the strength of his own magic still took him by surprise on occasion.

There was nothing wrong with seeking out the romance in life, he decided, no matter your age.

Movement caught his attention. Emrys shifted in his seat to watch the rest of the party as they had their overcoats and hats taken away. The wearisome expression on Wyndham's face was the perfect balance to the look of elation his husband wore as they shuffled to their seats in the intimate space. Emrys realized a bit belatedly that introductions were in order. He stood swiftly, Miss Stanton and her mother doing the same.

Pleasantries were exchanged, though one person was notably absent.

"Have you forgotten someone?" Emrys asked, leaning slightly to check behind where Wyndham and Roger stood.

"Torquil needed a moment," Roger explained in a hushed tone as he sat down in one of the open seats in the second row next to Mrs. Stanton. Wyndham was silent as he did the same. "They'll join us momentarily, not to worry."

It was far too late for that. Emrys considered how discourteous it would be to leave Miss Stanton sitting alone while he went to search for

Torquil. Would it be worth his mother's outrage if she found out? Wyndham's austere presence behind him was enough to keep him in his chair. He knew his brother would enjoy nothing more than to tattle on him for such an indiscretion.

Emrys' concern turned to frustration. Why had Wyndham and Roger left Torquil to begin with? They were the ones showing such little concern for their companion that evening, not him.

As the thick curtains on the stage parted, a hush swept across the room. Miss Stanton sat upright, somehow improving her already impeccable posture. Emrys knew he was being ridiculous. The purpose of the event was to spend more time with someone who could potentially be his future spouse, not his lover.

"Apologies," came a loud whisper, shaking Emrys from his deteriorating state. He turned just as the first notes of music filled the room. It was fortunate timing, for Emrys was helpless against the gasp that escaped him.

They had dressed Torquil in a slender tailcoat in the deepest shade of red. Wyndham had outdone himself with the knot of their cravat, creating a perfect cloud of fabric for Torquil to rest their chin upon. But the most striking change had been to Torquil's hair.

The loose curls Emrys so loved to run his fingers through had been brushed back into a neat style away from their face. The delicate points of their ears were on full display. A comb decorated with pearls and softly glittering gemstones completed the look.

As Torquil sank quietly into their seat—the last open one next to Emrys—he opened his mouth to say something, anything, but no words came. He stared until Torquil finally looked at him out of the corner of their eye; once, twice, and then finally they turned their face to him. The performance had grown too loud to speak over, so they were left to exchange a long, searching look.

Torquil was the first to break. It was only as he watched Torquil's attention return to the stage that Emrys realized how fast his heart was beating. He swallowed hard and pulled himself from his stupor, suddenly feeling very exposed and vulnerable in a way he had never felt before.

Luckily, it seemed that Miss Stanton was too enthralled with the performance to notice Emrys' lapse in focus. He shifted in his chair so that he could cross one knee over the other, leaning slightly closer to the young lady while still maintaining all appearances of public decency. Miss Stanton did notice this subtle change. She gave Emrys a coy grin, her gaze dipping to his lips and lingering for a moment longer than necessary.

Rather than intrigue, Emrys' chest filled with unease. Had Mrs. Stanton seen the unsubtle nature of her daughter's smile? Or worse yet, had Torquil?

When the performance concluded several hours later, Emrys escorted Miss Stanton and her mother to the pavement that had become slick with the cold rain. He helped them into their carriage and bid them a good evening, waiting just long enough for them to disappear from sight before he turned to try and catch Torquil before they left.

Wyndham found him first.

"Mind if we have a quick chat?" Wyndham asked, though it was far from a question. Emrys narrowed his eyes but followed him anyway. They walked until they reached a quiet alley away from the crowd.

"Finally found your opportunity to do away with me, have you?" Emrys teased. "I always thought you would find somewhere in the country to do it. They'll find me here eventually, you know."

Wyndham whirled on him. "I really ought to, after tonight," he said sharply. Emrys' eyes lit with his challenging tone, though he had no idea what Wyndham was so upset about.

Emrys lifted his chin daringly. "And why is that?"

"Don't be daft," Wyndham said. Emrys felt a breeze pick up around them. He couldn't be sure if it was the weather or his brother's magic, but either way it was biting against his exposed skin. Wyndham was known to lose a bit of control when he was upset. It was always a thrill to work him out of his typically calm demeanor.

"Get on with it then, before we both freeze," Emrys urged.

"Leave Torquil alone," he said plainly.

Emrys could do nothing to stop the bark of amusement that escaped him. "Leave them *alone*? Whatever do you mean?"

"For a man with so much responsibility to uphold, you certainly lack the ability to remain focused on the task at hand," Wyndham scolded.

Emrys' mirth faded. "Miss Stanton had a perfectly nice evening," he said, growing defensive. "Perhaps you missed the way she looked at me?"

"I'm surprised you even noticed yourself, what with your attention being directed the opposite way for most of the night." Heat bloomed across Emrys' face. Before he could come up with a response, Wyndham stepped closer and lowered his voice. "Grandmother has tasked Roger and myself with looking after Torquil while we all adjust to our new Council positions. In addition, we have work to do. I've very little interest in having *you* as an interruption."

Torquil's prior request for politeness between them was but a whisper now as Emrys tilted his head to one side.

"If you are trying to imply that I will somehow damage your working relationship by pursuing an attraction," he said, "then allow me to remind you of the absolute devastation your own such behavior has caused in the past. If either of us has done his share of creating disruptions and breaking hearts, it's you."

Wyndham huffed out a laugh. "Sweet that you would think to pay a lover enough mind to become attached." He reached out to pat the middle of Emrys' chest in a brotherly way, though there was enough force behind it to be considered a shove. "Leave Torquil alone, if for no other reason than to allow my husband his newfound friendship. If you scare them away and upset Roger, I promise I will make you regret it."

With that, Wyndham stepped around him in the direction of the street. Emrys turned to watch him go in time for him to call over his shoulder, "By the way, Miss Stanton looks as though she could be your daughter. Perhaps you should try again."

CHAPTER 20

TORQUIL

TORQUIL WAS quiet in the carriage from the opera. The evening had been…interesting. They expected opulence, they expected a sensational performance, they even expected to see opera glasses focused on their seat. But they hadn't expected to be so distracted as to barely register the performance at all.

Part of the distraction was due to the sheer wealth surrounding them, such a stark contrast to their own everyday life. The fact that Torquil had been trussed up to match the rest of the audience gave them mixed feelings of isolation and pride. They had been sitting in the Wrenwhistles' opera box, wearing a dashing suit, fashionably-tied cravat, and even *jewelry*. Everything about it felt so alien to Torquil's usual existence that they felt as though they spent the entire evening outside their own body.

The second and more powerful distraction came in the form of the gentleman sitting next to them. Torquil could *feel* every time Emrys turned his gaze to them. They could feel his eyes lingering. They noticed when he attempted to hide his interest by turning to Miss Stanton. They also noticed the coy smile she gave him and the way Emrys had gone just a little bit rigid in response. They tried not to notice the way their own stomach twisted at the sight.

In an effort to avoid the second distraction, Torquil had concocted a third distraction of their own: responding to the curious glances that were thrown their way by returning the curiosity. They looked with interest at the guests in the boxes around them, noting with pleasure that Lady Fitzhugh had the St. Clair family sitting around her, Mx. Hillcrest was seated in a box between Mr. Thompson and Miss Thackeray (a *very* interesting development), and Mr. Irving was seated next to another gentleman, occasionally murmuring commentary that his companion did not seem pleased to hear. Torquil allowed a small smile. Gerald Irving was not looking in the right places for his future spouse. They continued to look around and found Mr. Ravenwing as well, who was also sitting next to a companion, although Ravenwing's murmurings were met with much more interest, if his companion's expression was anything to go by. Both gentlemen disappeared in the shadows of the Ravenwing box in the second act. Torquil tsked quietly. Hardly the right way to mend a broken heart.

Torquil stifled a yawn during a particularly melodious scene and focused on sitting straight in their seat. It would not do for their companions to recognize their fatigue *again*. When the opera was finally over, Wyndham and Roger escorted Torquil home, despite their assurances that such a fuss was unnecessary.

As Wyndham helped Torquil down, he gave an assessing glance at the press building. Torquil cocked an eyebrow.

Wyndham shook his head in a vague way. "I thought it would feel less strange now that I know what your magic feels like. And it does. But there's something about it that feels familiar, though I cannot see how that's possible."

Torquil was, frankly, too exhausted to care very much about Wyndham's opinion on their security spell, so they had filed the remark away and headed inside.

⚜

DESPITE THE PROMISES that work would start later in the day, habits that had formed over the years were hard to break. Torquil woke when the London sky was still pink with the rising sun. Grumbling, they curled up on their bed, unwilling to get up right away, and thought back to the previous evening's events.

As they rubbed the sleep out of their eyes and blinked in the early morning light, they pondered Wyndham's words about the protection spell with more consideration. After practicing magic for hours on end several days in a row, sensing magic was no longer as much of a strain as it used to be. Cautiously, they felt out with their magic. They noticed little things: a secrecy spell on one of the scraps of gossip on the desk, the wind outside the building, but everything else felt too far away to analyze distinctly. Finally, they got up and dressed, wondering idly whether they ought to change up their regular route a bit.

This question was answered with the sound of someone hammering on the door. Warily, they opened it and were surprised to find Lex, once again looking out of breath on the stoop.

"Am I needed today?" Torquil said.

She nodded. "I tried to fetch you yesterday, but you weren't home."

"I was working," they explained. "Do you know what this is about?"

She shook her head. "You think they tell *me*?"

They sighed, locked the door, and followed her down the street. About halfway to the Council chambers, they realized she was looking at them nervously.

"Is something the matter?" they asked.

She paused and turned to them, wringing her hands a bit. "I was wondering…well, I'd heard that you sometimes give…that you pay people for gossip?"

They grinned. "I do. You have some?"

She nodded and pulled out a crumpled piece of paper. "I'd heard you prefer it in writing."

"I'm not particular, but it does make it easier for me." They handed her the usual amount and then gave her one extra shilling. "If any of the other aides have gossip, feel free to send it my way," they said with a wink.

She beamed in response and they continued to the chambers. To Torquil's surprise, Lex led them to Councilmember Williams' office.

"Finally," the man muttered as Torquil stepped inside.

"You wanted to see me?" they said.

Williams slapped a copy of the *Tribune* on his desk. "I'd like you to explain this."

Torquil bent forward and glanced over the issue. "Was there a particular bit of gossip you wanted more details on? I'm afraid that goes against my policy."

"I want you to explain *this*," he said sharply, pointing to the final paragraph.

"Ah," Torquil said lightly. "Was something unclear?"

"What's unclear is who gave you permission to discuss Council business in your ruddy paper?"

"I was not aware I needed permission to write about the Council, considering I have written about it multiple times in the past without express permission, and considering that I was asked onto the Council after doing so."

"Well, now that you're on the Council, you are being held to a higher standard."

"That has been quite obvious," Torquil said, taking a seat.

"Was that impudence?" Williams said.

Torquil raised their chin, realizing that they'd seen Emrys take up the same defensive posture when confronted with his brother's insults. They bit back a smile at the similarity and remembered their own advice to Emrys to offer a bit of civility. "That was merely an observation, Councilmember Williams," they said. "It has been patently evident that my presence here is unwelcome, despite the fact that I was invited to be here. I was asked to be on this Council, and I don't think it was because my writing skills suggested I'd make a good secretary," they added with a smile. "So let's be honest with each other: you don't like me, but I am here to do my work. As someone with access to a paper, it seemed a reasonable tactic to use. If I were a full-blooded person—on either side—I think we can both agree I wouldn't be spoken to in such a way."

"Now, listen here—"

"And furthermore, I was under the impression that I fell under Iris —that is—Councilmember Wrenwhistle's purview. So I rather think this censure should be delivered by her, shouldn't it? Or am I misunderstanding the hierarchy?" They gave him a sweet smile.

Williams glared and pointed a finger at them. "I don't like you putting words in my mouth, Pimpernel-Smith. And I don't like seeing Council business going to the public before it gets to me."

"I think your second point is fair enough," Torquil said. "I will be sure to send the Council an advanced copy next time." With that, they stood and left the room, ignoring Williams' calls to *come back at once.*

They strode to the other end of the hallway and knocked on Iris' office door. She looked up from her desk and beamed at them.

"Good morning! I didn't expect to see you today, but I'm glad you came in."

Torquil took a seat. "I was summoned by Williams."

She lifted an eyebrow. "Oh?"

They grimaced. "And I *might* have angered him just a bit."

She chuckled and sifted some papers into tidy piles. "Not a very difficult feat these days. He's been in a frightful mood for the past month. What was the infraction?"

"My recent issue of the *Tribune.*"

She seemed to pause. "You mean the last paragraph? I rather liked that."

Relief washed over Torquil. "Williams was upset that I didn't ask for permission first."

"This Council likes to say they want fresh and new ideas, but as soon as fresh and new ideas are introduced, they're annoyed. Don't worry about it. I'll talk to him."

"Thank you," they said and started to stand. "I'll be working with Roger and Wyndham again today, so if you need me—"

"How was the opera?"

Surprised by the question, Torquil sat back down with a thump.

"I heard you looked very becoming in a new suit and a comb."

"Wyndham loaned me the suit."

She smiled at them, her expression expectant.

"It was lovely," they said at last. "Em—Mr. Emrys Wrenwhistle was kind enough to include me in the invitation since I was present when he invited Wyndham and Roger."

Her smile widened and she sat back in her seat. "How nice."

"It was a perfect vantage point to see so many members of society. I have a nice bit of fodder for my next issue."

"What did you think of Miss Stanton?"

Torquil weighed their words carefully. "She seems very sweet. Although...er...perhaps a bit too young for Mr. Wrenwhistle. I'm not sure they would suit."

She nodded as if satisfied. "I'm sure I would appreciate it if you hinted as much in your next paper. My daughter-in-law is insistent on the match and I cannot understand it."

They chuckled. "I'm sure I can fit something in."

"Good. And how is your project going with Wyndham and Roger?"

"It's going well, I think. I have a much better understanding of my own magic now. A third rubric is decidedly necessary."

"Yes, I thought that might be the case," she said in a musing tone. Her gaze swept over them in a critical manner. "But please see to it that you don't work too hard. I know young Roger throws himself into projects. There's no rush on this one, what with the winter holidays approaching."

The advice brought back the memory of Emrys' concern and Torquil felt their face flush. "I don't mind it," they assured her.

"Hm," she said, sounding unconvinced. "Did you say you're working with them again today?"

They nodded.

She pulled out a reticule and then passed over a small pile of coins. "Be so good as to bring breakfast when you go. I want you all to keep up your strength."

Torquil eyed the pile. "I don't think I'll need that much."

She shrugged and nudged the coins to the edge of the desk. "Be creative."

They reluctantly pocketed the money. If it had been given by anyone else, they might have refused, but they didn't quite dare refuse Iris, much as they wanted to. "Thank you."

"Remind Wyndham that we have an appointment this week."

Torquil left and browsed the market, finally deciding on a basket of pastries, some fruit, and freshly cooked sausages. After some deliberation, they used the rest of the coins on sugared almonds. Something twisted in their chest as they took the parchment paper, warm with roasted nuts. When they reached the townhouse, the butler took all of the packages and promised to bring them to the study immediately.

Roger and Wyndham were already waiting. Roger sat with his head bent over the previous day's notes and Wyndham was sitting with his back against the armrest, watching his husband with a fond expression. They both looked up and smiled when Torquil walked in.

"I come bearing gifts," Torquil said. "Courtesy of your grand-mother. Your butler said he'd bring everything in with the tea. And your grandmother bid me to remind you of an appointment later this week."

"Oh, excellent!" Roger said, setting aside the notes and clearing away some space on the table. "That was very kind of her."

The corner of Wyndham's mouth twitched. "Yes, my grandmother is thoughtful like that. And I haven't forgotten my appointment. Which reminds me, how are you feeling?"

"I'm fine," Torquil assured him.

"Did you get better sleep last night?"

"Yes, thank you. Although I'm afraid I'm not good at sleeping late."

Wyndham's eyes narrowed slightly. "Hm."

"You look…that is, you seem more rested today," Roger put in. "I cannot forgive myself for ignoring the signs. I'm usually much better at that."

"It's fine," Torquil said. "I don't expect you to look after me."

"Of course not," Roger said, the brightness in his tone slightly forced. "But we really should be more careful of taking breaks in the future. I tend to get carried away."

"Yes, and I'm still annoyed that my brother, of all people, noticed before I did," Wyndham said. "Which reminds me—"

The butler came in at that moment, effectively cutting off the conversation. Torquil tried to hide their relief. Roger was properly distracted with the breakfast offering and he cheerfully served everyone a plate before pouring out the tea.

Wyndham, however, was not to be distracted. After Torquil had taken a bite of pastry, Wyndham said, "I'd like to talk to you about Emrys."

Torquil raised an eyebrow, unable to respond with their mouth full.

Wyndham's expression turned serious. "I think you should be careful about him. I've seen the way he looks at you and…I don't trust him."

Torquil coughed on their food. After recovering, they took a large gulp of tea. "Are you worried he'll damage my reputation, Wyndham? I'm hardly a blushing debutante, you know."

"No, I have a very apt example of *that*, thanks to seeing Miss Stanton last night," Wyndham said. "But I don't want him to break your heart. You're far too good for him."

Torquil cleared their throat, glancing between the two men. Wyndham was looking painfully serious and Roger looked anxious.

"To be fair," Roger said, "Emrys is far more polite to you than he is to us."

"He can be charming when he wants to be," Wyndham said.

Torquil tried not to laugh at their somber expressions. "Thank you for warning me. I'll be careful."

Wyndham breathed out. "Good. Now that that's out of the way, what are we doing next?" He paused and then frowned, turning back to Torquil. "Did you say you saw my grandmother this morning?"

They nodded.

"I've been giving her reports on our work. I'm surprised she called you in."

"She didn't. Williams was actually the one who did that. He took offense to my write-up in the *Tribune*."

Roger looked perplexed. "Whatever for—oh! Do you mean that bit about the fae-human magic? But that was brilliant! I meant to tell you yesterday."

Torquil couldn't help beaming at the compliment. "Thank you. I thought it a good strategy. Williams seemed to think I went about it poorly."

Wyndham rolled his eyes.

"He was always rather cutting to me," Roger admitted, "until our engagement."

"Yes, well that's when you became useful to him," Wyndham said. "I take it my grandmother was not of his opinion."

"No, thankfully."

"Good. Shall we get started then?"

Roger nodded, mid-bite, then shuffled through his notes and pulled out a page. He sucked the sugar off one fingertip and said, "I thought we might change strategy today, especially considering how hard you've been working the past few days. I think it would be good to see your spell sensing abilities. Wyn and I can do spells today and you can sense them and tell us what you notice. Will that work?"

Wyndham plucked the paper out of Roger's hand and flicked crumbs off the edge. "That will do nicely. Are we doing spells individually or together?"

"I'd like to see you cast together," Torquil put in. "I've only seen you do that at the wedding."

"Good," Wyndham said, standing. "You two finish eating. I'll send for the ingredients we'll need."

"I can help," Torquil said as they set their plate down.

Wyndham gave them a hard look and placed two more pastries on their plate. "No need."

Roger reached forward and placed another sausage on the plate too. "They're quite delicious," he said. "We should finish them all up while they're fresh."

Torquil knew charity when they saw it. But when Roger picked up another sausage and began eating it too, they conceded defeat and tucked into the second serving.

The afternoon was almost as exhausting as the previous days had been. Although Torquil wasn't doing any of the casting themself, they were unaccustomed to sensing magic for hours on end. But the magic that Roger and Wyndham cast together was so unique and so extraordinary, they couldn't bring themself to say anything about how exhausted they were; that their eyes were beginning to itch and their body was beginning to feel heavy. Combined, the couple's magic was fascinating to see. Roger would cast the initial spell and then Wyndham would tweak it, or add onto it, and then Roger would scribble in added details, so the spell became layered on itself, getting more and more complex. It was dizzying to watch.

In the end, Torquil didn't have to admit their fatigue; Roger glanced up in pride after a particularly tricky spell, and his good cheer was quickly displaced by a stricken expression. Wyndham moved quickly, ushering Torquil to a seat despite their protests, and Roger poured out a hefty helping of tea and pushed it into their hands.

"I'm fine," Torquil said, although they sipped the tea gratefully.

"Perhaps we should end early today," Roger said a little fretfully.

Wyndham was studying Torquil with a thoughtful expression. "Is sensing magic difficult for you?"

Torquil shrugged. "Not difficult exactly. But I'm out of the habit. It's…it's like stretching a muscle that hasn't been used in a while."

"So you're feeling sore and fatigued and stretched too thin?" Wyndham supplied.

"That is not an inaccurate description, but I don't mind continuing," Torquil said quickly. "I just need to adjust to it. That's all."

Wyndham huffed and turned to his husband. "I think you're right. Let's end early for today."

Roger nodded. "Would you like to join us for dinner?"

"It will be with my family," Wyndham put in.

"That is very kind of you to offer," Torquil hedged.

"I don't blame you," Wyndham said. "My family is a trial at the best of times. But we will have you stay for dinner one of these days. Would you like a ride home?"

"I can walk, but thank you."

Roger held up a tea towel that he had tied into a parcel. "The rest of the pastries are in here," he said. "And some of the other items that will still taste good tomorrow."

Torquil tried to protest but was overruled. They took the parcel of food and strode home. Inside the tea towel were three pastries, two apples, and the sugared almonds. Torquil stared at the small collection of food for a long moment. They felt uncomfortable with such generosity, particularly since they didn't know whether it was based on a general knowledge of their financial circumstances or if there were tells that they weren't aware of. They sat down at the desk and picked up the package of almonds. The scent alone reminded them of Emrys. Had all of those little treats been borne out of the same concern for their welfare? The thought made them equal parts touched and discomfited.

They had spent years living in stubborn independence. Even as a child, they had been trusted to entertain themself. Their parents had never dedicated much effort in helping Torquil find friends their own age—partly to shield Torquil from the inevitable bigotry, and partly because after Torquil's mother was shunned from society, she had determined that society was useless. Mr. and Mrs. Pimpernel-Smith only needed each other, after all. Why should their only child be any different?

Except, Torquil *had* been different. Shortly after their twentieth birthday, they'd expressed an interest in moving to London and starting a press. Their parents had balked at the idea, and attempted to persuade them out of it—warning of lack of funds, the cruelty of society, and the dirtiness of the city. But Torquil had been adamant and their parents had finally relented, going so far as to purchase the press building and equipment for them and setting up the initial protection spells. Then they had sold their own little cottage in the country and gone off to travel the world together.

Torquil had hardly heard from them since, except for a letter every few months describing colorful adventures. Torquil's independence had been somewhat imposed upon them when they arrived in London, but they had fought to earn it, working tirelessly to become London's foremost gossip column, and a name that everyone knew. And if a full stomach, fine clothes, and friendship were hard to come by? That was simply the price Torquil had learned to pay.

But now they had people looking after them, worrying about them, scheming on their behalf. It had never occurred to them that gaining friends would involve such overtures. They plucked an almond out of the paper and savored it. Perhaps a little independence was a worthwhile concession when it came with such friends as Emrys, Roger, Wyndham, and Iris.

With that, they set the food aside, retied the parcel, and began working on the next *Tribune*.

TORQUIL WAS awoken again with Emrys gently stroking through their hair. This time, however, they had fallen asleep at their desk. They blinked their eyes blearily and felt a soft kiss at the nape of their neck.

"I don't intend to stay long," Emrys said. "I only wanted to make sure you were all right."

Torquil huffed and sat up. "Of course I'm all right. Why wouldn't I be?"

Emrys grinned and traced a fingertip over Torquil's raised eyebrow, then trailed that finger down their cheek. "They're working you too hard."

"They're not. Only now they're exceptionally anxious about it, thanks to you. They even sent me home with food!"

Emrys brightened. "As well they should. It's the least they could do after the hours of work they put you through."

"I'm a willing participant, I assure you. And speaking of which, don't you dare come all the way over here just to kiss my neck and then leave. I'll never forgive you."

Emrys laughed and bent down to pull them into a kiss. Torquil cupped the back of his neck and deepened the kiss, making their intentions for the evening very clear.

Emrys pulled away and kissed their cheek. "You ought to rest."

"Perhaps I'll rest better if you're in bed with me," Torquil said cheekily.

Emrys swiftly started undressing by way of an answer. Torquil watched with amusement. "If I knew that would be the reaction, I'd have said that a long time ago."

Emrys rolled his eyes. "As if you have ever lacked the ability to get me naked."

Torquil hummed appreciatively as his shirt hit the floor. "It is one of my finer gifts, I think." They stood and gently shoved Emrys onto the bed, then straddled his hips and kissed him. "I've been warned about you. Your brother is very concerned about your influence on me."

Emrys groaned. "Yes, he warned me too. Told me not to *distract* you."

Torquil laughed. "Well, you must admit you're quite the distraction."

"Not an unwelcome one, I hope?"

"You'd know it if you were," Torquil assured him, kissing him again to prove their point.

Emrys pulled them both down to the mattress, winding their legs together and wrapping both arms around Torquil, who snuggled close in response. "I've always liked the idea of sleeping next to you," they admitted quietly.

"Now *that* you should have said a long time ago," Emrys said. He ran a hand through Torquil's hair. "I quite liked the comb. But I've always loved the unruliness of your curls."

Torquil chuckled. "I'm aware." They felt Emrys tweak a curl playfully. "You're supposed to be resting," Torquil reminded him.

Emrys promptly dropped the curl and cradled Torquil's head. "My apologies," he murmured.

Together, they settled into silence. Torquil enjoyed the way their breathing began to match Emrys'. They stroked a hand down Emrys' bare chest, wondering how long he'd stay this time.

They knew that Emrys was not looking forward to his obligatory marriage, and Torquil had spent a great deal of energy trying not to think about what that marriage meant for this friendship. Their friendship with Wyndham and Roger felt new and fragile, but full of promise. The friendship they shared with Emrys was…different. It felt comfortable and right, the way fabric softens after more use. Emrys felt—most terrifyingly—like home. Torquil quickly shoved that thought aside. It wasn't smart to settle down into a temporary home, especially one that had an ever-approaching deadline.

Emrys' breathing became slower and more even and Torquil tried not to feel pleased by how quickly the man had relaxed in their embrace. They felt a small and sudden niggling curiosity as to what Emrys' magic felt like. After hours of practice, the idea of sensing magic was not as daunting as it used to be. And now that they had rested for a few hours from the morning's strenuous work, they felt better equipped to explore. They closed their eyes and breathed out slowly.

They were surprised by how powerful a presence Emrys' magic was. They supposed they probably shouldn't be; after all, Emrys had inherited based on his magical abilities. His magic practically filled the room, quite like the man himself tended to take up space. But what was even more surprising were the tendrils of magic that were tentatively reaching for Torquil's own power. Not for the first time, they wished they could cast without a human spell to ground them. They wanted to coax their own magic to those small tendrils, reach out in return. They had to make do with sensing that magic with more intention, getting a better gauge on the personality of Emrys' power. There was something familiar about his magic although Torquil couldn't quite put a finger on what that was.

Before they could do any more sensing, Emrys awoke with a start and gave Torquil a long, unreadable look. "Are you…" He paused, licked his lips. "Is that your magic?"

Torquil nodded hesitantly. To their surprise, Emrys responded with one of the brightest grins they'd ever seen on his handsome face.

CHAPTER 21

EMRYS

He had felt Torquil's magic so few times that he'd never been able to pin down a way to describe it. In those instances, the sensation was not unlike the heaviness of a storm in the distance still hours from arriving, or the unmistakable scent wafting from a bakery window in the early morning hours. Emrys knew it, but it had always remained just out of reach.

But this was entirely different. *This* was the first drop of the storm falling onto his skin. This was a bite of fresh bread, covered thick with jam bursting sweetly on his tongue. It was so very faint, but it was everything.

Emrys brought his hand to the side of Torquil's face and rested their foreheads together. "Do it again," he whispered.

The emptiness in his moment of anticipation was enough to make his own magic stir wildly, searching for company in the small room. It knew every corner, every surface, but now there was something new. Emrys closed his eyes and tried to focus, realizing that such power could mask something so gentle with ease. He stroked his thumb across Torquil's cheek, waiting with more patience than he'd ever had in his life.

And then it came. The featherlight brush of Torquil's magic

reaching for his own set his body on fire, lit from within and strong enough to make Emrys tremble. He huffed out a laugh and pressed his mouth to Torquil's, sliding his fingers into their hair and pulling them close. The way Torquil leaned into him only made the heat burn brighter.

"I cannot tell you how jealous I've been knowing that Wyndham and Roger have had all this time with your magic," he admitted in between heavy kisses. "All this time with you."

"You can see me whenever you'd like," Torquil said, breathless.

"You know it's not the same." Emrys finally pulled back to look into Torquil's eyes, searching them just as he'd done at the opera. All at once, he felt as though his words were hurtling toward some sort of confession that he could not wrap his thoughts around fast enough. Before he could voice them, he kissed Torquil again, rolling them onto their back. Perhaps the safest way to avoid these heavy words was to not speak at all.

Emrys moved to straddle Torquil's hips. It was a position he did not find himself in very often, but he had to wonder why as he soaked in the way Torquil was looking up at him with hungry eyes and kiss-swollen lips. His attention shifted to the laces that had already been loosened at the base of their throat, exposing only a tease of what hid beneath. That just wouldn't do. Emrys eased Torquil to sitting and took the hem of the untucked shirt, pulling it up and off in one quick motion. Before it hit the floor, Emrys had his hands on Torquil's skin, exploring as he leaned to press a slow kiss to their shoulder.

Torquil shivered. At first, Emrys thought it was from anticipation, and he smirked against their shoulder before placing another kiss there. But the slide of Torquil's slender fingers along his back revealed the truth. They were freezing.

Without pause, Emrys called on his magic. The dirty window high on the wall was in enough disrepair that he could pull air from outside through the gap in the frame. The breeze *whooshed* past them on a direct path to the tiny stove that Torquil depended on to heat the room. It was not enough, and never had been, but Torquil had never allowed Emrys to replace it no matter how many times he'd offered. The dying fire inside glowed doubly as bright the moment his magic reached it.

Torquil chuckled softly. "Always the hero."

Emrys grinned down at them as he guided their head back to the thin pillow. "I'm only trying to get you to write more positive things about me in the *Tribune*," he said. "I spent the morning trying to convince my mother that it's not going to work between Miss Stanton and myself, but she won't hear it. I need all the help I can get finding a suitable alternative to capture her attention."

A small pout formed on Torquil's mouth. "And what of your own attention?"

Emrys had to consider his response. When he finally gave it, his words were quiet. "I am beginning to think that I will have to abandon all hope of being matched with someone who can provide everything I am looking for." Emrys watched as Torquil's fingertips traced lightly over his chest and stomach. "If I'm honest, Torquil, I did not think I would have such trouble with the whole thing. I have known my responsibility to my family since I was seventeen, and yet I cannot...I cannot bring myself to let go of whatever is causing me such hesitation."

Torquil's fingers stilled. "Wyndham did not want to get married. Perhaps you are like him that way?"

Emrys scowled. "And yet he still did. So did Auberon, and with your assistance I believe my sister will also find herself married before long." He took a breath and sighed. "I do want to be married. I suppose I just never imagined that I would find myself as a thirty-four-year-old bachelor with my *mother* trying to find a suitable spouse because I could not manage it on my own."

Torquil hummed before a small grin quirked the corner of their lips and their nose wrinkled. "That is a bit sad, isn't it?"

Emrys' mouth fell open in surprise before he laughed. "You cruel creature," he scolded as he leaned down to kiss Torquil in a playfully chaste way. Torquil moved to wrap their arms around Emrys' neck and shoulders, but he pulled away, taking Torquil's wrists and kissing the underside of each before he placed them above Torquil's head on the pillow. "Move those and I'll leave without hesitation."

Torquil gasped. "Now who is being cruel?"

Emrys was already busy placing a trail of kisses down Torquil's chest, his hands coming to rest on their hips as he moved toward the foot of the bed.

"Wait until I've finished—or until you've finished, rather—to decide if you still feel that way," Emrys teased in a low voice. Torquil's soft moan was all the encouragement he needed to begin working their trousers off, moving at a leisurely pace until the rest of Torquil's clothes found a place on the worn floorboards around the bed.

Emrys had always hated Torquil's bed. Not only was it too short for two people with fae blood to fit on comfortably, but it also brandished a headboard and footboard that made moments like this nearly impossible. With a grunt, Emrys pulled Torquil's body so that they were lying across the mattress at more of an angle. He leaned down to kiss Torquil's hip, then the other, before he took them in his mouth.

As much as he wished for Torquil's bed to suit them better, he had to admit that he enjoyed the way they gripped the headboard as they did now. Torquil had never been shy in their intimate moments, which often meant that their hands never stopped touching, searching. Sometimes Emrys had no choice but to make a demand like the one he had so that he could focus on Torquil's pleasure alone.

"So very cruel," Torquil managed on a whimper as Emrys brought them ever closer to the edge.

Emrys was desperate to feel their magic again. He reached out with his own; enveloped Torquil in it enough to make them shiver once more despite the warmth that had filled the room from the stove. Emrys switched to using his hand and considered.

"Perhaps that's been my problem all along," he said. "I'm actually a horrible partner in bed, is that it?" The first tickle of Torquil's answering magic brushed against his own. It sent a wave of pleasure between his legs.

"The worst," Torquil panted. Emrys used his free hand to still their hips from writhing in the mussed sheets. He felt a pang in his chest at the way their hip bone curved in such a pronounced way under his palm, but there was little time to focus on it. "I pity anyone who has to put up with your obvious lack of skills—*ah!*" Torquil's back arched as Emrys took them in his mouth again, deeper this time. Words gave way to more moans and whimpers until Torquil came with a shuddering exhale. Emrys' magic swirled around them both, capturing every last drop of what Torquil had to give of their own power, until the room settled into a state of sleepy satisfaction.

Emrys pulled the blanket out from under his lover's sated body and brought it up over both of them as he collected Torquil into his embrace again. It took a long moment for Torquil to turn into his arms, apparently lacking the energy to move. That's exactly what he had been hoping for. Emrys placed a slow kiss into their dark curls as Torquil slid their knee between his legs.

"I suppose I'll have to tell my mother we've discovered what's wrong with me," he said with a grin. Torquil made a soft sound of acknowledgement, not quite a laugh.

As Emrys waited to see if Torquil had one last witty remark, he moved his fingertips along the dip of their lower back, no longer able to restrain the flood of thoughts he had pushed away while he'd focused on Torquil.

Something had changed when their eyes locked at the opera. There was no denying that Emrys had been attracted to Torquil since the first night they met. They'd slept together in that very same bed and Emrys enjoyed it just as much then as he did now. He had seen every bit of Torquil's body, experienced nearly every kind of pleasure he could imagine with them. So why had his reaction been so intense the previous night? Was it the change in wardrobe, or the jewelry tucked into their hair?

Or was it simply the idea of Torquil existing in that quiet moment of his life? The idea of experiencing the opera together, knowing that the rest of society could see them together and feeling...content? Proud?

Emrys kissed Torquil's hair again. He held them close, allowing all of his questions free in his mind as Torquil slept in his arms.

CHAPTER 22

TORQUIL

Torquil slept so soundly, they didn't hear Emrys leave. They woke up to a half-empty bed as the early morning light crept into the room. They clutched the blanket to their chest, remembering the way Emrys had responded to their magic. His delight had been a surprise, but even more of a surprise had been the way his magic had reacted. Torquil had barely sensed Emrys' magic a second time before it seemed to explode, filling the room and surrounding them both. Emrys had been practically glowing. Torquil shivered at the memory. They had never experienced anything like that before, not even with Emrys. If it had been anyone else, they might have asked for advice from Roger and Wyndham. But they could just imagine how Wyndham would reply to the question. *So I was in bed with your brother and right before he brought me to immense satisfaction...* They nearly laughed at the glare they would most certainly receive.

Which brought them to the final two surprises of the evening: Emrys had been *affected* by feeling Torquil's magic. The effect had been very noticeable through his trousers. Torquil had even tested the theory with the last shred of their mental capacity, exploring the way Emrys' magic had expanded, and then observing how Emrys had...well, expanded as well. Yet another question they couldn't see themself asking their new friends. Roger would likely faint, poor thing.

The very last surprise had been the extraordinary tenderness Emrys had shown. He had always displayed his softer side to Torquil, but this had felt different, somehow. There had been unspoken meaning in the way he'd stared into Torquil's eyes, an earnestness in the way he'd held them. It felt weighted, this tenderness, and Torquil had no idea what to do about it.

At last, they got out of bed and ate a couple pastries and an apple before getting dressed. After some hesitation, they tucked the half-empty packet of almonds into their coat pocket and went downstairs.

They swept their hand over the cold metal of the press as they passed it. They paused at the door and looked around the room. Perhaps it would be wise to keep practicing their sensing, gently work the muscle so it was less strained by the end of the day. They leaned back against the door and closed their eyes, feeling their magic explore the room. There was magic in the press, which startled them more than it should have. They could feel the magic in the cabinet with their supplies, although that was to be expected. Emrys' magic lingered on the door at their back, the lock now acquainted with the way Emrys manipulated it to open for him. Torquil gave a little sigh and went out the door.

They paused on the stoop and looked up at their building. After years of patching up the spell haphazardly, Torquil was a little nervous about how it would feel now. To their surprise, it felt secure and seamlessly woven together. They frowned. That was impossible. They trailed their fingertips over the wall's surface. At the base of the magic, they could feel their parents' spells, faded from time but still a solid foundation. There were splashes of magic at all of the spots Torquil usually cast. It made them wince a little to feel the irregularity of it.

But what confused them most was the magic that had been cast around all of it like a net, fusing the different magical elements together. They closed their eyes and laid their palm flat against the wall and focused harder. The magic felt familiar. Their eyes flew open with realization: *Emrys.* Had Emrys been enhancing their security spell? And when had he started? They bit their lip, remembering the way they'd explained to him that the lock had compromised their safety. They turned their attention back to the magic; it felt layered. Torquil had an inexplicable certainty that Emrys had been doing this long before the lock had been broken.

Their hand dropped from the wall and covered the pocket with the almonds before they turned to leave. How had they missed all of the ways Emrys had taken up space? He had woven himself into the very walls of their home, fused himself into the lock. It was more than the smell of his soap on their pillow. That was a remnant Torquil was accustomed to. They shivered a little as they walked. What would happen when Emrys got married and stopped coming? How long would it take for his presence to fade? Torquil deeply didn't want to know the answer to that.

They took a slow and meandering walk to Wyndham and Roger's townhouse. They tried to distract themself by checking on more sources than usual, but even though they received ample gossip and cheery conversation, they couldn't completely shake their messy feelings about Emrys.

When they finally reached Wyndham and Roger's front door, they tried not to be grumpy about how jumbled their thoughts still were.

This grumpiness was clearly evident as Roger greeted them with, "Good heavens! What's wrong?"

Torquil immediately smoothed out their features. "Nothing."

Wyndham snorted. "Ah, yes. I always scowl when nothing's wrong."

Roger seemed to hesitate. "Well, you *do* sometimes. But I don't think I've ever seen Torquil scowl."

"Nothing's wrong," Torquil said. "Just…thinking. A lot on my mind this morning."

"Anything you care to share?" Wyndham said.

"No, it's fine," Torquil said hastily.

Wyndham raised an eyebrow and Roger said, "Oh, do sit, Torquil. You know you can tell us anything, don't you?"

Torquil sat and considered the question. *Could* they tell their friends about their discoveries from the night before? Perhaps if they didn't name names. They took a deep breath. "I suppose I can discuss some of it. But be aware that the topic is…er…indelicate."

Wyndham smirked. "My favorite kind."

Roger blushed but stammered for Torquil to continue.

Torquil cleared their throat. "I had a guest over last night. And… well, you know how I'd said yesterday that I'm out of the habit of sensing magic? Well, I decided to try sensing a little while my friend was with me. And he reacted in a way that…surprised me."

"What do you mean?" Wyndham said. "Did he react poorly?"

"Not at all. I mean…his magic reacted to my magic. It…it expanded, almost? And my friend…it was almost like he was glowing." They paused. "Then again, I've never sensed his magic before so maybe it's not all that unusual. But I am sure his magic was not quite so *loud* before I sensed it. If that makes sense?"

Roger looked thoroughly baffled but Wyndham looked pensive. "Is your friend fae, by any chance?"

Torquil nodded.

Wyndham hummed thoughtfully. "How familiar are you with wedding spells?"

Torquil was confused by the abrupt topic change. "I've only been to one fae wedding and that was yours."

Wyndham scrunched his nose. "Not a particularly good example, I'm afraid. You see, the origin of the wedding spells in fae tradition is rooted in the idea of magical compatibility. The wedding spell is supposed to display how compatible the couple is. When the couple is well suited for each other, according to tradition, their magic will be suited for each other too."

"I thought Councilmember Cricket said it was supposed to prove their love," Roger said.

Wyndham inclined his head. "Yes, well, love supposedly impacts how well the two magics blend. If the two people are in love, one magic will strengthen the other. If the lore is to be believed."

Torquil suddenly felt very uncomfortable. "Oh," they said quietly.

Wyndham gave them a long look. "I take it this friend of yours is one you know rather well?"

"Y-yes. Several years."

Wyndham's expression turned sly. "Is he eligible?"

Torquil rolled their eyes. "Very. It's a bit unfortunate, really."

"Why?" Roger asked at the same time that Wyndham said, "Anyone we know?"

Torquil heaved a sigh. "It's unfortunate because I am the sort of person that eligible people take to bed but I am not the sort of person that eligible people take to the alt—" They broke off and their face heated. "And no, it's nobody you know."

Roger and Wyndham's expressions had swiftly changed to sympathy.

"I'm sure that's not true," Roger said soothingly.

"No, it isn't," Wyndham said heatedly. "It's a complete lie. Both statements are, actually. Did he say that to you? He's a right bastard if he did. Tell me who—"

"No, he did not say anything of the kind. It's just something I know." Torquil stood, feeling uncomfortable under the attention. "When you're a fae-human and your mother was disowned for marrying your father and having you, when nobody in society wants anything to do with you, when you spend your days writing a gossip column, and live above your press room, and have no money and no connections…then you know you're the sort of person that eligible people don't marry." They ran a hand over their face. "Forget I brought it up. I'm sure I just imagined the whole thing anyway."

Roger stood and hurried to stand in front of Torquil. He placed a gentle hand on their arm. "You know there's more to you than that, don't you? Whoever he is would be lucky to have you."

Wyndham leaned back in his seat. "You didn't imagine any of it. Whatever sort of person you believe yourself to be, you are decidedly not the sort of person who imagines something as profound as the spark of magical compatibility." He reached into his waistcoat pocket. "As to your statement that nobody in society wants anything to do with you, need I remind you that *we* are in society? Even my rotten brother, who most certainly had the wrong intentions towards you, was willing to be seen in public with you. That is not nothing." Before Torquil could fully register those words, Wyndham held up a stiff piece of paper. "And here is another example to prove that particular statement wrong."

Torquil strode to Wyndham and took the offered paper. Dread

thickened in their stomach as they read it: an invitation to a dinner party hosted by Iris Wrenwhistle.

"My grandmother ordered me to give that to you," Wyndham explained, somewhat unnecessarily.

They swallowed and traced over the gold lettering with the pad of their thumb.

Wyndham stood and put a hand on Torquil's shoulder. "If you want my advice, I would suggest you not let go of this friend. A reaction like what you described is no small thing. I can't argue against your family's history. But as to your social standing—you're a councilmember. And you are our friend. And my grandmother is very invested in seeing you successfully become a more active member of society. You are *not* without connections, Torquil. And if your friend is as eligible as I suspect, your lack of money is not an issue either."

"Exactly," Roger said, returning to their side. "It's not impossible."

Torquil wanted to argue that it *was* impossible, that there was no way Mrs. Wrenwhistle would approve them as a spouse for her son, and that Emrys would have to disregard all of his responsibilities in order to marry them.

They pressed a hand over their pocket, feeling the packet of almonds inside. It didn't seem fair that Emrys could fill Torquil's life with his presence, while Torquil was unable to do the same.

"Will your friend be at the dinner party?" Wyndham said, his tone lightly teasing.

Torquil was grateful for the levity. They arched an eyebrow and pocketed the invitation. "If you think I'll tell you that, you vastly underestimate my capacity for mystery."

Wyndham snorted a laugh and cuffed Torquil's shoulder.

"Shall we get to work?" Torquil asked almost plaintively.

"What should we do today?" Roger said.

"You mean you don't have it all planned out?" Torquil teased.

"Well, I had some ideas," Roger admitted. "I thought it might be good to do another day of you sensing magic. Only this time, perhaps you can watch us do spells individually?"

"That sounds perfect, actually," Torquil said. "I'd like to get more practice in that."

"Yes," Wyndham added, "and maybe next time your friend visits, you can give us a more detailed description of how his magic—"

"Absolutely not," Torquil said, shouldering past Wyndham and taking a seat. They lifted their chin. "Now let's get to work or I'll devote my next issue to a commentary on how your waistcoat is frayed at the edges."

There was a small chirrup at Torquil's feet.

Wyndham chuckled. "It's like you summoned her. You can blame Peony for the fraying. I made the mistake of holding her while wearing it and she got caught on the fabric."

Peony rubbed her cheek against Torquil's shoes. They reached down and scratched behind her ears. She plopped herself over their toes, twisting so her belly faced upward, and began to purr. When she began sucking on Torquil's finger, they pulled her into their lap and stroked her fur softly.

The afternoon passed more agreeably than the morning had. Peony slept on Torquil's lap for over an hour as they watched Roger and Wyndham perform magic. Torquil was still fatigued by the end of the day, but lasted longer than they had previously. They went back home, head full of how Roger and Wyndham's magic had been fascinating to watch, but how their individual talents paled in comparison to how their magic blended together. It was not entirely unlike the way Torquil's magic had ignited Emrys' power; they felt a little sick at the realization.

Once they got home, they peeled off most of their clothing and flopped onto the bed, lying on their back with both legs hooked over the footboard. They dined on the rest of the sugared almonds, relishing each bite. They had turned down another of Roger and Wyndham's invitations to join them for an informal dinner with the Wrenwhistles. They wondered how long they could continue to reject such invitations before they started to appear rude. But the idea of being at the center of not only Iris' attention, but Mrs. Wrenwhistle's as well, was a rather harrowing thought. Best to put that off as long as possible. And now that they had confessed a friendship with an eligible fae gentleman, they were unsure how long they'd be able to be in Emrys' presence without Roger or Wyndham picking up on the connection. They sucked the sugar off of an almond and briefly imagined how it would be to attend a family dinner without so many fears.

CHAPTER 23

EMRYS

FAMILY DINNERS HAD ALWAYS BEEN a tedious affair. Forcing all or some of the Wrenwhistle siblings to sit around one table and make idle conversation was the quickest way to stir up a heated argument, or a string of insults at the very least. Emrys often enjoyed the banter, especially when his youngest brother was involved. But at other times, including when their grandmother was present as she was that evening, he allowed his thoughts to wander instead, removing himself from the situation entirely.

At his mother's insistence, Emrys had spent the early afternoon with Miss Stanton. The two sat in an open carriage for a lengthy ride around the Park. The thick blankets draped across their legs and layers of outerwear had done little to protect them from the brumal weather, but the young lady hardly seemed to mind as their equipage quickly became the talk of everyone they passed. She smiled, perhaps a bit too brightly, at the onlookers as they went.

The diversion left Emrys feeling relieved. With her attention elsewhere, he found that his role in their outing was rather simple. He sat and watched, allowing Miss Stanton her fun while his focus meandered between his current situation and the one he had discovered the night before.

Emrys was well aware of what the rest of society was whispering after their carriage passed by. Sharing a dance, attending the opera, *and* promenading together over the course of a few weeks? After another public outing or two, an engagement announcement would be fully expected. His mother knew what she was doing. Emrys knew he should feel stronger about it, but in that moment he could not bring himself to worry.

All he could think about was the touch of Torquil's magic. He was consumed by the memory of it. The experience had settled on him like the warmth of the rare London sunshine; something he would not dare take for granted.

Emrys had held Torquil after for as long as he could stand it, allowing them to sleep soundly until he felt as though he might shatter. He had returned to his own bed only to find that he could not escape the residual fervor. Even revisiting the moment in his mind as he worked to find his own release was not enough to satisfy him, though it did help him eventually fall asleep just as the sky started to brighten.

"Emrys, are you listening?"

His mother's words dragged him back to the dinner table.

"Hmm?" he asked absently, blinking at her.

"As though the dreamy look on his face was not answer enough," Aveline chaffed. "He must be thinking of Miss Stanton."

Emrys let the grin fade from his features as smoothly as he could, trying to avoid drawing more attention to himself than he already had. He reached for his wine and took a sip. "And if I was?"

"The pair of you look so lovely together," Mrs. Wrenwhistle chimed in. Her comment elicited such a large cringe from Wyndham that Emrys noticed it across the table.

"It seems Wyndham disagrees with you," he told her.

Their mother tutted. "What is so disagreeable about it, Wynnie? They are well matched."

Wyndham pressed his lips together. He had never been very good at letting an argument lie. The uncertain look Roger gave him indicated that he knew this about his husband, as well.

"You must admit that Miss Stanton is rather...youthful," Wyndham said finally.

"Since when is being vivacious an undesirable trait? I was Miss Stanton's age when I was matched with your father." She spared an affectionate glance at her husband. "Look how well our marriage has turned out. We've had years of happiness and four perfect children together."

Emrys and Wyndham groaned in unison, earning a glare from their mother.

"Were you pleased with the match, Grandmother?" Aveline asked with genuine interest.

Iris gave her a mild grin. "I did not have much choice, darling. The two of them were dangling after one another by the time the news of their engagement was published in the papers. It was obvious that they were compatible in every way one could hope for them to be."

Emrys wanted to chuckle at his grandmother's diplomatic answer, but he was instead overcome with a feeling of guilt.

Harmonious marriages were often something couples expected to develop over time. Lucky were the matches that also started with intense feelings of attraction or love. But the one undeniable requirement for a successful match in a fae union was compatible magic. Without that as a foundation, it was an unspoken certainty that the marriage would be an unhappy one.

Emrys thought back to the end of his ride with Miss Stanton. Curiosity got the better of him as he'd watched her wave politely to someone she knew. Without any forethought, Emrys called on his magic to stir a breeze around them. While it was certainly not *encouraged*, a gentle touch such as that was nothing compared to what he had done with other respectable ladies in far more intimate situations in his youth.

His companion had turned her attention to him at once, brushing a stray tendril of golden hair away from her rosy cheek as she offered a sweet smile. It was promising, although it told him next to nothing of their actual compatibility. When her gloved hand returned to her lap, she tucked it with the other and buried them deeper into the blanket over her legs.

"I do apologize for inviting you on another terribly cold outing," Emrys offered, realizing that using his magic had not helped the matter.

Miss Stanton's answering laugh clouded the air in front of her mouth.

"While I am grateful for your invitation, Mr. Wrenwhistle," she began, her jaw quivering slightly as she spoke, "I must admit that I do prefer warmer weather."

"Yes," Emrys agreed, glad to learn they shared that opinion. "Summertime provides far more opportunities for sport and relaxation." He studied Miss Stanton where she sat under her layers across from him. "Or, at the very least, provides far more agreeable conditions for a leisurely ride in an open carriage."

Miss Stanton seemed to remember herself and straightened in her seat, glancing up at where the top of the carriage might've been.

"I fear I would not have been allowed to join you otherwise, even with a chaperone." Her voice dipped as she continued. "Mama seems to believe I will pounce on you at the first opportunity." She studied his face briefly, then the rest of him. "If I may be so bold, sir, you are impossibly handsome. But I've every intention of doing this properly."

It was Emrys' turn to fog up the air between them with a huff of surprise.

"I assure you, Miss Stanton, we are aligned on that as well."

She gave him a satisfied nod, as though this had been a great concern and she was relieved to have settled the issue.

"I am glad to hear it," she said. "I wouldn't dare do anything that might give Mx. Pimpernel-Smith a reason to write something unfavorable about me in my debut Season. That is the greatest embarrassment I could possibly imagine."

Emrys recalled Miss Stanton's brief mention in the *Tribune*. If she was at all similar to Keelan, Aveline, and the rest of the hopeless romantics that called London home, she was likely wishing that her next mention would be accompanied by the words *proposal* and *engagement*. It seemed that she was satisfied with the idea of *Wrenwhistle* being printed alongside them.

Emrys felt caught in an impossible situation, only made worse by the way he could not focus under the shadow of his persistent thoughts about another. How could he possibly pretend to be looking forward to a marriage with Miss Stanton when he knew what it felt like to touch synergetic magic?

He grinned. That was another word he'd learned from Torquil.

Slowly, he realized the most impressive example of such magic he had ever witnessed was sitting across the dinner table from him. Emrys took another sip of wine as he studied the way Wyndham and Roger had disappeared into their own private conversation, as they often did. Had they known anything of their compatibility before becoming engaged? It had been largely unplanned on their part, of course, but they had spent countless hours working together in the weeks that led up to their announcement. Certainly they had to know *something* beforehand.

"What must it feel like, to be so compatible with another?" Emrys mused, drawing their attention back from wherever they had gone. They were not the only ones at the table who were capable of answering the question, but theirs was the answer he wanted to hear.

"It's...er...rather overwhelming, I suppose," Roger began uneasily, looking to Wyndham again. After a moment, Wyndham raised his eyebrows with a slight, encouraging nod. Roger met Emrys' intense gaze as he continued. "Compelling, in a way. At least, that's how it was for me. Still is, if I'm being truthful." His mumbled confession caused him to blush and look away.

"There is nothing else like it," Mrs. Wrenwhistle said with confidence. "Isn't that right, dear?"

"Nothing else like it," their father echoed in agreement from his seat at the head of the table. Emrys watched the way he gave their mother a familiar, closed-mouth smile before he took another bite of dinner. Mr. Wrenwhistle was a soft-spoken man, and when he did speak it was always with honesty.

Emrys allowed the responses to settle. He wondered if perhaps he would have been better off not knowing the answers to his question.

"How will you do it, then?" Aveline asked. "Will it be a private moment, or a grand gesture? Oh, how I would love for one of my brothers to make a public declaration! Auberon and Wyndham were so very quiet about it. Emrys, won't you please do this for me?"

Emrys laughed. "I am not doing anything yet, I'm afraid."

This earned him a clever look from his sister. "But Grandmother has already invited Miss Stanton to her dinner party. Her parents and sister will be there, as well. What better time to speak with her father?"

Emrys turned sharply to his grandmother, who offered him a knowing grin.

"It does not have to happen at the party, of course, darling. I thought it would be a fine opportunity for both your families to mingle, that's all."

"That's…" Emrys paused, not sure how to respond.

"A very thoughtful thing to do, thank you," his mother finished for him primly. "We want everyone to see that you are not simply trying to parade the young lady around for show. A more formal, intimate affair is an appropriate next step in your courtship."

Being aware of his mother's intentions was one thing, but to hear her speak the words made everything incredibly real. Emrys swallowed and stared down at his plate in silence long enough for the conversation to move on without him. He was only partially listening as they continued to talk about the party.

"Did you give Torquil their invitation?" his grandmother asked eventually, which pulled him from his stupor.

Not only would Emrys be expected to spend the evening with Miss Stanton, but he would also have to do it with Torquil present again? If his thoughts remained as they were, he was not sure he could manage both and survive the night.

"Yes," Wyndham answered. His expression softened a bit as he seemed to consider something, before he tilted his chin up at Emrys. "You may be in luck. It seems that Torquil is also exploring magical compatibility at the moment. Perhaps the two of you can discuss it at the party."

TORQUIL'S TRIBUNE

MONDAY 6 DECEMBER, 1813

Greetings, fashionable folk and harmonious humans,

We will start with the most important news: Lady Fitzhugh has proposed to Miss St. Clair. We all anticipated it and we send our heartfelt congratulations to the happy couple. May their union be a felicitous one. The date for the wedding has not yet been announced, but Mrs. St. Clair sent in the official news just yesterday. It is always a delight and an honor to be at the forefront of information such as this.

This humble writer was invited to join the Wrenwhistle family in their opera box this week. Considering all of the curious glances that were received, this writer feels bound to point out that they are now working alongside Mr. Wyndham Wrenwhistle and Mr. Roger Wrenwhistle on a Council project. The evening was a much appreciated reprieve from the challenge we have all been working to resolve.

Some observations that were made over the course of the evening:

Mx. Hillcrest was seated next to Mr. Thompson, an exciting

development. Miss Thackeray was seated on Mx. Hillcrest's other side. Hopefully this will quell all of the concerns that have been flooding our doorstep that Miss Thackeray and Mr. Thompson are in some sort of spat or that Mx. Hillcrest ousted the young lady in some manner. We believe that three such lovely people ought to be friends. If only the rest of London had such good sense. It is refreshing to see more fae and human social engagement.

However, there were two examples of fae and human engagement that this writer fears will not last long. Mr. Gerald Irving was seen with an eligible fae gentleman, but the pair do not seem well matched. We suggest Mr. Irving try again.

Additionally, Mr. Emrys Wrenwhistle and Miss Lydia Stanton attended the opera together. Many have speculated about this couple's inevitable engagement. But this writer has some qualms about the match. Miss Stanton is lovely and charming, and any promising young lady should enjoy a dazzling debut. Far be it from this writer to suggest the lady wait until the next Season to find a spouse. But it might be advisable for her to wait for someone closer to her age, of a more compatible disposition and temper, and who matches her unique flair.

Other items of note: Major Pemberton and Mr. Lowry were seen sitting quite close in one opera box. Is it possible the romantic performance on stage inspired feelings of romance between the two gentlemen? Or perhaps between Miss Everslee and Lord Oakleaf?

There was one pair in the boxes who were notably withdrawn into shadow. While we would usually caution readers against amorous activity in opera boxes—considering the boxes are as much a source of entertainment as the performers on stage—it can be presumed that at least one of the occupants of this box was hoping to be noticed...perhaps by the occupant of another box? If that is the case, we gently advise that the person in question give up that hope for lost and search instead for someone who will think of them first.

Miss Aveline Wrenwhistle was absent from the opera, which likely caused a great deal of disappointment. Let us hope she graces society with her presence more in the months to come.

Your esteemed editor,
Torquil Pimpernel-Smith

CHAPTER 24

TORQUIL

AFTER SPENDING the morning releasing the *Tribune*, Torquil was late getting to Wyndham and Roger's townhouse. When they entered the study, they were unsurprised to find a copy of the recent release on the table, but they were a little surprised by the glee with which Wyndham greeted them.

"Good morning!" he said jovially.

Torquil gave him a small smile. "Pleased are you?"

"Your recent issue was of particular interest to me."

"He's pleased that you single-handedly stopped an engagement between Emrys and Miss Stanton," Roger explained. "I'm still trying to reconcile the fact that you knew about my best friend's engagement before I did."

"I'm sure she said the same thing when you got engaged," Wyndham said. "And Torquil said exactly what I've been saying for over a week. Only now that it's in the column, my mother *has* to listen. Aveline told me that Mrs. Stanton sent a message to their house this morning and that my mother has been in her room with smelling salts ever since."

Torquil took a seat. "You were opposed to the match then?"

"She's half his age. Of course I was opposed to the match."

Torquil hummed thoughtfully. "Is that concern for your brother perhaps?"

Wyndham made a face. "Nothing of the sort. I was only worried about her. The poor child needs a better fate than being saddled with *Emrys* of all people."

They chuckled. "Well, I'm glad it met your approval. I daresay your mother will not feel the same way."

Wyndham shrugged. "She'll get over it. Your column is responsible for a great deal of our marital successes, as she well knows."

"You don't think she'll be unpleasant tomorrow, do you?" Roger asked, wringing his hands in his lap. "That would be very awkward."

"What's tomorrow?" Torquil said.

"My grandmother's dinner party," Wyndham said.

"Oh, that's right. I'd almost forgotten."

Just as Torquil started to match Roger's anxiety, Wyndham continued, "But I doubt it. For one thing, my mother can't abide a public scene. For another, you're my grandmother's guest."

"This is one of the many unfortunate aspects of me being out in society," Torquil said. "I'm not accustomed to having to talk to the people I write about."

Wyndham waved a dismissive hand. "Don't worry. We'll be there and we'll make sure it isn't too unpleasant for you, as will my grandmother. And I can tell you from personal experience that she excels at dinner party pairings. Furthermore, Aveline likes you, as does Emrys, for all that I distrust his intentions. Oh, and speaking of which, I should warn you: I told Emrys you two might have a topic of common interest. So don't be surprised if he broaches it."

"What topic was that?" Torquil said, torn between wariness and curiosity.

Wyndham smiled. "Magical compatibility. He was asking about it at dinner last night."

Torquil froze. Emrys was asking about it too? "Oh," they said at last. "Well...I'm sure it will be interesting to compare observations. Now, what is on our list to do today?"

Roger sat forward in his seat. "I would like to get back to you casting but considering today was a *Tribune* day, I thought it might be better to wait another day first."

"That is very kind of you," Torquil said, touched.

Roger gave a small smile. "You look exhausted, no offense. And tomorrow will be a long day, what with the dinner party and everything. So I thought it might be good for us to compile notes today. You can write down all of your observations of our magic, both individual and combined. While you're doing that, Wyndham will write down his observations of your magic—"

"I will?"

"Yes, and then I'll start a chart for the rubric. I suspect your rubric may look a little different than ours. But I also think your request in the *Tribune* will go a long way towards our project."

Torquil agreed to the plan and the afternoon was spent with everyone sitting in companionable silence. The crackling fire and the whisper of pen against paper filled the quiet, occasionally punctuated by one of them asking a question or musing aloud. Torquil had never had occasion to work quietly alongside someone in such a way and they rather loved it.

When it was finally time to leave, Roger said, "Tomorrow, we'll start working on spells with raw materials to see how that works with your magic."

Torquil nodded. "I've been curious about that."

"And you can come with us to the dinner party," Wyndham said, in a tone that brooked no argument. "I'll lend you another one of my suits."

"I still need to return the first suit," Torquil protested.

"Keep it," Wyndham said. "It looked well on you. But bring the comb if you still have it. You looked very dashing in it."

"I do have my own clothes."

Wyndham gave them a sly smile. "Yes, but what if your gentleman friend is there tomorrow?"

Torquil groaned. "I never should have said anything." They left before Wyndham could tease them further.

THE NEXT MORNING, Torquil left even earlier than usual so they could arrive at Wyndham and Roger's home on time, with the comb in hand, and a great deal of nerves. Both men were already at work preparing the room. Wyndham whisked the comb out of Torquil's hand as soon as they walked in the door, passing it to a servant who took it upstairs. Roger greeted Torquil with a cheery wave and beckoned them to the desk.

"Now," he said without preamble. "There are several spells we can try. I was thinking a breeze spell might be good to start. Partly because it was the first one *I* started using raw ingredients with, so I can give better advice, and partly because Wyn has experience with corralling this one, in case anything gets out of hand."

Torquil glanced nervously at Wyndham. "Right," they breathed.

"Will that work for you?" Roger said, brow furrowing.

Torquil gave him a warm smile. "Of course it will."

Roger pulled out a long willow leaf and a large sheet of spellpaper and laid it on the ground. Torquil knelt next to him as Roger walked them through the spell setup.

"There," Roger said as Torquil wrote in the final equation for the spell. "That ought to do it. Ready?"

They nodded and cast the spell. Considering the raw material, Torquil had been worried that the spell would explode or overpower them. They needn't have worried. Their human magic started off faintly as usual. This time, however, it wasn't so faint as to seem invisible. Even without their fae magic, the human spell was almost at the caliber of Roger's spells. Encouraged, Torquil coaxed some of their fae magic into the spell and the breeze took off. Wyndham tossed a handkerchief in the air and Torquil maneuvered the breeze to scoop it up. The handkerchief looped lazily around the room until Torquil let it drop into Wyndham's lap.

Then they let out a heavy sigh. "My word. I didn't expect that at all."

Roger looked delighted. "Was it just me or was it stronger this time?"

"Definitely stronger," Wyndham said, toying with his handkerchief. "Raw materials are famously volatile to use but when you used it…"

"It was about the strength of a normal person," Torquil finished for him.

Wyndham narrowed his eyes. "Let's say it was about the strength of a human, shall we? But yes. And the fae magic definitely gave it a significant boost."

Roger scrambled for his notes and began writing everything down.

Torquil sat back, leaning against their palms.

"How did it feel?" Wyndham asked.

"Exhilarating," Torquil said, beaming at him. "Tiring too, though. I'm not sure I'll be able to do this for a full day. But my magic has never felt like *that* before. I might have kept up with my practice if it had." They paused and cocked their head. "How did it feel for you? Still strange?"

Wyndham chuckled. "I'm too used to your magic now to think of it as strange. But you recall when we first began this project and you said your magic has often been described as pungent?"

They nodded.

"This time, it felt as though the power was more evenly dispersed. So rather than being given a spoonful of sauce with an abundance of spices, it was as if the spoon had swirled those spices into a bowl full of sauce instead. The personality of the magic was still there, but it had more room."

They considered this response. "I wonder how we shall determine if that is the case for others."

Wyndham shrugged. "We'll figure it out." He looked at Roger. "What do you want to do next? Another breeze spell?"

"Hm," Roger said, reading over his notes. "I *would* like that but I think it might be best to do a variety of spells today so we can verify our findings."

"That sounds reasonable," Torquil said.

"But we'll take breaks between each," Roger said decisively before pulling on the bell cord. "We've been remiss in offering you tea lately. Let's do that now."

Torquil complied and the three of them sat down and took a leisurely tea break. Between multiple breaks, Torquil performed a fire spell, a cleaning spell, and a shrinking spell. Each was more successful than any of their previous attempts with treated ingredients. By the end of the day, Torquil was exhausted but feeling remarkably pleased with himself, which was a first when it came to magic.

Wyndham glanced at the clock. "We have just enough time to get ready for the dinner party."

Torquil followed his gaze. "We have over two hours."

Roger laughed. "Yes, well, this is Wyn we're talking about. He'll take over an hour getting himself ready."

"And I've ordered a bath for you. I hope you don't mind," Wyndham said, putting an arm around Torquil's back and guiding them out of the room.

They didn't mind, but they did feel their difference in social status rather keenly as they were led to a familiar guest room. Wyndham left them to it, promising to return in an hour. Torquil luxuriated a bit in the bath, enjoying the fresh smell of the soap and soothing their sore muscles. A servant dressed them in a suit of forest green. Then their hair was pulled back and set with the comb. Torquil didn't want to admit how much they liked the accessory.

Finally, Wyndham came in, dressed in a muted gray suit accented with a soft pink waistcoat. He looked over Torquil approvingly. "Darker colors suit you very well. Your friend won't be able to keep his eyes off you."

"He might not be there."

"True," Wyndham said, throwing a cravat around Torquil's neck. "But if he's not, we'll be able to make him wish he was. Can you dance?"

"Not well."

"Hm. Pity. We should add dance lessons to our project time." Torquil glared at him and Wyndham gave a winning smile in return. "I expect I could persuade my sister to come help us teach you. Emrys probably would too, actually, but I'd prefer he visit us as little as possible."

"I don't suppose I have a say in any of this," Torquil muttered.

"You won't once I suggest the idea to my grandmother," Wyndham said cheerfully. "If you ask me, she wants you to become a darling of society."

"She has her work cut out for her."

"Which is why I'm confident she will be pleased by the idea of dance lessons. Now hold still. This knot is devilishly tricky."

Torquil groaned as Wyndham finished the cravat. "This is why I shouldn't become friends with the people I write about," they said, touching a finger to the knot as soon as Wyndham was done.

"What, you think this is revenge for you printing about my engagement before it had happened?" Wyndham said in mock surprise.

Torquil lifted an eyebrow.

"Let us instead call it: proceeding in the same spirit of the initial action. You knew we belonged together. I can appreciate that now. And *we* know that you deserve someone who will take you to the altar." He frowned at the cravat knot and tweaked it slightly. "For someone as remarkably intelligent as you are, you are astonishingly foolish when it comes to yourself."

His expression softened a bit and he lowered his voice as he put a hand on Torquil's shoulder. "I never knew I could love someone as much as I love Roger. And I didn't expect to find anyone who makes me feel as safe and as seen as he does. I know I'm not the first person to be matched up thanks to your paper. Don't you think it's time one of your little projects paid you back in kind?"

Torquil sighed and followed Wyndham out of the room. Roger was waiting in the hallway and he brightened when he saw them. "You look wonderful, Torquil. I hope your friend is there tonight."

Wyndham winked at them and led the way down the stairs and into the carriage. Torquil sat in the carriage, anxiety churning in their gut. Emrys would be there tonight, but they couldn't very well admit that he was the friend in question. What were they going to do for an entire evening now that Roger and Wyndham were on the watch for yearning glances? Perhaps they could just avoid looking at Emrys? Wyndham already knew Emrys found Torquil attractive, so as long as Torquil didn't return Emrys' longing looks with their own, they might be fine.

They were feeling a little encouraged with this line of thought by the time the carriage reached Iris' lavish home. She greeted them all at the door, bestowing kisses on not only Wyndham's cheeks, but Roger's and

Torquil's as well. Then she slipped her hand around Torquil's arm, like she had the night celebrating Roger and Wyndham's return.

"You look marvelous," she said, leading them into the room. "Wyndham does have a way with clothing, doesn't he? The comb is a nice touch." She squeezed their arm. "I know you're nervous, but you needn't be. I have everything well in hand. You know most of the people here already. Well, I should say you've met most of the people here. I don't think you've met the Stantons. Sadly, Miss Lydia was not able to make it. Poor child has a headache, apparently."

"Oh, dear," Torquil said.

She chuckled. "I haven't thanked you yet. It was well done."

"I didn't say anything I didn't believe to be true."

"Yes, I know. But I appreciate it all the same. My daughter-in-law is less than pleased, of course. But then I knew she would be. Emrys, on the other hand, looks lighter than he has in weeks."

"Does he?" Torquil couldn't keep the pleasure out of their voice. "I'm glad to hear it."

"Yes, I've paired you together for dinner. Wyndham mentioned the other night that the two of you might have some common interest to discuss."

Torquil felt as though they'd been plunged into icy water. "Oh." *So much for the plan to avoid looking at Emrys.*

She patted their arm. "Don't worry. Whatever Wyndham has said about his brother is likely exaggerated. Those two have never gotten along, sadly. But I am sure Emrys will make an excellent dinner partner."

To Torquil's horror, Iris walked them all the way to where Emrys and Aveline were standing. "Darlings, I believe you both know Councilmember Pimpernel-Smith. I trust I can leave them in your capable hands?" She gave Aveline a kiss on the cheek and left.

Aveline practically pounced on Torquil as soon as her grandmother had left. "I'm so glad I'm finally able to thank you in person for all of the lovely things you've been saying," she gushed. "It is always such a delight to read your paper."

They gave her a small smile. "I print the truth, Miss Wrenwhistle. I only wish I had a good idea of who would suit you."

"So do I," she said with a sigh. Then she smiled and glanced at her brother. "You certainly have a great many opinions on who doesn't suit Emrys though."

Emrys grinned. "You're cheating me of the ability to thank them myself, sister." He reached forward and took Torquil's hand in his, bowing over it gallantly. "I cannot tell you how much I appreciate you doing what I could not."

"I'm relieved to learn I did not break any hearts," Torquil said, with more levity than they felt.

Emrys chuckled. "You might have broken my mother's but you certainly didn't break mine. Miss Stanton is lovely, but she's not for me."

"So the quest continues," Torquil said.

Emrys' grin widened and Torquil felt their stomach flip at the sight.

"It looks like we're going to dinner now," Aveline said. "It was lovely to meet you again. Emrys, try to be your most dashing self."

"As opposed to—?"

"Your usual self." With that, she strode to her own dinner partner, a tall fae gentleman with a handsome face and a vapid smile.

Emrys offered his arm and, once Torquil took it, leaned over to murmur, "You look stunning."

Torquil's face heated. "You can blame your brother for that."

"Hm. The cravat does accentuate the sharpness of your jaw. And the color of the coat does bring out your eyes. They didn't pull your hair as tightly into the comb this time. I quite like it. It's more you."

Torquil swallowed. "Is this you at your most dashing?"

Emrys chuckled as he pulled out a seat for Torquil at the long table. "I'm just happy to see you." He sat down beside them. "I'm happy that my mother's plans to match me with a young woman who didn't suit me have been foiled, particularly since the lady in question was seemingly too perfect for me to object. And I'm happy that my grandmother seated us together. It's as though the different parts of my world have merged perfectly. I get to enjoy your company in front of my family and I'm truly delighted."

Torquil felt a strange mixture of giddiness and worry at his words. Their own world had been so small for so long. It had been easy to fit Emrys into it. Now their world had expanded and they had no idea how to fit a friendship with Wyndham and Roger along with whatever it was they had with Emrys into the same space. But the genuine affection in Emrys' voice filled them with warmth. "It's good to see you too," they said quietly. "Although it is strange to see you and not be able to…"

Emrys reached for a glass of wine. "Yes, I know. It is taking remarkable strength of will not to pull you into my arms and kiss you, especially when you're dressed like that. I hope you appreciate my self-control."

Torquil chuckled. "Ah, yes. Self-control. One of your finer virtues."

Emrys grinned at them and took a sip. "All right, I suppose you haven't had much occasion to see it in the past."

"No, not much. But I wouldn't worry about it," they went on, reaching for their own glass. "You have other qualities, I'm sure."

"Oh, yes? Anything of note?"

Torquil sipped their wine. "Nothing comes to mind. Ask me again at the end of the night."

"Do you mean the end of the party or…"

Torquil glanced at him. "Much as I'd enjoy your company afterwards, I'm not sure I'll be much good tonight."

Emrys' expression turned serious. "Are they running you ragged again?"

"On the contrary. They've been very careful about keeping me from exhausting myself. But all the same, it's been a tiring day."

Emrys gave them a long look. "How is your project going by the way?"

Torquil was surprised. Emrys did not usually inquire into the topic. "It's going well, I think. I performed magic with raw materials today."

Emrys stiffened. "Isn't that dangerous?"

"Apparently not for me. My magic is too…that is, my spells are rather faint. So the raw materials bring them more on par with… human spells."

"One of these days, I'm going to watch you perform a spell," Emrys said, with endearing decisiveness.

"I'll get the materials for a fire spell. That's one I'd like to practice anyway."

"And your room could use the added heat. Thank you," Emrys added. "I'm looking forward to seeing more of your magic."

Torquil worried for a moment that he'd continue the topic. Thankfully, a servant came by with a serving dish and Emrys spooned some onto both of their plates. Torquil glanced up at the servant, recognizing him as one of the usuals who delivered the Mayfair copies. The servant gave them a warm smile, which helped Torquil's nerves somewhat—at least the servants weren't concerned by whatever conversation they were overhearing.

Before Torquil could think of anything to say, Emrys spoke again. "Wyndham says you were asking about magical compatibility."

Damn, Torquil thought. They had no idea how to describe what they had learned from Wyndham. How to confess that if they understood correctly, it meant that they were a suitable match for Emrys. How to explain that their magic might have expressed what they had known for a long time but hadn't had the courage to say. How to tell Emrys that they didn't know what they were going to do when he got married to someone else. They took a bite of boiled potatoes, buying themself time to respond.

CHAPTER 25

EMRYS

Even Torquil's delayed response was not enough to dampen the immense relief Emrys had been feeling since he'd read the latest copy of the *Tribune* that morning.

He had trusted that Torquil would do what they could to aid in his request, and the letter they'd received from Mrs. Stanton less than an hour later only solidified Emrys' confidence that the situation would dissolve in his favor. While he did feel penitent for upsetting the girl so much that she did not want to be seen in public, or perhaps just seen by him, he could not bring himself to regret their courtship ending.

Emrys dished out the next platter brought to him onto both of their plates, a grin quirking the corner of his mouth as he realized that Torquil was not only chewing slower than any person normally would, but that they were also working very hard to avoid his gaze. After the servant moved on, Emrys gently bumped his thigh against Torquil's under the table.

"Sensitive topic, I take it?" he asked before taking his own bite of food. Torquil finally looked at him then, and Emrys' teasing smirk faltered a bit at the serious expression they now wore.

He had assumed that Torquil brought the topic up with Wyndham and Roger in a positive way. They likely had not divulged any information that was too telling, though Emrys understood perfectly how tempting it might have been to do so. But with a look as sullen as that, Emrys began to wonder if it had not been such a happy conversation, after all.

Emrys leaned forward slightly to peer down the table at where Wyndham and Roger were seated together. His brother's words at their family dinner had not indicated anything beyond it being a curious overlap of conversation from both sides. Wyndham was famous for giving a sly grin or crafty remark when he knew more than he was letting on. Had Emrys missed it?

He sat back in his chair and followed Torquil's lead, allowing silence to settle between them as they both ate. A small part of him was thrilled simply to watch them from the corner of his eye as they worked steadily at a real meal for once, rather than the small treats and other random bits of food he normally saw them eating. The rest of him, however, was quickly consumed with uncertainty.

What if Wyndham had done this on purpose? Had Torquil confessed what happened between them, and Wyndham had taken the opportunity to force them together in a public place knowing Torquil had not been pleased about feeling Emrys' magic?

Emrys struggled to swallow down his mouthful of dinner.

What if the sensation had been unpleasant for Torquil? Perhaps it was the intimate situation that prevented them from revealing the truth. Emrys had told Torquil to reach out again. He was the one who so self-ishly begged for more because *he* enjoyed it. Had Torquil? Or had they simply wanted to accept what Emrys was offering and get a restful night of sleep? That was what their arrangement had been for years, after all. Why would it change now?

Distracted by his own thoughts, Emrys reached for his glass of wine without really looking. His lips were already on the rim when there was a whisper at his side.

"That's mine," Torquil said softly.

Emrys' eyes went wide as he rushed to look at the glass he was holding, and then at the one that he'd been using. He set Torquil's wine back where it belonged and picked up his own, draining it. Emrys couldn't bring himself to look at Torquil. Normally, he could not keep his eyes off them, but his embarrassment was too strong to even risk a glance.

He had to explain himself somehow. Apologize for being so careless and inconsiderate. He would offer to make amends however necessary, although he knew Torquil would refuse everything he could possibly think of.

Emrys tried to wait patiently as his wine glass was refilled. He proceeded to empty it as soon as it was in his hand again. Begging someone's pardon was not something he was very skilled at. He'd had very few instances to practice. But he knew this was important, so he would try.

THE SLOW PACE of the meal was excruciating. When it finally concluded, Emrys was on his feet in seconds to guide Torquil's chair away from the table. Before he could say a word, Iris was there to whisk Torquil away, claiming that she wanted to introduce them to some of her dear friends. With a heavy sigh, Emrys watched as they walked out of the room together. He tried to put out of his mind the way Torquil did not glance back at him as they went.

With his thoughts such a mess, Emrys knew he would be useless in trying to make polite conversation. He settled for wandering instead. There were just enough people in attendance that he could get away with gliding quietly from one room to another without drawing attention to his uncharacteristic behavior. He even managed to convince Keelan to let him be alone for once, requesting that he go and entertain Lady Proust instead.

To his surprise, Emrys found that it was rather interesting to move around the edges of the festivities, rather than being in the center of them. He noted which guests had formed the larger and louder groups in the main room, and which others had scattered off to quieter places. The topics of conversation he overheard varied widely. It came as no surprise, however, that the *Tribune* was mentioned more than once. He even overheard his own name at one point, though the discussion shifted a bit after the speaker noticed that his topic of choice was standing nearby.

When he could no longer avoid it, Emrys allowed himself to look for Torquil. He found them instantly across the crowded room. The emotions he'd been stewing in washed away, replaced fully by the staggering realization that Torquil was staring right back. The connection lingered longer than it should have. His grandmother's hand settling on Torquil's upper back as she said something to them finally shook their shared moment apart.

With a newfound heat beneath his cravat, Emrys left the room as quickly as he could without running. He stepped into the hallway that separated the two main rooms being used that evening. There he found Roger perusing the sideboard decorated with a number of finger desserts.

"I daresay you've got the right idea," Emrys told him. The poor man startled so badly that he nearly dropped the small plate he was holding.

"W-what idea is that?" he asked after he turned a cautious look at Emrys.

"Seeking respite with some sweets." Emrys stepped closer to Roger and reached for one of the little cakes. He popped the entire thing in his mouth and turned to lean heavily against the wall next to the table.

"Wyn asked me to get enough for both of us," he started to explain, but Emrys waved his hand to stop him.

"I'm not judging you," he said as he looked down at the plate, then at Roger. "I envy you. Nobody expects either of you to be anyone but who you are at parties like this." He gestured vaguely in the direction of the room he'd just left. "We all know that Wyndham and Roger Wrenwhistle will join in for *exactly* as long as society expects, and then the two of you will wander away to enjoy each other's company for the rest of the evening." Emrys sighed a bit wistfully and rested his head back against the wall. "I fear I am getting too old to enjoy such gatherings as a bachelor."

"It seems as though your mother is trying very hard to remedy that for you." Roger placed another dessert on his plate. "If I may be so bold," he paused, "it appears that you are trying equally as hard to reject all of her matches."

"I am *not*," Emrys challenged, though he quickly realized that hearing it put so plainly felt an awful lot like the truth. "It's just that...that my mother clearly does not understand what type of spouse I am looking for."

Roger adjusted his spectacles. "Have you told her that?"

Emrys was not certain at which point he had started losing the upper hand on their conversation, but his emotional state mixed with the amount of wine he had consumed left him feeling too open to care very much.

"I think I am afraid to," he admitted, reaching for another sweet and shoving it into his mouth.

"Why is that?" Roger followed Emrys' lead and ate one of the little desserts he had already piled onto his plate. Having Roger's undivided focus was a bit unnerving, but something told him to continue.

"Because if my mother knows exactly who it is I am looking for, she will tear London apart to find them. And that thought is almost more terrifying than marrying someone who is not right for me."

A long silence stretched between the two of them. Emrys was not used to being so vulnerable with anyone, even Torquil, but somehow the admission left him feeling relieved. That is, until he turned his head to look at Roger again and found the widest grin on his face.

"What?" Emrys demanded, brows pinching together. He pushed away from the wall when Roger's expression shifted even more toward unbridled joy. "What is that look for?"

"Nothing!" Roger reassured him, just as Wyndham came through a doorway to join them in the hall.

"Is everything all right?" Wyndham asked, a protective hand coming out to rest on Roger's arm.

"Everything's just wonderful," Roger told him as they exchanged a glance. "Come along, I think I've filled the plate to capacity. Lovely chatting with you, Emrys," he called over his shoulder as the two disappeared to enjoy their shared confections. Emrys rubbed a hand over his face as he let out a small groan. Why had he told Roger so much? And why had it felt so nice to say it?

Emrys spent another hour lurking about, waiting for the right moment to take back what had been stolen from him at the conclusion of their meal.

He knew his grandmother's intentions were good. Torquil was in society now, and who better to get them acclimated than one of society's pillars? Still, it had given Emrys far too much time to think and refill his glass and consume small bites of cake.

In the end, it was Torquil who stepped away. Emrys only noticed when there was a blur of dark green making haste toward the front hall. He set his half-empty glass on a nearby table as he followed, hoping to reach them before they disappeared into the night.

"Mx. Pimpernel-Smith," he called out as soon as he could see them again. To his relief, Torquil came to him rather than moving even faster in the opposite direction as he'd feared they might. It took every bit of self-restraint he possessed not to pull them into an embrace when they got close enough.

"I need air," Torquil said shakily into the space between them.

Emrys escorted them out to the back garden. The vibrant blooms of late summer had given way to the hardier plants that could survive the harsh winter weather. Camellia bushes and clusters of bright red winter-berries lined the path that led them to a place that only a member of the family would know about. He had spent his childhood playing in his grandmother's garden, learning all of its secrets and finding the most wonderful places to hide. He'd never expected to use that knowledge to help a friend.

As desperately as Emrys wanted to sit with them, he guided Torquil to the small stone bench and took a few steps back, giving them the space they had asked for. He realized belatedly that it would have been wise to ask for their overcoats before dashing out into the cold night air. Their breath was visible and only made it more apparent how erratic Torquil's breathing was.

Emrys crossed and uncrossed his arms. He shifted his weight from one foot to the other. He started to step closer, but found the strength to stay put.

The words he wanted to say were there. He had been thinking them all evening, and now his time had come to say them, but he found he could not. Emrys gritted his teeth and paced two steps away, then two steps back. Just as he found the courage to voice his apology, Torquil's words filled the air instead.

"I do not think I can do this, Emrys."

The emotion in Torquil's voice split him apart, straight down the middle. He sank to his knees in front of them, his hands coming up to cup their face.

"You can," Emrys said in a harsh whisper. "Of course you can."

Torquil refused to meet his eyes. "I am not suited to be under such scrutiny," they went on. "Even with Iris' protection, I am nothing but fodder for their intrusive questions and uneducated judgements."

Anger swelled inside Emrys. His respect for his grandmother had apparently also put Torquil in an unsafe position, but all he had done was stand around and watch. He thought back to who had been with them. Several members of the Council, of course, as well as people from both sides of society that his grandmother knew quite well. What could they have said to upset Torquil so? And how could she have allowed it?

"And my grandmother said nothing to stop them?"

"Of course she tried to. But it always ends the same."

"You will teach them," Emrys said. He stroked his thumbs along Torquil's cheeks, leaning a bit to try again and make them look at him. "Just as you have taught me so many things, you will use your skill and your paper, and you will help them understand how wrong they are."

"But will they listen?"

"We will make them listen. This work you are doing with Wyndham and Roger will make them listen." Emrys paused to take a steadying breath. "You deserve far more respect from everyone. Myself included. I recognize that I do a terrible job of asking your thoughts and feelings, which is something you have always done for me, and for that I am sorry."

Torquil finally looked up. "You do not have to apologize for that."

Emrys swallowed. "Well, I already have, and I will not take it back."

Unexpectedly, Torquil let out a sad little laugh. Something like hope bloomed in Emrys' chest; his magic swirled at the sound. With nothing profound left to say, Emrys moved closer to Torquil where he had landed between their parted legs.

"Can I please kiss you now?" he asked with an innocent grin. "I'm rather foxed, you see, and you are quite irresistible."

Torquil's mouth twisted into a small grin of their own, and they barely had time to nod before Emrys pressed their mouths together, hands still on either side of Torquil's face.

He wanted so badly to pull Torquil down with him onto the stiff winter grass and keep apologizing in other ways until he was certain Torquil understood how much he meant it. But he also knew there was a part of him that would be happy for Torquil to kiss him just as they were for the rest of his life. No matter who else came along as a match for him, Emrys knew that giving Torquil up would never be an option.

TORQUIL'S TRIBUNE

Greetings, frightful folk and horrid humans,

Iris Wrenwhistle hosted a dinner party last night. The guest list included some of the most fashionable people in London. The Stantons were present, which surprised nobody. Miss Stanton was notably absent, which disappointed many partygoers. It was evident, however, that what was once anticipated as a formal courtship has dissolved practically overnight. We are sure this news will be received with relief by some and dismay by others. Thankfully, other than some slight awkwardness, there were clearly no hard feelings by either party.

The food was sumptuous and the guests were elegant, exactly what one would expect from an event hosted by Iris Wrenwhistle. There were few promising potential couples, unfortunately. However, as this humble writer was honored to be invited, there were several noteworthy conversations over the course of the evening. After much thought, here are our conclusions:

If London society can be so celebratory of two families joining together in marriage, why does that same society seem determined to shun the offspring of such marriages? We will never move forward until we are able to accept and nurture the disenfranchised.

It is interesting to observe that when families are separated through disinheritance, the disinherited shoulder the blame and ridicule. Is the loss of money and connection not enough?

Topics that are not particularly engaging: what schools a person may have attended, the magical scores a person may have earned, and where a person shops for clothing. Instead, consider: intriguing books that have been read recently, interesting gossip that has been heard, how one takes their tea, who sells the best sugared almonds in town, what people hope for the future in terms of themselves or society as a whole.

This writer implores the *ton* to do better.

Your esteemed editor,
Torquil Pimpernel-Smith

CHAPTER 26

TORQUIL

TORQUIL HAD NEVER WRITTEN a *Tribune* with the level of bitterness with which they wrote this one. They had attempted to take Emrys' advice, teaching the truths they held most dear. But Emrys had always accepted Torquil for what they were. They were certain society *could* change, but would it change in their lifetime? Nevertheless, they printed the paper before they could second-guess themself. No one said anything about it until Sal came back to report that distribution was complete.

As Torquil began putting everything away, they noticed Sal still standing in the room. "Was there anything else?"

Sal seemed to hesitate. "This last one…it was a bit different, wasn't it?"

Torquil sighed. "Yes. I'm not sure it was wise, but we'll see."

"Treating you poorly, are they?"

They shrugged. "They're treating me the way they think I deserve."

"Because you're a writer or because of your birth?"

"Both, I suppose."

Sal was quiet for a moment.

Torquil waited for her to respond and then finally said, "Why do you ask?"

Sal stuffed her hands in her pockets and leaned against the press.

"I've just been wondering. You've always been the sort of person who gets up before the sun and then goes to bed before most people have dinner. Now you're working for the Council. You're going to all these fancy parties. Are you sure you can do all of it?"

Torquil bristled and crossed their arms. "Of course I can."

"No offense meant. I'm only saying…" she huffed out a breath. "If you need help, you only need to ask. You know that right?"

Torquil was taken aback. "Thank you," they said slowly. "Although what I really need help with is getting these people to stop treating me like I don't belong. Or maybe I need to stop trying to belong." They scrubbed a hand over their face. "Somehow I don't think you can help with that."

"I couldn't. And I don't think you need to stop trying, but I do think you might try looking at these problems from a new angle, that's all." Sal straightened and rapped the press with her knuckles before walking away. "I've always been curious how you run this thing, you know. Take care of yourself."

Torquil blinked at the door closing behind her. They ran a finger over the edge of the press. Sal had not been particularly subtle in her advice, but Torquil wasn't sure they could bring themself to follow it. Let someone else do the *Tribune*? But it was their whole life—or it had been. They heaved a sigh and ran a hand through their hair. A problem for another day. They stowed the moneybox and put on their coat to go to Wyndham and Roger's home.

As they stepped into the brisk air, they noticed a small stack of letters by the door. Stooping to pick them up, they read over the direction and then opened the first one:

Dear Mx. Pimpernel-Smith,

I am writing in response to one of your recent Tribune *issues about fae-human magic. My father was a fae and my mother was a human.*

They scanned over the rest of the letter and quickly opened the second one. It was also from a fae-human, as was the third.

An unfamiliar bundle of feelings kindled in Torquil's chest. A full week had passed since that issue was released, and they had begun to lose hope that they would get a response. But this was exactly what they'd hoped for. They read over the three letters again and noticed their hands were shaking slightly. *I am so pleased to learn someone is researching this,* one said. *I've always wondered if anyone else shared my style of magic* and *Please publish your findings. I would very much like to know if anyone else does magic the way I have* and *I hope this is helpful to you. Although I'm afraid I've always been told my magic is too weak or too strange to be any good.* And finally: *I was so pleased to read your column. My cousin sent me the issue in question and, for once, I felt less alone in my magic.*

Torquil wiped at their eye and swallowed as they carefully folded the three letters again. After such a disastrous evening and doubt-riddled morning, receiving such words turned out to be the reminder they needed. *This* was why they did what they did. This was why they had accepted the Council position, why they wrote the gossip column, and why they had braved society at all. They pocketed the letters and locked the door before striding down the street to Wyndham and Roger's townhouse.

As they entered the study, they pulled the letters out and said, "Look what arrived this—" They stopped on the threshold as they took in the chaos.

Peony was climbing up a long velvet curtain. Shredded bits of fabric showed the trail she had taken. Four servants were attempting to reach for her, Roger was trying to tempt her with treats, and Wyndham was standing to the side, looking amused. When the kitten reached the curtain rod and clambered onto it, Torquil sensed her triumph. But then she looked around the room and gave a very sad and pitiful meow.

"Oh, Wyn," Roger said. "She's frightened!"

Wyndham uncrossed his arms and a breeze buffeted the curtains as his magic traveled up the fabric. Peony gave a little meow of surprise as the breeze scooped her up off the curtain rod and into Wyndham's hands. He gave her an affectionate scratch behind the ears and then kissed her nose. "My little hellion," he said with pride. "I'll go deposit her in our room. Don't give your news yet, Torquil," he said as he brushed past them. "I want to hear it."

The servants filed out after him, some of them giving Torquil subtle nods or smiles in greeting. Torquil glanced at Roger. "It looks like it's been an eventful morning."

Roger chuckled as he straightened his spectacles and tugged on his vest. "It was actually very leisurely until about five minutes ago. Tea?"

Torquil took their usual seat as Roger poured out. They began to settle into the familiar comfort of their friend's presence. Although the expression on Roger's face as he passed the teacup gave them pause.

"Was Emrys a suitable dinner partner?"

"Er…" Torquil said, taking the teacup. "He was very gracious."

"I had worried, you know, because Emrys can be a bit… provocative."

Torquil relaxed. "Ah, I see. No, he was perfectly gallant."

Roger's smile grew. "I'm glad. He certainly seemed in a more companionable mood when I found him after dinner. Best conversation I've ever had with him, I think."

"That's good. I have noticed that he and Wyndham do not share much brotherly affection."

"No," Roger said. He cut a glance at Torquil and then stirred his tea in a *very* casual way. "Did the topic of magical compatibility come up?"

"We…er…seemed to skip over that subject."

"Hm. I confess I have found it very interesting that the subject came up twice in one day. Don't you? Perhaps it's just a matter of being around more fae folk than I'm used to. Then again," he went on. "Emrys seemed more curious than knowledgeable on the subject. He was asking me and Wyn what we knew about it."

Torquil felt frozen as they tried to come up with a suitable response.

Roger took a sip of tea. "I suppose I could have asked him what made him think about it in the first place. I've been under the assumption that he didn't know what he wanted or what he was looking for, so I had guessed he wanted more guidance in that way. But, as it turns out, he seems to know *exactly* what he wants." Roger smiled at Torquil over the rim of his cup. "Or should I say *who*?"

Torquil was saved from having to answer that when Wyndham breezed back into the room. "So sorry for the delay. Cook chopped up some fish for her so that should calm her down a bit. Then again, it might make her think that climbing up curtains results in fish." He shrugged. "Ah well. We already spoil her rotten. Can't imagine adding fish will make it that much worse." He poured himself some tea. "You seemed to have news?"

Torquil roused themself from their momentary shock and put the teacup down. They glanced at Roger as they pulled out their letters, but he didn't seem intent on continuing the previous topic, thankfully.

"I received these this morning," they said, passing them over.

Wyndham took them and Roger looked over his shoulder. "Ooh!" Roger squeaked. "Are they all about fae-human magic?"

"Yes."

"They gave different responses," Wyndham said in a thoughtful tone as he started the second letter.

"Yes, I thought that was most interesting."

"But it's always a combination," Roger said. "One person performs magic the opposite way that you do—starting with fae magic and then transferring that power into a human spell."

"And this one," Wyndham said, shuffling the letters, "cannot perform fae magic at all but has particularly strong sensing skills. That's fascinating."

"I was particularly intrigued by that one," Torquil said. "It looks like he uses it alongside his human magic to improve the balance and determine what to change as he works."

"Goodness," Roger breathed. "How on earth shall we make a rubric for such varied talents?"

"It will be a challenge," Wyndham murmured.

Roger clapped his hands together. "Notes!" He hurried to his desk, extracted a few sheets of paper and a pencil from the mess, and then sat back down. He licked the tip of the pencil and began writing a list. Torquil recognized their own magic style at the top of the page. "I think," Roger said as he wrote the last example down, "the first thing we need to do is determine what everyone has in common—even if they are at varying strengths."

Wyndham gave a hum. "So sensing magic, manipulating magic the way fae do, and human spells?"

"Exactly," Roger said as he wrote those three items down. Then he sketched out a little chart and filled in the boxes. "It may not look exactly like the rubrics we did before, but I imagine we can do something similar. I confess I'm concerned as to who could even test such a variety of skills, but I suppose that is a problem for a later day."

Torquil reached for their teacup, pondering the issue, when a servant came in with a note on a silver tray. To their surprise, the tray was held in front of them. They picked it up. "It's from Iris," they explained. "Perhaps she wants a report on the project."

"I've been giving her reports," Wyndham said. "But it's possible she wants to hear them from you."

"Well, the timing is good, at any rate," Torquil said as they gathered the letters and pocketed them again. "I can show her these."

"Why don't you use our carriage?" Wyndham asked, standing. "Then you can return more quickly."

"I don't mind the walk," Torquil protested, but Wyndham waved a dismissive hand.

"It's no trouble. And it will be much faster." He rang the bell cord. "Besides, think of all the casting we'll be able to accomplish if you conserve your strength."

Torquil sighed, recognizing the logic. The carriage was sent for and in the time it took to be brought around, Torquil, Roger, and Wyndham planned out how they would proceed with the project. By the time Wyndham helped Torquil into the carriage, they were feeling pleased with how much they'd have to report to Iris.

However, when they stepped into her office, she asked them to close the door and began the conversation with, "I read your column this morning. Are you all right?"

"Oh," Torquil said. "I'm sorry. I didn't mean to suggest any—"

She shook her head before they'd finished speaking. "I didn't take offense. You were very complimentary about my hosting. But you did look rather wrung out before you left and then I read what you wrote after. Was there anything particular that prompted it?"

Torquil let out a long breath. They thought back to how they'd been practically running for the door when Emrys found them, and the subsequent conversation in the garden. Emrys' hands on their face had been grounding in a way they had desperately needed. "Nothing particular, no," they said at last.

She gave their face a searching look.

"I…I'm not sure I'm cut out for this sort of life, Iris," they admitted quietly.

She was silent as she tapped her desk for a long moment. "I think that is exactly what some people want you to believe."

"Maybe they're right."

"I don't think you really believe that," she said with a small smile. "If you did, you wouldn't have written this." She lifted the *Tribune* briefly.

"I'm not sure it was the most *tactful* way for me to respond."

She chuckled. "Oh, I don't know. I've always appreciated your candor. Admittedly, you've never been as open about your personal experiences, although I think it would be good for that to change."

Torquil bit their lip. "Except that now I'm facing the public who will be reading about my personal experiences."

"Is the public as bad as that?"

"No, of course not. You aren't. Roger and Wyndham aren't. The Barneses have always been very kind. And Miss Aveline and…Mr. Emrys were both very gracious."

She cocked her head. "Oh? I'm glad to hear it. That was the other thing I wanted to ask you, actually. How did Emrys suit as a dinner partner?"

Torquil had a brief moment of panic that she was hinting at the same thing Roger had, but they pushed it aside. "He was very companionable."

She smiled warmly. "Good. I had hoped that would be the case. You two looked very well together."

Torquil hesitated. "That sounds like the sort of thing I'd write."

"Yes, it does, doesn't it? I was almost surprised that your paper didn't include a new list of attributes that Emrys is looking for in his spouse. It seemed like a good time to learn that."

"Almost?"

She laughed. "Well, I wasn't entirely surprised. I do have some suspicions on the subject."

"Anything you care to share?" Torquil said, attempting a light tone. "You know I'm always keen for new gossip."

She gave them another broad smile. "Well, I would, but it's nothing you wouldn't already know. Besides, you don't like writing personal things."

Torquil felt their stomach plummet. Icy shock trickled down their spine as the implication of her words hit them.

"Iris—"

She raised an eyebrow.

They lost the nerve to ask what they'd really wanted: *does it bother you? How do you know? It is hopeless, isn't it?* Instead they said, "I think I have a better understanding of what Mr. Wrenwhistle isn't looking for. But I don't think it's what my readers wish to read."

"Perhaps not," she agreed. She looked thoughtful for a moment and then said, "I understand that Wyndham and Roger have invited you to join us for dinner recently."

Torquil gave her a wary glance. "They have. I haven't accepted. Working on the project has been very exhausting."

"Well, it occurs to me that perhaps you were right after all: we ought to ease you into society with more intimate gatherings. I'll be joining my son's family tomorrow night for dinner. You should come."

"I'm not sure that—"

"And perhaps you will be able to learn the information your readers will want to know about."

They could tell from the look in her eye that they weren't going to wiggle out of the invitation. "Are you sure I'll be allowed in the door? I don't think I'm a particular favorite of Mrs. Wrenwhistle's."

She laughed. "I'm sure she'll be over it by then. Besides, Emrys' good mood can't have escaped her attention. I'll see you tomorrow, Torquil."

Thus dismissed, Torquil glumly left the office and returned to Wyndham and Roger's study. The two men were sitting together on the sofa, with Peony asleep on Roger's lap. Wyndham had his arm around his husband's shoulders, stroking his arm as they read over Roger's notes together.

When Torquil strode into the room, they collapsed onto their usual seat and said, "Well, she didn't want a report on the project. She wanted to ask me how I was after having read the *Tribune* and…invite me to dinner tomorrow night."

Roger looked delighted. "That's wonderful! We've been hoping you would."

"Did she give any particular reasons for the invitation?"

"She wants to ease me into society in a different way," Torquil said. It was partially the truth after all.

But then Wyndham and Roger shared a look that filled Torquil with certain dread. It wasn't possible for Wyndham to suspect as well...was it? Torquil wasn't sure they could handle so many people knowing their secret.

"How nice," Wyndham said with a sly grin.

CHAPTER 27

EMRYS

AFTER A RATHER UNRESTFUL night following the dinner party, Emrys woke the next morning hopeful that his escape from the situation with Miss Stanton would provide a fresh start in the search for his future spouse. Unfortunately, his mother had not yet completed her lamentations, which Emrys discovered the moment he sat down to take his breakfast in the family dining room.

"How frightfully unpleasant it was to be in the same room with the Stantons for an entire evening after your news was in the *Tribune*," she moaned over her plate of food. "Such gall to still accept the invitation, and without Miss Stanton! Certainly her headache must've been the result of her shock over her own family's actions."

Emrys considered the ramifications of standing up without a word and returning to his room. He took a deep breath and closed his eyes for a moment, searching for strength.

"They still had every right to attend the party, Mother." Emrys sat back as servants filled his plate. "Just try to imagine the scandal that would have come if none of them had been brave enough to show their faces after what happened. I thought it was very appropriate for them to be there."

"You did not read the note Mrs. Stanton wrote to me," Mrs. Wren-whistle spat in his direction.

"And I am glad of it. I do not wish to be involved in the intricacies of whatever sort of deals you are working out without my knowledge as you continue your search." Emrys took a bite of toast and pulled the latest copy of the *Tribune* out of his breast pocket. He had lost count of the number of times he'd read over Torquil's words that morning.

Part of him was proud of Torquil for being so candid. Though it had not been what Emrys might have expected them to say on the matter, they had obviously taken the advice to heart. They had to start somewhere. But the other part of him was left feeling...something. He could not identify what it was, even after more than an hour of careful consideration. The decision that eating might help him think more clearly was what had ultimately brought him downstairs.

When Emrys looked up again, his mother was still quietly fuming in her seat. He sighed and waved his toast at Aveline, who he realized had been far too silent.

"Why don't you pester Aveline about her evening," he suggested. "Even if mine did not play out the way you hoped, you can still be pleased that your other children seemed to have a wonderful time." Emrys stopped himself before he could sound too bitter. Aveline had also been matched with an intriguing dinner partner. He'd watched the two of them over the course of the party, and he had to admit that his sister had seemed quite satisfied. Upon further inspection, he realized that her silence was matched with a dreamy, distant look. He chuckled and gestured at her again before giving his mother a pointed look. "You see? Not to worry. You'll have another wedding to plan in no time at all."

Emrys did not give her time to respond. He took his toast and retreated to his room to save himself from being exposed to any more strong emotions that might mix with his own and ruin his day entirely.

Only after the sun had set and the house had settled did Emrys venture out again. He held his hat and scarf against the wind as he hurried across town. During the warmer months, there would have still been plenty of activity happening in the streets at such a time, but he found himself alone as he crowded close to the lock of the press building and let his magic grant his entry.

Emrys removed his outermost layers as he focused on the set of steps in the far corner of the room. He listened as he approached, taking far more care than he usually did. He thought of all the times he had infringed upon Torquil's private space like it was his right to disturb them. Carefully, he pulled the curtain aside and peered in. The desk chair sat empty. Emrys took another step and found Torquil sitting on their bed, legs bent close to their body, cheek resting against their knees. One arm was wrapped snugly around their shins while they used their other hand to turn the page of a book that was open on the bed.

Torquil glanced up at him, but did not move otherwise.

"I came to check on you," Emrys said, feeling the need to explain himself. After they had lingered in the garden at the dinner party, they had returned inside separately to avoid drawing unwanted attention. Torquil left soon after. Emrys was the only one who knew that it was for a reason other than getting home so the *Tribune* could be released on time.

"I'm fine," Torquil told him.

"Then why do you have the look of a scared animal hiding in the woods?"

Torquil huffed out a silent laugh and closed their book, setting it aside. They unbent their legs and crossed them instead, hands coming to rest in their lap. A small shrug followed. Emrys needed nothing more to understand.

"Have you slept?" he asked as he moved a bit closer to the bed. One look at the stove told him Torquil might've also been huddling for warmth.

"I spent the day working with Wyndham and Roger," Torquil said. The avoidance brought a grin to Emrys' lips. At least they were not too tired to be their usual self in that way.

"Stressful dinner party, *Tribune* distribution, a day full of research, and now here you are reading. It's a miracle you're still upright." Emrys extended his hand and waited for Torquil to take it. He guided them to their feet beside the bed and, after a quick assessment, worked until

Torquil was left in nothing but their long shirt, which he knew was self-ish, but he decided it was all right to take that for himself.

Emrys pulled back the covers. He did not have to ask Torquil to climb under, but he did shush Torquil's whimper of protest when he did not join them. Instead, he tucked the thin blanket up around their chin and braced his weight on his hands on either side of them so he could press a slow, gentle kiss to their forehead.

"Get some rest," he said, tone indicating that he would not hear any more opposition on the subject. In the time it took for him to brush the ragged curtain aside again, he'd used a breeze to stoke the fire and snuff the candles that had been burning around the room. While he worked the lock back into place, he took a deep breath and spread his magic across the entire building, fortifying what little protection he was able to provide.

⚶

EMRYS COULD NOT EXPRESS how grateful he was that his mother's mood had improved by the time dinner was served around his family's table the next evening. It seemed as though everyone else was in high spirits, as well, which was emphasized tenfold as Wyndham and Roger arrived just as they were taking their seats. Emrys had failed to notice the additional place setting next to his until he realized who followed them in.

"Hello, darlings. So lovely that you could join us tonight, Torquil," his grandmother said as her son helped her into her chair. Emrys blinked at Torquil as they came to his side, mild amusement showing in the crooked grin they wore. He remembered his manners in time to pull the chair out for their guest. A quick glance around the table told him that he was the only one who had been unaware of the addition to their family gathering.

"After so many invitations," Torquil said as they sat, "I felt as though declining once more would give you all the wrong idea."

Iris laughed. "Nonsense, but I am sure I can speak for everyone and say we are glad you finally relented to the Wrenwhistle charm."

"More like the Wrenwhistle stubbornness," Wyndham said.

"Perhaps we can agree it is a bit of both," Iris decided.

There was a lull in the conversation as platters and serving dishes made their way around the table. Emrys glanced at Torquil and was pleased to find that they looked far more rested than they had when he'd left them the night before.

He made sure to fill Torquil's plate as much as he could. It earned him a hard look when a particularly rounded scoop of pickled beets decided to abandon the serving utensil and fall onto the tablecloth between them. Emrys grinned apologetically at them as one of the servants stepped forward to clean his mess, though the deep purple stain left behind would need more attention.

When he turned away, his grin disappeared. Wyndham and Roger were both watching his antics. The smirk his brother wore was unsettling. Even more unsettling was the look he and Roger exchanged after. Emrys thought back to the conversation he'd shared with Roger at the party. The details had since faded, but he could not forget the way Roger smiled so brightly at the end of it. What sort of inferences had the man made at the dessert table?

To further heighten his unease, his mother chose that moment to speak up.

"I would love to know what inspired your change of tone in the latest copy of the *Tribune*," she said, speaking to Torquil without looking at them. "It seems to me that such a statement must have been inspired by a specific event."

"Which statement are you referring to?" Torquil asked evenly.

"Oh, the part about shunning the children of fae-human marriages." Her flippant choice of words was matched with the arch of her delicate brow. "You are the only person of such a background that I know personally, and look at you. Attending parties, sitting on the Council."

"All very new situations for me, you can be certain," they told her.

"And for the children of such circumstance who you do not know," Wyndham added. "Plenty of them exist, Mother."

Mrs. Wrenwhistle made a face that Emrys thought looked far too much like a blend of pity and disgust, and something within him snapped. The thought had crossed his mind before, but he'd not had reason enough to voice it until now.

"You do realize that Miss Stanton is human," he said.

The statement drew everyone's attention.

"Of course I do," she responded after a pause.

"So you also realize any children we might've had would be both fae and human, just the same as Torquil."

The heavy silence that settled over the table was broken by his mother's incredulous laughter. "It's hardly the same at all," she muttered as she reached for her wine.

"Isn't it?" Emrys demanded.

Mrs. Wrenwhistle took her time setting her glass down. The way her lips pressed into a thin line was telling of how angry she was becoming.

"This isn't the appropriate time to speak of such things," she said finally.

"You brought it up," Wyndham cut in.

Emrys was surprised at his brother's show of support in such a tense moment, but he was grateful for it. How could their mother be so cold? As horrid as her implications were, to voice them in front of Torquil was unthinkable. Emrys wouldn't have blamed Torquil if they wanted to excuse themself from dinner and never see him again. He turned, prepared for the worst, but instead found them looking back at him with a small grin.

"Thank you," Torquil mouthed at him.

Emrys nodded. It was all he could manage. For someone so worried about not being able to handle society, Torquil was one of the strongest people he'd ever known. His desire to reach out and take Torquil's hand was so intense that he had to tuck his fingers beneath his thigh to keep them to himself.

CHAPTER 28

TORQUIL

TORQUIL WAS unsure if they should continue the topic or not.

Then, to their surprise, Iris spoke. "It is interesting that you brought up Torquil's position on the Council, Odella. Despite the fact that they are a councilmember, the majority of the Council has been resistant to any of Torquil's contributions." She paused. "Not only Torquil, but Wyndham and Roger have been met with opposition in practically everything they have suggested. Strange, is it not, that a group of people in need of fresh ideas would discount every proposed solution as unsuitable?"

Mrs. Wrenwhistle gave a little sniff of disapproval. "Just because an idea is fresh does not mean it is good, Iris."

Iris gave a slow smile. "I think Councilmember Williams said exactly those words earlier this week."

Torquil fought back a laugh; they could distinctly imagine the gentleman saying such a thing.

Iris took a sip of wine. "In my mind, it is a similar issue to that of parenting."

Mrs. Wrenwhistle frowned. "What could you possibly mean?"

Iris shrugged. "Well, I've always found it odd that people would have children, give them the resources to think and feel deeply, and then be upset when their children turn out to have minds of their own."

"You mean like my parents?" Torquil cut in.

Mrs. Wrenwhistle looked as though she might combust from agitation so they continued, hoping to deflect some of her temper. "From what my parents tell me, my mother was a debutante the year she met my father. Everyone was certain she'd make a match. But when she did, her parents were so opposed to it, they cut her off without a penny and without a word."

Iris beamed. "Exactly."

"That's hardly a fair comparison," Mrs. Wrenwhistle said. "Your mother married below her station. Her parents had every right to disapprove."

Out of the corner of their eye, Torquil noticed Emrys stiffen at his mother's words.

"Do you mean because Miss Pimpernel married a human?" Wyndham said, tilting his chin up.

His mother tsked. "Of course I don't mean that. She married outside of her social circle. That's all."

Torquil felt a mix of emotions at this. They were relieved that Mrs. Wrenwhistle was less concerned with their mixed blood status, but she was still prejudiced, and her prejudice was one that had dogged Torquil all of their life. After all, their mother had made a massive step down, socially, in marrying a nobody like their father. The fact that the couple had betrayed all convention by spurning the Pimpernels' disapproval and leaving all of London society behind had seemed to cement the idea that Mr. Smith had fully ruined his wife's prospects. Being poor and inconsequential had been almost as challenging for Torquil as being fae-human.

"I married outside my social circle as well," Wyndham said.

"Roger's father is on the Council," she protested. "He works with your grandmother. Meanwhile, the Pimpernels are one of the wealthiest families in the *ton*. Sienna Pimpernel would have outranked practically anyone who offered for her—in fact, it's hardly surprising that her name comes first, considering. And then for her to abandon her family to marry someone so far below her station as to not even be in the same drawing rooms—it was entirely different. They were from completely different worlds. It's a wonder they met at all. You'd known Roger since childhood. You were at all of the same parties. It made perfect sense for you two to be together."

"How did your parents meet, Councilmember Pimpernel-Smith?" Aveline asked. "Was it terribly romantic?"

They chuckled, relieved at the evident attempt at a break in the tension. "It was, rather. My father had been commissioned to print some scientific illustrations for a botany text. I don't remember the exact details, but he was having difficulty with printing one particular piece, so he went to a florist to buy some flowers in order to see if that helped his perspective."

Aveline leaned forward. "And your mother was there?"

"She was. According to my father, he couldn't take his eyes off her the moment she stepped up to the stall. And according to my mother, she thought he was the florist, and launched into a full story as to why she was there and what she needed. I suppose my father was so tongue-tied, he simply held up the flowers he had in his hand and offered them to her."

Everyone laughed.

"How sweet," Mrs. Wrenwhistle said in a tone that was not quite sincere.

Torquil took a sip of wine to disguise their hurt. They'd always loved that story of their parents.

"I have long been of the opinion that young people often know their own minds," Iris said. "Even when it means marrying below their station or outside their social circle. Fresh ideas do not always mean good ideas. But fresh ideas are always worth hearing. I rather think it's time most of the councilmembers listened for a change. It's also time we set aside some of our old-fashioned ideas about suitability when it comes to marriage. Don't you agree, darling?" she said, turning to her son.

Mr. Wrenwhistle looked thoughtful for a long moment. "If I recall correctly, Mother, you told Odella and I that we were too young to be married. And I cannot imagine being married to anyone else. So I think I'd have to agree with you."

Mrs. Wrenwhistle looked torn on whether to be triumphant at her husband's remark or irritable. "How is your little project going, Wynnie?"

"It's going well," Wyndham said, glancing at Roger.

Roger nodded. "Oh, yes. It's been fascinating learning how Torquil does magic. They just started receiving letters from other fae-humans the other day. Every time I think I've learned all the facets there are to magic, I discover I've barely scratched the surface."

"What do you mean?" Emrys said. "What is your magic like?"

Torquil hid a smile at the question. "I used to think that I was barely competent in either magic system. But it turns out my fae magic requires my human magic and vice versa. I can't perform fae magic without a human spell first, and my human spells have practically no power without my fae magic to add to it."

"And," Wyndham said, "they can sense magic as easily as any full-blooded fae. Which, as we learned, is not a universal trait for all fae-humans. So, in a way, Torquil can perform two different types of fae magic while also performing human magic."

"It's extraordinary," Roger breathed.

"My curiosity is certainly piqued," Emrys said. "I'd love to visit and see this in person, but I'd hate to distract you all from your work," he added with a meaningful glance at his brother.

Torquil expected Wyndham to express a similar irritation to the last time Emrys had come into the study. But instead he shared a glance with Roger, turned to Torquil, and said, "It might not be a bad idea to have an outside opinion. Don't you agree, Torquil? Fresh ideas, and all that?"

Wyndham's smile was decidedly untrustworthy, but all Torquil could say was, "You know I'm following your and Roger's lead. You both have a great deal more experience with this sort of thing than I do."

Iris sighed happily. "I knew the three of you would work well together."

Emrys gave Torquil a grin and said, "I'll visit tomorrow then."

"You really ought to be focusing on finding a spouse," Mrs. Wrenwhistle cut in. Torquil thought she sounded more cheerful now that she was back on firmer ground.

"Wouldn't that seem callous of me after such a public almost-courtship with Miss Stanton?" he replied.

"Of course not," she said blithely. "It will simply prove that you have moved on."

Emrys was silent for a long moment. "Then again, if I were to be seen with someone else, it might suggest that I'm desperate for a spouse. Perhaps it could wait a few days?"

She pinched her lips together. "Very well. A few days."

The topic finally changed and Torquil was beginning to think the rest of the evening would proceed without incident. But just as they were getting ready to announce they ought to leave, Iris spoke up.

"I've been thinking that Emrys might have the right idea about how he should proceed in his search," she said, turning to him. "Perhaps it might even be wise to be seen without someone, show everyone you're searching again. Another night at the opera even? You could take your siblings with you."

"Oh, yes!" Aveline said. "I should love to go. I was not invited last time," she added with a pointed look at Emrys.

"I thought you were busy!" he protested. He glanced at Wyndham. "I know you both enjoy the opera."

Roger beamed. "I never tire of it."

Emrys turned to Torquil and their stomach dropped in dread of what he would say. "Perhaps you would like to join us as well?"

Out of the corner of their eye, Torquil saw Mrs. Wrenwhistle stiffen.

"Thank you, Mr. Wrenwhistle," they said evenly. "It is very generous of you, but I could not possibly—"

"You don't even know when we'll be going," Emrys laughed.

"I think I've intruded in enough family gatherings," they said quietly.

"Don't be absurd, Torquil," Wyndham said.

"I think I'd better leave now," they said, standing.

"Yes, I think that might be best," Mrs. Wrenwhistle murmured.

They left the room as quickly as they could. The dinner had been even more of a disaster than they'd expected. They nodded at one of the footmen standing in the hallway, another familiar face from their morning route. The sound of footsteps behind them caused anxiety to flare in their chest. Before they got to the front door, however, there was a warm hand on their arm and they were gently tugged around. They turned to see Emrys.

"Torquil," he said, grabbing their shoulders. "I didn't mean to upset you."

"You didn't," they said hastily.

"Then come with us."

"You know that's impossible, Emrys," they whispered.

"Why?"

Torquil glanced around, uncomfortably aware of the servants in the vicinity. "If I attend the opera as the only guest of the family, people will assume—"

"They'll assume we're friends. You're friends with my brother and his husband after all."

Torquil took Emrys' hands in their own. "They would assume a great deal more and you know it."

"Is it so wrong for me to want to see you outside of the confines of your room?" Emrys said, his brow furrowing. "Now that my grand-mother has taken you under her wing, it seems only natural that we would become better acquainted. No one would think anything of it."

Torquil glanced at one of the footmen, conspicuously standing at attention by the wall. The man gave Torquil a small, reassuring smile. Torquil supposed it was fortunate that they had spent years earning the trust of London's domestic staff, even if only to aid them in this moment of vulnerability. They turned back to Emrys. "Your mother would."

"She isn't everyone. And she thinks the worst regardless. Please come to the opera with me."

Being with Emrys would make any social outing a great deal more bearable. Torquil could readily imagine their hand around his arm, the way he'd merrily take over the conversation, how he'd argue against any criticism they'd receive. But Torquil could also imagine the looks they would get. They could already hear the whispers. Being with Emrys would make everything better while also making everything much, much worse. They shook their head. "I can't," they whispered.

Emrys pulled his hands from Torquil's grip and framed their face. "Torquil," he breathed, his tone gently admonishing.

"Please—" They extricated themself and stepped away. "I should go."

Emrys sighed. "I'll see you tomorrow?"

They nodded distractedly. "You'll be watching us work."

Emrys gave a sly grin. "But I'll still visit you soon and watch you perform your fire spell too."

They couldn't resist the weak smile that came unbidden. "Good."

CHAPTER 29

EMRYS

EMRYS WOKE at a wildly unreasonable hour. There was no question as to why; he had been invited to come and observe Torquil openly perform magic. This had been a thing of his dreams for years before he'd discovered the truth of their compatible magic. Admittedly, he had never expected it would happen under the watchful guidance of Wyndham and Roger, but he was more than willing to overlook that small compromise.

After struggling to find something to occupy himself with, Emrys sent out a note just as the sky began to shift from black to a slightly less miserable gray. Of all his connections in London, Emrys only knew of one other person who would be awake at such an hour *and* be willing to dress for an outing.

When he arrived at the coffeehouse, Keelan had already found a table near the windows and had a steaming cup waiting for him.

"You really are a wonderful friend," Emrys murmured as he took his seat.

"I know," Keelan said smugly. "Now tell me, should I be worried?"

Emrys blew gently on his drink before he brought the cup to his lips for a slow sip. The ambient noise of the modest establishment was comforting as he felt the coffee go down. It was one of the few remaining coffeehouses on their side of town after most had been abandoned or transformed during the growing popularity of exclusive clubs. Emrys was not particular about visiting either, but the clubs would not be open for another several hours.

"Why would you be?" Emrys asked warily.

Keelan's eyebrows went up. "Your note simply said *Harrison's, urgent.* Such little detail can only leave a man to wonder."

"And did your intrigue not get you here in record time?"

Emrys watched over his cup as Keelan leaned in conspiratorially, nearly far enough to dip his cravat into his coffee.

"Get on with it, then. Has it something to do with Miss Stanton? Are you having second thoughts about ending things? I am certain she would take you back if you asked, the poor thing."

"It has nothing to do with Miss Stanton," Emrys sighed.

"Have you decided on one of your other suitors, perchance?"

Emrys looked down into his cup. "Quite the opposite, actually."

Keelan gasped softly. "You've found someone all on your own, is that it?"

The coffee roiled in Emrys' stomach as he realized that he'd put himself into another impossible situation. What had he been thinking, asking Keelan to meet him when he was feeling so uncertain? He should've known he would be pressed to answer questions that he simply could not.

Perhaps he could spin things as he always had, providing just enough information to satisfy without revealing too much.

"How many times have you felt someone else's magic during an intimate moment?" Emrys asked, keeping his voice low.

Keelan sat back at the question, peering over his shoulder before he whispered his response. The coffeehouse was not yet full, but there was a group of drowsy students two tables over chattering in hushed voices, and several other patrons with eyes on their morning papers and ears primed for overhearing gossip as fresh as their morning brew.

"Certainly more than an unmarried person should," he said. Keelan knew as well as anyone that it was highly inappropriate to do such a thing, and even more so to speak about it later. "As much as our elders would try to deny it, we all know fae have been breaking that particular rule for centuries looking for our perfect match. You cannot tell me you've never done it yourself."

"Of course I have," Emrys agreed, before he went silent. His thumb worked the smooth surface of his cup as he stared at Keelan, trying desperately to think of the best way to explain himself in the pause that grew heavy between them. In the end, it wasn't necessary. The sly expression his friend wore faded slightly. Then it disappeared completely, replaced by one of surprise and delight. Emrys hated the way it reminded him so much of the look Roger had given him at the dinner party.

"Who?" Keelan demanded in a harsh whisper. It was still loud enough to draw the attention of the students sitting nearby. Emrys glanced at them before giving Keelan a look of distress that did nothing to sway his friend's excitement. "And more importantly, what was it like? Was it as brilliant as they all say?"

There was no use in diminishing that detail. Emrys' features soft-ened as he thought back to the experience he'd shared with Torquil. He allowed himself to remember the way it made him feel, the way it consumed him entirely in the moment and long after.

"Nothing could ever possibly match it," he admitted.

"You lucky bastard," Keelan said finally, shaking his head as he reached for his forgotten drink. "How will you tell your mother she can end her search?"

Emrys huffed. "I cannot tell her."

Keelan nearly choked on his sip of coffee. He set the cup down with a clatter and wiped at his chin with the heel of his palm to catch the dribble.

"What do you mean you *cannot tell her*? You must!"

"She will never approve of the match," Emrys explained, trying his best to keep his tone neutral. "I fear I would be disowned for simply mentioning it."

"You are set to inherit," Keelan argued. "Certainly it cannot be as bad as you're making it sound. Who are they, Emrys, some sort of beggar? Do not tell me you slept with some criminal in between their stints in prison and just happened to discover that you're magically compatible?"

Emrys glared at him, and Keelan took that as answer enough.

"See? You must tell her and end your suffering."

Emrys wished he could explain why it would never be as simple as that. In truth, he wished that he could get the thoughts out of his head completely.

Torquil was his *lover*, his friend. Yes, they had known each other for many years, and Emrys had to admit that the comfort he felt with Torquil was unlike anything he had ever experienced with anyone else. The same could be said for the passion in their moments of intimacy, or their understanding in moments of support.

There was just one issue that Emrys kept returning to as he had thought about all of this for hours when he should've been sleeping.

Not once had Torquil ever mentioned wanting to be married to *anyone*. Of course, their position in society left Torquil free to make that decision. Many people did not marry, especially if they had a career and were able to look after themselves. But Emrys found that he could not recall a single time when Torquil had indicated their feelings on the matter, unless he had forgotten, but he found it hard to believe that he would have forgotten something like that.

Emrys decided he would make it a point to ask them. It was a fair question, he thought, and there was no reason why he would have to explain himself or why he wanted to know beyond the sake of curiosity.

"I suppose you're right," Emrys said finally. "I shall have to tell her."

♨

WYNDHAM HAD INSTRUCTED Emrys on the time they would be expecting him. He was a few minutes early, but he could not help wondering if his brother had told him the wrong time entirely to make him look like a fool. He tried to shake his worry as he climbed the front steps of the townhouse. When the door was answered and he was welcomed inside, he felt a bit better, but it was not until he was announced at the door of the study that he could finally relax.

That is, until he was met with a wall of residual magic so strong that it nearly knocked him back. The fluttering in his chest intensified, and he decided that perhaps the second cup of coffee had been a poor choice.

"Good afternoon," he greeted, pushing through. Wyndham and Roger were seated close together on the sofa with Torquil on a chair nearby. Emrys helped himself to the last open spot on a chair close to the fire, which he was grateful for. It appeared he had found them just as they were finishing tea.

"Please, do sit," Wyndham said dryly.

"Would you care for some tea?" Roger asked, leaning forward to pour him a cup regardless of his answer. Emrys accepted it and then promptly set it on the side table next to his chair.

"I fear that would be an unwise choice at the moment," he said. "But I do appreciate it all the same." Emrys met Torquil's gaze and gave a small nod before his attention shifted to the servant entering the room. They moved a few of the items on the table to clear a space for the plate they had carried in.

"Courtesy of Mr. Emrys Wrenwhistle," they said before stepping away.

"I hadn't realized my timing would be so perfect," Emrys said. "I was out this morning and decided I should pick up something on my way over."

"That was very kind of you," Roger said, reaching for one of the fresh ginger cakes that had been neatly arranged. "Thank you." He hummed his approval after the first bite and reached for another, handing it to Wyndham. "They're still warm," he enthused.

They were no sugared almonds, but Emrys had picked the ginger cakes because he knew Torquil enjoyed them. When they didn't take one, he wondered if their interaction from the night before was still lingering between them. Then Emrys noticed the kitten that was curled up on Torquil's lap.

He grimaced. "At least that thing is kind to someone." He tried to ignore the flickering of jealousy he felt. Of course the kitten would find comfort with Torquil, though. How many times had he gone to them for exactly that reason?

"*She* is rather sweet to almost everyone," Wyndham said. "The only people she does not like are you and Mother. Imagine my surprise."

Emrys scoffed and sat forward in his chair. He picked up the plate and held it out to Torquil so they could take one.

"And who says chivalry is dead?" Roger asked a little too pointedly for Emrys' comfort.

"I'll do whatever it takes to keep that th— *her* asleep," Emrys said, eyeing the little cat again before collecting a cake for himself and changing the subject. "It feels like you've already been hard at work in here. What do I get to see?"

Glances were exchanged between the three of them. Roger brushed a few crumbs off his waistcoat and pushed his spectacles up his nose with a bent knuckle before he looked at Emrys.

"Torquil has been using raw ingredients. I expect that's why you're able to feel it lingering so strongly. We've been trying to keep a window open, as the space is rather small, but with the weather it's been...er...cold."

Roger continued on into a speech that nearly bored Emrys to death. He hoped that his expression did not give away his disinterest as Roger explained more about all of the human spells and fae magic combinations they'd tried, the results of each, and how they related to their work for the Council and the new rubric they were struggling to create. Emrys was fairly certain he fell asleep at one point, but it was painfully obvious that Roger cared deeply about their work, and he hoped that all three of them would be rewarded for it in the end.

When Emrys could not stand one more moment of listening to words he didn't understand, he sat up from where he'd slumped in his chair. "Excellent," he said as he clapped his hands once in a show of appreciation, talking over Roger and scaring the cat awake. She jumped off Torquil's legs and scrambled under the sofa.

"Oh," Roger said clumsily. "Thank you."

"Now," Emrys said as he rubbed his hands together. "Impress me."

Wyndham got up first, joining his husband where he'd stood near the desk during his lecture. Without a word the two of them began ripping spellpaper and gathering ingredients, clearing away the used items and replacing them with the new. Watching that alone was impressive. Emrys had never seen anyone prepare for human magic in such a way. He knew it happened all around him, even in his own home, but he'd never had a reason to be there to see it.

When they were finished, Wyndham and Roger turned to Torquil. Neither of them wore a look that indicated uncertainty or apprehension. If anything, Emrys thought they both looked quite proud.

Torquil got up from their chair and moved to the open side of the desk. It was too tall for Emrys to see what exactly had been laid out, so he also stood and wandered closer without crowding any of them. He crossed his arms for good measure, still near enough to the fire to feel the heat of it on his back, and watched closely as Torquil began.

Emrys wished to know the intricacies of what he witnessed. At one point, Roger offered Torquil praise for remembering something without needing one of the five open reference books spread out across the desk. Their slender, ink-stained fingers worked to cover the papers with various lines and markings that translated into items moving and shrinking and all sorts of things. After lifting a goose quill and making it twirl in the air, it only took three tries for Torquil to dip it into the inkwell before drawing it across the paper to scribe a rough version of their name.

It required every bit of restraint Emrys possessed to keep his own magic contained so that Torquil could work without interference. He found it was even more difficult to restrain his desire to wrap his arms around Torquil's middle and rest his chin upon their shoulder so that he might watch from a better vantage point behind them, or perhaps swipe the desk clean of magical ingredients in favor of pressing Torquil back against it and kissing them until they understood just how proud he was of them.

"Roger and I found our first real success in blending fae and human magics with the next spell," Wyndham said after a while, shaking Emrys from his intense focus. He swallowed and nodded his understanding, never looking away from what Torquil was doing.

Emrys recognized it as a breeze spell. It was so faint at first that it almost wasn't there at all, but he could see when Torquil's human spell was enhanced by their fae magic as the candles guttered and the curtains swayed.

"Torquil is still working on building up their strength. I've been assisting on spells like this to help them feel the appropriate amount of power needed." Wyndham took a breath, and Emrys watched as some of the used papers on the desk fluttered before they were lifted into the air.

Instantly, Emrys felt the magic in his chest become as vicious as the kitten still hiding under the sofa. The reaction surprised him at first, but not for long. How dare Wyndham be the one to touch Torquil's magic right in front of him? How dare *anyone* touch Torquil's magic except for him?

"Allow me," Emrys said as he stepped forward, proud of himself for not shoving Wyndham out of his way as he came around to where Torquil was standing. Their eyes met, and Emrys let his magic free.

It was there. It had been there from the moment he arrived, lingering and teasing. But now it was fresh and alive and Emrys silently begged Torquil to reach out, to seek his magic just as he was seeking theirs.

Please, he thought, *show me I'm not alone in this.*

Emrys' magic rushed behind the curtains, underneath the furniture, wilder than he'd felt it since he was a child. It was intoxicating all on its own.

But then it happened. Their magics brushed, and Emrys felt a spark so raw it made him jump as Torquil gasped sharply and reached for Emrys to steady themself as though they were about to fall. The candles went out first, then the fire. Only the heaviest book remained in place as the other items on the desk were whisked away in a sudden crash.

Everything went silent and still after that, long enough for Emrys to realize that he had pulled Torquil into his arms. He let go and they stepped apart, Torquil looking away as they pressed a hand to their forehead.

"I'm so sorry," they began breathlessly, crouching to pick up two of the books that had landed by their feet.

Emrys blinked and turned away as well, inspecting the mess behind him. Everything left over from their tea was shattered across the floor. A painting had fallen off the wall.

Movement at the window caught Emrys' attention. It took him a few seconds to realize that the shaking of the curtain was not their magic, but the kitten frantically trying to climb to safety.

Wyndham sighed. "I'll get her," he said as he stepped over the broken teapot in her direction.

Emrys expected to find Roger nearly as shaken as the poor cat. He looked up to offer an apology of his own, but instead found him smiling.

CHAPTER 30

TORQUIL

Torquil resisted the urge to look at Emrys. They felt as though their whole body was still buzzing after the burst of magic. They focused on trying to pick up as many books as they could carry.

"Don't worry about that, Torquil," Roger said.

"I practically destroyed your study," Torquil protested, gesturing around them.

"We've done worse," Wyndham said, plucking Peony off the curtains and holding her against his chest. "It can take a while to get the balance right, especially when you're casting with another person."

Torquil did *not* point out that this hadn't happened when they'd cast with Wyndham.

"Of course," Wyndham went on, "it would help if the other person had a tighter rein on their magic. When I said I've been showing you how much power to reach, I didn't mean quite that much."

Emrys raised his chin. "You're hardly one to talk about controlling magic."

Wyndham gave a snort.

Emrys opened his mouth to retort and then closed it. Instead he turned to Torquil and put a hand on their back. "Are you all right?" he said softly.

Torquil gave a jerky nod. "Yes, of course. Just surprised, that's all."

Roger took the books Torquil had collected and set them on the desk before he led them back to their usual chair. "Let's get you some tea—oh." He glanced at the shattered tea set and then rang the bell cord. "Thankfully, we have spares. As Wyn said, we've done worse."

Torquil sat in the chair and attempted to replay the catastrophic moment in their head. All they'd done was try to feel Emrys' magic, as Wyndham had shown them to do, so they could get a gauge on the level to strive for. But one brush of their magic against Emrys' and everything had practically exploded. What did that say about their compatibility? Torquil couldn't be sure which answer they dreaded more.

Emrys hovered over their chair, looking uncertain.

"Would you like to stay for more tea, Emrys?" Roger said politely as he sat across from Torquil. "Or…er…stay as we drink more tea?"

Torquil gave Emrys a wary glance, which seemed to help the man make up his mind. "Very kind of you to offer, but I think I'd better take my leave. I'll rest a bit before the opera. Are you sure you won't come with us?"

"Quite sure," Torquil replied in a soft but even voice.

Emrys sighed. "Very well."

After Emrys stepped out, Wyndham waved his hand lazily toward the door and it shut. He plopped onto the sofa next to his husband and set Peony on his lap. "So," he said, drawing out the word.

"I really am sorry about the study," Torquil said quickly.

Wyndham gave them a long look before looking down at Peony and stroking her back. "Did the same thing happen in your room? From what I remember of the building, it would hardly be standing after such an explosion."

Torquil pressed their lips together.

"You had described him as glowing," Wyndham went on, his gaze still on the kitten. "I think I'd agree with that description. Your magic acted like a match to a prepared hearth. His magic burst into life. I've never seen his magic so powerful before."

Roger glanced at him. "Isn't he the most powerful one in your family?"

"Yes," Wyndham said in a musing tone. "And you cannot imagine how galling it is to see someone so foolish with so much power. What a waste. He was practically falling asleep during Roger's explanation of our project." He chuckled. "I used to make up words when I was younger, just to trick him into thinking he had an even smaller vocabulary than he has. It's a cruel irony indeed that the most powerful person in my family is also the most stupid."

"He is not—" Torquil started before snapping their mouth shut.

Wyndham's gaze shot up to meet theirs and he gave a slow, sly smile. He raised an eyebrow. "Isn't he?"

Torquil clenched their hands together.

A servant walked in with a tea tray and set it down, making no comment on the disastrous mess, and left.

Roger poured a cup of tea and handed it to Torquil with a kind expression. "You can tell us, you know. We've had our suspicions since Iris' dinner party."

"What gave it away?" Torquil said wearily.

"The way you two look at each other. There's definite fondness between you. And you talk to each other with an evident familiarity." Roger shrugged. "And I spoke to Emrys after dinner that evening and he said things that…confirmed my suspicions."

"Roger put it all together before I did," Wyndham admitted. "Although I certainly would have known after today."

Torquil winced. "I can't imagine what you saw could possibly be evidence of a good thing."

"It's just a matter of getting accustomed to each other," he said easily. "You'll figure it out. I do have questions though."

Torquil sighed. "Yes?"

"How long has it been going on? And what could you possibly see in him?"

Torquil gave a weak chuckle. "I met him before I opened my press."

Wyndham blinked in surprise. Roger laughed at his husband's expression. "You didn't expect Emrys to be capable of that much discretion, did you?"

"I certainly did not." His eyes went wide. "Is that why you never wrote about him in your paper?"

Torquil nodded.

He huffed out a laugh. "Stars above. That brings me back to my second question. How could someone as clever as you see anything in someone like him?"

"There are different types of intelligence, Wyndham," Torquil said softly. "Your brother is kind. At least to me. And generous." They grinned and cocked an eyebrow. "And he has a great many qualities as a lover. For instance—"

"Absolutely not," Wyndham said loudly.

They smirked. "You asked."

"I withdraw the question."

There was a long silence and then Torquil said quietly, "He knows how much I like ginger cakes."

Roger gave a little gasp. "That's so sweet."

"I knew he wasn't being generous for our sake," Wyndham mumbled.

"What does it matter?" Roger said. "Torquil brings out the best in him. That's wonderful. And how it should be," he added, with a satisfied little nod.

"Why did you turn down the invitation to the opera?" Wyndham said with a small frown.

Torquil shrugged. "I had to. You know how it would look."

"It would look like my brother has set his sights on you. With the way he looks at you, it would very much look like he's in love with you, wants you to get to know his family better, and wants to see you as much as possible."

Torquil didn't want to examine the feeling they got at the casual assessment of Emrys being in love with them. "Exactly."

"And why is that a problem?"

"Because it's impossible!"

Roger cocked his head. "Is it?"

Torquil stared at them both. "Were you not at dinner last night?"

"You mean my mother?" Wyndham rolled his eyes. "Don't worry about her. She'll come around. If she were to witness what we just witnessed in terms of your magic, she'd come around *very* quickly."

Torquil didn't believe that in the slightest.

"Besides," Wyndham went on. "Despite your mother being

disowned, she comes from a very powerful and influential family. I wouldn't be the least bit surprised if my mother orchestrated a family reunion just to make herself look good."

"All the more reason why this could never happen. I've never met my grandparents and I'm quite sure I don't want to."

"Can't say I blame you," Roger said. "They sound dreadful."

Dreadful didn't even cover it, as far as Torquil was concerned. Like many of the well-to-do fae families, the Pimpernels were both wealthy and powerful. They were even more influential than the Wrenwhistles. From what Torquil had learned from their mother, friendship with the Pimpernel family was a strong social currency; resentment from the family could result in social ostracization. Apparently Mrs. Pimpernel was particularly adept at wielding gossip, creating waves in the *ton* with a mere comment, a stray observation. Torquil liked to think that they had inherited a gift and transformed it into something good. As far as they were concerned, their grandparents were nothing less than vile.

Torquil drained their teacup. "Shall we put the study back together?"

"Why?" Wyndham said. "We'll have the servants help us do that. And this is far more interesting."

"Besides, you must be exhausted after such a morning." Roger paused. "Perhaps we should end early today so you can go home and rest."

"That might be best," Torquil said. They stood and both men stood as well.

Wyndham laid a hand on Torquil's shoulder. "I mean this with all sincerity, Torquil. What your magic looks like alongside Emrys' is extraordinary. If he could learn to control his power when he cast with you, he—" Wyndham winced as he continued, "he would *almost* deserve the inheritance. That's how remarkable it is."

Torquil lifted an eyebrow. "Praise indeed."

"I mean it," Wyndham said, squeezing their shoulder. "Furthermore, you make my least favorite sibling considerably more bearable. You're good for him. And from what I've seen of you two together, I'd hazard a guess that he's rather good for you, too. This is not as impossible as you seem to think."

Torquil had nothing to say in response to that, so they left as quickly as they could.

⟡

WHEN THEY REACHED HOME, they found four more letters from fae-humans had been delivered. They read the letters as they let themself into the building, locked the door behind them, climbed the stairs, and sat down on the bed. One letter even expounded on how delighted the sender was to write a fae-human on the Council. *I hope you know that you are giving all of us hope that we may someday be as much a part of society as you are.* The words settled like a stone in Torquil's stomach. They knew with a letter like that, they could never completely quit society. Iris had, unsurprisingly, been right all along. They set the letters on the desk and curled up in bed, too weary to even undress first.

For years, they had operated in the background, making changes happen by manipulating the gossip to make the right impact. But being at the forefront of change felt different. Now they felt as though they were being manipulated into action. They were becoming a figurehead, an emblem of what was possible. When they had accepted the position on the Council, they had expected to continue making quiet changes on the sidelines. The Council was not known for being a particularly powerful body, nor a particularly active one. Torquil had hoped to gently push the Council in the right direction; it hadn't occurred to them that they might get pushed into a new direction too.

But after all of the letters they were receiving, it was evident that this was where they needed to be, this was the change that was needed. They only hoped they were up to the task.

⟡

WHEN TORQUIL MADE their rounds for gossip the next day, they found that many of their sources were also full of information about Emrys: "Mr. Wrenwhistle tips very handsomely," and "all of the Wrenwhistles' servants say that the heir is very respectful to the staff." They were even assured multiple times that Emrys hadn't had a single dalliance in years.

Torquil couldn't decide whether to laugh at the show of support or cry at how obvious they had been.

As soon as they arrived in Wyndham and Roger's study, Wyndham handed them a purse full of money, explaining that Iris had instructed him to dole out their wages appropriately. He also handed Torquil another invitation.

"It's tradition," he explained. "My family always goes skating in the park this time of year."

"And there will be a market!" Roger said.

Torquil thought about the letters they had received. "Very well," they said. "I'll be there."

"Emrys will be pleased by that," Wyndham muttered.

Torquil narrowed their eyes.

Wyndham attempted a sorrowful expression. "You should have seen how miserable he was last night. All alone at the opera."

"He was surrounded by his siblings."

"Yes, and we all would have been grateful if you had come. He practically snapped at Aveline for sniffing in the third act. If I had known that your presence makes him a moderately decent person, I would have encouraged you to join us years ago."

"You didn't even know me years ago."

Roger chuckled. "Well, I'm glad you'll be there for the outing in the park. From the way Aveline was talking about it, it is a big event for the fae population. It more or less begins the winter holiday festivities."

"Yes," Wyndham said. "We have fairy lights everywhere, the lake is covered in ice for skating. There are magical and musical performances. It is *quite* romantic."

"Are you trying to talk me out of going?"

"You've already accepted," Wyndham said hastily. "My grand-mother was most insistent."

Torquil forebore grumbling about it. Instead, they pulled out the letters they had received and the afternoon was spent in note-taking and discussion.

When Torquil left the townhouse, they found themself oddly disappointed that they hadn't practiced any magic that day. They wandered to the market and purchased everything needed for fire spells, better quality spellpaper, and even a new spellbook. They returned home and leafed through the book, making a list of spells they'd like to try. It was a strange feeling, being excited to do magic.

They had no idea when Emrys intended to visit, but they were torn in how they felt about it. They were looking forward to seeing him, as they always were. And part of that excitement had to do with the prospect of doing magic together again. Would it be better this time? More polished? Would it result in disaster? There was a significant part of them that was anxious at the idea of doing magic with Emrys that might result in a destroyed home. But there was also a small but very strong voice in their head that told them Emrys would never let anything harm them. They thought of the way he had pulled them into his arms when the magic had burst in the study. It had been instinctual, automatic. He hadn't even seemed to mind that his brother was in the room, observing. It was strange, really, that with everything he had at stake, Emrys didn't seem to worry if people noticed his affection for Torquil. And Torquil couldn't entirely chalk that up to absentminded-ness. It was almost humorous the way Torquil was more concerned about Emrys' reputation than he was.

With that in mind, Torquil sat down at their desk and began polishing their draft for the *Tribune*. There were some fascinating new developments about Aveline that they were keen to write, and after their discussion with Roger and Wyndham, they had a nice bit of information for the fae event coming up. As usual, they lost themself in their work, and didn't even notice when Emrys entered the room until he bent down to kiss their cheek.

"I was hoping you'd be in bed. It's after midnight."

Torquil rubbed their eyes and moved their foot out from where they'd been sitting on it. It tingled with disuse. "If I'd known you were coming, I'd have prepared things for you."

"Oh?" he said with a grin. He ran a hand through their hair. "What would that have entailed? I hope it means you would have had less clothes on."

Torquil laughed. "I believe I promised you a fire spell. I could hardly be expected to focus on magic if I were undressed. *You* would be too much of a distraction in that case."

Emrys scoffed. "Can I help it that you look delectable when you're down to your shirt?"

They tugged on his waistcoat and pulled him down for a kiss, smiling against his lips. Emrys broke off the kiss and scooped Torquil up, plopping himself onto their seat and pulling them onto his lap. He nipped their earlobe lightly. "That's better."

Torquil wrapped their arms around his neck and kissed him again. "Perhaps we should forgo the magic tonight."

"Absolutely not," Emrys said. "I have been wanting to see your magic for years. I'm not about to pass this up." His forehead wrinkled. "Unless you're too tired, of course. Are they working you too hard?"

Torquil chuckled and kissed him. "I'm not too tired. We didn't even do magic today actually."

"Good. I don't like you exhausting yourself."

Warmth blossomed in Torquil's chest at Emrys' words. They were so accustomed to rejecting his generosity, confident it was only charity. But his words were too heated to be charitable. They leaned their head against Emrys', enjoying the way he didn't rush them. On the contrary, Emrys settled into the seat, bringing his hand to stroke between Torquil's shoulder blades. They kissed his neck.

"How was the opera?"

He grunted. "Everyone seemed to have a good time."

"I heard you didn't."

"Yes, well, the opera box was notably lacking one guest."

"I'm sorry."

He sighed. "Don't be. I missed you. That's all."

They wondered briefly if they ought to confess that Wyndham and Roger knew about this relationship. But a small, selfish part of them worried it would mean Emrys would leave. So instead they said, "I missed you, too."

Emrys' hand stroked through their hair. "It's strange. You've only just started entering into society and now it feels like you've always belonged there. There's a...a lack when you're absent."

They twisted one of his buttons between their fingers as they processed his words. "That's a very kind thing to say," they said at last.

"You know I mean it."

"I know. You're not one to say things you don't mean. I've always liked that."

Emrys shifted to encourage Torquil to sit up again. They obliged. He looked searchingly into their face. "Are you sure you're all right? You seem very...I don't know...sad?"

Torquil gave a small smile and traced Emrys' jaw with their fingertip. "Not sad. Just...it's been...I don't know. With the Council and the project and all of these events. Not to mention the *Tribune* on top of it. It's a lot."

He caught their wrist and kissed their palm. "Too much?" he asked quietly.

"I'm not sure yet. But I have a feeling that if it is, I won't be able to go back to how it was before. I think the Council and the social events will...I think they'll always be a part of my life now. It's too important."

Emrys rubbed a hand up Torquil's side soothingly. "What about the *Tribune*?"

Torquil looked over Emrys' shoulder at the draft on the desk. "I'm still working that out, to be honest. It was everything I had for so long— well," they added with a smile, "almost everything. But I'm not sure it's...compatible with my future."

Emrys was quiet for a long moment, rubbing his cheek against Torquil's palm almost absently. Torquil thought he might be trying to think of a subject change so they were surprised when he said, "And what do you imagine your future will hold?"

They considered the question. "If I'm lucky, more projects like this one. I'm hoping the social things will get easier. Maybe I'll meet more people like you, Wyndham, Roger, Iris, and Aveline. I'd like to get to a point where I can help other people like me integrate into society."

Emrys seemed to hesitate before asking, "And marriage?"

Torquil looked at him in surprise. "What?"

"Do you want to get married? You've never really talked about it."

Torquil was quite certain there was only one person in the world they could possibly marry. "Perhaps," they hedged. "If the right person asked me."

Emrys gave a bright grin in response. "I'm glad to hear it."

Torquil laughed, surprised. "Well, you know I always aim to please."

Emrys kissed them, deepening the kiss with unexpected tenderness. When they broke off, they felt as though they were dangerously on the cusp of some frightful confessions. "Speaking of aiming to please, I believe I promised you a fire spell."

"Do you have everything you need for it?"

Torquil nodded. "I just went to the market today."

They both stood and situated themselves on the floor, with Torquil facing the stove and Emrys sitting behind them to watch closely over their shoulder. As Torquil began preparing everything, setting up the ingredients and writing on the spellpaper, they felt a buzz of magic stirring around them. They glanced up at Emrys.

He shrugged self-consciously. "Don't want a repeat of yesterday."

"Protection?"

He nodded.

They hesitated. "You seem quite proficient in that."

"Oh," he said with a smile. "You noticed?"

"Only recently."

He brushed a lock of hair behind their ear. "I'd do more if I could, you know."

They quickly turned back to the spell and finished writing it, their hands shaking slightly. "Right," they said in a brusque tone. "Have you ever seen a human fire spell before?"

"A couple of times. We have some human servants. But nothing in detail."

"This one is a little simple. Only a few ingredients. Roger started me off with a one-ingredient spell but we're working up to more complex ones. Sometimes the more complex ones last longer, sometimes they'll smell nicer, or sometimes both." They were babbling and they hated it. They weren't used to feeling so vulnerable. Torquil had always felt so safe with Emrys, but they felt as though they were teetering towards a strange new sort of intimacy, one more terrifying than making love had ever been.

Emrys' hand landed on their waist and began rubbing gently up and down. "That makes sense. I'm glad Roger is easing you into things. What else do you need to set it up?"

"That's it."

Emrys leaned into their space and pressed a soft kiss to their jaw. "Go ahead," he whispered against their skin.

They took a deep breath and cast. The fire sparked into life and they reached out to sense it. They felt Emrys' magic instantly, filling the room, surrounding them both. It felt more familiar now and Torquil allowed themself to relax and sink into the familiarity as they coaxed magic into the spell. It burned brighter. Emrys nuzzled against their neck. "More," he breathed.

They increased the power slightly.

Emrys' kisses moved down to the bottom of their neck as his hands roamed over their thighs. "More," he demanded.

Their breathing grew labored as they increased the magic again, feeling Emrys' magic swirling around them like a heavy perfume. They tilted their head back and murmured his name. The fire blazed as Emrys' magic filled the stove, building on the spell. They could feel their own magic winding in and through Emrys' in a way that felt tantalizingly *right*. They turned into his arms and kissed him.

CHAPTER 31

EMRYS

THE ONLY WORD Emrys could focus on was *heat*. Heat radiating from the stove where they'd both fed Torquil's spell with their fae magic. Heat that had been smoldering within him since the encounter the day before, when he'd nearly destroyed his brother's study for the chance to feel Torquil's magic again. Heat as Torquil leaned into the kiss, moving to straddle his lap there on the floor so swiftly that Emrys had to put a hand behind him to catch himself from falling.

He used his other arm to wrap around Torquil's lower back, hauling them closer as Torquil's hands came to the sides of his neck. More heat began to pool in all the right places as Torquil rocked their hips in a way that made Emrys groan and break their kiss.

"I've been desperate for you since yesterday," he managed, keeping his eyes closed as Torquil's fingers moved to the buttons on his waistcoat.

"You've always been weak for a bit of destruction," Torquil teased, and Emrys grinned.

"That was not my intent. I sent replacements this morning for everything that was broken." Emrys felt his waistcoat slide down his arms and sat up enough to move it out of their way. "I would've offered for them to go and pick out what they wanted themselves, but

Wyndham would have refused, so I did the best I could from memory."

Torquil's answer was a hum against his mouth as they kissed him. His cravat disappeared before they pulled back again, and Emrys forced his eyes open to watch as Torquil continued to undress him. The glow from the stove cast shadows that sharpened their features; the strong line of their jaw and brow, the curve of their lips. How could anyone fault Emrys for being overzealous when it came to someone so stunning?

Emrys allowed himself to be guided onto his back before Torquil got to their feet and began to tug their shirt free from their trousers. Ordinarily, Emrys would've had the restraint to lie back and enjoy the teasing for as long as Torquil wanted to drag it out, but he'd been telling the truth when he said he'd been positively ruttish and barely able to conceal it. Sitting through the opera surrounded by his family in such a condition had been torture.

As such, he unfastened his trousers and lifted his hips just enough to shove them down his thighs. He propped himself up on one elbow and reached for Torquil after they'd removed their own and kicked them aside. As they returned to their knees, the loose fabric of their shirttail brushed against his erection. Emrys drew in a sharp breath through his teeth.

Torquil leaned to kiss the side of his neck. "Sensitive, are we?"

"Embarrassingly so, I'm afraid," Emrys admitted, though he was far from bashful about his current state. "Reminds me of the way I used to find you when all of this between us was new," he added with a playful fondness in his voice.

"How's that?" Torquil asked between placing soft kisses down Emrys' neck to his bare shoulder. "Hard and burning for a wealthy older gentleman to come and ravish me?"

Emrys snorted a laugh. "Exactly." His hands slid beneath Torquil's shirt and up their back.

"And how do you find me now?" Torquil sat up enough to meet Emrys' gaze, and the lightness of their conversation faltered. Emrys swallowed as his hands settled on Torquil's hips. Did they want the truth? Could Emrys give it?

Could he tell them that he looked forward to seeing them even more now than he had all those years ago? Could he admit that he hadn't been with anyone else for nearly two? Could he look Torquil in the eye and say that finding them had been one of the best things that had ever happened to him?

Emrys made a thoughtful face. He reached for one of Torquil's hands and brought it up to inspect. "A bit more ink-stained," he began, before kissing their fingers. He set it back where he'd taken it from and cupped their cheek. "A bit more tired." He leaned up to kiss them. "But still rather perfect."

Torquil grinned and rolled their eyes before they pushed Emrys back down to the floor and pressed their mouths together. Hips moved and hands wandered until their hair was wrecked and both of them were panting. With the fire still burning brightly beside them, Emrys wondered if the room had ever been so hot before. Not that he minded the effect it was having on both of them, and the way his palms slid over Torquil's damp, silken skin.

"How do you want me?" Torquil asked.

Emrys shifted his shoulders and winced. "Unfortunately, the price you pay for sleeping with wealthy older gentlemen is a lack of spontaneity," he groaned.

Torquil laughed lightly and got up. "Bed it is, then."

Emrys followed, bracing his weight on the desk to pull his trousers and shoes the rest of the way off. His gaze wandered absently over Torquil's notes and a stack of letters as he reached for the drawer where he knew he would find the small glass bottle he was after.

"Looks as though you have plenty of material for the *Tribune* tomorrow," he said as he turned around. Torquil had arranged themself in a most tempting way on their stomach, shirt exposing just enough of their backside that Emrys forgot everything he'd just been saying.

"Get away from there, you busybody," Torquil warned. "I cannot have you spoiling the gossip before I can properly release it."

"I wouldn't dare," Emrys promised as he joined Torquil on the bed. "Besides, the people of London would not care to hear it from me. Yours is the only voice they wish to listen to on matters of such importance."

"Your flattery is not necessary," Torquil said, slightly muffled against the pillow they'd wrapped an arm around. "You've already got me naked."

Emrys grinned as he shuffled closer on his knees, leaning forward to kiss the back of Torquil's neck. "Just accept the compliment, would you?" he murmured against their ear.

He nearly lost himself at the way Torquil responded to the combination of the fragrant rose oil and a couple of his fingers. The heat of the room continued to intensify, making Torquil's breathy moans that much heavier. Emrys felt his own perspiration rolling down the center of his back as he reclaimed his hand to collect more of the oil.

"It's bloody stifling in here," Torquil said on an exhale. They let go of the pillow to push a hand back through their hair, which Emrys could see had started to stick to their forehead.

Emrys made a distracted sound of agreement as he rubbed his hands together. "Hope you've had the chimney sweep come by recently." He knew nothing of what was involved in the proper maintenance of fireplaces and the like, but both his family's townhouse and country estate had one in nearly every room, so he knew that frequent visits were for the better.

"You think I can afford a chimney sweep?"

That got Emrys' attention. The cheeky grin Torquil gave him in return earned them a hard look. As he worked the oil on himself next, he took a deep breath and called on his magic to pay a visit to the candles scattered around the room. They slowly blinked out, one at a time, until there was only one source of light and warmth left in the room.

Torquil looked at Emrys over their shoulder. "Why don't you put the stove out, as well?"

"And ruin your hard work?" Emrys asked. He frowned as he tucked his fingers into the bend of Torquil's legs and pulled their hips up just roughly enough to make them gasp. "I think not."

He kept one hand on Torquil's hip and used the other to guide himself as he brought them together, slow but purposeful. Torquil pressed their face into the pillow and let out a strangled cry, but the way they pushed right back into Emrys told him to keep going.

Before long, Emrys regretted his decision to leave the stove lit. The heat was bordering on uncomfortable; it was so distracting that he could scarcely form a clear thought. Something had to be spurring it on.

"Are you still using your magic?" he panted.

Torquil whimpered softly in response, fingers wrapped tightly in whatever fabric they could reach. "No. I'm not trying to, anyway."

As hesitant as he was to have a repeat of the last time their magics touched, he'd tried to use what he could of his own to prevent it. Something had to be done about the stove before both of them fell unconscious. He supposed the other option was to stop what they were in the middle of, but he had a feeling neither of them wanted that. Emrys reached out with his magic again, drawing air from the crack in the window, and his entire body instantly lit from within as the room went dark.

"Emrys!" Torquil yelped, just as Emrys used his body to shield them from whatever was about to happen around them. Perhaps Torquil's small shelf of books above the bed would fall, or a beam would collapse from the roof overhead.

But it was quiet, save for their ragged breathing.

"Are you all right?" Emrys asked, using a hand on Torquil's shoulder to guide them to their back on the bed. He could hear Torquil swallow hard.

"Yes," they said after a pause, chest still heaving. "Are you?"

He was more than fine. He was awestruck. He was speechless.

He cupped the side of Torquil's face and choked back a sob of a laugh.

He was in so much trouble.

Emrys pinned Torquil to the bed with a crushing kiss, supporting his weight on his forearm as his other hand disappeared into their limp, wet curls after bringing them together again. Torquil wrapped themself around Emrys in response, one hand on his side, the other fisted against the back of his neck as they moved together like nothing had happened.

Oh, but it had. Feeling the spark of Torquil's magic brought Emrys to life in a way he never knew was possible.

They found such a rhythm that the pitiful excuse of furniture Torquil called a bed started sounding its protest, creaking and swaying in a way that it was rather fortunate Torquil lived alone. As much as he did not want to, Emrys tried to slow himself down before the thing collapsed beneath them.

"Don't stop," Torquil breathed. Emrys hadn't noticed when they'd brought their legs up around his hips, but he certainly felt the way their heels pressed against the backs of his thighs, urging him on and holding him even closer.

Emrys let out a groan of frustration as he pressed his face against Torquil's neck and rocked into them the way they'd asked. This was a perfect example of why it vexed him to no end that Torquil would not allow him to buy them anything. Countless times he'd offered to replace the bed with a nicer one, and each time they refused. So instead, they got to pretend they belonged to some ancient army and call up the battering ram against Torquil's poor bedroom wall.

"This is ridiculous," Emrys muttered against their skin. "If you will not allow me to fix your bed, then I will simply have to find a way to get you into mine."

Emrys' declaration sent Torquil's quiet, amorous sounds to a higher, more erratic place. He placed a long kiss against the side of their neck and sat back enough to allow Torquil to work themself to their release. His eyes had adjusted to the low light just enough to see a rough outline of what was happening beneath him, and it was enough to get him there, as well. He pulled out and came with a few vigorous strokes, heart pounding, magic still swirling.

The two collapsed into a heap of tangled limbs and drenched bedclothes. Emrys was glad for the heat lingering in the room then, since it meant neither of them needed to move to reach for the blanket. The thought did cross his mind, however, that it would've been nice to be able to call down for a glass of water for each of them. There were no servants to call upon, though. Only Torquil and him and the growing silence around them as their breathing returned to normal.

Emrys knew he should leave so Torquil could at least attempt to get some rest before they had to be up to work on the *Tribune*. Torquil knew it, too, but somehow Emrys was always the one sneaking out after they'd fallen asleep in his arms after asking him to stay just a little longer.

His brows furrowed. Torquil hadn't moved from their spot on the bed.

"Are you asleep?" he asked, just above a whisper. When there came no response, Emrys sat up and began carefully untangling himself so that he could find his clothes. After stumbling around a bit, he sighed and snapped his fingers as quietly as he could. A small cluster of fairy lights came to life near his shoulder and provided just enough of a glow for him to see.

Emrys was finishing the last buttons on his waistcoat when the silence was broken.

"You didn't really mean it, did you?" Torquil's voice was soft. Emrys turned to look at them, surprise and then confusion coating his face.

"Mean what?" he asked, stepping closer to the bed so he could sit on the edge of it. The fairy lights drifted toward the ceiling.

"What you said, about...about your bed."

Emrys huffed a silent laugh, grinning a little in the dark. He leaned toward Torquil and placed a kiss on their forehead.

"You said it yourself," he began, forcing himself to his feet so he would not be tempted by his own want to stay. "I do not say things I don't mean."

Emrys left before he could say any more.

TORQUIL'S TRIBUNE

Greetings, fetching folk and hearty humans,

Tomorrow marks the official beginning of the winter holiday festivities here in London. The fae community will be gathering for their annual skating party and winter market. Both the rink and the market will remain open to the public after tomorrow evening. For tomorrow, the Birch family is hosting the celebration and sources say this will be a veritable who's who of fae circles.

Many are already speculating who will be in attendance, but what is more intriguing to this writer are the possibilities of romantic interludes. There are a number of eligible fae folk. Will tomorrow night be the night they find their match?

A great deal of attention will likely be on Miss Aveline Wrenwhistle. At a recent dinner party, she was seated with Mr. Arlen Buckthorn. Mr. Buckthorn has long been known for his fashion sense and his gentle nature. Sources say the conversation was somewhat one-sided. But that doesn't seem to bother Miss Wrenwhistle, considering Mr. Buckthorn's recent visit to the Wrenwhistle home for tea earlier this week. There have been rumors of flowers being sent as well. Could these two find love under the stars tomorrow? We can all but hope.

Speaking of the Wrenwhistle family, we have received a number of inquiries regarding a more intimate acquaintance. It is true that this writer has been honored to be included in family dinners and other informal gatherings. However, it must be noted that Mr. Wyndham and Roger Wrenwhistle are collaborators on a Council project that this writer has been fortunate enough to be assigned. While closer friendship with the family is certainly appreciated, we ask that readers not read too much between the lines, particularly in regards to Mr. Emrys Wrenwhistle. We do not know what the gentleman is looking for in a spouse, and we certainly do not know who. If any readers have a theory, be so good as to forward it on.

In addition to the as-yet-unmarried Wrenwhistle siblings, guests will likely be curious as to whether Mr. Cricket will be attending with anyone on his arm. Will Mx. Hillcrest be bringing guests? Considering they have lately been seen on friendly terms with some notable humans of genteel birth, many are curious if they will be invited to attend the fae event. We do not doubt Mr. Ravenwing will be accompanied, although we have a great many questions as to who that will be.

We want to express our sincere gratitude to those who have submitted replies in response to the query about fae-human magic. It has become increasingly evident that those with mixed blood have a unique and extraordinary magic. It deserves more study and more appreciation. Please believe that we are working tirelessly to achieve both.

Your esteemed editor,
Torquil Pimpernel-Smith

CHAPTER 32

TORQUIL

TORQUIL DOZED on and off after Emrys left. The evening filled with vulnerable discussion, powerful magic, and enthusiastic activity in bed had well and truly wrung them out. When they finally dragged themself out of bed and down to the press, they kept hearing Emrys' words in their head. *There's a lack when you're absent* and, later, his exasperated declaration that he would have to get them into his bed.

Even as the statement had been made through panting breaths and gritted teeth, it had sent a tremor through Torquil and they had yet to fully process it. Emrys wanted them in his bed. On the one hand, they knew they shouldn't be surprised. He'd been coming to their bed for almost five years. On the other hand, there had always been an unspoken boundary between them. Emrys visited when it was dark, when it was safe, when he was unnoticed. Would he expect to sneak Torquil up the back stairs? Would they creep out of the house before the sun came up like Emrys did? Somehow, they weren't sure they'd be capable of it.

They resolutely pushed the thought from their mind as they released the *Tribune*. When Sal came in, she took one look at them and said, "You look terrible. Isn't your lover treating you right?"

Torquil glared at her.

She crossed her arms and leaned against the press. "You think I didn't know about that? We've all been talking about it. No one minds. Lucky for you, the upper class is more oblivious than the lower class."

"At least some of them," they agreed.

"You could stand to be a little more obvious in the *Tribune*," she mused. "He might not know how you feel. You keep going on about who he should be marrying. Maybe you should start hinting at yourself." She gave them a wink.

"Any more sage advice?"

"Sleep more."

They snorted. "Helpful."

"Isn't there anything you can have someone else help you with?"

They cast a long look at the press, giving the question proper thought. "I like making my rounds to gather gossip, but maybe you can take over that for the time being?"

She brightened. "I'd love to! I already know who you talk to and how often you go to different spots. I'll start tomorrow!" She left promptly as if she expected them to take back the request.

Wyndham and Roger were just as appallingly nosy as Sal had been about what Torquil had written ("What do you mean you don't know what Emrys is looking for in a spouse?" and "Maybe you should interview him tomorrow night."), but Torquil managed to steer the conversation to the topic of their project. For two full days the three of them worked on the rubric, with Roger suggesting spells to be used for testing and Wyndham observing Torquil's casting.

By the time the sun started to set on the evening of the fae event, Torquil regretted agreeing to the invitation. Their apprehension grew when Wyndham announced that they would be wearing his clothes again.

"You really need to stop lending me things," they grumbled as they followed him upstairs.

He scoffed. "I will when you have someone to spoil you with clothes of your own. Tonight we need to dress for the occasion," he added with relish. As it turned out, dressing for the occasion apparently meant a velvet suit of deep scarlet and matching waistcoat. The waistcoat had gold threads sewn in little flourishes all over the fabric.

"Are you sure you wish to part with this?" Torquil asked.

"It's a bit too understated for my tastes," Wyndham explained.

"I might ruin it. I haven't skated since I was a small child."

Wyndham seemed amused. "Oh, I doubt that will happen. Besides, you'll be wearing a coat over it for at least part of the evening anyway."

"Then why do I need to—"

"When it comes to matters of haberdashery, I think I have some expertise," he replied in a tone that brooked no argument.

Torquil sighed. "Very well."

Wyndham brightened. "And I took the liberty of acquiring an additional item for you."

"You needn't have done that," they protested.

He gave them a quelling look. "My brother could hardly take his eyes off you when you wore a comb in your hair…both times. Besides, you look very becoming in hair accessories. But it will be cold and I don't wish you to catch a chill." He beckoned to a servant, who brought forth a hat box. Wyndham opened it and pulled out a hat. It was a more feminine style, much like the comb had been. Torquil couldn't resist running a fingertip over the brim, hardly daring to believe that they would get to wear something so beautiful.

Wyndham carefully set it on their head. "This will sit at an angle so your hair will still be shown to advantage. But it will keep your head warm." The servant passed over a comb and Wyndham set it into their curls in a way that displayed the comb, held the hat in place, and pulled their hair out of their face. Wyndham tied their cravat knot and added a pin to match the comb. "Perfect. He will be completely oblivious to the rest of his surroundings for the whole of the evening, if we're lucky. Now why don't you wait downstairs with Roger while I get dressed? Won't be a minute."

"I'm not entirely sure why you want him so distracted. It isn't as if we could get married."

"Isn't it?"

"And I'm not sure he wants to," they added, lifting their chin.

Wyndham snorted in response.

Torquil made their way downstairs where Roger was waiting. "You look marvelous!" he breathed.

"Wyndham insisted."

"Emrys won't be able to take his eyes off you."

Torquil glared at him.

Roger stifled a laugh behind his hand.

"His mother will be there," Torquil said, carefully touching a hand to the hat. "I am sure she will see to it that Emrys is occupied. You two are getting your hopes up for nothing."

Roger gave a sly grin and said nothing.

After significantly longer than a minute, Wyndham joined them downstairs and they left for the festivities. As soon as they arrived, Torquil was relieved that their companions brought them to Iris instead of Emrys.

Iris looked them over appraisingly. "My word, you do look well, Torquil," she said. "Wyndham has such a good eye for these things, doesn't he?"

Torquil moved to touch the hat again self-consciously but Wyndham batted their hand away. "I'm not used to such…" They gestured vaguely. "Fripperies."

"Roger fell in love with me for my waistcoats," Wyndham said matter-of-factly. "Never underestimate well-placed fripperies."

"It was *not* because of your waistcoats," Roger muttered.

Iris laughed and tucked her hand around their arm. "I know it all feels very strange still, but you really are doing much better than you think. We're aiming to make you a fashionable member of society in your own right. Is there anything not to your taste? There's a market tonight. I'm sure we could—"

"No, no," they said hastily. "Everything is lovely. It's just…a great deal *more* than I'm accustomed to."

She smiled. "I understand. But as long as you don't dislike anything in particular, I think this will do quite nicely. It's a perfect mixture of blending in and standing out. It suits you."

They were so touched by the compliment that they could think of nothing to say in response as they were led through the crowd.

"Now," she said, "I have arranged for you to have a companion this evening. Someone to make sure you talk to people, but that you also have a pleasant time." She gave a graceful grimace. "I can ensure the former but I fear I am not always successful in the latter. And Wyndham and Roger, bless their hearts, are quite gifted in the latter, but they will hide you away for the entire evening and I don't want that either."

Torquil chose not to say that Wyndham and Roger would likely do nothing of the kind considering their current matchmaking proclivities. Instead, they said, "That was very considerate of you, but I don't want you to go to any trouble."

She tsked. "Nonsense. It's no trouble. You two seemed to get along very well during the dinner party. I'm sure he'll take good care of you tonight."

Torquil felt alarm bells ringing in their head. "What?"

"Ah, there he is," she said, leading them directly to Emrys.

Torquil had no idea whether they felt more dread or exhilaration at the idea of spending the entire evening with Emrys. What would his mother think? What would everyone say? They were going to look like a complete fool after what they had printed in the *Tribune* the previous day. But considering how wonderful he had been in the garden at the dinner party, Torquil knew they could trust Emrys to keep them safe and that realization made them nearly dizzy with relief.

Emrys turned as they approached and Torquil noted with interest the obvious approval as his gaze raked slowly over them. Iris placed a hand on her grandson's arm. "Thank you, darling, for accompanying Torquil. I know you'll take good care of them." She gave him a peck on the cheek and glided off.

They stared at each other in silence for an agonizingly long moment.

Finally, Emrys said, "You look incredible," in a voice that was more gravelly than usual.

"Thank you," Torquil said quietly. "I was, once again, Wyndham's personal fashion plate."

Emrys gave a small smile and touched a fingertip to the comb. "Far be it from me to compliment my brother on anything, but he chose well." He held out an arm gallantly. "Shall we?"

Torquil slid their hand into the crook of his elbow and was shocked by how comforting it was to walk through the crowd at his side. At first, most people seemed to ignore Torquil in favor of greeting Emrys. But

Emrys was fastidious about introducing them as "the newest member of the Council for Fae & Human Relations" and "the writer of the best paper in London." It would have been embarrassing if it hadn't been so gratifying. They were almost feeling optimistic about the evening when Mrs. Wrenwhistle found them.

"There you are," she said, bustling over. "I've been looking all over for you," she said to her son. "I'd like you to escort Lady Cynthia Proust this evening."

"I cannot, Mother."

Her eyes narrowed. "I promised you a few days. But you really need to focus on the matter at hand."

"I already promised Grandmother that I would escort Councilmember Pimpernel-Smith tonight."

She looked at Torquil as if she had only just noticed them. "Oh. I didn't realize you were coming this evening."

"Iris asked that I attend."

"I'm sure she did," she muttered. "Well, I'm certain she can find someone else to walk you around. After all, this is more of a fae event anyway. So you really—"

"Torquil *is* fae, Mother. And Lady Proust, might I add, is not."

"I invited her expressly to spend the evening with you."

"Well, I'm very much afraid you will have to entertain her. As I said, I've already given my word to keep Torquil company."

Torquil wanted to sink into the ground with the way Mrs. Wrenwhistle looked at them. They wondered if Emrys had realized he'd used their first name.

"And what would you have me say to Lady Proust? And what will people think when they see you all evening with this—"

"Councilmember? I suppose they'll think we're becoming better acquainted," he said, laying a hand over Torquil's. "And I'm sure Lady Proust will understand when you tell her I was not aware of your plans."

She made an exasperated sound and stormed off.

"You didn't need to do that," Torquil said.

"Do what?"

"Get on your mother's bad side. And for my sake."

Emrys rolled his eyes. "It is frightfully easy to get on her bad side these days. Aveline is currently making calf eyes at that Buckthorn fellow, so I'm sure my mother will be properly distracted by that in no time. Besides, I don't like the way she talks to you. It isn't right."

"It's how a great many people talk to me, Emrys."

"It isn't right," he repeated harshly.

"She's not wrong, you know," they said quietly. "People will talk."

"I'm used to being talked about."

"Your reputation—"

Emrys turned so that he was facing Torquil and put his free hand on their shoulder. "You are too much my friend for me to abandon you in a large event like this. I know how much you hate these things and I know how hard you're trying to get used to them. When Grandmother mentioned that she was looking for someone to keep you company all evening, I volunteered."

Torquil blinked up at him. "You did?"

Emrys looked exasperated. "Of course! As for my reputation," he went on, giving a small tweak to Torquil's cravat, "I can think of worse things than to escort a stunning creature like you all evening. You're far better company than most of the people my mother is attempting to saddle me with. So do stop fretting about it. I have the whole evening planned out." He turned back to be on Torquil's side and continued leading them through the crowd.

"Do you?" Torquil said, trying to hide how touched they were by his words. "And what plans are those?"

"We're going to complete our circuit for the sake of socialization. Then we're going to skate. After that, I expect you'll need something hot so we'll get some mulled wine. Then we can wander through the market."

"That sounds rather nice."

"I know," Emrys said, puffing his chest out a little. It was adorable.

Torquil laughed. "I hate to ruin your plans, though. I'm quite terrible on the ice. I fell when I was little and went right through and into the water. Got a dreadful chill. I haven't attempted it since."

Emrys looked horrified for a moment before he collected himself.

"Well, I'll see to it you don't fall tonight." He sounded so confident that Torquil didn't have the heart to argue further.

Just as they were nearing the end of Emrys' proposed circuit, they were waylaid by Councilmember Cricket.

"Emrys!" She greeted him warmly. "Keelan's been looking for you."

"I've been here for over an hour. He's just not looking hard enough."

She laughed. "Well, that's my son for you." She noticed Torquil on his arm and her smile dropped. "I had no idea you would be here tonight, Mx. Pimpernel-Smith."

"Iris requested that I attend."

"Councilmember," Emrys said.

"Yes?" she asked, looking up at him.

"It's *Councilmember* Pimpernel-Smith," he said.

"Oh," she said faintly. "Yes, of course. How silly of me to forget. It's just been *so long* since you were in the chambers."

"They've been working every day on that rubric project," Emrys said. "I can't remember the last time my brother reported taking a break."

"Ah, yes. How is that project coming along?"

Torquil gripped Emrys' arm for comfort and raised their chin. "It's coming along quite well, thank you. A great deal more work than any of us anticipated, I think. It seems as though fae-human magic has been largely neglected for far too long. We have a great deal of catching up to do before we can determine the best way to measure a magic system that no one has bothered to study." They gave her a charming smile.

"I thought you said you weren't very skilled in magic," she retorted. "It hardly makes sense to study a lack of skill."

"My mistake," they said. "We've come to learn it isn't a lack of skill. It's an entirely different skill set."

"And it's extraordinary," Emrys put in.

She stared up at him. "You've been joining, Emrys?"

"My brother invited me to observe recently. I've never seen anything like it."

"Oh," she said. "Well, carry on, I suppose. Oh and do see to it you find my son so he can stop pestering me."

Emrys bowed and led Torquil swiftly towards the ice. "Are they all like that to you?" he said, his voice heated.

"They're usually worse," they admitted.

"Insufferable," he muttered.

"Thank you for standing up for me. It was very kind of you."

Emrys frowned at them. "I corrected her for not addressing you properly. You stood up for yourself, although you damn well shouldn't have to."

Torquil wanted to laugh at how stony Emrys' expression was, but they didn't quite dare. There was a light, bubbly feeling in their chest at how upset Emrys was on their behalf, how immediately he had corrected Cricket, how he had stood up to his mother, and how he had *asked* to be with them all night.

Torquil had a strange and sudden suspicion that Emrys would not expect them to sneak up the backstairs to join him in bed. And, for some reason, that mattered a great deal more than it should have.

Emrys rented them both skates and guided them to a bench to put them on. He knelt to secure the skates to the bottom of Torquil's shoes. Torquil lifted their feet to inspect the skates and verify the tightness, noting that the blades ended in decorative curls at the front.

Emrys tapped the curl at the toe. "Reminded me of your hair," he said with a grin. Then he sat down beside them and strapped his own skates on. He stood and held out a hand. "Ready?"

"No," they said simply.

He rolled his eyes and pulled them to their feet. "You'll be fine."

As soon as the skates hit the ice, Torquil was absolutely, entirely certain that they would *not* be fine. Their arms started to pinwheel as they attempted to gain balance. Just as they were about to fall back and embarrass themself completely, Emrys slipped an arm around their waist, bracing himself at their back. Torquil gripped his arm tightly.

"It's all right," he murmured in their ear. "I've got you. Let's start with our left feet, shall we?"

They took a deep breath and nodded, carefully following Emrys' lead. Emrys slid his free hand into Torquil's grasp, as if they were dancing. Torquil could tell by the speed of the people around them that they were traveling slowly but it still felt too fast. They tightened their hold in Emrys' hand.

Emrys made a humming sound. "If I'd known you'd react like this, I would have taken you on the ice much sooner, socializing be damned."

"Cruel creature," Torquil bit out.

Emrys laughed and pulled them closer as he increased their speed slightly. "Well, when it results with you in my arms like this I don't see how you could possibly blame me."

Torquil smiled a little despite themself. The teasing was familiar, like being back on solid ground. This was Emrys, after all. As they started to gain more confidence, they relaxed enough to lift their gaze from the ice and look around. They wanted to drop their gaze back down to the ice immediately when they noticed all of the curious looks pointed in their direction. They had no idea how they were going to explain this away in the *Tribune*. Absolutely no one would believe them if they started speculating about Emrys' prospects now.

They tilted their face back a little and said, "If you're going to hold me like this in public, the least you can do is give me something to write about later."

"What did you have in mind?" Emrys said teasingly.

"I shall have to find some way to explain this to my readers. Perhaps if you gave me an exclusive interview about what you're looking for in a spouse, they'll be so impressed with my conniving ability of persuasion that they'll forgive me for the dalliance they are most certainly privately accusing me of."

Emrys was quiet for such a long moment that Torquil started to worry they'd offended him.

"Emrys?" they said at last.

"Sorry," he said hastily. "I'm afraid I may need you to repeat that. I got lost a bit halfway through."

They laughed. "Perhaps we'd better continue the conversation after we're done skating."

"Well, it would help if I could see you better," he said, pulling away.

Torquil gasped and reached for him.

Emrys swung around so he was facing them, skating backward. He took their flailing hand in his. "It's all right," he said gently. "I'm right here."

"A little warning next time, if you please."

"Oh, will there be a next time?" he said brightly. "I was beginning to think you'd never let me bring you on the ice again."

They rolled their eyes. "That's a definite possibility."

"Hm. I may have to insist that you let me anyway. Your cheeks are so rosy right now." He gave them a twinkling smile. "I like it."

Torquil found themself ill equipped to respond to such charm. They grappled for something to say. "Aren't you worried you'll run into someone like that?"

Emrys shrugged. "I've done this for years."

"But you're not even looking behind you."

"There are other ways to sense things."

Torquil's eyes widened. "Are you using magic right now?"

"Just feeling behind me to make sure I'm not going to hit anything. And a bit of protection around you," he added, squeezing their hands. "Why don't you see for yourself?"

"Isn't that dangerous? What about—"

"I won't blow up the ice."

Torquil huffed. They knew they probably shouldn't, but they really were curious, so they cautiously reached out with their magic. They could feel the protection around them first. It wasn't like a human protection spell, but as if Emrys had called upon the wind to surround Torquil like an invisible cushion. They could feel the eddies and swirls of the breeze rippling through the magic. Emrys had similarly manipulated the breeze to guide his back. They closed their eyes and focused, noting the way the wind shifted as people glided around them. They looked up at Emrys, impressed.

"You can do all of that while skating backwards?" they said incredulously.

He shrugged. "Used to do it all the time as a child." He gave a small grin. "Mostly to taunt Wyndham. He couldn't do it this well."

"Ah, I see. Skill borne out of enmity."

Emrys' expression shifted in that way Torquil had come to learn was bafflement. He smiled, a familiar one that suggested he didn't want

Torquil to know he didn't understand something. Their heart melted a little at the sight.

A snowflake drifted into view and Torquil tore their gaze away from Emrys' face. "I didn't realize it was going to snow tonight."

"Well, even if it wasn't, I'm sure someone would have orchestrated it."

"The fae do love an impressive outdoor event with the elements at their whim."

"Precisely."

Torquil noticed their pace slowing although they certainly didn't complain. Then Emrys reached up and brushed lightly through their uncovered curls, and Torquil's breath caught. He stilled with his fingertips against their cheek. Emrys was staring at them with something like wonder and they were definitely no longer moving at all. They felt their heart stutter at the look in his eyes. He looked as if he might kiss them, which would be both delightful and catastrophic.

"I'm afraid the hat is not entirely practical in terms of keeping the snow off," they managed.

Emrys licked his lips. "Well," he said, his voice husky again. "My brother has never been one for practicality when it comes to fashion. I've seen him wear silk in the rain."

Torquil smiled.

Emrys' fingers slid gently down their cheek. "Although I can't find it in me to complain in this case." He paused and then his forehead crinkled. "Unless you're cold?"

They shook their head. "No, not cold."

Emrys looked unconvinced. He seemed to shake himself mentally. "I'd better get you that wine I promised," he said. He looped their hand around his arm and led them off the ice.

CHAPTER 33

EMRYS

EMRYS KEPT his grip on Torquil's hand as he guided them toward the edge of the ice. He'd been pleased to find that they had acquired some beeswax-treated leather gloves to wear for the evening, rather than the thin cotton ones they typically wore. He suspected Wyndham had played as much of a role in that as he had the rest of Torquil's accessories. His younger brother's newfound generosity was quite surprising. Wyndham had never been known to go out of his way to help anyone when it did not directly benefit him, but it seemed to have become a new hobby of his. Perhaps it was yet another way that his marriage to Roger had changed him for the better.

Torquil bobbled a bit and Emrys gripped their hand tighter. He gave them what he hoped was a reassuring grin when their eyes met, though he couldn't be sure exactly what his face was doing. Despite the sturdier gloves and layers of outerwear, Torquil's cheeks and nose were still flushed with the chill of the air, and Emrys struggled to look away from them for any length of time. It was growing more difficult with each passing moment as snowflakes continued to settle on their dark hair and hat.

A shriek was what finally drew his attention away. He and Torquil both looked to find Roger flat on his back on the ice nearby. Emrys changed their course and glided to a stop before he let go of Torquil's hand.

"You're meant to use the skates, not your backside," he teased lightly as he reached for one of Roger's hands; Wyndham took the other. They got him sitting upright and Roger let out a shaky little laugh.

"I warned Wyn that I've always had a dreadful time with this," he said before he reached up to his face. "Oh dear, my spectacles."

"I've got them." As unsteady as they were on their own skates, Torquil had managed to pick them up from where they'd landed. It was fortunate that someone hadn't skated over them on the packed ice. Roger took them from Torquil with a sigh of relief and put them back on before he looked around, and then up at Wyndham.

"Er...I'm not certain I know how to get up."

"You'll have to get on your knees," Wyndham directed him.

Emrys snorted. "First on his back, then on all four. I daresay, Wyndham, you'll wear him out before the night has even begun."

Wyndham gave him a flat look as he stood protectively over Roger while he turned over. Each with a grip on his hands and elbows, Emrys and Wyndham were able to get him back up on his feet, but the moment Emrys let go Roger flailed and squeaked in alarm. He looked over his shoulder to make sure Torquil was doing well enough to follow behind on their own as he helped Wyndham get Roger safely to solid ground.

"Sorry to ruin everyone's fun," Roger muttered. He sat slumped on a bench as Wyndham removed his skates for him. Emrys and Torquil did the same on either side of him.

"Nonsense," Emrys said. "We were just coming off the ice ourselves to go and find something to warm up with. I promised Torquil some mulled wine."

"That does sound nice," Roger said, recovering slightly. "Wyn and I will join you."

"We will?" Wyndham asked. There was a look exchanged between the two of them, another unspoken conversation that shifted his brother's expression from aversion to one of sly intrigue. Emrys leaned back slightly to glance at Torquil, but they were hardly paying attention. Their focus was on the crowd that had nearly doubled in size while they'd been skating. Something tightened in Emrys' chest. He'd never been happier to be doing his grandmother a favor, for it meant that he had every excuse to keep Torquil close.

After returning their skates, Emrys held out his arm for Torquil to take and they set off for the winter market with Wyndham and Roger trailing close behind. The air around them was thick with excitement and holiday cheer. Bare branches of the trees along the path were lit with thousands of fairy lights charmed to stay put, though some had still broken free and were floating lazily about. Evergreen boughs had been fastened to the trunks, tied with ribbons, and adorned with clusters of red berries and tiny bells that chimed all on their own from time to time.

Wyndham let out a long sigh. "Have some discretion, dear sister."

Emrys turned to look out on the ice. Aveline was indeed making a fair spectacle of herself as she and Mr. Buckthorn danced together on their skates, twirling and showing off the way only two fae could. Even from a distance, he could see that they looked sickeningly happy. Emrys chuckled and raised an eyebrow down at Torquil.

"Ready yourself to announce another Wrenwhistle engagement," he said.

"If she keeps acting like that for all of society to see, they'll have no choice but to be married," Wyndham added a bit grumpily.

Emrys gave him a pointed glance over his shoulder.

"You do realize you're the youngest sibling, correct? What does it concern you if she's off gallivanting?" They were hardly the only ones being indiscreet. All around were friendly hugs and cheek kisses that lingered a bit too long, subtle hand touches disguised by greatcoats and thick shawls. There was an unmistakable undercurrent of *desire* and *want* and *romance* so strong you could nearly taste it, as was the case with most any public fae event, especially one around the holidays.

"Do you care nothing of her reputation?" Wyndham countered.

Emrys barked out a laugh. "Since when do you care about reputations? In case you've forgotten, yours was rather frightful and yet you still managed to find a spouse."

"What's your excuse, then?"

Wyndham's words sent an unpleasant chill up his spine.

"Wyn," Roger warned softly.

It was enough to quiet him, but Emrys could still feel the heat at his back. As though he needed any more reminders of how his brothers had both married before him, and now it seemed that his sister was close behind. He knew how it looked, to be the last to find a match despite being the most magically powerful sibling. If the promise of wealth and power and a secure place in society were not enough to tempt someone, then what could possibly be wrong with Emrys Wren-whistle?

Torquil's hand squeezing gently on his arm pulled Emrys from his thoughts.

As they approached the first stalls of the market, Roger broke their silence with a gasp of wonder. All the decorations they'd seen before carried over into the neat rows of vendors selling their wares. The strong scent of pine was quickly masked with warm spices and freshly baked bread. They passed by a small gathering of people who had stopped to listen to someone playing a bright tune on their flute.

Emrys looked forward to the event every year, but he soon found himself in the same position he'd been in on the ice, taking more interest in watching what Torquil thought than in his own enjoyment of what was happening around them. It didn't take long for Torquil to notice, and they gave him a questioning look.

"Is it anything like you expected?" he asked.

Torquil shrugged. "Yes. It's very loud."

"The wine will help," Emrys said. He guided them toward the stall that had sat in the same spot during this event for nearly a century, run by several generations of the same German family. There were other vendors selling a similar product, but Emrys had always liked theirs the best.

Drinks in hand, the four of them crowded around one of several rudimentary standing tables that had—rather conveniently—been set up near to where a country peat farmer was demonstrating the steady, low burn of the fire their product could create. Emrys took his first sip of the spiced wine and savored the warmth as it spread through his middle and across his face.

"Lovely, isn't it?" he asked after Torquil had done the same.

"It's delicious," Roger agreed. "It's a wonder why we only have it around the holidays. I could never tire of such a hot burst of comforting flavors."

"You might at the end of summer, when you're sweating through your clothes simply sitting and doing nothing," Emrys reminded him.

Roger's enthusiasm faded. "Oh, yes, I suppose you're right."

"It seems the weather was prepared for us to enjoy it fully this evening," Wyndham said as he peered up, squinting against the snowflakes that continued to fall. Emrys tilted his face toward the sky, as well, and closed his eyes. The contrast of the cold air and delicate snow against his rapidly warming skin was quite wonderful.

He pulled in a slow breath and thought of Keelan's advice. There were hundreds of people wandering around, shouting and laughing and even singing. A violinist was busy with a slower, dreamier piece somewhere nearby. Through it all, Emrys recognized it as one of life's quiet moments. A pause.

When he opened his eyes, Torquil was still there.

"Tipsy already, are we?" Wyndham asked.

Emrys blinked at him and furrowed his brow. "Me?"

"You're rather flushed," Roger added helpfully. "The both of you are, come to mention it. Perhaps you should remove your overcoat until you're walking around again, Torquil, so that you do not start to feel unwell."

Torquil gave Roger a long look before they set their wine down on the table. With a small wiggle of their shoulders, they worked the overcoat down their arms to reveal an outfit that Emrys was entirely unprepared for. He'd been taken with the hat and comb combination, but matched with the dark red fabric and details on the well-fitted waistcoat, it was as though the whole ensemble had been custom made for them.

"You've expanded your wardrobe, I see," Emrys said, still distracted.

"Only borrowed," Torquil said as they folded their coat over their arm and picked up their drink again. Emrys frowned a bit.

"Borrowed from where?" He looked at Wyndham. "Certainly that did not come directly from your endless supply. It fits them far too well."

That seemed to give Torquil a reason to question it, too.

"You said—"

"Forget what I said," Wyndham cut them off with a wave of his hand. "You look fabulous and I wanted you to feel confident this evening."

"You cannot just buy me clothes on a whim!" Torquil argued.

"I can and I have. Consider it an early solstice gift."

Torquil started to say something else, but then stopped, ending with a huff instead. It hadn't been fair of Wyndham to do it that way, but Emrys knew exactly how difficult it was to gift Torquil anything. It burned that Wyndham had figured out how to manage it in several weeks when he'd been trying for years.

"Well," Roger said after finishing his last sip of wine, "Wyn has promised to show me where I can find the best holiday cakes he's ever had, so perhaps we'll catch up later." Roger's hand curled around Wyn's arm effortlessly as they turned and slipped into the crowd.

Emrys stared after them for a moment before he turned to Torquil.

"You do look fabulous," he said with a cheeky grin. Torquil gave him an unimpressed look, which pulled a bubble of laughter from him as he reached to take both of their empty cups. "Let's go see what the market has to offer."

Emrys walked Torquil down the main path, explaining what he knew about the vendors that had returned from previous years and pausing to learn more from those he'd never seen. There were all the usual stalls selling any sort of clothing item you could think of, from stockings and gloves all the way up to furs and bejeweled hats. They were taken by surprise when a scarf seller looped one around Torquil's neck so quickly there'd been no time to protest.

"Looks lovely on you, dear, just lovely! Only cost you 2 shillings." The seller stuck out their hand at Emrys expectantly. Torquil looked up at him in mild distress as they started to remove the scarf.

"Oh, no thank you," Torquil tried carefully, but Emrys shook his head subtly and reached for the small purse he'd brought with him. He dropped the coins in their waiting palm and placed a hand on Torquil's back to guide them along.

"Before you protest, because I know you will," he started as soon as they were out of earshot, "you must understand that these vendors travel great distances to sell at markets such as this. For some, they might earn more tonight than they will the rest of the year combined." Emrys nodded and offered a polite smile to an acquaintance as they passed. "A few coins I will never miss mean a great deal to someone else. I know you can appreciate that. So please, allow me to do what is expected of me tonight. You can keep what you like and give away the rest. There must be someone in your life who would appreciate a warm scarf such as this." To his relief, Torquil only nodded.

They passed toymakers and booksellers, more clothes, and a stall selling orchids that had been charmed into full bloom, despite the cold. There were tables lined with jars of preserves and fruit jams alongside rows of magical ingredients and unique tea blends. Emrys thought to pause and look at some watch fobs, but lost interest as Torquil stepped closer to a cart nearby.

"See something you like?" he asked as he stopped beside them. At first, he wasn't quite sure what Torquil was looking at amongst the seemingly random collection on display.

"Ah," the man sitting behind the cart said with a smile and a thick accent. "I had a feeling the right person would come along tonight."

He picked up one of the pots of ink and held it out as though it were nothing important; Torquil reached for it with both hands like it was made of gold. They opened the jar and looked inside, rotating it just enough that it must've moved the ink around. They handed it back to the man, and Emrys finally realized what it was that had caught their attention.

Even with his basic level of interest in writing, he could appreciate the beauty of the inkstand, what with its dark wood finish and intricate brass details. Two swirled glass ink pots sat on either side of the delicate handle. The seller reached forward and pulled a small knob, revealing a drawer underneath the glass top for storage.

"Stunning craftsmanship," Emrys told the man. "Did you make this?"

"My father did," he said with evident pride.

Emrys hummed and smoothed a gloved fingertip along the curved design of the brass inlay. Just as he was about to ask the price, Torquil stepped away. Emrys looked after them and realized they weren't planning on stopping, either. He thanked the man for his time and hurried to catch up.

"Where are you off to?" he asked, but Torquil did not slow their pace. After bumping into several people in his effort to follow them, he let out a frustrated grunt and reached for Torquil's arm. He pulled them aside and into an alcove between two of the stalls. Torquil pulled out of his grip but remained still, thankfully.

"Do. Not," was all they said, staring up into Emrys' eyes. Emrys couldn't pretend that he did not know what Torquil meant.

"You like it," Emrys tried to reason, though more of his frustration came out than he'd intended.

"Of course I like it," Torquil said, looking away. "It's beautiful."

"Then why would you not wait at least long enough to hear the cost?"

"Because it's too much! Whatever it is, it's too much."

The hurt in Torquil's voice quelled the emotions Emrys had been struggling to hold back just moments before. He took a breath and let it out, further calming himself as he stepped closer. Emrys hooked a finger under their chin and pulled their face up so he could see them again. Torquil reached out to grab the fabric at the front of his coat and held on tightly.

"You deserve nice things," Emrys began gently. "Things that I have wished for many years to be able to give you." Torquil tried to look away again, but Emrys caught their chin in his fingertips this time. "You are my friend, Torquil, and I care about you very much. Why will you not allow me to show it?"

Torquil's response was a whisper. "What will people think?"

Emrys let his hand drop from Torquil's face as his heart sank. *Damn them*, he wanted to shout, *I do not care what they think of me!* Then, a realization brought a wave of uncertainty so strong his knees nearly buckled.

Perhaps Torquil was not concerned about what people thought of him, but what people thought of them. Was that it? Had Emrys become so distracted by his own feelings that he'd forgotten Torquil had a business to run, and respect to uphold on the Council, and a reputation of their own to maintain?

Torquil was right. For years, their relationship had remained as it was from the very start: quiet, private, uncomplicated. But from the moment Torquil entered society, Emrys had struggled to separate their private and public interactions to the point where he had volunteered to escort them that night. How could he have been so thoughtless?

"I'll make you a deal," Emrys said finally. "Allow me to buy the inkstand for you." Torquil's eyes went wide as they started to protest, but Emrys held up a hand to quiet them. "In exchange, I'll give you the interview, but I get to decide when. Until then, you can continue to leave your readers guessing." He pressed his palm flat over where the latest copy of the *Tribune* was tucked into his breast pocket. "Or perhaps you'll have readers send in their theories as you requested. That should be entertaining for the both of us."

Torquil stared up at him, arms crossed, jaw set. Emrys arched an eyebrow.

"Oh, very well," Torquil relented, though they did not sound particularly settled with the idea. "I cannot see how you're getting anything out of it, though."

"I am getting far more than what I deserve," he said.

Emrys sent Torquil to find whichever stall was selling the most delicious looking cinnamon bread as he returned to the cart to purchase the inkstand. He asked the man what else he thought might be important to go with it, and after selecting a few more items and the bottle of ink Torquil had looked at, Emrys walked away carrying a parcel wrapped with twine and a feeling of accomplishment so invigorating that he could not wipe the grin from his face.

As the event came to a close in the early hours of the morning, they were reunited with Wyndham and Roger. They offered to take Torquil home, but Emrys was already guiding them toward his own carriage. He had made a decision and intended to follow through with it, whatever the outcome.

Emrys was careful to allow Torquil to give the directions to the press building, even though he knew them just as well. They were quiet during the ride, sitting close but not too close, and Emrys kept his hands planted firmly on his thighs until the carriage eased to a stop just outside the familiar alley.

He got out and offered his hand to Torquil, which earned him a suspicious, albeit tired look. For the first time since the night they'd met,

Emrys did not care who saw him on the quiet side street. He did not check to see who was peeking at him from the windows above. He did not care about anything other than escorting Torquil safely to the door.

When they reached it, Torquil dug their key out of a pocket with the hand not holding the package and turned the lock with a quick glance over Emrys' shoulder.

"Are they going to wait for you?" they asked, sounding uncertain.

"I hope so," Emrys chuckled. "I'll only be a minute." Torquil's brows went up slightly, and Emrys couldn't miss their quick glance at the front of his trousers.

"Oh, right then. Do you just want me to—"

"Torquil," Emrys said, reaching for their hand. He brought it up to kiss their knuckles; the gloves had come off the moment they sat in the carriage. "I enjoyed our evening together. I hope you did, as well." When Torquil said nothing, he went on, ignoring how hard his heart was thumping. "I would very much like to call on you again. Or perhaps I could join you for dinner at Wyndham and Roger's home soon? I'll send a note in the morning and ask when they're available."

"Emrys," Torquil managed, a bit breathless, but Emrys only kissed their hand again and turned to leave. He did not look back, even after he'd settled in his seat and the door was closed. He did not look back, even as the carriage pulled away. He did not look back, because the only thing he wanted to look at any longer was his future.

CHAPTER 34

TORQUIL

As soon as Torquil reached their room, they carefully unwrapped the package from Emrys. He had bought far more than just the lovely inkwell; he had purchased ink and new quill pens to go with it. They placed everything carefully on the desk and traced their fingertip over the brass. Unbidden, tears pricked at their eyes and they sank to the bed and hung their head in their hands. It was all too much. Emrys had treated them like some sort of suitor, purchasing gifts, walking them to the door, asking to call on them. A sob wracked through them. What were they supposed to do now? It was too much and yet not enough. Emrys might court them but he would never marry them. Surely he realized that? Cruel creature, indeed.

They sniffed. That last thought helped to derail their current spiral. Emrys was never cruel. Careless, perhaps, but never cruel. Torquil could not have described anything Emrys did that evening as careless. It had all felt so intentional. They heaved a sigh and began to slowly undress, which did little to help their spirit. Everything they were wearing had been a gift. By the time they had laid the suit, the waistcoat, the cravat, the comb, the hat, and the scarf on the chair, they felt raw and wrung out.

They lit a small fire spell in the stove, allowing a fresh wave of sorrow to wash over them. They sat hunched in front of the oven for a long moment until their eyes started to itch with fatigue. Then they crawled into bed and tossed and turned. It was hours before they fell asleep.

&

WHEN TORQUIL WOKE, they had to admit they were relieved that they had asked for Sal's help as they were able to roll over and sleep some more. It didn't help as much as they'd hoped, though. By the time they strode into Wyndham and Roger's study, they still felt as though they'd been run over by a carriage. Their sleep had been fitful, haunted by dreams of Emrys in the alcove leaning down to kiss them and then disappearing in a puff of smoke, Emrys getting married to someone else as Torquil stood by and watched helplessly, and another paper reporting everything as the *Tribune* went unpurchased. The last one was almost the most troubling because Torquil woke up feeling a tinge disappointed that it wasn't true, and *that* caused another flurry of wretched thoughts.

By the expressions Roger and Wyndham gave them when they walked through the door, they clearly looked as bad as they felt.

"Good heavens," Roger said, hurrying over to lead them to their chair. "Are you all right?"

"Did my brother keep you up all night?" Wyndham asked. "I might have thought he'd give you the courtesy of a little bit more sleep."

Torquil shook their head. "No, he didn't stay. He dropped me off at home."

They could feel Roger and Wyndham exchange a look.

"That surprises me," Wyndham said slowly.

Torquil sighed. "He said he'd like to see me again. Said he'd ask you two if he could join us for dinner some night."

They both brightened considerably. "Why, that's wonderful!" Roger said.

Torquil glared at him.

"Torquil," Wyndham said gently. "I think Emrys means to court you. That *is* wonderful."

"But he cannot possibly—I'm not—we're not—his mother—"

Wyndham poured a cup of tea and passed it over swiftly. "Right, well until you finish those sentences, I'm afraid I can't entirely argue against them. But my mother *will* come around."

"Your mother detests me."

"My mother is…difficult sometimes. However, if she saw you two perform magic together, I promise you she would be asking you what flowers you want for your wedding before you had finished the casting."

Torquil stared at him, puzzled.

Wyndham seemed to think through his next words carefully. "Not only is it evident that yours and Emrys' magic are compatible, but you enhance his power…significantly. Trust me when I say that my mother would be more taken with that than she would with your occupation or your birth." He leaned forward. "And if my brother learns to control his power when he casts with you, then the two of you would be a force to be reckoned with."

Torquil swallowed. "His control is improving," they said quietly. They felt tears threatening again so they hastily took a sip of tea.

"Quite frankly," Roger said, cutting a slice of cake and passing it over, "you are more eligible than I was when our engagement was announced."

"That is decidedly untrue," Torquil said. "Your parents were not disinherited."

"But I was not a member of the Council. My father was, but I was already in my majority, with a very poor magical score and a modest dowry. I know your dowry is probably not very grand either," he went on hastily, "but you have a career, both as a writer and as a councilmember. And yes, your mother was disinherited, but you do come from a very impressive fae bloodline. I do not think this is as impossible as you seem to believe."

But if I'm really as eligible as all that, why hasn't he asked me to marry him? Torquil wanted to say. Their lip trembled.

"If my brother doesn't propose to you before the Season is over, I might kill him," Wyndham said before taking a bite of cake.

Torquil gave a watery laugh. "I'd rather you didn't. Even if he marries someone else, I'm quite fond of him." They took a steadying breath. "You're both being very kind, but could we please discuss something else?"

"No offense, but I'm not sure I trust you with magic right now," Wyndham commented.

Roger tsked. "More importantly, I think attempting to cast would cause you to faint. Are you sure you want to work today?"

Torquil thought of their empty room, of the desk still strewn with Emrys' gift, and the chair still covered with clothing. "Yes," they said, straightening. "I want to work."

Roger looked sympathetic. "That bad, is it?" He gave a small smile. "Well, we can definitely help with distracting, I think. As Wyndham pointed out, it would be best to not perform magic today. However, I think we're nearly to the end of that part of the project, don't you? So perhaps we ought to go over our notes again, as well as the notes from the letters. I've drafted out ideas for the rubric, but we'll need to discuss if that will work for all the varieties that are out there."

Roger was talking so quickly that Torquil was sure he was speaking solely to keep them from thinking too hard. They were so grateful for the kindness that they applied all of their energy to focusing on the task at hand.

The three of them worked diligently through lunch and tea, going over notes, discussing spells, and comparing ideas. When a servant delivered a note to Wyndham, Torquil had buried themself so completely in work that they had briefly forgotten their troubles. That is, until they saw Wyndham's sly expression.

He waved the note. "My brother is formally expressing a desire to have dinner with you, and requesting that we act as chaperones."

Torquil's eyes widened. "Chaperones?"

"Well, you are quite young, you know——"

Torquil snatched the note out of Wyndham's hand. "I'm an only child, you goosewit. Only children and heirs gain their majority faster than most. And we've been seeing each other without chaperones for years."

"Yes," Wyndham said as Torquil read the note several times over. "But as you have both fae and human parentage, I think it's safe to assume we should treat you under the human traditions of courtship."

Roger peeked over their shoulder. "He makes it sound very formal. I've never heard Emrys speak in such a courtly way."

"Love does cause us to do strange things sometimes," Wyndham said pointedly.

Torquil groaned and flopped onto the sofa.

Wyndham laughed and ruffled their hair.

Torquil glared up at him. "Don't you dare make that a habit."

"If you're going to marry my brother, you're going to practically be a younger sibling, and you cannot imagine how much I have wanted a younger sibling to torment."

"If I'm marrying your older brother, I think you'd give me a bit more respect. And besides, nobody has spoken of marriage." They tossed the note onto the table.

Wyndham picked it up. "Not yet. But this is a proper start. Now, the question is, when can we have you both to dinner? I'm afraid we're getting to a rather busy time of year."

"Oh dear, are we?" Roger said.

"Yes, we have dinner plans for the next three nights, and then an invitation to the opera, a ball, a dinner party, and then the solstice, of course. And then we shall have to start preparing for *our* party on Christmas Day. It may have to wait until after Christmas."

"Not really!" Roger said. "You cannot mean for them to wait that long. Can't we reject some invitations?"

"I imagine both Emrys and Torquil will have commitments of their own," Wyndham said. "I shall write to him and see when he will be available and we'll figure something out."

Torquil couldn't decide if they felt relieved or disappointed by the wait. They were fairly sure that after the excitement of the previous evening had dulled in everyone's memories, Emrys would come to his senses and go back to courting people his mother actually approved of. But the thought of that made them almost more ill than the thought of being formally courted by their dearest friend.

With Wyndham's assurances that he would let them know as soon as a date had been determined, they left and trudged back home. To their surprise, they found a number of letters waiting for them. Some were the usual messages from readers and gossips, as well as a hefty stack of notes from Sal. But others were invitations. They leafed through them and found an invitation from the Buckthorns, the Barneses, and the St. Clairs.

Mind still boggling at this turn of events, they hurried up to their room, carefully moved the pile of clothes from the chair to the bed, and sat down at their desk. They gave the gifted inkwell a long look and then finally dipped a new quill into the ink, blotted it, and wrote three acceptance letters. Then they hastily wrote down the dates for each event. It was strange to suddenly have to keep track of a social calendar. They chuckled to themself, amused by the change. Then they put away their new clothes and set about drafting the next *Tribune*.

CHAPTER 35

EMRYS

W HEN E MRYS STEPPED into his grandmother's study the morning after the winter festival, he felt like he was seventeen all over again, sick with nerves and excitement and the weight of a new and great responsibility sitting on his shoulders. It was just after he'd learned of Wyndham's results on his Sciurus Exam, securing Emrys' position as the most magically powerful of the siblings. He would inherit the family title and estate when the time came, but from that moment forward he would be expected to uphold the family name in every other way he possibly could. All eyes would be on him.

He felt that scrutiny more now than ever before.

"Darling," Iris said with a tilt of her head and a smile after he'd been announced. "What a nice surprise. Are you well?"

Emrys kept his hands clasped behind his back as he made his way to one of the large windows overlooking the back garden. Snow had continued to fall for most of the night, resulting in a miserable, slushy carriage ride from the townhouse, but the places that had remained untouched were something out of a storybook. For a long moment, Emrys watched the songbirds dart from one place to another, knocking bits of snow from branches and calling to one another.

Iris came from behind her desk, gathering her skirts in one hand. "Emrys?"

"Tell me the story of how you and Grandmama met," he said.

"Oh," Iris said on a sigh, her gentle grin returning. "Come and sit."

Emrys turned from the window to join her in one of the twin chairs by the hearth. The warmth and gentle popping noises coming from the fire took Emrys right back to the last night he'd been with Torquil in their room. He looked away, settling his gaze on his grandmother instead.

"Breyelle was a dear friend," she started. "We had known each other since we were children, always attending the same dinner parties and dances. It would have been rather unfortunate if we did not get along." Iris paused for a moment. "During her first Season out, she had so many callers that I wondered if she'd forgotten about me. I was happy for her, of course, but I also missed her something terrible. I had not realized just how much time we spent together until she was not there.

"It seemed very likely that she would accept a proposal before the end of the Season. Everyone was talking about it. She was rather like Wyndham, you know, a bit of a mystery that they all wanted to figure out." Iris gave him a knowing look. "But when spring came and no announcement had been made, the rumors began. I knew I had to reach out to my friend and make sure she was all right. I went to call on her for tea, and was turned away. She did not want any visitors. So I went home and wrote her a letter."

"What did you say?" Emrys asked.

"I told her she'd better let me come and visit her at once, or else I would keep writing until she did."

"And did she?"

"I wrote her twenty-seven letters before she sent a reply."

Emrys scoffed. "How could you possibly come up with so much to say?"

"I told her everything. What I'd had for breakfast that morning, the color of the new dress Mama had bought me, what song I was learning to play on the piano. All the silly little things we used to talk about." Iris laughed warmly. "I was certain she would give in eventually and allow me to come and visit her. Imagine my surprise when she wrote back and said how much my letters had meant. It turns out that she had fallen quite ill and was bedridden but did not want anyone's pity, so she settled for the rumors instead.

"We continued to correspond over the summer. It took several days for the letters to arrive, of course, as we'd both returned to the country. Eventually our conversations became so muddled that we couldn't make any sense of them, but I looked forward to them all the same."

"Wasn't it quite scandalous of you to be writing back and forth so much?"

"Oh, absolutely," Iris said with a feverish nod. "But at the time, we thought nothing of it. We were just friends."

"Hmm," Emrys said, a grin tugging at the corner of his lips.

"When it was time to return to London, we agreed to meet as soon as we were both settled. I'd never been more anxious about anything in my entire life—and I was set to make my debut that Season!" Iris caught Emrys' gaze and held it, the wrinkles at the corners of her eyes revealing all. "I'm certain you can draw your own conclusion from there."

Emrys' focus returned to the fireplace. He watched the flames dance as he considered his next words carefully, something he was not always very good at.

"How did you know your feelings for her had changed?"

He could practically hear the pieces falling into place as Iris worked out what was really on his mind. It was the reason he'd come to see her. If anyone could help him navigate the situation with grace, it was his grandmother.

"I'm not certain they ever did."

"But you were *just friends*," Emrys emphasized, brows furrowing.

Iris smiled. "I loved her as my friend. I loved her as my wife. I love her still, even though she's been gone for so long." She placed her hand on her chest, near the base of her throat. "The heart does not know the difference between the kinds of love. All it knows is how to feel. It's your mind that tells you the rest."

"So what changed your mind?"

"Life," she answered simply. "Society demanded that we each find a spouse. It was particularly important for me, as I was set to inherit, just as you are. Given the choice, why would I not pick someone my heart already loved?"

Emrys stared at his lap. "And what if someone is unable to choose?"

"Not able and not allowed are two very different things," Iris said, her tone becoming more serious. "If you value your happiness at all, Emrys, you will tell your mother how you really feel."

Emrys' face heated at his grandmother's words. How could she make it sound so simple? He looked up to search her eyes, swallowing thickly at the emotions coating the back of his throat.

"You heard her at dinner," he said, voice raw. "The only thing that matters to her is how things will look."

Iris reached across the space between them and put her hand atop his.

"On the surface, yes, your mother is a very proud woman. She takes herself far too seriously in all the ways that do not really matter in the end. She might show her love in the most overbearing, relentless way possible, but I was there at her bedside when you were born. I witnessed the tender way she held you and promised you the world. That's all she's trying to do, is keep her promise."

Iris patted Emrys' hand a few times before she stood and rang for tea. When she sat down again, the mood lightened considerably, as though the air around them had been swept clean. Emrys felt her magic brush his cheek as she smiled at him.

"Now," she said with purpose as she smoothed her hands over her skirts, "tell me all about your evening with Torquil."

Emrys grinned despite himself. He let his head rest against the high back of the chair for a moment as he studied the painting above the fireplace. It was a piece that Wyndham had done, a near perfect recreation of the garden he'd been admiring out the window. It reflected a springtime scene with vibrant blooms and lush greenery encroaching on the familiar path.

The word stuck in his mind. Familiar.

He'd listened to his grandmother's story countless times before. Aveline had requested to hear it repeatedly when they were children, claiming it was the most romantic thing she'd ever heard. Grandmama Breyelle had died when Emrys was only an infant, so he had no memories of her, but the way Iris' eyes lit up when she spoke of her late wife was enough for him to know that she must have been very special to her.

Perhaps that was the truth of it. There was no malevolence—he'd looked it up—in his mother's actions as she searched for his perfect match. It was simply that Emrys already had one. His mind refused to accept the thought of anyone else because his heart already knew where it belonged: somewhere on the far side of London, in a dreadful little room above the press, wrapped up in the arms of someone special and *familiar* and right.

"I'm rather in love with them, you know," Emrys told her.

Iris chuckled. "I thought you might be."

"Our magic is…" he paused, grip tightening on the armrests of his chair as he tried to think of the best way to describe it. "Terrifying," he admitted with a miserable little laugh. "But I think it will get better, with time."

"How did you meet?" Iris asked just as the tea was brought in.

Emrys waited until the servant left to give her a rueful grin. "I drunkenly stumbled upon the press one night, and they were witty, and charming, and…well, what was it you said about drawing your own conclusions?"

Iris tried to hold back her grin as she poured out. "Oh my," she murmured.

"That was nearly five years ago," Emrys said, his confessions peeling away like layers of clothes he'd been wearing for far too long.

"Quite a long time to keep things a secret," Iris mused. "Though I imagine you both had your reasons."

"Yes, well I—" Emrys paused, mouth open. He closed it slowly into a small frown. "I suppose I was comfortable with the way things were."

"And now?" Iris encouraged as she handed Emrys his tea.

He thought for a moment. "Now you and Wyndham and Roger have gone and pulled them into society so fully that I feel as though something has been taken from me."

Iris made a thoughtful sound. "Best get it back, then, before someone else comes and scoops it up for themselves." She tipped her chin up at one of the bookcases framing the fireplace. "Do you see that small box there?"

Emrys turned to look for it. "Yes," he said. Iris raised her eyebrows expectantly. He set his tea on the table between them and went to collect it. As he sat back in his chair, he opened the lid and was met with a few lingering notes of a sweet tune. The music box was empty, save for a tiny drawstring bag. Emrys set the box on the floor by his feet as he removed it.

"I suspect you'll be needing that," Iris said.

His grandmother still wore a plain gold band on her finger, but there was another, more delicate ring that hadn't been seen for over thirty years. Emrys didn't have to ask to know it was in the bag he was holding.

Suddenly, his heart was racing.

He knew better than to wonder if she was certain she wanted him to have it. It was his to take when the time was right. If anything, he'd let the precious heirloom sit for far too long.

Emrys tucked the bag into his breast pocket with care and reached for his tea. His fingers trembled only slightly at the thought of what came next.

TORQUIL'S TRIBUNE

THURSDAY 16 DECEMBER, 1813

Greetings, formal folk and hallowed humans,

The fae community came out in style for an ice skating party and holiday market. Nearly every fae of consequence was in attendance. Noteworthy guests include Miss Aveline Wrenwhistle, who looked fetching in a fur-lined coat and matching muff. In what is now becoming expected, she spent most of the evening with Mr. Buckthorn. The two were formidable on the ice and quite a sight to behold. Many are hoping that this pair may be the next big engagement announcement.

This writer has received a number of comments about their appearance with Mr. Emrys Wrenwhistle that evening. To quell any additional rumors: no, there is still no announcement as to who Mr. Wrenwhistle intends to marry. However, the gentleman did promise this column an exclusive interview. We are at his disposal, where that information is concerned. We welcome any and all guesses, theories, or bets on the matter.

For those still visiting the market between now and Christmas, we can recommend the mulled wine at Keller's stall and the cinnamon bread at Blanchet's stall.

We received a special report about two more guests at the event. While some were disappointed that Lady Proust did not accompany Mr. Wrenwhistle for the evening, it would appear she was not left to her own devices. She was observed in the company of Mr. Keelan Cricket. Sources say the two were very cozy and enjoyed several glasses of cider together. The evening was certainly geared for romance. Did those two find love under the fairy lights and snowfall? One can only hope someone did.

Your esteemed editor,
Torquil Pimpernel-Smith

CHAPTER 36
TORQUIL

Torquil stayed up late writing the *Tribune*, frustrated by their own lack of gossip. It was becoming frustratingly difficult to have news to share when they were so busy with their project. Adding social obligations on top of that and they were beginning to worry how they were going to accomplish everything. Sal came in while they were still setting letter tiles into place.

"Oh," she said, sounding oddly disappointed. "You're already putting it together."

Torquil glanced at her over their shoulder. "Did you expect otherwise?"

She shrugged. "I had a bit of gossip, that's all."

Torquil straightened and held out their hand. "Give it here then."

Sal pulled out a worn piece of paper out of her pocket. It was a larger scrap than the bits of gossip Torquil usually received. As they unfolded it, they noticed more writing than usual as well. They gave her a puzzled look before reading over it. It was more than a bit of gossip. It was a whole paragraph, written in a style very similar to their own, but with a slightly different tone.

"You wrote this?"

Sal shuffled her feet. "I don't mean to be presumptuous, of course."

"Not at all," Torquil said hurriedly. They read it over again. "It's quite good. And your handwriting is very neat. I never knew that."

Sal scratched at the back of her neck. "Well, that's my nicer copy."

Torquil smiled. "Can I include it in today's edition?"

Sal shrugged. "If you like."

"Thank you," they said softly. "Would you like to help me get the letters in?"

She nodded a bit hesitantly and stepped forward.

Torquil took out a pencil and made a mark on their own draft. "We'll put your piece right here, yes?" Then they showed her how to put the tiles in place. It was a fairly easy part of the process so they let her take over. As they watched Sal carefully pulling out letters, her tongue between her teeth in concentration, it occurred to them that they had never considered taking assistance in such a way.

They leaned against the press, feeling the cold of the metal biting against their palms. They had briefly mentioned to Emrys their concerns about the *Tribune*, but not all of it. It was becoming increasingly evident that they would soon have to decide between their paper and their life as a councilmember. It hardly seemed fair. But if the latter would result in better opportunities and better acceptance of fae-humans, then it would be worth the sacrifice. They watched Sal work steadily through her own paragraph. Perhaps the sacrifice would be less painful if they could hand everything over to someone capable. It was worth considering, at the very least.

Once Sal was done, they showed her how to operate the press. In the end, the delivery people were all a bit delayed because Sal hadn't managed to round them up before helping Torquil, but Torquil couldn't bring themself to mind very much. After everything was done, they divided the money in half and scooped it into their hand to give to her.

Sal looked mildly horrified. "What is that?"

Torquil blinked. "It's payment. You did half the work. You should get half the income."

"Are you barmy?"

Torquil frowned in confusion.

Sal sighed and dug her hands into her pockets. "If you want to pay me, then give me some extra coin as a contributor. But unless I can have a say in the price of the *Tribune* and how much you pay for deliveries and information, I'm not taking the rest."

Torquil weighed the money in their hand for a moment. "You want to raise the price, don't you?"

"Yes. I'd still pay out the same though. You don't charge for your full worth. I've said that for years."

They were surprised by her word choice but they said, "Yes, you have. How much would you say a contributing writer is worth then?"

Sal considered. "Three shillings."

Torquil laughed and handed the money over. "Consider yourself formally invited to provide any writing for the *Tribune*. I've found myself a bit dried up for gossip lately."

"Would have thought you'd have more since you started rubbing elbows with the upper classes."

"Yes, well," they said as they began cleaning up, "the upper classes are less inclined to gossip when they think it will appear in print. And they're less likely to rub elbows with those that spread the gossip."

Sal looked thoughtful.

"You look as though you have a solution."

Sal blushed. "I might. But I need to think on it a little longer."

They chuckled. "All right then. Let me know when you've thought it all out."

After Sal left, they changed and went to Roger and Wyndham's home. They worked steadily on the rubric until dinner, and then went to the Buckthorn family's townhouse.

It turned out the Buckthorns were very eager to provide gossip to Torquil, as long as that gossip was about their son and his very promising prospects with Miss Aveline. Torquil passed a surprisingly pleasant evening, learning all about how perfectly the two suited each other, how much in love Mr. Buckthorn was falling with the lady, and a very long story about their acquaintanceship. Torquil suspected a great deal of it was made up, but they weren't about to complain, especially when they agreed that the two were well suited. They assured their hosts they would continue to promote the relationship, as long as it felt right to do so.

They left feeling strangely satisfied, as if they'd passed some sort of test. They had attended a social function without Iris' help, or even Roger or Wyndham's help. And they'd managed it without too much suffering or damage.

The next day Wyndham announced that a date had been set for them to present the rubric before the rest of the Council. The three of them began to work through all of their notes, double-checking spells and verifying decisions.

Afterwards, Torquil went to the St. Clair family for dinner, feeling uncharacteristically popular. The St. Clairs were similarly enthusiastic about Torquil's work on the *Tribune*, ascribing a great deal of the engagement's success to their frequent gossip. Torquil asked about the upcoming wedding, whether a date had been set, if the couple planned to go on a honeymoon. They were delighted to be given free rein to be as inquisitive as they wanted and took full advantage, while avoiding indiscrete or impolite questions. By the time they left, they were enjoying that satisfied feeling again, now coupled with actual news to share in the *Tribune*.

When Torquil showed up at Roger and Wyndham's home the following morning, they were not sure how they were going to handle more magic. But with one week to go, there was no time to waste, so they threw themself into their work. By the time Wyndham announced they needed to leave for dinner with the Barneses, Torquil had worked themself into a blistering headache. Wyndham gave them something for the pain, which turned it into a dull throb. It was not an ideal position to be in for a social obligation, but Torquil had no desire to disappoint one of the few members of the Council who was actually nice to them.

They were not surprised that Roger and Wyndham joined them with the Barnes family for dinner. Roger's siblings were in town, ready to celebrate the winter holidays with their family. Torquil had never had occasion to meet Roger's sister or brother, or their respective spouses. It was shockingly less daunting than dinner with the Wrenwhistle family. The Barneses turned out to be very much like their patriarch, kind and gentle people, with an avid fascination with magic—well, most of them; Torquil suspected Mrs. Barnes had barely a passing interest, but she was so polite and encouraging that it was hard to tell.

Frederica took after her parents, soft-spoken and warm-hearted. She came across like another mother figure in the family, which Torquil rather liked. Bernard was as keen to discuss magic as his father and brother. When Councilmember Barnes invited Torquil to describe their work on the project, Bernard had as many questions about it as his father. Torquil noticed that the younger man was not as tactful as his father or brother. Sometimes his commentary came across as downright abrasive or condescending. Wyndham seemed to bristle every time that condescension was angled toward Roger or Torquil, but Torquil found it less offensive than Mrs. Wrenwhistle's criticism. They suspected Bernard Barnes was not acting out of malice, but a lack of care about how polite his tone was. Carelessness was easier to handle than outright disdain.

Torquil stayed late into the evening, discussing the nuances of fae-human magic in comparison to human magic and fae magic. They sipped port with the family, said goodbye to Frederica and her wife's children as they trooped through the room to say their goodnights, and even left with an armful of borrowed books from Councilmember Barnes.

"Do come again soon," Barnes said as he stacked the last book on top. "This was delightful, and much overdue."

So it was a third night in a row that Torquil returned home feeling satisfied with a full day and evening's worth of work. For once, they began to hope they might actually be able to manage the social obligations now required of them. They had even succeeded without Iris or Emrys' help!

The downside, of course, was that the later nights meant less and less sleep. The headache remained all night and into the morning. Torquil began to grudgingly accept it as a constant companion. They worked all the way to dinner, even staying with Roger and Wyndham for the meal. Emrys did not join as he had a prior commitment with Lady Proust. The twinge of disappointment that Torquil felt gave them the answer they'd been seeking for days: they *did* want Emrys to join them. They did like the idea of more evenings spent on his arm, drinking mulled wine and eating cinnamon bread. They sat at the dinner table, thinking dreamily about whether conversation for the inevitable chaperoned dinner would be stilted or flow as easily as it ever did when they were with their friends. They began to imagine Emrys and Wyndham becoming better acquainted and losing some of their shared animosity.

"Thinking about my brother?" Wyndham said after a long lull in the conversation.

Since Torquil *had*, in fact, been doing just that, they blushed and shook their head. "Not at all. I was thinking about the *Tribune*. I have to publish the next one tomorrow, you know."

Wyndham scoffed. "Little liar," he muttered.

Torquil ignored him and turned to Roger. "I've been thinking about our conversation with your family. I might dedicate some of tomorrow's issue to discussing our project in more depth. What do you think?"

"I think it's a marvelous idea," Roger said, graciously allowing Torquil their mistruth. "It worked for our previous project after all."

"Yes," Torquil said, thinking back. "It did, didn't it? I probably *ought* to get permission first but…"

"But when did that stop any of us?" Wyndham said, clinking his glass against Torquil's. "There are three of the Council present. We are all in agreement. We know my grandmother and Roger's father wouldn't mind. So that's five members."

"Good enough," Torquil said, grinning.

Wyndham returned the smile, took a sip of wine, and said, "But don't think I didn't notice your dreamy expression. I cannot believe you have brought me so low as to actually talk to my brother on a regular basis, but we really are trying to find a time to have you both over."

"It's honestly a miracle that he's inviting Emrys at all," Roger said in a mock whisper.

"Yes," Torquil said, "I am surprised you've been so supportive of this—whatever it is. After all, if you succeed, you'll have to see him even more than you do now."

Wyndham grimaced. "Don't remind me. He is almost tolerable around you. And I'm cheering myself up by imagining how bored he'll be when we're all inevitably invited to the Barneses for dinner again. He'll probably fall asleep in the potatoes."

Torquil gave him a mock glare. "I don't think Mrs. Barnes would allow that to happen. She's far too adroit a conversationalist. And I don't think she cares much for all of the academic discussion of magic either, so I'm sure she'd be pleased to have someone who shared her lack of enthusiasm."

Roger beamed. "That's a lovely thought. It's like you two are part of our family already."

Torquil blushed again. "Just trying to mitigate your husband's enthusiasm for seeing Emrys embarrassed. That's all."

But they couldn't deny that they imagined the hypothetical dinner as they attempted to write the *Tribune* that night, and spent hours thinking about it rather than sleeping.

TORQUIL'S TRIBUNE

Greetings, formidable folk and haughty humans,

Iris Wrenwhistle's annual winter solstice party will likely be the next big event of the Season. We do not have access to the guest list, but we can anticipate prominent names from both the fae and human side of society. This writer has been fortunate enough to be invited and will be sure to provide a thorough report. To those who criticized our most recent report on the fae event at the park, you are more than welcome to share your own gossip if you think it so very valuable.

Sources say that Mr. Buckthorn called on Miss Aveline Wrenwhistle again. Many are beginning to say that it is not a matter of *if* an engagement is forthcoming but rather *when*. Some may argue that it is, perhaps, too soon to speak of such things, considering they've only had their names linked in this paper for less than a fortnight. However, as Mrs. Buckthorn herself will tell anyone who wishes to know, Mr. Buckthorn and Miss Wrenwhistle have enjoyed a friendship since childhood. It is hardly surprising that they are dancing around each other with such intention now. We are all eagerly looking forward to more news. And, perhaps, more importantly, what the two will be wearing to the solstice party.

The St. Clair family is eagerly preparing for their daughter's upcoming wedding. Sources say the wedding will take place in January. The couple is expected to go on a honeymoon to Lady Fitzhugh's country estate. It is reasonable to suppose that neither lady will be seen much in London for the rest of the Season. And we all wish them a very merry time in the country.

The date has been set for the next rubric to be presented to the Council for Fae & Human Relations. This third rubric has been somewhat contested even within the Council itself. Fae-human magic has been so under-researched that it is hardly surprising how little was known about it. Based on the information received from such wonderful readers as yourselves, we have determined that study on this particular system of magic has been too long overlooked. Fae-human children are often refused testing and, when they are allowed to test, they are held to the standards of their fae or human peers. Those of us who have been working on this project have only scratched the surface of what there is to learn and we are eager to learn more.

Your esteemed editor,
Torquil Pimpernel-Smith

CHAPTER 37

EMRYS

EMRYS ARRIVED to collect Torquil for the solstice party with more anticipation than he'd realized on the ride over. He hadn't seen them for several days, which at one time had been nothing out of the ordinary. But now it felt like an eternity had passed since he'd left them standing in front of the press building.

It was still early in the evening and he'd assumed that Torquil would be expecting him, so Emrys was surprised to find the door locked. He called on his magic to fiddle it open and let himself inside. He did not pause to think about how he probably should have waited for them to come and open the door until he was already at the top of the stairs brushing the curtain aside.

Torquil was at their desk, one knee bent up to their chest, the other foot hooked precariously around the leg of the chair at the floor. They were resting their head in a nest of their own arms; the candle by their elbow burned down to nearly nothing. Emrys huffed out a silent laugh as he grinned at the sight.

"I could swear we agreed that the only one allowed to bend you over that desk was me," he said as he stepped closer, words bawdy despite the lack of time to act on it, as much as he would've liked to. Come to think of it, they hadn't involved the desk in quite some time. They would have to remedy that.

When Torquil did not respond with a witty remark of their own, or even a little laugh, Emrys' grin faded a bit. He moved to the other side of the chair so he could see Torquil's face, but their hair was in the way. He brushed it back with his fingers to find their eyes closed. Emrys tucked what he could behind their ear and slid the pad of his thumb along their cheekbone.

"Pretending to sleep will not get you out of this event, I'm afraid. I've got strict orders. I'll throw you over my shoulder if I must."

Emrys braced his weight on the edge of the desk as he crouched beside the chair, his other hand moving to rest on their upper back. He'd rubbed a couple of small circles there before he realized what Torquil was wearing. They were down to their shirt and tattered old trousers, feet bare, certainly nowhere near ready for a party.

"Torquil," Emrys said, the confusion in his voice quickly spreading across his face. There was still no response. He brought his hand to their shoulder and shook it lightly. "Torquil?" he tried again with more urgency. Something like panic splashed cold in Emrys' stomach as he shoved their shoulder back and reached for the other so he could shake them properly. "Torquil!"

"What is it?" Torquil said harshly, brows bunched together over eyes that remained shut. They leaned against the back of the chair, though they were far from being awake enough to remain upright. Emrys cupped their cheek and searched their face desperately.

"Are you sick?" he demanded. "Hurt? What's the matter?"

Torquil blinked several times and looked at Emrys blankly for a moment. "Whatever do you mean?" they asked as they brought a hand up to rub at their eyes, a yawn following close behind.

"I thought you were pretending to sleep to avoid going to the party," Emrys explained, heart still beating hard. "It appears you were not pretending."

Torquil looked at the candle. "I was reading a book I borrowed from Councilmember Barnes," they said, still a bit distant. The book was there on the desk. Torquil sat up straighter and closed it, finally coming around. "After I finished with the *Tribune* this morning, I went to continue working on our project, but instead Roger and Wyndham practically forced me to learn every dance that's ever been danced in a matter of hours." They leaned forward and blew out the candle before they looked at Emrys and pushed a hand back through their hair. "It must've taken more out of me than I thought."

Emrys stood and held Torquil's face with both hands this time as he pressed his lips to theirs, eyes squeezing shut as he tried to shake off the way his nerves had been thoroughly rattled. He kissed Torquil until they made a soft sound of surprise in the back of their throat. Emrys kept his eyes closed as he rested their foreheads together.

"You scared me," he whispered.

"I did not mean to," Torquil whispered back.

Emrys would've given almost anything to pick Torquil up out of that chair, carry them to the bed, and hold them until they could not even recall the meaning of the word tired. But the thought of disappointing his grandmother forced him to settle for one more kiss before he took a step back.

"We need to get you dressed," he said, turning his attention to Torquil's small wardrobe on the far wall beneath the window. "What were you planning to wear?" He looked at each suit and matching waistcoat with feigned interest, waiting for Torquil's reply so he could take out the requested items. "I'm afraid I'm not as good at picking accessories as Wyndham, and he can tie a better knot, but—"

Arms wrapped carefully around his waist from behind, and he felt the press of Torquil's body against his. "Emrys," they said, cheek against the back of his shoulder. Emrys took Torquil's wrist so that he could lift their hand and kiss the back of their fingers.

"I'm trying to be a gentleman for you," he said quietly. "I should have waited at the door." He was still scolding himself for the lapse in etiquette.

"I'm glad you didn't," Torquil murmured as they stretched up on their toes to kiss the back of his neck. The touch of their lips sent a spark down his spine that made him shiver.

"Torquil," Emrys warned half-heartedly as their hands moved to the front of his trousers. "There isn't time."

"I'll be quick," Torquil promised as they slipped around to face him and sank to their knees on the worn floorboards. "I cannot imagine that either of us will enjoy ourselves tonight with that many worry lines creasing your forehead."

᪣

THE SELF-SATISFIED LOOK was still on Torquil's face when they arrived at Iris' townhouse. As Emrys helped them from the carriage, he avoided eye contact with the footman they'd kept waiting for entirely too long. He had blamed the delay on an unfortunate wardrobe blunder and left it at that.

They could both see their breath the moment they stepped out, so Emrys hurried them toward the door, still uncertain about the extent of Torquil's condition. He had never seen them sleep so deeply before. Were they truly only exhausted from being overworked, or was it something more serious? Regardless, he planned to have a chat with Wyndham about it before the night was over.

As they were welcomed inside, a wash of warm citrus and spice instantly took Emrys back to his childhood. He had fond memories of lighting altar candles and drinking wassail with his family gathered around the fire. Some traditions had changed over the years as he and his siblings had grown older, including the addition of dark rum to their glasses, but at the root it remained a time to celebrate the turn of winter and fresh beginnings.

It felt oddly appropriate for Torquil to be on his arm on such a night.

They gave up their coats and Emrys couldn't help but watch as Torquil's head tilted back slowly, taking in the magnificent display of solstice décor in the foyer. Candles were nestled amongst the evergreen swags on the stairs, placed thoughtfully on every windowsill, and there were some doing their best fairy light impressions where they'd been magicked to float around the chandelier.

"Did your family not decorate for the winter holidays?" Emrys asked as he held his arm out for Torquil to take again. They let out an incredulous little laugh as their eyes met.

"I have never seen a home as decorated as this."

"Grandmother's favorite time of year," Emrys explained as he walked Torquil toward the low chatter of a party in progress. "My mother can do all she likes with flowers, but she will never top an Iris Wrenwhistle Solstice."

"She might hear you," Torquil scolded under their breath as they entered the room together. Emrys felt them start to shy away as several people turned to look, but after being met with polite smiles and nods, Torquil seemed to relax.

"She would be wrong to deny it," Emrys assured them in a hushed tone as he searched the crowd for familiar faces. "I cannot believe I'm saying this, but let's try to find my brother."

Wyndham and Roger had already settled themselves near one of the fireplaces, each with a glass in their hand. Emrys fought back a fresh flood of discomfiture at the realization that, for the first time ever, Wyndham had arrived at an event before him.

Roger spotted them first.

"Happy Solstice!" he cried out as his hands went up. It was fortunate his drink was mostly gone, or else he would've been wearing it. The look of mild amusement and concern on Wyndham's face indicated that perhaps this was not their first round, either.

"Where can I find a couple of those?" Emrys asked, forgoing a proper greeting in favor of matching the jovial mood of his brother-in-law as soon as possible.

"I'll show you," Wyndham offered. "I trust that you'll look after this one for a moment?" he added in Torquil's direction. They nodded and took Roger's arm, guiding him to a nearby sofa.

Emrys arched a brow as he followed Wyndham through the rest of the partygoers. "I wouldn't have taken Roger for a——"

"Leave him be," Wyndham said. "It's so infrequent that he allows himself to forget that he's...well, Roger." They approached where the wassail was being served, cinnamon and cloves overpowering the air around them, and both took a fresh glass in each hand. Emrys wasted no time in sipping from his.

"*Mmh*," he managed against the burn in his throat. "It's no wonder he's merry! This is more spirit than cider." He took another pull.

"Grandmother has never been one to deny her guests," Wyndham said mildly as he brought one of the glasses he was holding to his lips.

Emrys turned to him. "Speaking of denying people of things, when I arrived to collect Torquil this evening they were asleep at their desk. I narrowly managed to wake them."

"Is that why you were so late?" Wyndham asked, a smirk forming.

"You're working them too hard," Emrys argued quietly, ignoring his brother's prodding. "They've not had enough time to adjust to keeping a social calendar on top of their existing obligations. You and I have been doing this since before we could walk."

"And what does it matter to you if Torquil is tired or not?"

Emrys let out a frustrated sigh. "You're the one who warned me not to do anything to ruin the friendship forming between them and Roger. It will be difficult for them to remain friends if Torquil meets an early grave."

Wyndham chuckled and swirled his drink a few times before he took another slow sip. "A fair point," he said, catching Emrys by surprise. "Unfortunately, Torquil is quite stubborn. Roger and I do what we can, but there's only so far our guidance in this endeavor can go. They've been refusing to slow down on our project, accepting more invitations. I think they're finally coming around to the idea of being out in society."

"Well, you ought to try harder," Emrys said.

"Duly noted," Wyndham told him.

When they made their way back, Roger was sitting by himself, though he seemed quite pleased about it. Wyndham offered him the new drink, which he readily accepted.

Emrys could not stop himself from blurting out, "Where did Torquil go?"

"Oh, wonderful news," Roger said. "They've gone and nearly filled their dance card while you were away. It seems you're not the only one who wants to spend time with them this evening."

Jealousy flashed hot in Emrys' chest before he could fully comprehend what Roger had said. He turned to look for Torquil just as the musicians started to play the first song in the adjoining room.

CHAPTER 38
TORQUIL

No sooner had Torquil sat down next to Roger, than a number of people appeared wanting introductions and asking to dance with them. Then Roger told the growing crowd that Torquil was "a marvelous dancer" and soon their dance card was all but full. It was highly embarrassing. They were decidedly not a marvelous dancer, but after spending the entire afternoon being drilled in assorted dances by Roger and Wyndham, they felt moderately prepared for the evening's festivities. Torquil had no idea if their sudden popularity had to do with the dark red velvet suit they were wearing again, or the fact that they had been seen with Emrys at the fae winter festival, or perhaps people had simply grown accustomed to the idea that Torquil was now a fixture in society.

As they were led onto the dance floor by Mr. Brooks, they couldn't resist looking around to try and spot Emrys. They had been pleased to see him and Wyndham getting along, but it felt like a betrayal to dance with another man. Mr. Brooks was charming in a bland sort of way and Torquil was beginning to understand why the gentleman was always seen with assorted fashionable men, but only ever briefly.

"You dance divinely, Mx. Pimpernel-Smith," Brooks said.

Torquil didn't bother to correct him, either for the compliment or the omission of their councilmember status. "Thank you," they said with a smile. "It is a pleasure to meet you at last, Mr. Brooks. After hearing so much about you, I confess my curiosity has been piqued."

Brooks' smile broadened. "The pleasure is all mine, I can assure you. Besides, I had to save you from your dull human companion."

Torquil frowned. "Roger? He's delightful."

"That's not what I've heard."

"Well, then you've been listening to the wrong sources."

"I should probably just stick to your paper," he said with a chuckle.

Torquil forced a grin. "That's the idea."

When the dance was over, another partner stepped forward. Torquil was passed from one person to the next for over an hour. By the time they reached one of their few empty spots on the dance card, they were feeling dizzy. Although whether they were dizzy from the dancing, fatigue, or the crowded room, they couldn't determine. They spotted Emrys standing near Wyndham and Roger and couldn't help the smile of relief that took over their face.

"I'm sorry I abandoned you," they said as they approached.

Emrys gave a tight grin in response. "Nothing to apologize for. You look stunning. No one is surprised that you are popular."

Torquil arched an eyebrow at Emrys' tone. Was he jealous?

Wyndham snorted. "Jealousy isn't a good look on you, brother."

Emrys opened his mouth to retort and then closed it. He seemed to consider for a long moment and then said in a softer voice, "I really am not surprised that so many people wish to know you better. It's long overdue. But if you have any dances left on your card, I would be honored to have them."

Torquil felt themself blush as they fumbled for their card.

"Dances?" Wyndham said. He tsked. "Have a care for propriety, will you?"

"Would you stop with this newfound obsession with propriety?" Emrys hissed, although he gave Torquil a warm smile as he took the card. He frowned over it for a moment and then added his name to the three blank spots remaining.

Wyndham looked over his brother's shoulder and then rolled his eyes.

Emrys handed it back and said, "We do not have to dance for all of them, of course. But I'd like you to have some time to rest." As if to prove his point, he gestured to a chair beside him.

Torquil was grateful as they sank into the seat. "That is kind of you," they said. "I'm not accustomed to dancing this much."

"You could have fooled me," Emrys said. "You dance very well."

Torquil laughed. "I most certainly do not."

Emrys cleared his throat. "Then let's say you dance very well for someone who just learned." He stood next to the chair and braced his hand on the back of it, with his hip hitched on the arm.

Torquil looked up at him, thinking about how easy it would be to rest their head against his side. Just as it had been easy to bring him to swift satisfaction before the party. Only they were in a crowded ballroom, people were watching, and nothing was easy anymore. They missed that ease with Emrys. They sighed a little and rubbed their eyes.

"Are you well?" Emrys asked, immediately bending closer.

"Yes," they said, recalling how terrified Emrys had been as he'd shaken them awake in their room. "Only tired."

Emrys cast a baleful look at Wyndham, who shrugged in response.

The set ended and Torquil's next partner came to lead them to the dance floor. It was a couple of hours before they were back at Emrys' side for the last two dances of the evening. The dizziness had worsened and it took everything they had not to collapse into his arms as they strode up to him.

"You look pale," he said. "Should I take you home?"

"Will you take me to bed or will you drop me off at my door again?"

Emrys swallowed. "I think you need rest more than anything else."

They sighed. "Then I'd prefer to stay, please. I've barely gotten to see you all night."

"Would you like to dance or do you need to rest?"

"Both?"

He chuckled. "Let's get you some fresh air." He held out his arm and led them through the crowded rooms, to a darkened hallway that was clearly not open for the party, and into a private little garden at the back of the house. "I should have gotten your coat," he said as Torquil shivered in the cold night air.

"No," they protested. "It's fine. You were right. The fresh air is… helping."

"Perhaps you should sit…" Emrys said, glancing at the stone benches, covered in a glaze of frost. "…or…er…this was a foolish idea."

"No," they repeated, more forcefully. "It wasn't. This is lovely." They squeezed his arm. "I've missed you," they said softly.

"I've missed you too," he whispered, placing his hand over theirs. "I've been torn all evening over being pleased to see other people recognizing how wonderful you are, and…wishing I had you all to myself still."

They looked up at him, studying the embarrassment and earnestness on his face. "If it helps, as much as I appreciate the sudden approval, I would have preferred to dance with you."

Emrys smiled. "Really?"

They leaned up and kissed his cheek. "Really." They sighed and leaned into his side. "But I don't know if I can bear another set on that dance floor. It's exhausting to have so many people watching me all the time. I'm not used to it."

Emrys hummed. "Well, perhaps we can remedy that."

"What, me being accustomed to being watched?"

"Well, that too. But I was thinking more about the dancing. What is the last dance anyway?"

Torquil pulled out their dance card. "The waltz. Should I be shocked that Iris has waltzing at her party?"

"Oh, she's very modern. But that does make things easier." He dropped his arm and slid it around their waist, pulling them in front of him and close to his chest. He scooped up their free hand in his and began to gently guide them in a quiet waltz. "How's this?"

Torquil smiled. "Perfect."

Snowflakes drifted down lazily. The garden was so quiet, they could hear the sounds of chatter from inside the house and, if they listened carefully, the lilting tones of the music drifting over the voices. Louder were the soft shuffles of two pairs of shoes against the stone pavement.

There were so many things Torquil wished they had said to Emrys before the wedding, before the Council, and before their lives had gone so topsy-turvy. It would have been so simple to whisper into the dark as Emrys curled up beside them on their rickety bed: *I love you. I need you. Please don't leave me.*

The dizziness was getting stronger so Torquil closed their eyes and leaned their head against Emrys' chest, willing him to understand the words they didn't have the courage to speak out loud.

CHAPTER 39

EMRYS

It came as no surprise that breakfast the morning after the solstice party was a mild affair. Aveline appeared to be the most unaffected as she gazed dreamily at her food, no doubt thinking about her new beau, but Mrs. Wrenwhistle looked as though she might retch onto her plate at any moment. She had requested her coffee to be as strong as possible. It was not the ideal time to broach important topics, he knew, but Emrys' restraint had worn completely through.

"Mother, Father, I need to speak with you."

Mrs. Wrenwhistle swallowed thickly and grimaced as she set her cup down on the table. "Oh Emrys, can it not wait?"

"It cannot," he said resolutely.

She closed her eyes and sighed. "Very well. Aveline, please give us some privacy." This normally would have been met with some level of protest, but his sister was apparently too distracted by her own romantic thoughts to mind. She stood from her chair and flitted out of the room without a word. Emrys blinked after her. Perhaps this would go better than he feared, after all.

"Is there a problem?" his father asked, brows pinched. The holidays kept him home longer than at any other time of the year. Investing in businesses, it turned out, was even more rewarding when the people running them were allowed time to see their loved ones on occasion. As nice as it was, it still felt strange to see him picking at his buttered bread in the chair at the head of the table that so often sat empty.

"I suppose you could call it that," Emrys said slowly. "But certainly not from my perspective."

His mother brought her hand up to rub gingerly at her temple. "Do get on with it. I haven't the time or stomach for twisted words."

He took a steadying breath and set his shoulders. "I am requesting that you stop your matchmaking for me at once. It will no longer be necessary."

Mrs. Wrenwhistle's eyes snapped open with a sharp gasp. She sat up in her chair as her expression shifted from the brink of death to surprise to pure delight in a matter of seconds.

"You've made a decision?" she asked excitedly, tossing a look in her husband's direction. Emrys couldn't determine if it held more relief or pride. "I had a feeling it wouldn't be long! It's the perfect time of year for such connections to be made, what with the romantic nature of the winter holidays. It can leave most anyone wishing to be a little less lonely, isn't that right dear?"

"Indeed," Mr. Wrenwhistle added with a single, satisfied nod before he went back to his toast. Emrys decided to ignore his mother's implications about him being lonely. Instead, he pressed on, making good use of her improved mood and his own wavering confidence while it lasted.

"I've collected Grandmother's ring. It's in excellent condition, as I expected it would be, but I left it with the family jeweler. I was unaware that it is so very intricate. I thought it best to have a thorough inspection and cleaning."

"I believe it was redesigned with more stones," his father mused.

"Yes, that's what she told me," Emrys said quietly.

He had been expecting something beautiful, but he'd been entirely unprepared for what he'd found when he opened the drawstring bag and carefully emptied the contents onto his palm. A cluster of brilliant rubies gave a unique shape to the setting, offset with a stunning dark opal that held a flash of fire in the correct light.

The jeweler had promised to find the perfect velvet box to put it in for when the time was right. Emrys had never been so worried over a fashionable accessory in his life.

"We can start wedding planning as soon as the new year arrives," his mother said. "Fortunately, there will be plenty of time to work out the finer details. We will wait a few months to have the ceremony so we can take full advantage of early spring at the estate."

"That seems like something we should discuss—"

"Of course, invitations will still need to be printed and sent out as soon as possible. We do not want to give anyone the chance to fill their social calendars and miss the opportunity to attend the wedding of the Season!"

"I thought Wyndham and Roger already—"

"Have you spoken with her father? I can send a note out and invite the family for dinner this evening—"

"Mother!" Emrys bellowed, silencing her. They stared at each other across the table as her words settled. Mrs. Wrenwhistle's smile faded to confusion as Emrys struggled to maintain his composure, magic swirling uneasily in his chest. "What did you say?"

"I said I can send a note to the family."

"Which family, exactly?" he asked tightly.

"Why, the Proust family, of course," she said with a slight laugh, as though it were obvious. "Who else?"

Emrys pressed a finger and thumb to his eyelids as he took a slow breath and let it out. When his hand returned to his lap, he watched his mother sip her coffee without hesitation. It seemed that the best remedy for overindulgence was smug satisfaction. He wondered if that was the reason Wyndham never seemed to struggle with such issues.

"I am not asking Lady Proust to marry me," Emrys said. That was enough to catch even his father's attention. His mother's cup moved slowly from her mouth back to the table as her forehead wrinkled.

"I beg your pardon?"

"I am not marrying Lady Proust," he repeated. Mrs. Wrenwhistle's mouth began to open, likely in wild protest, and he had no time to give in to his apprehension. "I am not marrying any of the people you set me up with, nor anyone who has come to call on me with that express interest in mind. To be quite honest, Mother, you have done a terrible job of finding me a suitable spouse, but I cannot blame you for it without also blaming myself."

"Emrys," she warned, voice almost a whisper.

"I realize I have failed to inform you of what I am looking for. I thought for the longest time that I did not know the answer either. I told myself I would be pleased to accept anyone who fit the role. Anyone who would embrace the role as expected."

"And have I not brought you every eligible member of society? Have I not worked tirelessly to find you a perfect match?"

"You have," Emrys said, allowing her that. "But I have since discovered that I do know what my heart is after. Or who, rather. Speaking with Grandmother made it clear."

His mother scoffed and rolled her eyes, shaking her head dismissively. "Naturally. That old woman has made it her mission to challenge me in every possible way from the moment I married her son." Emrys held his tongue, keeping his opinion on the matter to himself. "What has she done? Clouded your mind with silly thoughts of romance outside your station? Made you think you're allowed to marry anyone you please?"

Resentment sent Emrys to his feet in an instant, his chair making a horrible scraping noise against the floor as it was shoved backward, nearly toppling over. A servant stepped forward to steady it.

"Am I not?" he demanded. "Wyndham married as he wanted to, and so did Auberon. So did you!" He threw a hand out in his father's direction, chest heaving. "Why is everyone in this family allowed to marry for love rather than duty except for me?"

His mother's expression had moved beyond anger, into a calm that he knew meant she had stopped listening with any feeling. She sipped her coffee.

"You are set to inherit, Emrys. You are the one carrying the family name. A good match is more than important, it is a necessity. A match like that does not often happen by chance."

Emrys let out a broken sob of a laugh at how wrong she was. He wished so badly that Torquil was there so he could show her. So that their magics could touch and light up the room and his soul and prove to her that he had made his own perfect match years before, drunk and heedless as he'd taken his wordsmith upstairs for the best first knock he'd ever had. He'd been hopelessly unable to forget them from that night on.

He laughed again weakly. His heart really had known all along.

"Are you not even interested to know who it is?" he asked finally, his words laced with defeat.

His mother's face had grown pallid once again. "Do not try to pretend that you've been at all subtle," she said primly. Emrys felt his entire body flush. "A mother cannot be expected to ignore the irresponsible actions of her son."

"But a son should be expected to sacrifice his happiness to obey the antiquated rules of society?" Emrys let his gaze drop to the breakfast he'd barely touched. "You must know that I have never wanted to disappoint either of you. I have done everything you've ever asked of me. I've even tried to look past my own desires and accept that I would likely have to settle for whichever partner best satisfied your wishes for the future of our family." He lifted his chin. "In this, I have failed. I understand if this failure is met with repercussions. But I will not apologize, and I will not change my mind. I can only hope that you will give me the opportunity to show you why I have been altogether captivated, because I know that if you could see them the way that I do, you would love them, too."

With that, he left. He could do nothing more. As much as he did not want to live the rest of his life in the shadow of his mother's disapproval, the memory of dancing with Torquil in the garden the previous night was enough to reassure him that he already had everything he would ever need.

"Emrys," his father said. He looked back to find that he was also standing now. Emrys fisted his hands at his sides, preparing himself for anything. Mr. Wrenwhistle closed the distance between them and patted Emrys' shoulder as he continued walking by. "Just promise me one thing."

Emrys turned after him. "Yes?"

"Do not force them to sign the *Tribune* as Torquil Pimpernel-Smith Wrenwhistle. Ink is too damned expensive for all that."

TORQUIL'S TRIBUNE

Greetings, festive folk and holidaying humans,

Iris Wrenwhistle hosted another successful event, this one her annual winter solstice party. Everyone agreed that the decorations were sensational, all of the guests were beautifully dressed, the refreshments were delectable, and the music lively and sweet. All in all, another feather in the councilmember's cap.

Everyone who is anyone was present. Noteworthy guests included Lady Fitzhugh, who danced multiple times with her betrothed. No one could bat an eye at that, considering how clearly the two ladies are in love. Lady Proust was also present and seemed to enjoy the attention of multiple gentlemen, including Mr. Keelan Cricket, again. Sources say the two danced together twice. Mr. Wyndham and Roger Wrenwhistle were present, of course, and danced a respectable two times. Some may be disappointed by the lack of entertainment, considering how much the gentlemen danced during their courtship phase. However, as a friend of the family, this writer can assure readers that the romance between the two is alive and well, dances notwithstanding. Miss Aveline Wrenwhistle shared one dance with Mr. Buckthorn, but before readers express dismay that it was not more, the two were practically inseparable throughout the whole of the evening. Mr. Emrys Wrenwhistle danced rarely, which was sure to disappoint the readers of this paper. Mr. Brooks danced with a pleasant variety of partners, as did Mr. Ravenwing. Mx. Hillcrest danced once with Mr. Thompson and once with Miss Thackeray.

All in all, a marvelous time was had by the entire guest list, and there were so many intriguing pairings as to keep the whole city wondering about what will come next.

To turn to the considerably less exciting topic of politics, a new rubric will be presented to the Council for Fae & Human Magical Relations tomorrow morning. This rubric is intended for those of mixed parentage, whose magic may not fit in either the human or fae rubrics. While the existing rubrics have been used as a model, this third rubric is as unique as the magic it is meant to test. More to come after the Christmas holiday is over.

Your esteemed editor,
Torquil Pimpernel-Smith

CHAPTER 40

TORQUIL

TORQUIL SPENT the entire day after the solstice party preparing for their presentation before the Council with Wyndham and Roger. They felt sick with nerves, and Roger was pale and fidgety, so Torquil stayed all the way past dinner and into the evening as the three of them worked through who would say what. Wyndham wrote down all of their notes, copying everything out with meticulously nice script. By the time Torquil collapsed into their bed, they had a headache on top of the nervous stomach.

They didn't feel any better the next morning. They were, frankly, grateful when Sal showed up early and offered to help again.

"I don't have any new gossip," she admitted.

"Don't worry about it," Torquil assured her. "Do you still want to help with the printing?"

She nodded eagerly. Torquil was impressed when they stepped aside and Sal did almost the entire process with very little prompting. When the *Tribune* had been fully distributed and they locked the door of the press, they were torn between relief that they had found someone so capable to take over their precious paper, and despair at what that meant for the future.

They met Roger and Wyndham at the doors outside the Council chamber, still distracted by these thoughts.

"Good heavens," Roger said when he saw them. "Are you ill?"

They shook their head wearily. "I've barely slept in days."

Wyndham frowned. "When this is over, you need to go straight to bed and sleep until tomorrow. Do you understand?"

They scoffed and rolled their eyes. "Trust me when I say I'd like nothing better. But you needn't be so patronizing about it. I'm not that much younger than you."

"Yes, well, my brother will have my head if you fall ill because of this project."

They scrubbed a hand through their hair. "This is too important. Sleep can wait."

Wyndham sighed. "Are we ready then?"

"As ready as we'll ever be," Torquil said.

Roger squeezed their shoulder and the three of them filed into the chamber. The rest of the Council was already seated at the long table, which was set up again with the chairs all on one side.

Wyndham cast a critical glance at the arrangement. "Are we not sitting at the table with the rest of the Council?"

"We usually hear proposals in this manner," Gibbs said testily, "as you may recall."

"Yes, but is that typical of those who are also on the Council?" Wyndham replied.

"It *is* a bit unprecedented," Cricket said. "That is, usually these sorts of projects are completed by the entire Council. Or if only some of us do it, we have regular reports."

"Exactly," Williams said. "This whole affair has been done in a most unorthodox manner."

"I believe I passed on all of my grandson's reports to everyone," Iris said.

"I have not had any issues with the manner in which this project was done," Applewood said.

"Nor have I," Barnes said, smiling at the three of them as they still stood awkwardly beside the table. "Perhaps we ought to accept that things will be changing on this Council, considering the fact that we have new members, and we're taking on so many new and unique projects."

"Very well put, Norman," Iris said, smiling at him. "I second that opinion."

"So do I," Applewood said.

Cricket shrugged. "I suppose it makes sense."

"And if our votes still count," Wyndham said in an acid tone, "I daresay we would all be in favor of that opinion as well."

Williams glared at him. "Don't be impertinent, young man."

"We only just joined the Council," Roger put in. "No one ever told us we needed to do anything differently. How were we supposed to know that we were acting against protocol?"

Barnes smiled at his son and looked at Williams expectantly.

Williams huffed. "Oh, all right. I suppose we can bypass formality this time. But I will not accept a shuffling around of the furniture again. It is the outside of enough."

Torquil raised an eyebrow and dragged a chair to the center of the table, opposite the rest of the Council. They took a seat and folded their hands on the table in front of them, willing themself not to faint with nerves and exhaustion. Wyndham and Roger followed suit, taking seats on either side of them. Wyndham took his stack of carefully written notes and handed them to Applewood, who took one and passed it to Cricket. As the notes were passed around the table, Roger took out his notes, which were significantly messier and a little crumpled from so much handling. He laid them on the table in front of Torquil and gave them an encouraging nod.

"As you likely already know," Torquil said, lifting their chin and raising their voice. "We have come to the conclusion that a third rubric for those of mixed parentage is, in fact, necessary. We did our best to follow the same model of the Barnes-Wrenwhistle Method—"

Gibbs scoffed at the name.

"—but we determined it was impossible to hold to the exact same rubric. You see, magic manifests differently in every person born to fae and human parents. Some can only cast if they start with human spells, like me. Others can only cast if they start with fae spells. Some use fae magic to enhance their human spells, like I do. Others use human magic to build on their fae spells. Some can sense magic in the fae tradition, others cannot. As you can imagine," they went on with a smile, "this made it very difficult to determine a consistent measurement for magic."

Wyndham leaned forward and took over. "So we decided to keep with Roger's initial rubric of five skills, although we did alter course in how those will be measured. In the Barnes-Wrenwhistle Method," he said, shooting Torquil a grin, "we outlined specific spells for each child to perform. But since every child in this case will be using magic differently, we decided to make the rubric a bit more open. We will be giving children the option to perform any of the spells outlined in the other two rubrics. After all, it wouldn't be fair to judge a child who uses fae magic as a foundation by whether or not they can start a fire spell. Fae do not create fire out of nothing."

"Nor would it make sense," Roger chimed in, "to expect a child who uses human magic as a foundation to cast fairy lights. For humans cannot do that." The two men exchanged a look and Roger took over. "So we will expect those who conduct the tests to exhibit flexibility. They will need to allow each child to choose which five spells they wish to perform, and then they will be judged by the same criteria in the other rubrics: power, focus, control, understanding, and intuition."

"And for children who use fae magic as a foundation," Wyndham added, "they will have the option of exhibiting their knowledge the way fae children do."

Roger nodded to Torquil to take over again. "In addition to this proposal, we would like to expand on the other two rubrics. You may recall that Roger and Wyndham concluded their previous proposal with the discovery that fae and human magics are compatible. We recommend that children be tested on this as well, performing magic with someone of a different magic system. It will further demonstrate their knowledge and their ability to think on their feet, as well as collaboration. All of which are skills that would be good to identify at a young age. To align with this, we are recommending that fae-human children be tested on how well they balance their own two magic systems." They raised their chin again. "After all, we would like to encourage these children to be empowered by their own unique blend of magic."

There was a long silence.

"A creative and unique proposal," Iris said at last. "I think it is an excellent one."

"Agreed," Barnes said. "Although I do worry about children being tested on collaborative magical performance. That could prove dangerous."

Roger wrote that down.

"I think if those who administer the tests are appropriately trained, it could work," Applewood said. "We still need to further understand how the two magic systems blend, of course, but I believe it would be prudent to add that skill to magical curriculums on both sides."

"Yes," Cricket said, turning to Roger and Wyndham. "Especially after that performance at your wedding. Extraordinary," she whispered.

"I think the proposal has merit," Williams said. "Although I am reluctant to give an opinion until we can prove we have a plan for how to launch any of these rubrics."

Roger deflated a little beside Torquil. "That is understandable," he said morosely.

"As much as I hate to defer this decision," Iris said, "I do think Councilmember Williams makes a good point. Why don't we agree to reconvene after Christmas? We can discuss the prospects for launching all three rubrics and identify any changes that may need to be made."

Around the table, everyone nodded.

"That is reasonable," Williams said.

"I still think three rubrics is exorbitant," Gibbs said.

"Why?" Wyndham challenged. "There are three magic systems. Why shouldn't each be tested individually?"

"It's never mattered before," Gibbs said. "Moreover, the population of fae-human children is insignificant in comparison to—"

"It is not insignificant," Torquil said quietly.

Gibbs glared at them. "I dislike being interrupted, and I wasn't intending any insult by—"

"Nevertheless," Torquil said. "What you said was insulting. We may be a small population in comparison to fae and human children. But that does not make us insignificant. Our magic has been unstudied, we have been kept out of every institution, we have been forbidden from being tested. The system is set up *intentionally* to keep fae-human children from having good futures. They are kept out of polite society. They are disinherited. They are disgraced. And for what? Because their parents had the audacity to fall in love?"

They sat back in their seat. They had a feeling they were being a little too honest and outspoken, but they were too tired to curb their tongue. "Only months ago, all of you were applauding a marriage between a human and a fae. Was that celebration purely because you knew they would not have children? We are aiming to correct a wrong. And you wish to stand in our way because you don't think a small community such as mine matters."

"I never said I was standing in your way," Gibbs said mulishly.

Torquil huffed. "No, but you have demonstrated a dislike of me and everything about me since the moment I walked in these doors. I am here because I represent the unrepresented. I am here to break ties." Their headache throbbed and they touched a finger to their temple, rubbing it irritably. "I did not ask to be on this Council. I was approached and my presence was specifically requested. You have all known of my opinions on the inaction of this body. Goodness knows I haven't made a secret of it in my paper. You have all known that I prioritize making the public aware of what happens here. Some of you have even used me to that end."

They shrugged and dropped their hand back to the table. "As well you should. But I have worked too damn hard on this project—we all have worked bloody hard on this project—for it to be dismissed as unimportant simply because it doesn't affect you personally. It affects a lot of people. It will improve a great many people's futures. If you could see the letters I've received since joining this Council—and especially since starting this project—you would not call any part of this work insignificant. Nothing that improves the lives of others could ever be insignificant."

There was silence for a long moment, but before Torquil could begin to regret their words, Iris spoke up. "I think I can speak for all of us when I say that was very well said, Torquil," she said, beaming at them. "Thank you for, once again, reminding us of why we chose this work to begin with." She said this last with a meaningful glance in Gibbs' and Williams' direction.

Williams cleared his throat. "Indeed. Very well spoken. And a fitting end to the session, I believe. We will reconvene in a few days."

Iris stopped Torquil before they could walk away from the table. "I'm proud of you," she said, smiling at them again.

They swallowed, feeling as if they might cry. The tears prickling their eyes made it abundantly clear how desperately they needed to sleep. "Thank you," they whispered.

They attempted to leave but Wyndham and Roger waylaid them as well.

"You were marvelous!" Roger said.

Wyndham grinned. "Perhaps you ought to come to Council sleep deprived more often."

They chuckled. "Heaven forbid."

He clapped them on the shoulder. "You really were wonderful. Now do go home and get some sleep. You look like you might faint."

They nodded wearily and stepped away, only to be stopped *again* by Councilmember Applewood.

"I've been meaning to tell you," she said in her usual quiet way, "I'm glad you're on the Council. Even before that speech," she added with a laugh. "You're exactly what we need. Well, you and the young Wren-whistles, of course. You three will be the next generation to take over, I think. And it's a very good thing."

They smiled. "Thank you, Councilmember."

"I know Iris has taken you under her wing, so I've been hesitant to reach out. But I hope you know if you ever require help on anything, you need only ask."

"Thank you," they said again.

"What are your plans for tonight?"

"Sleep."

She laughed. "Yes, you look like you need it, poor thing. Well, I was just thinking if you are alone in the city, you might want some company on Christmas Eve. It's more of a human tradition, of course, but my children love it. And I thought you might celebrate it as well. So if you wish, you are welcome to join us for dinner tonight."

Torquil felt a lump in their throat. "I'd like that very much," they said softly.

She squeezed their shoulder. "We'll expect you then." She gave them her address and they finally left the chamber.

Torquil trudged back home, thinking fondly of their creaky old bed. They passed a carriage as they entered the alley to their door, giving it a wary look as they pulled out the key.

"Are you Mx. Pimpernel-Smith?" asked a polished voice from inside the carriage.

"It's Councilmember Pimpernel-Smith," they said.

"Oh, excellent." The door opened and a woman about Iris' age stepped out. Her hair was pulled back into a fashionable updo under an expensive-looking bonnet, making her pointed ears visible. "May I speak to you?"

Torquil stared at her for a good long moment. They recognized her. Even if they hadn't made a career of writing about the goings on of the upper class, they would have known who she was. She looked too much like their mother to be mistaken for anyone other than a relation. The woman was Leonora Pimpernel: Torquil's grandmother.

They considered for a moment, their sluggish brain making the action more difficult than usual. Seeing how she had waited for them, it was unlikely that she intended to inflict damage to the building. And she was speaking to them in friendly tones, which suggested that she did not intend to inflict damage on *them*. "Very well," they said at last, unlocking the door and stepping aside.

She breezed past them, holding a valise. They pulled the only chair in the pressroom forward for her and leaned back against the press, willing the conversation to be speedy so they could get to bed.

She took a seat, placing the valise on her lap. On closer inspection, Torquil realized the item was rather old, the leather worn and the straps much used. Although the material of the piece was of such good quality that it was holding together despite its age. Once seated, the woman fidgeted with her hands for a moment. Torquil registered with surprise that she was nervous.

"I just returned from abroad and I came here directly to see you."

"Why?" Torquil asked flatly. "You hate me."

Her mouth pinched. "I don't, actually. My husband…my *late* husband was very close-minded, though. He disinherited your mother and sent her away as soon as he learned that she was with child and that she intended to marry your father."

"You didn't stop him," they said, with more bitterness than they liked.

She folded her hands on the valise. "I wanted to. But I spoke to your mother about it, and we agreed this was the best course of action. She left with your father and I stayed with my wretched husband. It was not what either of us wanted, of course—well, she was happy to be with your father, don't mistake me—but it was the best way to ensure everyone was safe."

"Safe?" they echoed. "I grew up in the country. No one from my mother's past ever spoke to her. We were outcasts."

She nodded sadly. "Yes, but it was the only way. We had to bide our time until my husband died. And in the meantime, I saw to it that you were all cared for."

Dizziness began to cloud Torquil's brain and they squeezed their eyes shut for a moment. "What do you mean?"

"I mean that I gave your parents money for the cottage, I sent them money every year, I even gave them the money to help you start this press."

Torquil's hand slipped on the side of the press and their eyes flew open as they straightened. "You what?"

"I know how it sounds. But you see, if I had spoken in favor of my daughter, I would have been cut off financially as well. We agreed between us that it was better for me to stay put and do what I could to give them money and make sure you were all safe."

Torquil's head started pounding. "But my mother always told me that it was both her parents that—she never mentioned—" They swallowed. "Why would she lie to me?"

She opened the valise, but rested her hand on the open bag. "I didn't care for that, myself. But Sienna was adamant that it was easier to explain to a child that both of their grandparents were against the match, than to explain that their grandmother still loved them but could never see them." She drummed her fingers on the top of the valise.

"She was also concerned about our safety, should you decide to reach out to me. Even when you moved to London years ago, I wanted to establish communication. But Sienna was sure you would wish to meet or correspond. She worried your grandfather would pose a danger to you, or even myself, if we were found out."

Torquil was no longer sure that the dizziness was due to fatigue. Not only was the room spinning, but it felt as though their whole *life* was spinning. "Was all of it a lie?" they asked softly.

"No, of course not," she said soothingly. "My husband was a horrible man. That was all true. So, simply take everything you ever heard about both of us and attach it all to him."

"I see," they said weakly.

She made a distressed sound. "I'm so sorry to spring all of this on you. I haven't been in town because I've been in mourning. There are some absurdly strict rules about that, you know. But as soon as my mourning period was over, I came here immediately. You cannot imagine how much I've wanted to talk to you. I believe Iris Wrenwhistle has been seeing to your social debut—bless the woman—but I'd like to officially recognize you as my grandchild. It will open even more doors for you."

Doors that had been closed all of their life, simply because of their birth. "Why would you do that? You don't even know me. I could be horrible."

She laughed. "I know you aren't horrible. I've subscribed to the *Tribune* since its first publication. And Iris is an old friend and has kept me somewhat informed. And of course your mother—" She reached into the valise and pulled out a thick stack of papers. "—Your mother has been writing to me since before you were born. She's told me all about you." She stood and held the stack out.

Torquil took it, hands shaking. It was true. Of course it was. There was no reason for the woman to lie. Although they were still trying to wrap their head around why their parents had lied to them all their life. But it was evident they had. They recognized their mother's curly writing on page after page, letter after letter. They caught glimpses of reports on their childhood, their adolescence. Their vision blurred as they leafed through the pages, an entire lifetime's worth of correspondence that they had never known about. It was all too much.

"Excuse me," they said. "I think I need to…I need to think…"

"Of course, dear," she said hastily. "Please take as long as you'd—"

The dizziness and the tears were practically blinding as they reached behind them to put the stack on the press. They missed and the letters cascaded to the floor. Torquil stood and stared at them, and then, abruptly, turned and fled up the stairs.

They sank onto their bed and put their head in their hands. The room was still spinning and they closed their eyes as the tears continued to fall. They heard their grandmother close the door behind her and heard her carriage leave. It occurred to them that they didn't even know her address. And then they realized that they now had to decide what on earth they were going to do with the decision she'd laid at their feet. They fell back onto the bed, the dizziness becoming vaguely more tolerable when horizontal. They laid there, unmoving, for hours, replaying the conversation over and over, remembering stories from their mother, wondering how many of those stories were even true.

As the sun began to set, they remembered Applewood's invitation. Being upright and around people was, frankly, the last thing they wanted. But their mind was too busy to sleep and they couldn't countenance any more time spent with nothing to distract them. So they carefully hauled themself out of bed, changed into something less wrinkled, and walked to yet another dinner engagement.

CHAPTER 41

EMRYS

AROUND NOON, a note arrived for Emrys with an urgent request to meet at the club he and Keelan both belonged to. It was the perfect excuse to slip away from the townhouse as his mother worked to promote holiday cheer while also simmering with poorly disguised irritation every time they were in the room together.

After a brisk walk down St. James' Street, Emrys was escorted inside to one of the busier rooms on the second floor. The heavy curtains were drawn to keep out the scant midday light, the hearths were alive, and a spirited game of cards was being played around a table large enough to easily accommodate the fifteen people seated there.

Keelan was tucked into an alcove by one of the fireplaces, surrounded by shelves full of books and art sculptures that had never held his interest, despite their value. Emrys took a seat in the open chair and accepted the drink Keelan offered him, eyeing the stack of tomes on the small table between them.

"Finally decided to learn how to read, have you?" he teased lightly before he brought the glass to his lips.

Keelan laughed high and crisp in the back of his throat. "Those were there when I arrived. They do make me appear rather intelligent though, do they not?"

"Only to those who do not know you," Emrys assured him. "Your note would've had me believe you were in trouble. It seems that you're rather well."

"I had to escape for a while," Keelan explained, his expression sobering. "You know how my father gets around this time of year. He wanted us to join him in *hand-making* wreaths to hang on every door in the house this morning. The man is absurd. I am not a child."

"At least you are allowed to participate in the joy somehow," Emrys muttered. "Our home becomes a veritable museum of Christmases past every year, and for more than a week we are not even allowed into the family sitting room as Mother prepares it for guests. I cannot tell you the number of times I've been scolded for accidentally touching and inevitably ruining some sort of display while I was trying to play."

"And that's just this month alone," Keelan quipped.

They both laughed and sipped at their drinks, watching for a moment as the game of cards became heated. Emrys had never been particularly interested in games or gambling. Wyndham had told him more than once he hadn't the mind for it, which was probably true, if he was honest.

"To make matters worse, we are not even hosting this year. Mother decided that it would be exciting if everyone gathered at Wyndham's new townhouse instead."

"Auberon did not want the honor? He's newly married, as well."

Emrys scoffed. "None of us wanted to travel that far for a feast."

"I cannot imagine living in the country exclusively," Keelan said, his face twisting a bit in aversion. "It's so dreadfully boring."

"It seems that only those of us who are seeking something feel that way. The commonality I have found amongst people who enjoy a quieter lifestyle as such are those who have settled. Perhaps not always with a romantic partner or spouse, but something within them is happier with the slowness of country life."

Keelan seemed to sit with that for a moment, and then shook his head. "No, I really do not think I could manage it, even after I'm married."

Emrys set his empty glass atop the stack of books and sat back a bit in his chair, one hand smoothing down the top of his thigh toward his knee as the other came up for him to rub a fingertip over his bottom lip, a small grin forming there.

"I suppose I'll soon find out for myself."

Keelan turned to him with a look of surprise. "Not really."

Emrys nodded, and Keelan sat up, leaning closer across the space between them. "You rascal! How did it go?"

"I haven't asked yet," he said.

"No, I mean telling your mother."

"Oh. As you would have expected."

Keelan made a sympathetic sound. "Still, you've done it!"

Emrys reached into his pocket and pulled out the small velvet box he'd collected from the jeweler that morning. He'd only looked inside several dozen times since then. When he held it out for Keelan to take, the man gasped dramatically and placed a delicate hand at the base of his throat.

"Dearest, I told you not to ask me in public. You know I'm shy," he said coyly as he accepted the box and carefully opened it, tilting it a bit toward the fire to see it better. "It's incredible," he added in a more serious tone as he closed the lid and handed it back with a smile. "Torquil is going to adore it."

Emrys' face went hot. His brows furrowed as his mouth dropped open.

"How—"

"Emrys, please," he said with a chuckle. "I saw you dancing with them at the solstice party." He gave a knowing look. "*And* I saw you kiss them when the dance was over. If you were trying to be discreet, you did a very poor job of it. But I must say, if the chemistry between the two of you is that intense on the dancefloor, then your magical compatibility must be as indescribable as you say."

Emrys was still stuck on the fact that they'd been caught that night out in the snow. His magic swelled at the memory of Torquil resting their head against his chest as they followed the steps to the waltz he knew by heart. It was a good thing, too, because he'd been unable to think of anything other than holding them close and sharing such a perfect moment.

"When are you going to ask them?"

"Tomorrow night," Emrys said faintly, finding his voice again. He cleared his throat and tucked the ring away. "If my nerves do not kill me before then."

He knew nervousness was the least of his concerns. He'd made his decision, and he would follow through with it. There was only one thing that truly made him worry if he would survive long enough to ask his question: he still wanted to speak with Wyndham.

🔥

It was later than he'd planned when he arrived at his brother's townhouse that night. Tasteful bursts of mostly silver and green decorations were scattered throughout the main rooms, working alongside the existing palette of colors that could've inspired one of Wyndham's watercolor paintings.

Emrys was busy looking at one of the two hanging in the sitting room when the artist joined him.

"I see Mother sent her team to clutter your home with holiday cheer, as well," Emrys said as he turned to face him. "I'll have to let her know that I much prefer this understated look over what we have at home."

Wyndham's brows went up slightly. "Roger and I decorated ourselves. But please make sure I'm there to see it when you tell her that."

Emrys pressed his lips together. Wyndham sat on the sofa and crossed one knee over the other before he gestured to the open seats with an upturned palm, indicating for Emrys to take one. Emrys sat with a huff and tried to smooth his thoughts out enough to voice a coherent one. He decided to pick something safe.

"Is Roger well?"

"I sent him to bed with a tincture hours ago," Wyndham said a bit wearily. "He spent the entire day fretting over everything being perfect for the party tomorrow. At one point, he was so distracted while casting a cleaning spell to remove a stain that he made the entire rug disappear. I had to cut him off."

Emrys couldn't help the laugh that escaped him. To his relief, Wyndham's lips curved into a grin, as well.

"It must've been a rather large stain," Emrys mused.

"A very small rug," Wyndham corrected.

Emrys hummed. "Human magic is quite fascinating. I never knew."

"Yes," Wyndham agreed. "It's been an intriguing adventure, learning about what they are capable of." He paused. "Though I suppose I do not need to tell you that."

Emrys' gaze fell to his lap for a moment, before he looked up to find his brother staring at him. He'd seen that expression countless times. It was one of amusement, of challenge—the kind someone used when they knew something you did not. That was not a unique position for Emrys to be in. In truth, Wyndham had always looked at him that way, even as an infant. But there was something about that assessing gaze that had shifted over the last several weeks, and it wasn't until that moment that Emrys finally accepted what it was.

"How long have you known?" he asked quietly.

"Long enough," Wyndham said. "How long have *you* known?"

"Quite a bit longer than I truly realized, I'm afraid," he admitted, struggling to get the words out at first, but then they kept coming. "Mother is furious with me, of course. And I do regret having her go through all the trouble of finding me a suitable match, only for me to turn each and every one of them down. But…" Emrys' magic curled tightly inside him. "But it's not fair! I want to marry someone who makes me feel like I can accomplish anything, as long as they're by my side. I want to marry someone who I cannot stop thinking about. I want to marry someone who I can do everything and nothing with and be happy either way."

"And you do not think any of Mother's suitors could provide you with those things?"

Emrys sighed. "Not without me somehow forgetting that I already have someone who gives me all of that and more. So much more."

Wyndham made a face. "No need to elaborate on what *more* entails, if you don't mind." He smoothed a hand down the front of his waist-coat as he seemed to ponder his next words. "The compatibility of your magic is undeniable. What I witnessed that day in the study is worthy of recognition, no matter what else might transpire. Under different circumstances, I might've even suggested that the two of you continue some sort of magical partnership to find out exactly what you're capable of together."

Emrys' expression softened into something more hopeful.

"However," Wyndham said pointedly, "it seems as though you find yourself in a similar position to the one I found myself in not so very long ago."

"What position is that?" Emrys asked carefully.

Wyndham's jaw worked as he shifted a bit in his seat. "One in which your magical compatibility and your affections for someone cannot be easily separated."

Emrys tried to hide the smirk that came unbidden as he shook his head.

"You really are impossible, aren't you? I think the word you're trying for is *love*. You love Roger, and he loves you, and that's what made your wedding spell so impressive."

Wyndham tilted his head slightly. "And do you *love* Torquil?" he asked in a faintly mocking tone.

"Yes," Emrys answered without hesitation. "And do you want to know one of the things that helped me realize it?" Wyndham arched a brow, encouraging him to continue. "It was one of your paintings. The one you did of Grandmother's garden that she has in her study."

Wyndham cringed slightly. "Ugh. I painted that so long ago. I wish she would take it down and let me replace it with another."

Emrys ignored his self-criticism.

"That garden represents exactly how I feel. Maybe it's not perfect, but it's detailed and simple all at the same time. It's full of life and color, but it's private too, and there's a sense of familiarity that could only be understood by someone who has experienced the real thing." He brought a hand up and placed it over his heart. "There are thousands of gardens in London, Wyndham, but there's only one like that. And if I do not keep it for myself, then I will regret it for the rest of my life."

His brother was silent for a long moment. Emrys was sure that he was working up some sort of smart remark to make about the ridiculous comparison, but in the end, he only offered another small grin.

A soft blubbering noise caught their attention, and both men turned to find Roger standing in the open doorway clad in nothing but a night-shirt. He sniffled loudly and wiped at his nose with his sleeve. "That's so lovely," he choked out, more tears coming immediately after.

Emrys and Wyndham exchanged a look before Wyndham strode to Roger's side, wrapping a protective arm around him.

"What's got you up?" he asked softly before placing a kiss against Roger's temple. The gesture was so intimate that Emrys felt himself blush. "Have you had an unpleasant dream?"

"I came searching for you," he explained tearfully. "You always join me in bed, so when I woke to find you not there, I got worried."

"I've yet to come upstairs," Wyndham reassured him. "It's still evening."

"Oh," Roger said with a pitiful frown, sniffing again.

"Let me finish with Emrys and I'll be up in just a moment." Wyndham used his handkerchief to wipe some of the tears away from Roger's cheeks and carefully turned him around in the direction of the stairs. Emrys couldn't help but look at Wyndham differently when he returned to his seat. He'd never seen such tender behavior from his youngest sibling.

"What was in that tincture?" he asked with a little laugh in an attempt to lighten the mood.

"He sleepwalks on occasion when he's feeling particularly over-whelmed," Wyndham said with care. "When the elixirs are not quite strong enough to keep him asleep, it sometimes leaves him a bit out of sorts."

Emrys studied him for a moment. "I take back what I said. You're not impossible, just very particular about who gets to see your senti-mental side."

"Yes, well." Wyndham looked away. "I suppose now you've caught a glimpse of my own garden." He stood again and took a couple of steps toward the door. "If there wasn't anything else, I'll need to go and check on him."

Emrys followed him out of the sitting room. They both paused at the stairs. "I'm not entirely sure what I came here to say," Emrys managed. "Or if I've said it. I suppose I just wanted you to know."

Wyndham placed a hand on the bannister and put his foot on the first step, looking up toward their bedroom before he angled his body toward Emrys. His lips bunched to one side as he chewed the inside of his cheek, a quirk Emrys recognized from their childhood.

"A month ago, I would've told you to leave well enough alone," he said.

"I'm fairly certain that's exactly what you told me, actually."

"I thought you were after another easy target. Torquil was new to the Council, new to society, and new to our family—or so I was led to believe. I did not want you interfering with our work, and I most certainly did not want you to become someone who used Torquil for a spot of fun and then left me and Roger to clean up the mess you left behind."

"And now?" Emrys ventured.

"Now I see that you are one of the few consistencies in their life. I am the last person to divulge on things I have been told in confidence, but you must know that Torquil cares for you deeply. The destruction you caused in our study is proof enough of what has remained unsaid between the two of you. So who am I to try and deny what is meant to be?"

Wyndham turned and climbed the stairs without another word. Any uncertainty Emrys had felt dissipated, leaving him with nothing but hope. As he left for home, he laughed at himself, for his first thought was to hurry across town to share with Torquil how excited he was, just as he had done so many times before.

CHAPTER 42

TORQUIL

ON CHRISTMAS MORNING, Torquil awoke with a pounding headache. However, they could not find it in them to regret going to the Applewood family's home. The evening had been filled with tender family affection and joy, and being invited into the environment had soothed something in Torquil.

Growing up with parents like theirs had meant forgotten holidays, forgotten birthdays, and a general disregard for society. Their mother was a free spirit who had been relieved to have an excuse to leave her social obligations behind, and their father was an idealistic dreamer who had no interest in practicality. As soon as Torquil had expressed an interest in moving to London, they had sold their little cottage and embarked on a trip around the continent, reaching their only child through sporadic letters and packages. Torquil had often wondered how the two managed to keep a roof over their heads for all those years. Now they knew.

They had slept fitfully, thinking about their grandmother's visit and all that it entailed. They were too practical to believe that reuniting with the woman would result in the sort of warmth they had witnessed the previous night, but that didn't mean her offer was lacking. Reuniting with their grandmother would send a very clear message to the world:

even the most illustrious of families could move past their prejudice and accept their fae-human relations.

Torquil groaned, got out of bed, and wearily made their way down-stairs. The letters were no longer in a mess on the floor; a detail they'd overlooked in their hurry to leave the previous night. They were all stacked neatly on the press, with the valise placed nearby. They picked up the stack and the valise and returned to their room. Perching on the end of their bed, they looked through the letters with more care than they had before. They recognized their mother's flippant way of speaking in her recounts of Torquil's assorted milestones: walking, speaking, writing, reading, swimming in a lake, and learning spells. It was easy to read between the lines and guess at the questions that had prompted the responses. Their grandmother had worried for them, had sent gifts, had wanted to know every detail of their life. Some of the letters were more worn than others, suggesting she had often reread the words.

They reached the end of the stack and opened the valise to return them inside when they noticed another stack of papers. They pulled them out and felt emotion well up inside when they recognized copies of the *Tribune*. They leafed through them. Years of publications and, from what they could tell, every single issue was accounted for. Tears pricked their eyes as they set the papers on the mattress and buried their face in their hands.

It was all so deeply unfair. Why had she been kept from them for so long? Surely they would have managed to write to her secretly. Surely they would have been able to establish some form of connection. Surely...they might have been a little less alone living in London for years.

Torquil scrubbed at their face and got dressed, picking out their best outfit for daywear. Then they put all of the papers back in the valise, picked it up, and left. They walked with purpose for over a quarter of an hour before they realized where they were headed; without really thinking about it, they had started the trek to Iris' townhouse.

As they passed holiday merrymakers, they remembered with a jolt that it was Christmas morning, and stopped in the middle of the road. Could they call on Iris on such a day? They weren't entirely ready to face their grandmother yet. After a long moment of hesitation, they continued, resolving to request an audience and leave immediately if she proved busy.

It was almost strange to approach the door without a party on the other side. Torquil knocked and told the footman that they were requesting to speak with Councilmember Wrenwhistle, but only if she wasn't too busy. To their surprise, they were promptly led into an elegant sitting room.

Iris looked up and beamed at them. "What a delightful surprise," she said as she stood to greet them.

"I'm sorry to bother you this morning. I'm sure you're very—"

She waved away their concerns before they'd finished expressing them. "It's always a pleasure to see you. My family won't be celebrating the holiday until this evening."

"Roger's party?"

"Yes," she said, gesturing for them to sit. "I confess I would prefer a more intimate gathering but, well, you've met my daughter-in-law. She doesn't do anything by halves."

They allowed a small laugh. "No, that she doesn't."

Iris waited expectantly.

They took a deep breath. "My grandmother called on me yesterday."

Iris seemed to still for a moment. "And?"

"She explained—well, I assume you already know everything."

She nodded slowly. "I do. But I must admit that I've never cared for the arrangement."

"It sounded as though she didn't either."

"She certainly did not," Iris said, with more heat than usual. She seemed to collect herself. "I hope you understand, Torquil, that not everyone has the luxury of marrying for love. Leonora—your grand-mother—did not. She was married to a cruel and greedy man. There was no affection between them."

"I understand," they said quietly. "She gave me the letters my mother wrote to her over the years." They gestured to the valise at their feet. "She saved every issue of the *Tribune*. She...she told me she wishes to formally recognize me as her grandchild and make it known that we've reconciled."

Iris' smile was slow, but genuine. "That's wonderful."

Torquil clasped their hands in their lap. "It is. It will mean a great deal for the work we've been attempting to do." They hesitated and then said in a small voice, "I know it is foolish of me but…I'm terrified."

Iris' expression turned sympathetic and she reached forward to put a hand over theirs. "It isn't foolish at all. I'm well aware of how uncomfortable you are in social events." She squeezed their hand. "This will mean even more of them."

"Yes. And not to mention…she's essentially a stranger. I…I have no idea how to…how to conduct myself or—or what she'll think of me."

"Leonora has loved you since before you were born, Torquil," Iris said gently.

"She doesn't even know me."

"Anyone who has read your papers with more than an eye for gossip knows you, or at least aspects of you," she countered with a smile. "You pour yourself into your writing, whether you intend to or not. Your principles, your romantic ideals, your desire to help people, your sense of humor, your mind for solving problems—it's all there."

Torquil felt a tear slide down their cheek and quickly wiped it away.

Iris gave their hand another squeeze. "You've spent your entire life believing her to hate you. I can only imagine how difficult it must be to trust at this point. But I hope you trust me when I say that she has spent a long time waiting for this opportunity. From what I know of you, there is nothing you could do to make her dislike you. And," she added, "I'm not going anywhere. You don't have to do any of this alone. You'll still have me, Wyndham, Roger…and Emrys."

Torquil remembered the conversation in her office, when she'd hinted that she knew of their feelings for Emrys. It seemed like a lifetime ago. Now it was as though everyone knew about their secret relationship, and they were too weary to feel the usual frisson of panic. "How long have you known?"

She laughed. "Oh, I've suspected for some time."

They rubbed their eyes. "I suppose we weren't as subtle as we thought."

"No, not very," she said with evident amusement.

They sighed, unwilling to pursue the subject. They already had plenty to worry about without adding their worries regarding Emrys to the mix. They reached into the valise and pulled out a letter. "Is this still her address in London?"

Iris leaned forward to read the direction. "Yes, that's the one."

Torquil read it more carefully. "Oh. It's down the street."

The prospect of having this next conversation so soon made their stomach roil and their head pound even more. They rubbed at their temple. "I don't think I can do this."

"Of course you can," she assured them. "Although I'm not sure you should do it on an empty stomach. Perhaps I should—"

"I don't think I could keep anything down right now."

"Are you all right?"

They shook their head with a humorless laugh. "I'm not sure I've been all right for days. I have the most dreadful headache, the room won't stop spinning, and I think I might be sick—although that last one is likely from nerves more than anything else."

Iris wasted no time in sending a servant to fetch a tincture. They returned promptly and Torquil took it gratefully. The pain started to recede almost instantly. They stared at the bottle. "What is in this?"

She laughed as she took it from them and handed it back to the servant. "I'll teach you how to make it sometime. Are you sure you don't want something to eat?"

"Quite sure."

"Very well. Then why don't you go now before you lose your nerve. Oh!" she said and then strode to a writing desk and picked up a paper. "It is entirely up to you, of course, but if you wish, you can invite her to join us tonight." She handed them the paper, an invitation to Roger and Wyndham's Christmas party. Torquil's invitation was still on their own desk back at the press building. They pocketed the invitation.

"Thank you…for everything."

She took their hand again and gave them a fond look. "I cannot tell you how proud I am of the person you've become, and the person you're still becoming, Torquil. You are one of the bravest, cleverest, and kindest people I've met. An unexpected reunion and elevation in society couldn't befall anyone more worthy."

They laughed, a little tearfully, thanked her, and left.

On the stoop, they gathered their bearings, shifted the valise in their grasp, and strode down the street to the number on the letter.

The footman who opened the door to the Pimpernel residence took one look at Torquil, raised his eyebrows expressively, and then stepped aside to hold the door wider. "Do come in."

Torquil walked into the foyer, bemused.

"You will forgive me," the footman said. "You look very much like your mother."

Torquil huffed a laugh. "Ah, yes. I've been told. But not in a long time," they admitted.

The footman smiled and then led Torquil to a sitting room every bit as elegant as Iris'. "I'll tell her you're here."

Torquil felt too uneasy to sit, so they wandered around the room. It felt strange to look at portraits and know they were likely related to the subjects, to see knickknacks and wonder if they were family heirlooms. But they felt so disconnected from it all.

"You came."

They turned to see their grandmother standing in the doorway, beaming. She held out her hands and approached them, but stopped just short of reaching for them. Torquil offered their hand and she clasped it gratefully.

"I was worried you wouldn't. Of course, I wouldn't have blamed you."

"I just…needed some time to think about it. I'm afraid I was in such a state of shock yesterday that I…I didn't properly…that is…"

She shook her head and led them to a sofa, where they sat next to each other. "You weren't at all improper. I have spent months trying to imagine how I might break the news to you. There wasn't any way I could think of that might be gentle enough."

"The news itself wasn't gentle enough for an easy delivery," Torquil said. They took a deep breath. "I…I looked through your letters. I had no idea you'd been reading the *Tribune* all along."

"Once your mother stopped reporting on how you were doing, your paper was the best way for me to learn anything about you. Although Iris did write to me once you joined the Council. I wanted so much to tell you."

"I know."

"Have you given any thought to my offer?"

"I've barely thought of anything else. I mean to accept it, but I should admit that I'm not very good at social…functions. I'm sure Iris could tell you. I've been trying, of course, and I mean to go on, but… but it's been very difficult."

"I understand," she said. "You were not exactly prepared for this sort of life."

"No. I imagine my parents would be very surprised if they knew how much I was engaging in society now."

"How did Iris persuade you to do it?"

They laughed. "I'm a member of the Council. So it's more of a duty than anything. And the reason I'm on the Council…the reason I started the paper, and, frankly, the reason I came to London at all was to try and do what I could to improve things for people like me."

She gave them a sympathetic smile. "I know how much that means to you. Iris has been very complimentary of your work on the Council."

"I think this," they said, gesturing between them, "will go a long way towards helping that."

"I know it will. I am prepared to do whatever you need to aid in that endeavor."

"Truly?"

"Of course."

They took the invitation out of their coat pocket. "Perhaps we could start with this? I know it's very last-minute but—"

She smiled and covered their hand with hers as she took the invitation, giving it a cursory once-over. "I would like nothing better than to go with you. If you'll indulge me, I'd like to gift you with something to wear as well."

"Oh," they said, blushing. "But the party is this evening. I can't imagine anyone will be able to—"

"Well, I took the liberty of purchasing some things for you."

"You did? When? How?"

"Before my return to London. Iris told me she'd recommended a tailor to you. I wrote to him and asked him to make some pieces to your measurements. It was highly presumptuous, of course. I hope you don't mind. I had planned to give them to you, even if you didn't wish to know me."

"I don't mind," they said slowly, their mind reeling. "You did all of that for me?"

She leaned forward and kissed their cheek. "I was not permitted to spoil you rotten as a child. Please allow me to do so now."

They laughed. "I'm not accustomed to being spoiled. Historically, I'm quite bad at it, actually."

She smiled and cupped their cheek. "Well, we'll ease you into it. Let's start with food. Have you had breakfast?"

They shook their head.

She gestured to a servant and led Torquil into a breakfast room. "You caught me before I had eaten, fortunately. So your timing is very good. I keep London hours, you see. So I typically eat breakfast around noon." She gestured for them to sit and took a seat at the head of the table.

Torquil noticed that her expression had turned hesitant. "Is there something more?"

"Well...yes. I've been trying to decide when to tell you. I don't want to give you too much information at once."

Torquil huffed a laugh. "I think we're past that point. As I said before, there is no gentle way around this conversation." They sat straighter and with more courage than they felt, they said, "Do I have a secret sibling or something?"

She chuckled. "No, not quite that alarming. I've spoken to my solicitors and they've managed to ensure that you will inherit everything. Your mother has no interest in any of it, you know. She's far too happy gallivanting around Europe with your father."

Torquil could only stare. Finally, they managed, "I rather think that's more alarming than a secret sibling."

A servant placed a plate full of food in front of them. Their grandmother poured out tea. "I'm sorry for the onslaught of new information," she said, sounding truly contrite.

Torquil took a sip of tea. "Please don't be. Though...is there anything else?"

"Well...I would adore it if you came and lived with me. Your mother told me how you've been living in the press building and I'd feel much more at ease if you were somewhere safer. If you didn't feel comfortable with that arrangement, I could get you some rooms of your own."

"Oh, please don't do that," they said hurriedly. The idea of moving into Mayfair was alarming at first, but they gave it due thought. They'd no longer have to worry about break-ins, or traveling so far for their work on the Council...or to see Emrys. Perhaps it would be a nice sort of change, albeit a strange one.

"You don't have to answer right away about moving in," she said softly. "But do think about it, if you would."

"I will."

"And I recognize that it might be challenging for you to travel back and forth to do your work. I imagine you need to get up much earlier than I do for the *Tribune*. We can determine a schedule to ensure you always have food ready before you leave, and you would have a carriage at your disposal, should you want it."

"That's very kind of you. Unfortunately..." They paused, feeling a fresh wave of grief at the prospect of saying it out loud. "I'm afraid I'll have to give up the *Tribune* soon."

"Give it up? Why? Not because of me, I hope."

"No," they said, smiling at her. "No, I've been coming to the decision for a long time. With the *Tribune* I often get up before the sun. Now that I work at the Council, I'm busy throughout the day. And since I've started to be more engaged socially, I'm busy late into the night." They shook their head wearily. "It is too much. I've kept it up for as long as I could, but I don't think I can bear it any longer."

"I did worry about those circles under your eyes," she murmured. "So what will become of the *Tribune*? Do you intend to sell it?"

"I actually mean to give it to a friend of mine. She has proven capable of the work, and she seems to enjoy it. Not to mention she has a clever way with words. I think she will take good care of it."

She smiled at them with such affection, they felt another surge of emotion. Before they could wipe away the tears that started to fall, she put a hand to their cheek and wiped the tears away gently. Then she politely returned to her food.

"So, what can you tell me about yourself that I haven't read in the papers? I know you are a rising star on the Council, you're on the cusp of taking London by storm, and that you know everything there is to know about everyone."

"I'm not so sure about all of that. What is it that you'd like to know?"

"Do you have any plans? Schemes? Any friends of note? Any *lovers* of note?"

They coughed on their food a bit in surprise. "You wish me to tell you about my lovers?"

She gave them an amused smile. "Well, I don't anticipate a detailed account, of course. But I am fae. We're very open about that sort of thing."

They cleared their throat. "Well, I do have some friends that I've made recently: Roger and Wyndham Wrenwhistle."

She nodded. "I've known Wyndham Wrenwhistle a long time, although not exactly well."

"He is much kinder than he seems."

She laughed. "Anyone else?"

They hesitated. "I do have a friend who is very dear to me but... well, it's a very confusing situation."

"How so?"

"We've been friends for a long time. Lovers too," they added, feeling themself blush. "But he's going to inherit and his mother has been working diligently to find him a spouse. His brother thinks he means to court me but...but I'm not sure I believe it."

"Why not?"

"His mother hates me. Even if he wanted to propose, I'm sure she would never permit it." They swallowed. "She...er...said once that she thought it was very appropriate for my mother to be disinherited."

Leonora's lips pinched together for a moment. Then she smiled and patted their hand. "She sounds dreadful, but I'm sure she'll have no objection now."

"What do you mean?"

"You will be inheriting your own fortune. We will be publicly showing everyone tonight that we have reunited. I imagine her opinion of you will change very quickly."

"Oh," Torquil said. "I hadn't thought that far yet."

"So who is the gentleman?"

"Emrys Wrenwhistle," they murmured.

She seemed to think for a moment. "I believe I've spoken to him more than his brother. He is a very charming young man. Very handsome. Although, perhaps not quite as clever as Wyndham," she added hesitantly.

They laughed. "No, he isn't very clever. But I love him all the same." Her eyes widened and Torquil realized with a jolt what they'd said. "I mean…that is…"

She smiled. "It seems I returned just in time. I do love matchmaking."

They groaned.

She laughed. "I think you inherited that skill from me. Just think what fun we'll have once you're married. We'll be able to match up the entire *ton*."

They grinned despite themself and stifled a yawn as they said, "I shall take the matter under consideration."

She frowned and said, "Would you like to rest, my dear?"

"I'm not sure I should. I don't know if I'd wake up in time for the party."

"You know invitations can be turned down, don't you?"

"I couldn't do that to Roger and Wyndham," they protested. "This is their first time hosting an event. It will be fine. After tonight, I'll sleep for as long as I need to."

"Very well. But perhaps some relaxation is in order? I can have a bath sent up for you."

The idea of a bath sounded lovely, but doing so in a strange house gave them pause. "I don't know…" they hedged.

"You can take as long as you like," she pressed. "And it will give me a chance to show you the room I've selected for you and you can see if you like it."

"I'm sure I'll like it. Anything will be better than the room I've been living in."

"And I can show you the clothes I've purchased and you can choose your outfit for this evening? If you don't have any other obligations today, you could stay and ease into the idea of living here. You can have your bath, I can give you a tour of the townhouse. I'll have someone help you to dress and we can have dinner together before we go to the party."

She sounded so eager and they had to admit that her logic was sound. Spending a full day in the house would go a long way towards making them comfortable about moving in. "All right," they acquiesced.

After breakfast, Leonora gave them a tour of the townhouse, starting in the kitchens and leading them all the way up to the top floor, before bringing them to a bright and sunny bedroom. "This has always been my favorite bedroom in the house. It overlooks the garden and the bed is lovely."

The four poster bed had curtains around the edges that reminded Torquil of how they imagined royalty sleeping. There were plush blankets and plusher pillows in various hues of blue. They ran a hand over the fabric, noting the softness of the texture.

While their first thought was how luxurious and comfortable it would be to sleep in it, their very next thought was wondering what Emrys would think. They could just picture him testing the soundness of the bed, commenting on the lack of squeaking, and maybe he'd pull the curtains down so that it was just the two of them in their own little world. They flushed at the thought and attempted to think of something else.

Leonora smiled at them as she strode to a wardrobe. "Your friend needn't sneak in, by the way. It is perfectly normal in fae households to have lovers spend the night. It will ease my mind, really, to know that you are not depriving yourself of company."

Their face heated even more, but they didn't trust themself to speak so they simply nodded in response.

She opened the wardrobe. "I purchased a variety of items, things I thought you might not buy for yourself. There's an outfit for riding,

some formal attire—I think this one would do very well for tonight—
and some bed clothes, as well as more everyday pieces."

They looked through each piece, astounded by the expense that had
been put forth. Each article was made with undeniably quality material.
There were embroidered embellishments, gold threads, gemstone
buttons. They ran a hand over the riding trousers, smiling to themself at
the memory of Emrys in his. How would he react if they showed up
one day in such an outfit? They pulled out the piece that Leonora had
identified as a possible one for the evening. It was a forest green suit with
a silk waistcoat in a lighter shade. The waistcoat had silver embroidery
all across it. They rubbed a fingertip over the embroidery.

"You bought all of this for me…even though you weren't sure I'd
accept this? That I'd accept you?" they said, turning to her.

She gave them a sad smile and cupped their cheek. "Nothing I give
you—now or ever—will be contingent on you behaving a certain way or
living up to any expectations. I hope you know that. If I'd been in your
life more properly, I would have given you gifts and showered you with
affection, no matter how many temper tantrums you threw, no matter
how much you talked back in anger. You have lived your entire life
under the weight of so many expectations—you were not given the
grace to be poorly behaved, ignorant, or common. You have been under
scrutiny ever since you arrived in London, even before you entered
society in a more official capacity. I should like to provide you with one
space where there are no expectations and no scrutiny."

They wiped at their eyes. "You're going to think I weep a great deal
more than I ordinarily do. Thank you. You've been so kind. I…I don't
know how to accept such gifts, but I'm grateful for them."

She kissed their cheek.

Two servants came in carrying a bathtub, while several more trailed
behind with buckets of water.

"I shall leave you to your bath," she said, patting their cheek. "Take
as long as you'd like. The servants can reheat the water for you, should
you need it. And you can put this on when you're done." She indicated
a banyan hanging on a hook on the wardrobe door. Torquil had
completely missed it, too distracted by the other clothing.

Once the bath was prepared, they sank into the warm water,

exhaling in relief. A towel was placed behind their neck so they could lean their head back against the tub's edge. They thought again about Emrys. It was strange to go so many days without an evening visit from him. Not for the first time, they wished he would stop being so damned proper all of a sudden, and take them to bed. They had so much to tell him and it had only been a few days since they'd last seen him.

They turned their head to look at the bed. Would Emrys come visit them here? Would he knock gently on the door and slip inside, starting the conversation as he usually did with no preamble, as he casually discarded his clothing onto the floor? Or was such ease between them gone now? When Emrys married, what would happen then? Torquil knew it was common for fae to keep lovers after marriage. Would Emrys keep them? Living here would likely make the trip feel less tawdry. They would be peers, almost.

They wondered if their grandmother was correct about whether this new change would impact their eligibility. Was it too late to impress Mrs. Wrenwhistle sufficiently? Were they still too lowly for her son? They bit their lip at the thought. It would be dreadful if Mrs. Wrenwhistle snubbed Leonora too. Had it been a mistake to invite her to the Christmas party?

They felt the dizziness returning and they splashed water on their face, hoping to keep it at bay. It didn't work. And when the headache started to return as well, they decided to get out of the bath. They did not have the courage to ask for an elixir, as they had no idea what Iris had given them. They put on the banyan, tying it snugly around their waist. It fit perfectly, with the sleeves ending just at their wrists, and the back giving them proper room to move their arms. Leonora really had been thorough. They briefly wondered if they ought to wear something underneath the banyan but decided against it. They had no idea what one wore under banyans anyway. Besides, from what they had gleaned over the years from their mother, and Emrys, and observing the fae of society, such modesty was more of a human trait than a fae one. A servant offered them a pair of slippers and then led them back downstairs.

They enjoyed a leisurely pot of tea with their hostess as they discussed how the Season had been since she'd been out of the country.

They spoke about Roger and Wyndham's courtship and subsequent marriage, confessing their own role in that romance. They talked about the relationship between Miss St. Clair and Lady Fitzhugh, about the budding romance between Miss Aveline Wrenwhistle and Mr. Buckthorn, and all of their theories for the various single people in London. Leonora was an avid listener and a skilled gossip. By the time the teapot was empty, Torquil was beginning to suspect that she'd been in earnest about working together as matchmakers, and they were also beginning to think of it as a viable occupation.

♦

WHEN THERE WERE ONLY a few hours left before the party, Leonora sent Torquil upstairs to get changed. As with the banyan, the green suit fit perfectly. They marveled again at the intricacy of the waistcoat and reveled a bit in imagining Emrys' reaction to the garment. When they were fully dressed, Leonora came in, dressed for the party as well, and offered some finishing touches: an emerald cravat pin, a pocket watch and a watch fob in a coordinating shade.

She tilted her head and looked at them assessingly. "It still needs more, I think, but the color looks well on you. It brings out the green in your eyes. You look so much like Sienna," she said, smiling.

"I've been told," they said with a chuckle. "Same eyes, although they're more hazel than green thanks to my father."

"And the same chin, the same nose. Your smile is just like hers." She touched light fingertips to their curls. "But this is entirely from your father. Do you ever wear anything in your hair?"

"Wyndham has been slowly supplying me with hair combs. And there was a hat at one point."

"You enjoy feminine styles as well then?" she said eagerly.

"I'm beginning to. It is a bit more difficult to explore fashionable options when one is struggling to pay for food. But I've enjoyed everything Wyndham has attempted."

An expression of horror flitted over her face at their statement, but she recovered quickly and said, "I think I have just the thing." She took their hand and led them down the hall into an even larger room with an even larger bed. There was a conspicuously empty space on the wall above the bed that caught Torquil's eye. She noticed and said, "I had every portrait of my husband taken down as soon as the grieving period was over. It was such a relief."

For a moment, Torquil very nearly asked her if she'd killed him. But that seemed entirely unwise, not to mention unkind, so they didn't. As they stared at the empty spot on the wall—a large one that must have housed a huge portrait—they decided they wouldn't have blamed her at all if she had. Imagine having to spend every night staring at the painting of a man who had separated her from her only child and grandchild? Not to mention what other forms of cruelty the man had inflicted on her over the years. They repressed a shudder and turned their attention back to the matter at hand.

"Will this do?" she asked, holding up a silver hair band.

"That's beautiful," they said. "I don't think I've worn anything so fine."

She carefully set it on their head, arranging their curls just so. "There," she said. "It looks perfect. Your hair is rather charming so I don't wish to upset that, but this adds a touch of elegance."

They looked at a full-length mirror and stared at their reflection for a long time. It struck them quite suddenly that this was different from all of the other times they'd dressed up in the past. These were not borrowed clothes—or perceived borrowed clothes—this was not a temporary look. They were attending the party with their grandmother to make a statement, and this outfit would add to that significantly. This was who they were now, a Pimpernel as much as a Smith. "You're right," they said softly.

"Would you be opposed to some powder on your face? It might help cover up the circles, poor thing."

They agreed and a towel was placed over their clothes as Leonora's lady's maid applied a light layer of powder over their skin.

Afterward, they enjoyed a quiet supper in the dining room until it was time to leave. Torquil's stomach became fluttery with nerves by the time the carriage arrived at Roger and Wyndham's townhouse.

Leonora put a hand on their arm. "Are you all right?"

"Just nervous. This…er…this is going to change everything."

She smiled. "I'm not sure it will change *everything*. Your friends won't change at all, I imagine. Just the people whose opinion never mattered in the first place."

They laughed.

A servant opened the carriage door and helped them both out. Torquil offered an arm to their grandmother and walked up the steps, feeling strange about entering a space that had become so familiar but was now filled with unfamiliar faces. Everything had been decorated for the season: evergreen boughs wound around banisters and framed doorways, silver and green decorations gave everything a sense of cohesion.

The two hosts stood at the doorway, greeting guests. Roger looked nervous but otherwise in good spirits. Wyndham seemed too distracted by checking on Roger to be as tense as he usually was during social gatherings.

When Torquil and their grandmother stepped forward, Torquil said, "Roger, Wyndham. Please allow me to introduce my grandmother, Mrs. Pimpernel. She recently returned from the continent and was kind enough to reconnect with me."

Roger's jaw dropped in surprise. Wyndham recovered from his shock more quickly, offering a hand and kissing Leonora's knuckles with impressive elegance. "It is an honor to have you as our guest this evening, Mrs. Pimpernel." Roger stammered that he was delighted to meet her and any friend of Torquil's was welcome.

Iris found them before they'd stepped much further into the foyer. She greeted Leonora as an old friend and complimented Torquil on their outfit. As she walked away, Torquil could feel the gazes of the other partygoers. As they moved farther into the room with their grandmother, they could hear the whispers and murmurings following them. Leonora gave their arm an encouraging squeeze. She offered friendly greetings to everyone she passed, without stopping for chatter.

Torquil hadn't known where they were leading her until they found Emrys. When they saw him coming toward them, they felt as though a missing piece had been slotted into place. Emrys was there and everything would be all right.

Before he could say anything in greeting, Torquil launched into introductions, anxious to get the news out of the way as quickly as possible. "Mr. Wrenwhistle, I believe you are acquainted with my grandmother, Mrs. Pimpernel. She returned to town recently and was good enough to call on me."

Emrys glanced between them, bewildered. Leonora extended a hand and said, "Mr. Wrenwhistle, a pleasure to see you again. My grandchild has told me much about you."

It had been a long time since Torquil had been embarrassed by a family member and they realized suddenly that having their grandmother in their life would likely incur a great many more instances of embarrassment. They blushed and looked worriedly at Emrys.

But Emrys gave a bright smile in response. "How nice to see you again, Mrs. Pimpernel. Can I interest either of you in some punch? It is quite warm in this room."

Leonora eagerly accepted the invitation and Emrys' offered arm. When Emrys turned and offered his other arm to Torquil, they latched onto it. People gave way as he led them to the far end of the dining room, where refreshments had been set up.

"It looks wonderful in here," Torquil commented.

"Yes," Emrys said as he served them both a cup of punch. "I made the mistake of telling Wyndham that I liked his decorating style better than my mother's. I'm not sure if I'll ever live that down."

Torquil laughed, relieved that Emrys was still his usual self, even with their grandmother present.

Leonora gave them an amused look. "And how is your mother, Mr. Wrenwhistle?"

He grimaced. "She is well. Although she has been a little irritated with me for the past couple of days."

"Perhaps if you didn't insult her taste, she'd feel better," Torquil teased him.

Emrys' expression softened as he looked down at them.

Leonora patted Torquil's arm. "Since you seem to be in such good hands now, I think I'll go and chat with some of my friends. Is there anything particular you'd like me to say?"

They shook their head, grateful for the question. "I trust you to explain things."

She smiled, kissed their cheek, and, appallingly, gave Emrys a wink before gliding away.

Emrys stared after her. "So…I take it you reconciled with her then?"

Torquil chuckled. "No, she still hates me."

Emrys rolled his eyes. "Seriously."

"Seriously, yes. She visited me yesterday and explained. Apparently I've been lied to all of my life. My grandfather *did* hate me, but my grandmother was against the notion of my mother being sent away. She paid for the house I grew up in, paid for a great many of the things I had as a child. She was even the one who bought my press building. She wrote to my mother constantly, asking for updates about me as I grew up. She collected every single issue of the *Tribune*. My grandfather not only deprived his daughter of her inheritance and me of social standing, he deprived his wife of a relationship with her only grandchild." They sighed. "It's been a rather trying couple of days."

Emrys put a comforting hand on their lower back. "I'm sorry."

"I suppose at some point we all have to recognize that our parents are fallible and liable to make mistakes."

Emrys gave a small huff of laughter. "Yes, I have certainly been made aware of the fallibility of my own parents as of late."

Torquil shook themself mentally. "Anyway, I suppose it all worked out in the end. She's very kind, as you can probably tell. Or perhaps you already knew. It's strange to think that you know my grandmother better than I do. She means for me to inherit everything and she's invited me to come and live with her."

Emrys' entire face lit up. "But that's wonderful! You won't have to sleep in that horrid little bed anymore." He gave a satisfied sort of sigh. "It is good to know that you'll be better fed and more comfortable now."

Torquil took a sip of punch. "It is. I'm still getting accustomed to the idea though. She bought me a great deal of clothes, including this outfit, and it has taken everything in me not to reject it all."

Emrys' hand moved from their back to the front of their waistcoat. "She did a marvelous job." Then he leaned forward and said, "Does this mean I can buy you gifts now too?"

Torquil laughed a little. "Let's take it one thing at a time, shall we?"

Emrys patted his pocket, almost absently, before nodding. "Right. One thing at a time. How are you feeling?"

"All right. Overwhelmed by…everything. And very, very tired. I've barely slept in days."

Emrys frowned and held out his hand. "Give me your dance card."

"What?" they asked as they handed it over. "Why?"

"Because I'm going to make sure you don't overdo it again." He began crossing out dances. "How much would you like to dance tonight?"

"I'd like to dance with you," they said quietly. "Other than that, I'd be fine with not dancing at all."

Emrys looked pleased. He wrote his name down and crossed off the rest of the dances.

"I'm not sure that's allowed," Torquil said. "Won't people say something if I only dance one time? And won't people comment on the fact that my card is completely crossed out?"

"Do you want to dance more than once?"

"Not really."

"Then it doesn't matter what people think. Besides, I don't intend to leave your side tonight, unless you ask me to."

Torquil grinned. "That sounds nice. I've missed you."

Emrys stared at them for a long moment and Torquil thought he might be about to pull them into a kiss. He cleared his throat and said, "I've missed you, too." Then he glanced up, grimaced again, and said, "My mother's coming."

Torquil set down their punch and turned, attempting to prepare themself for Mrs. Wrenwhistle's inevitable coldness. She was probably annoyed that her son was spending yet another evening with them. They wondered if he'd be able to convince her to allow it again.

However, they were surprised when Mrs. Wrenwhistle greeted them cheerfully and told them how well they looked. "Did you ask Wynnie about the decorations?" she said in a teasing voice. "You match!"

Torquil sent a confused look at Emrys before smiling at her. "Thank you. I wish I could take credit for such forward-thinking. But the credit must all go to my grandmother. She gifted me with this outfit just this afternoon."

Mrs. Wrenwhistle's smile widened. "Ah, yes! I just spoke to your grandmother, dear Mrs. Pimpernel. I think her time abroad has done wonders for her complexion. She looks ten years younger! It was such a surprise to see her tonight. I had no idea she had returned to town."

"She just returned," Torquil said.

"And you two have reunited. It is just wonderful," she said with a sigh. "What a delightful Christmas gift, is it not, Emrys?"

Emrys blinked at his mother, clearly as surprised as Torquil by her change in attitude. "Indeed it is."

"Well, I won't keep you. I hope you both enjoy the party."

Torquil watched her walk away. "It appears my grandmother was right."

"Hm?"

"She predicted your mother would like me better now that I'm to inherit."

Emrys grunted. "That explains a great deal. That's the most she's spoken to me in days."

"Why is she angry with you?"

Emrys blushed and poured Torquil another glass of punch. "Come on, let's go sit down."

They took a settee to the side of the ballroom. Torquil was kept surprisingly busy, speaking to well wishers who wanted to comment on how nice it was to see their grandmother in town, how well she looked, and how well they looked.

Anytime someone asked for their dance card, Emrys would lean forward and say in an apologetic tone, "I'm afraid the councilmember is very fatigued this evening. I've recommended they rest a bit tonight." To Torquil's surprise, people seemed to take this explanation in stride, although there were a number of knowing looks and amused smiles in response.

They couldn't deny that they were grateful for his intervention. The dizziness and the headache had yet to subside since the bath. And while the pleasant conversations were a nice change, it made Torquil uncomfortable to be greeted with politeness only because their grandmother had deemed them worthy.

Their discomfort must have shown because after an hour or so, Emrys leaned closer and asked, "Are you all right?"

"Just tired." They looked up at him. "How could you tell? I'm wearing powder. Supposedly it covers up the circles under my eyes."

Emrys' lips pinched. "I noticed the powder. But I can tell when you're not feeling well. Your posture changes. And the set of your mouth. Perhaps you should go to bed."

They shook their head and then quickly regretted it, placing a hand over their forehead. "No, I don't wish to go to bed. I like sitting here with you."

"You're not well, Torquil."

They sighed in exasperation. "It's these people. They're suddenly so pleased to see me, after over a month of ignoring me."

"It's because of your grandmother."

"I know. I don't like it." They gave a huff. "I *do* appreciate what this means for other people like me. This means that everything I've been trying to do is finally working and we're on our way to better acceptance. But…it's still hard."

Emrys took Torquil's hand in his. "I know."

Torquil looked up at him, wishing the room would spin a little less as they did so. "One thing I am grateful for is that you've never looked at me differently. My grandmother said that would be the case."

Emrys smiled softly. "I think you knocked me off my feet the first time you grinned down at me from that rickety ladder of yours. I've yet to regain my footing."

Torquil beamed, trying to ignore the pang in their chest at the thought of losing this friendship when Emrys married. They swallowed. "I rather think you've been holding me steady ever since you helped me hang that sign."

Emrys murmured their name and leaned closer. Torquil put a hand on his chest. "Too public," they whispered. They clenched the fabric in their fingers though, despite themself. "But I wish we could."

Emrys gave them a long look. "Perhaps…perhaps we can do that interview I promised you."

Torquil blinked in surprise at the change of topic. "What, *now*?"

"Why not?"

"Because we're at a party!"

He smiled and patted his pocket again. "You're tired and not feeling well, but you won't go to bed. You get a little paler every time someone comes up to talk about how nice it is to see your grandmother. Why don't we dance, I'll give you my interview, and then I can escort you home? This way you can feel better about any so-called obligations you've decided you have to fulfill and I will feel better knowing you're resting."

They looked wearily around the room. "I hate to leave early. It's Roger and Wyndham's first time hosting."

"It won't be their last time hosting. And of all people, they will understand."

Torquil saw his point. "All right."

Emrys helped them to their feet and they stumbled a little as the dizziness increased. Emrys' forehead creased in concern. "Perhaps I should just take you home now."

"No. One dance. Our interview. Just like you suggested."

He sighed, patted his pocket again, and then nodded. "Right." He led them onto the dance floor and they took their places.

Thankfully, the dance was a slower one that allowed for better conversation. Not a waltz, unfortunately, but not a country dance either. Torquil was grateful and wondered if Emrys had planned it out that way.

"Now, what is your first question?"

Torquil considered as they stepped to the side in the first movement. As their head spun, they focused hard on the interview. "Will you be spending your time in the country like your older brother, or splitting your time between the country and town, like your younger brother?"

Emrys smiled. "I was just discussing this with a friend of mine. I think I could enjoy the quiet of the country with the right person. Although I do like being in town. So I imagine splitting my time would be best."

Torquil was uneasy with the way Emrys looked at them as he said *the right person*. They swiftly tried to think of another question. "Do you want children?"

"My mother wants me to have them."

"That's not what I asked."

"I thought you were going to ask me what I'm looking for in a spouse," Emrys said, grinning. "You have yet to ask me about *that*."

"We'll get there," Torquil said miserably, already dreading the answer. "I want to make sure my readers have their curiosity satisfied in all matters pertaining to you."

"The interview will be that long?"

Torquil chuckled. "Just answer the question."

"I like children. But I'd much prefer to focus all of my attention on my spouse."

Torquil considered their next question as they moved through the next step. "Do you intend to pursue a profession, as your father and brother have done? Or do you intend to be more of a gentleman of leisure?"

Emrys frowned in concentration. "I'm not sure I'd be much suited for any occupation." He gave a seductive smile. "I'm *very* good at leisure, though."

Torquil couldn't help but laugh. "Yes, I'm well aware of your skills in that arena. It is known that you are attracted to people of every gender. Do you have any particular preferences?"

Emrys shook his head. "I prefer specific people. But not because of their gender."

"I see. And…er…how do you imagine married life to be for you?"

Emrys smiled as his expression turned thoughtful. "I've been thinking about the quiet moments for the most part. Taking a leisurely walk around the estate in the mornings. Enjoying a quiet breakfast, side by side. Sitting curled up in front of the fire and talking about everything, or nothing at all. Falling into bed with someone after a long day and seeing the face I love most smiling back at me."

Torquil suddenly realized that this had been a very, very terrible idea. They were listening to Emrys expound on his ideal life and it sounded most dreadfully perfect. How were they going to print any of this? And how on earth were they going to stand by and watch Emrys walk away from them and into this perfect life with someone else? Their head pounded even more and they tripped a little as the room continued to spin.

"Torquil?" Emrys said, catching them by their elbow. "Are you all right? Do you need to sit down?"

Torquil looked up at him and saw the worry in his eyes. Emrys was their dearest friend. He was spending his entire Christmas night keeping Torquil company, instead of the myriad of suitors his mother would have preferred he speak to. He *deserved* this perfect life, even if Torquil wasn't a part of it. The least they could do was help him obtain it. They forced a smile and shook their head, trying to ignore how much the motion made them feel sick. "Not at all. Just clumsy." They found their footing and continued the dance, swallowing down the feeling of nausea and focusing on Emrys' face to combat the dizziness that was making it progressively more difficult to see.

"Now then, the question all of London wants to know: what are you looking for in a spouse?"

Emrys' face relaxed into a grin. "Now that is a question I have been asking myself for over a month, Councilmember. Let me think." He put upon a thoughtful expression, so comically fake that Torquil laughed. Emrys' grin widened. "I would like someone I can talk to. Someone who makes me laugh. If I can make them laugh, that would be very nice," he added, with a meaningful look that Torquil tried very hard not to read into.

"I am not the cleverest of men, as I'm sure you know. And I've spent a great deal of my life feeling rather foolish around people who *are* clever, like my brother. But there are some people, certain people, who are very clever and never make me feel foolish. They make me..." Emrys licked his lips, his eyes focused in a way that suggested he was truly thinking through his answer, and not merely pretending to. "I want someone who makes me feel comfortable being me. Who never expects anything other than what I am. But I don't mind that they're— *if* they're different. I like that I—that is, I'd like to be with someone who uses words I don't understand. Or who dazzles all of London with their wit."

Torquil felt as though their ears were roaring. Was it the party? Was it their dizziness? Or was it the fact that Emrys was most definitely describing *them*?

Emrys went on. "I would like someone who is kind. I would never have expected to want someone who wants to change the world, but I've found that to be a very attractive quality."

The room wasn't just spinning; it was tilted on its axis and Torquil had no idea how to put it to rights.

"I'd like someone I can take care of—and I don't mind if that's a lesson we have to learn together. I've been told all my life that I have many responsibilities, but I've found myself rather enjoying the idea of being responsible for someone I care about." Emrys looked at them with such earnestness that Torquil stumbled again. Emrys caught them easily. He smiled and ran a hand through their curls, not bothering to continue dancing. "And if they could have beautiful hazel eyes, a cheeky grin, and unruly curls, that would help a great deal."

"Emrys," Torquil whispered.

"Torquil," Emrys said. "I've met the most eligible people in London, according to my mother. People who look perfect when described in your column. But I've known who I want. I've known for a long time, even when I didn't *know* that I knew." He frowned. "If that makes sense. I want *you*, Torquil. I've wanted you since the moment you led me up the stairs that first night we met. I knew when I felt your magic for the first time that I couldn't be happy with anyone else. I want you, and I want you all to myself. I love you, Torquil."

The tears and the dizziness were making it impossible to see his face but Torquil leaned up to kiss him with the familiarity of years. Emrys' arm slid around their waist and they gripped his lapel as they kissed him. The room was still spinning, but it hardly mattered as long as Emrys was holding them steady at the center of the motion.

They broke off the kiss and whispered, "I never want to lose you, Emrys. I can't tell you how long I've wanted to hear you say all of that."

Emrys smiled and kissed them again. "Perhaps we should sit down for the rest of the set?"

"Yes," they breathed. "I think I have enough for my interview."

Emrys chuckled. "Good."

As they stepped out of his embrace, the quiet of the moment fell away. The floor seemed to lurch under them as their vision blurred even more. Emrys murmured their name, and then shouted it, as everything went black.

CHAPTER 43

EMRYS

EMRYS HAD NEVER FELT such immense relief in his life, kissing Torquil in the middle of a crowded room for the first time, holding each other tight without a care about who was watching. It was nearly as addictive as feeling their magic.

"Perhaps we should sit down for the rest of the set?" he asked. He didn't want to let go of them, but also recognized that they were somewhat in the way of the people who were still trying to dance.

"Yes, I think I have enough for my interview," Torquil agreed.

"Good," Emrys said as he released them in favor of taking their hand, encouraging them in the direction of the settee they'd been using before. His free hand pressed carefully against his pocket, and he realized that they'd been so caught up in the moment that he'd completely forgotten to actually present the ring and ask the question.

"Torquil," he began quietly, hoping that everything he'd already said was enough of a prelude to him getting down on one knee. He also hoped Aveline was watching from wherever she was, because here was his public declaration.

Emrys' cheek-achingly large grin was gone in an instant as their eyes locked when he turned around. Torquil's face had gone ashen and unfocused.

"Torquil!" Emrys reached for them as they stumbled once again, terror slicing through him as they went fully limp in his arms. He hauled them up so that he was supporting their weight, but the awkward angle made it difficult to do much more. Everyone around them had stopped to watch what was happening, though none of them seemed eager to step in and help.

It was Wyndham who finally came bursting through the crowd as the music stopped, with Roger close behind.

"We'll get them upstairs," his brother said calmly before he turned to Roger. "Bid everyone good night. The party is over."

Emrys was able to get Torquil into his arms with Wyndham's help, and he was directed up the stairs to one of the guest rooms. It wasn't until the door shut behind him that Emrys realized how grateful he was for the quiet. He carefully placed Torquil on the bed and sat by their hip in one swift motion, leaning over them to start removing the delicate silver accessory from their hair and the pin from their cravat. He discarded them on the bed with little care.

"What happened?" Wyndham asked as he stepped closer to touch the back of his fingers against Torquil's cheek first, then their forehead.

"I don't know," Emrys told him, voice shaking nearly as much as his hands as he struggled to untie the strip of fabric around Torquil's neck. "One moment everything was fine, and the next they...they—"

"Allow me," Wyndham said, placing himself between Emrys and Torquil so that there was no room for argument. Emrys got up and began pacing the room, one hand on his forehead and the other fisted on his hip. He watched Wyndham gently remove the cravat and set it aside, working next on the buttons of their waistcoat. "Perhaps they became overheated. These fabrics are quite thick."

"I asked them to marry me," Emrys blurted. "I-I mean, I tried to."

Wyndham's fingers slowed briefly on his task. "You proposed," he said, dragging the words out, "and then they collapsed?"

Emrys gave him a hard look as he went to the other side of the bed, sitting beside Torquil again as he pushed the hair back from their face.

"I'm not sure if that's terribly funny or incredibly romantic," Wyndham mused. "Help me get them out of these clothes."

They worked until Torquil was down to their underclothes and tucked securely under the blankets. All of the jostling roused Torquil enough to attempt a weak protest, but not much else. It took everything Emrys had in him not to crawl onto the bed and hold them in his arms. He settled for a chair so he could sit close by and hold their hand instead. Some of the color had already returned to Torquil's face, and their features were relaxed, which Emrys hoped was a positive sign.

There was a knock at the door. Wyndham opened it to reveal a very concerned Roger wringing his hands together.

"Everyone is gone," he said quietly as he came into the room. "I sent for the apothecary. Mrs. Pimpernel also insisted on sending her doctor to come and check on them. I barely managed to get her out the door, but I thought it was better for there to be as few people as possible crowding around them." Roger frowned as he stepped closer to the bed. "Is there anything else I can do?"

"Not at the moment," Wyndham said. "It appears that rest is helping."

"They've been so very tired," Roger agreed.

Guilt sat like a jagged stone in Emrys' stomach as he thought back over the previous couple of hours.

Torquil had seemed unsteady on their feet the entire evening. He had done what he could, keeping them from dancing with anyone else, but theirs was the dance that caused the catastrophe for everyone to witness.

"It's my fault," Emrys said miserably. "They refused to let me take them home, so I suggested we compromise and share one dance first."

Roger made a sympathetic noise. "Stubborn little creature, are they not?"

"There's more to the story," Wyndham added. "Go on."

Emrys sighed and lifted their joint hands so he could rest his forehead against them, squeezing his eyes shut for a moment.

"And then I told them I love them," he muttered. Roger gasped loudly. Emrys returned Torquil's hand to the bed and sat back so he could reach into his pocket. He pulled out the tiny velvet box and stared at it. "I was just about to give them this, when…" he shrugged.

"My vote is that he's sent poor Torquil into shock," Wyndham said.

"Oh, stop that," Roger admonished, flapping a dismissive hand at his husband. "Do not listen to him, Emrys. We happen to know that Torquil was quite hopeful for such an outcome."

"I did not mean it in a negative way," Wyndham countered defensively. "How often do those silly romances end with someone fainting into someone else's arms after a confession of undying love? It's practically the done thing."

Emrys furrowed his brows at his brother. "You read romance novels?" he asked skeptically.

Roger's face brightened as he started to reply, but Wyndham cut him off by placing a hand over his mouth. "Nobody asked you," he warned quietly before removing his hand and placing a kiss on his forehead. "Come along, let's give them some privacy until the apothecary arrives." Wyndham guided Roger from the room and shut the door behind them.

Emrys turned his attention back to Torquil. He let out a slow sigh and picked their hand up again, pressing his lips to the back of it before resting his cheek on the spot after.

"I do love you," he whispered. "I'm sorry it took me so long to realize it. Perhaps if I had told you how I felt long before now, it wouldn't have been so overwhelming." He brought the ring box up between them and turned it slowly back and forth between his fingertips. "This is yours, whenever you're ready, just as I have been yours and will continue to be yours for as long as you'll have me."

WHEN THE DOCTOR arrived sometime later, Emrys answered each question about what happened that night as carefully as he could. His heart ached as Torquil spoke through the haze of their tired mind to reveal the severity of the symptoms they'd had over the previous weeks. The doctor and apothecary eventually agreed that Torquil was suffering from extreme fatigue.

It was more than what one good night of sleep could resolve, but the more rest they could get, the better. The apothecary left a tincture to aid in that endeavor, while the doctor recommended that Emrys take great care in making sure Torquil's diet improved and that they worked to reduce stress. Emrys thanked them both and was secretly grateful to have medical professionals on his side to guarantee that Torquil started eating and sleeping more.

Only after Emrys made certain that Torquil was still resting comfortably did he give in to his own stomach's complaints. He was unwilling to disturb Torquil with the sounds of clanking silverware, so he slipped out in search of whichever room the smells of breakfast were wafting from.

He found Wyndham and Roger sitting rather close together in front of a roaring fire in the sitting room. Several platters of food were situated on the low table in front of them, and Roger was busy with a bite of something as Wyndham sipped his tea. The scene made something squeeze in Emrys' chest. He cleared his throat before he stepped into the room, not wanting to disturb their quiet moment. They looked up in unison, and Roger's forehead wrinkled.

"How are they?" he asked.

"Still resting," Emrys said, wandering a bit closer. "They'll likely be out the remainder of the day after the tincture the apothecary had them drink. It was so strong it nearly had *my* eyes watering."

"Come and have some breakfast," Roger offered. "Would you like tea?"

"Please," Emrys said with a small nod. He accepted the cup Roger poured for him as he sat in the same chair he'd occupied several nights prior when he had come to speak to Wyndham. "Thank you for allowing me to stay the night. I'm certain I would have just been back pounding on your door otherwise."

"Understandably," Wyndham said over the rim of his own cup.

Upon closer inspection, Emrys realized that his hosts looked as though they had not gotten much sleep, either. They were Torquil's friends. Of course they would have been restless and worried about them, too.

Emrys filled a plate and joined in their easy silence. He could not remember the last time he'd been in the same room with Wyndham for so long without making some sort of heated exchange or snide comment, or at least had one sitting ready on his tongue. His first instinct was to try and think of something, but then he realized he did not know why.

His brother had been the only one to come running in his time of need the night before. He had offered to help with Torquil's clothes when he'd been unable to do it himself. He had been vulnerable when Emrys came to speak with him. He'd been excessively kind to Torquil, offering them accessories and fashionable outfits to wear, giving them a certain social confidence that had, in hindsight, been one of the many changes that had happened to make Emrys see that he could never possibly live without them.

"I suppose this makes us friends by association," he said finally, a small grin curving the corner of his mouth.

Wyndham blinked and stared at nothing for a moment, before his gaze shifted slowly until their eyes met. He took another long sip of tea before he looked away, one brow arching slightly.

"How lovely," Roger said brightly as he put a hand on Wyndham's leg and patted it affectionately. "It's always nice to have more friends. Even if they are already family." When neither brother had anything to add, Roger moved on. "We were thinking of going to collect some of Torquil's belongings. Perhaps a change of clothes that would make them more comfortable while they recover. Of course we're happy to have them stay here as long as they need."

"I can go," Emrys offered. The selection was limited, but he knew which clothes would likely be their choice. He always seemed to find them wearing the same ones, especially when they were working on something for their column. "The *Tribune*," Emrys said suddenly. "Another one is due out tomorrow."

"Oh dear, that's right," Roger said. "I don't believe they've ever missed a publication."

"I don't know the first thing about working the press," Emrys added regretfully. In all the years he'd been walking past the enormous machine, he had never stopped to learn anything about it. "And who knows where they are with their notes. I would hate to disturb them just to ask what they intended to write."

Wyndham huffed out a laugh. "Certainly you already know," he drawled.

Emrys thought for a moment before he realized.

"Oh," he said. "I suppose I do."

"Were you able to give them the ring?" Roger asked quietly, as though someone might overhear.

Emrys shook his head. "Not yet. It's not official."

"Not until we read about it in the *Tribune*, it's not," Wyndham said. "I daresay few know that better than we do." He and Roger exchanged a look, and Roger grinned up at him fondly as he adjusted his spectacles.

"What are you suggesting? That I somehow learn how to use the press *and* publish my own engagement announcement before Torquil has even accepted?"

"It cannot be that difficult," Roger reasoned with a one-shouldered shrug. "Let's all go and have a look, shall we?"

"You can't be serious," Emrys protested. "I am not a writer!" The thought of his own, far simpler words taking the place of Torquil's eloquent ones made him cringe. He would never forgive himself if he forced readers away or upset Torquil somehow. This was their career. He knew how much it meant to them.

Wyndham got to his feet after setting his empty cup on the table.

"I say it's the perfect plan. Do you not think Torquil would be more upset to miss a publication than to have someone else release it? All of London is waiting to hear this exclusive interview they've been promised, in any case. We are simply going to give everyone what they want. And I do mean *everyone*," he said pointedly.

TORQUIL'S TRIBUNE

Greetings, radiant readers,

Our illustrious editor is not currently present so instead of our usual gossip, we wish to present an exclusive interview with Mr. Emrys Wrenwhistle. This interview was given to Councilmember Pimpernel-Smith during the Wrenwhistle Christmas Party. We are publishing the gentleman's words here with his permission.

When asked whether he prefers country life or city life, Mr. Wrenwhistle said that he imagines he will split his time between both, like his younger brother. "I could enjoy the quiet of the country with the right person, although I do like being in town," he said.

He admits that while he likes children, he does not see himself adopting any, unless his spouse wishes for it.

Mr. Wrenwhistle anticipates being a gentleman of leisure rather than one of occupation. "However," he hastened to explain, "I would be very open to having a spouse who pursues an occupation. Not that my spouse would need to have one if they didn't want one, of course."

We are sure this will come as a relief to many readers. Even more of a relief will be his explanation of his usual preferences. "As I said the other night, I prefer specific people, but not because of their gender."

Mr. Wrenwhistle went on to explain his ideal life: "How did I put it? I'm most drawn to the quiet parts of married life. Leisurely morning walks. Quiet meals together. Idle conversations. And with the right person, a little companionable silence can be very…companionable. And, of course, going to bed at the end of a long day and seeing the face I love most on the pillow beside me."

We did not realize Mr. Wrenwhistle was such a romantic at heart, although it certainly does explain why the gentleman has remained so elusive of the marriage state.

For the final question, what are you looking for in a spouse, we anticipated Mr. Wrenwhistle to have a variety of vague and impossible attributes. We were surprised, therefore, when he had a very specific list in mind: "I would like someone I can talk to. Someone who makes me laugh. I want someone who does not make me feel foolish, even if they are very clever. I'd like someone I can take care of—and I don't mind if that's a lesson we learn together. And I have come to learn that I prefer large hazel eyes, cheeky grins, and unruly curls."

Naturally, after this response, we inquired if there was someone the gentleman had in mind. He smiled and replied, "Yes, there is. Councilmember Pimpernel-Smith." We asked if a proposal has been made, to which Mr. Wrenwhistle admitted, "Not yet. Although I intend to propose at the earliest opportunity. I could never have imagined falling in love with someone as much as I love Torquil."

While we are sure this response will break many a heart, today's humble writer admits that they are quite pleased and, candidly, it's about time.

Hopefully our editor will return soon and report on the results of the proposal. In the meantime, we wish everyone a Happy Christmas and a Wonderful New Year.

Your Temporary Writer,
Sal Bailey

CHAPTER 44
TORQUIL

TORQUIL AWOKE IN A STRANGE BED, feeling groggy and confused. Their grandmother was sitting in a chair beside the bed, reading. As they shifted under the covers, she looked up from her book.

"Oh, thank goodness," she murmured. "You're awake."

"What happened?" they asked, attempting to take stock of the unfamiliar space.

"You collapsed at the Christmas party."

It all came rushing back: their grandmother joining them, all of the whispers, the sudden friendliness, the memory of the headache and the dizziness, and Emrys—*Emrys*—Emrys crossing out their dance card, dancing with them, giving the interview, telling them he loved them. Their hand flew to their mouth. "Where's Emrys?"

They grabbed the coverlet to push it aside, but Leonora stayed them with a hand on their wrist. "He's not here, dear. His brother said he'd be back this afternoon."

"Where is he?" they asked again, almost desperately. "I have to talk to him."

There were too many things unsaid. They hadn't told him they loved him back. And then they'd collapsed? What must he think of them?

"Wait," they said slowly. "How long have I been…out?"

"Over a day and a half now."

"*What?*" They frantically did some mental calculations. "It isn't the 27th, is it?"

"Yes, that's right, it's—"

"Oh no," they groaned. "The *Tribune*. I've never missed a publication since I started it."

"I'm sure your public will forgive you," she said soothingly.

They knew she was right, but that wasn't the point. They rubbed their eyes, grateful that, if nothing else, the dizziness appeared to be truly gone. They realized that the room was not the same one they'd changed in on Christmas Day. "Where am I?" they said, almost afraid to know the answer.

"We're in Wyndham and Roger's home. I'd better send word that you're awake. They've all been quite worried about you." She stepped out of the room.

Torquil let out a long breath into the quiet. They had collapsed just after Emrys had declared his love, they'd been sleeping for over a day in Wyndham and Roger's home, and now they'd missed a publication of the *Tribune* for the first time in nearly five years of running it.

After what felt like an impossibly long time, Leonora returned with Wyndham and Roger in tow.

"Thank goodness you're all right," Roger said, beaming at them. "We've been so worried."

"How do you feel?" Wyndham said, stepping close and pressing the backs of his fingers against Torquil's cheek and then forehead, making them feel like a small child.

"Drowsy. But mostly confused. I collapsed and I've been here for nearly two full days? And I missed the *Tribune*," they added miserably.

"Any more dizziness or headache?" Wyndham asked.

"No, thankfully."

Roger visibly relaxed and Leonora gave an audible sigh of relief.

"Good," Wyndham said. He gave Torquil a sly look. "Would you prefer the good news or the bad news first?"

"You cannot possibly be serious. What sort of a question is that?"

When Wyndham merely smiled, Torquil sighed and muttered. "Bad news, please."

"Right," Wyndham said, adopting a business-like tone. "The Council convened this morning."

A feeling of icy cold dread filled the pit of Torquil's stomach. "Without me?" they asked, their mouth feeling dry. "Have I been removed?"

Wyndham frowned in confusion. "My word, no! It isn't as bad as all *that*. No, we met and they've formally agreed to adopt the rubric we put forth."

"Oh," Torquil said, letting out a sigh of relief. "Wait, how is that bad—"

"The bad news is that they've also agreed that changes need to be made to the Council as a whole." At Torquil's confused look, Wyndham went on, "A sort of overhaul."

"I've been referring to it as spring cleaning," Roger added helpfully.

"But what does that mean?"

Wyndham sat down in the chair Leonora had vacated. "My grandmother has decided to step down from her position."

Torquil sat up in shock. "What? Why?"

Wyndham leaned forward and gently pushed Torquil back down. "If you exhaust yourself too quickly, I'll make you sleep before I tell you the rest."

"You think I could possibly sleep with this little information?"

Wyndham smiled. "My grandmother thinks that it's time for some new faces and fresh perspectives. With all of these rubrics we have to launch, she was concerned that the Council was holding itself back. She is stepping down, and so is Councilmember Williams."

"And so is Gibbs," Roger chimed in. "Although that could hardly be categorized as bad news."

"Why are they stepping down?"

"Williams agreed with Grandmother, surprisingly enough. And Gibbs dislikes just about everyone other than Williams, so he left in something of a huff. Roger's father is taking over the head of the human side, considering he's the only remaining senior member. Applewood and Cricket are going to wait until you return to put it to a vote on who will lead the fae side. The Council is going to reconvene some-time in January to discuss how we wish to go about adding new members."

Wyndham exchanged a look with Roger before he continued, "And they all agreed that we should add two additional fae-human members, and that you should be the head of your group when that happens."

Torquil's eyes widened. "Is that still the bad news?"

Wyndham laughed. "No, that's the end of the bad news."

"The bad news was Iris leaving," Roger explained.

"She's rather looking forward to the rest, I think," Leonora put in. "We've been making plans about what sort of havoc we can wreak together." She chuckled. "Never underestimate the power of two old biddies with nothing to do."

Wyndham gave an amused huff. "No one would dare call either of you biddies, and I'm personally familiar with the havoc my grand-mother can wreak alone, much less with a friend."

"Oh my," Roger said. "You two will be a force to be reckoned with."

"That's the plan," she told him with a wink.

"Is there more?" Torquil asked warily, still trying to make sense of it all.

"Yes, actually. It's about the *Tribune*."

Torquil bit their lip. "I can't believe I missed a publication."

"Well," Wyndham said, drawing out the word.

Torquil looked up. "Oh, did…did Sal publish it without me?" They felt some relief at that, tinged with the pain of their paper moving on without them.

"Yes…but she had some help. You see, we went to the press building yesterday, Roger, Emrys, and I, to try and figure it out ourselves."

Torquil sat up again. "You *what*?"

Wyndham cocked an eyebrow.

Torquil huffed and laid back down, crossing their arms over their chest.

"We quickly came to the conclusion that not a single one of us has the slightest clue how to run the blasted thing."

A laugh escaped before Torquil could help it. Wyndham gave them another mock serious look and Torquil covered their mouth with their hand, attempting to hide the surprised grin that was still on their face.

"I don't think I've given you nearly enough credit now that I know how much work you've put into that every week."

"Twice!" Roger said. "They do it twice a week! Imagine!"

"Anyway, we were at it for hours. Couldn't figure it out at all. Roger and I left before Emrys did. He was determined that you shouldn't miss it."

Torquil smiled behind their hand. "He was?"

"Yes. And we went back this morning to try again, but the press was already running. The friend of yours—Sal, was it?—apparently came in, woke Emrys up from where he'd fallen asleep, and proceeded to shame us all with her knowledge."

"The *Tribune* went out after all?" they asked, sitting upright.

"Torquil, really!"

"You cannot possibly expect me to take this news lying down!"

Wyndham sighed. "Fine. But after this conversation, you're to get some more rest. Understand?"

"I've done nothing *but* rest," they protested. When he simply stared at them expectantly, they grumbled, "Fine."

"Now, as to your question: yes, the *Tribune* went out after all. It would appear there was an exclusive interview that had been promised to the public and we were all quite sure you wouldn't want to keep them waiting."

The whole world seemed to freeze for a moment. "What?" Torquil whispered as they clenched the coverlet in their hands.

Wyndham grinned and reached into his pocket, pulling out a familiar-looking piece of paper with a flourish. Torquil snatched it out of his hands and read.

And read.

And read.

I intend to propose at the earliest opportunity. I would never have imagined falling in love with someone as much as I love Torquil.

Torquil read with a hand over their mouth, hardly believing the words. Emrys had publicly declared his intentions to propose to them? More than that, he had publicly declared his love?

Tears began to fall down their cheeks. They hadn't ruined everything by collapsing at precisely the wrong moment. He still loved them. He still wanted them. Thoughts that they hadn't yet managed to process on the night of the party finally began to crowd their brain. They wouldn't have to stand by and watch Emrys marry someone else. Emrys was going to marry *them*! They weren't losing him. They'd get to spend quiet mornings with him, sit in front of the fire next to him, go to bed with him, and wake up next to him.

Someone sniffed and they looked up to see Roger and Leonora with equally teary expressions. Wyndham remained dry-eyed, but his smile was fond as he watched Torquil.

Torquil swallowed. "This went out to—"

"To all of London," Wyndham said. "Yes."

"Iris says it's going to be the wedding event of the Season!" Roger said.

"That was your wedding," Torquil said, wiping their face.

Wyndham laughed. "I think you might have us beat, Torquil."

And then a new voice came from outside the room. "They're awake?"

Hurried footsteps came down the hall and the door was pushed open to reveal Emrys. His face broke into the widest smile they had ever seen. "Torquil!" he breathed.

CHAPTER 45

EMRYS

A LEOPARDESS FROM the Royal Menagerie could've been prowling the room and Emrys would not have noticed, for all he could see was Torquil. They looked so small there in the middle of the bed, pillows fluffed behind them, blankets piled high to fight off the slight chill coming from the large windows. Outside, a thick fog had settled over London, trapping an intense cold that coated every surface with hoarfrost and left Emrys' nose and cheeks red after his arduous journey back from the press building on foot.

His smile faltered as he sat beside Torquil on the mattress, both hands coming up to hold their face. Belatedly, he realized that his fingers had also succumbed to the intense winter weather, even through the thick leather gloves he'd been wearing. Torquil did not seem to mind as they leaned into his touch and covered his hands with their own.

"Why are you crying?" he asked softly. "Are you still feeling poorly?"

Torquil gave a weak, wet laugh. "I feel wonderful."

Emrys sighed in relief, his smile returning.

"You put your interview in the *Tribune*."

Torquil raised a copy between them. Emrys took the paper, his eyes skimming the words only briefly. He'd become intimately familiar with each of them as he worked to compile what he believed was a fair and honest recount of the conversation they'd had while they danced. He had little interest in reading over them again anytime soon.

"Now I know why you sign each one the way that you do," he said. "You deserve every bit of that respect and admiration."

"Did you not think that I did before?" Torquil chaffed.

"Of course I did," Emrys urged. "But I hadn't the faintest idea of what it takes for you to publish each one, and with such little assistance. Sal and I shared a very thorough conversation about it. It's no wonder your body gave out on you."

Torquil looked down and away, but Emrys caught their chin with a curled finger and lifted their face back up, searching their eyes.

"You are truly remarkable," he told them. "And I want to kiss you so badly right now."

"Everyone out," came Wyndham's voice from somewhere behind him. Emrys looked over his shoulder just in time to see his brother leading the way for the small number of people gathered in the room. Torquil's grandmother was followed out by two servants, and Roger was the one to pull the door shut with a very triumphant look on his face.

Emrys rolled his eyes good-naturedly as he turned back around, prepared to use his light touch still lingering under Torquil's chin to close the distance between them.

He did not get the chance.

Torquil's lips were against his before he had time to shut his eyes, their arms wrapping tightly around his neck. Emrys chuckled and moved his hand to the back of their head instead, fingers combing into their dark curls as he brought his other arm around their waist.

He was grateful for the opportunity to replace the memory of the last time Torquil was in his arms.

"I love you," Torquil whispered against the corner of his mouth before placing another kiss there. "I cannot tell you how sorry I am that I was unable to say it before."

"I'm just glad you're saying it now," Emrys reassured them. He twirled his fingertips against their nape in languid circles. "I was so worried about you."

"I know."

"I meant what I said," he went on, kissing them again. "I do want someone I can take care of. Although I must admit, I was thinking of something much less terrifying than you falling unconscious in my arms when I said it."

Torquil laughed and hid their face against Emrys' shoulder.

"But, should it happen again, I always want to be the one to catch you."

Torquil went very still. Emrys slipped carefully out of their arms and reached into his pocket. The velvet box was there as it had been all the other times he'd checked. He hoped this would be the last time.

He pulled it out and glanced up to catch Torquil's expression. They were watching intently, eyebrows bunching together as they brought a hand up to cover their mouth.

"You do not have to wear it all the time." He paused. "You do not have to wear it at all, if you choose not to. But the larger stones have been passed down in my family for many generations. They belong to me now."

Emrys paused again as he lifted the lid, revealing the ring inside.

Something like a sob came from the back of Torquil's throat. More tears pooled in their eyes, one blink away from rolling down their face.

"I would be honored if you would accept this as a token of my affections for you, my commitment to you, and my promise to always look after you and provide for you." A small grin quirked the corner of his lips. "Even though it seems you'll not be needing my help in looking after yourself financially now."

Torquil let out a pitiful little laugh, forcing their tears free. "No," they agreed, "I suppose not."

Emrys used a bent knuckle to wipe their cheeks dry before he carefully removed the ring from the box and held it up between them.

"Dance with me at our wedding, Torquil, and I'll never ask you to dance in public again," he whispered.

Torquil nodded and held their hand out. Emrys placed the ring on their finger—a perfect fit, imagine—and scarcely had time to let out a shaky breath before Torquil was kissing him again.

◊

HOURS LATER, after Emrys had threatened to close his eyes for only a moment or two, he awoke with a start at the purposeful knocking coming from the closed door. He breathed in deeply as he blinked hard a few times, taking in the vaguely familiar surroundings.

"Come in," he called out. The door opened just slightly at first, then wider as the man he recognized as Roger's valet stepped into the room.

"Messrs. Wrenwhistle are requesting your presence downstairs."

Emrys grunted as he sat up more fully, supporting his weight on one arm.

"Only me?"

"Both of you," the valet clarified before he turned and left.

Emrys peered down at the figure beside him, tucked under so many layers that they were hardly recognizable. He frowned a bit at the thought of waking them, and even more at the thought of getting them out of bed when they were clearly still needing the rest. However, he knew that neither of them could remain in Wyndham and Roger's guest room forever. Perhaps it was time to discuss what happened next.

"Torquil," he said gently, rubbing his hand along their arm where it was hidden beneath the coverlet. Emrys smiled to himself as he watched them wake, as he had done countless times before when it had been time for him to take his leave after falling asleep in their bed. He waited for the way they arched their back first, then unbent their knees, all before their eyes ever opened.

"Hm?" they asked.

"It seems we are being summoned. Do you think you're well enough?"

Their forehead wrinkled, eyes still closed. "Where?"

"Downstairs. That's all the information I've been given."

Torquil sighed. "Can they not come and speak with us here again? I'm so very comfortable."

Emrys chuckled. "Apparently not."

There was a stretch of silence that made Emrys want to forget the request, as well. All he really wanted was to fall back into place behind Torquil and keep them warm and safe and unbothered for as long as possible.

"Very well," Torquil said finally.

After helping them dress in the clothes he'd brought back for them, Emrys kept a supportive hand on Torquil's back as they ventured out into the hallway. They were met by a servant who guided them down the stairs and past the sitting room Emrys expected to be taken to. It was only after they passed through the next doorway that he realized why they'd been called down.

"Good evening!" Roger said cheerfully from his place next to Wyndham where they stood behind their chairs. "So glad you were both able to join us."

The dining table was set in such a way that Emrys wasn't quite sure if they'd been aiming for spectacularly formal or intimate and casual. He couldn't help but laugh at the way such a combination represented them as a couple so accurately; different and yet somehow, it worked.

The flatware was new enough that it reflected the candlelight like a mirror. The bouquets of red roses and white winter flowers were sprouting from vases that looked like something his mother would've been wildly jealous of. But as he pulled a chair out for Torquil, he recognized that the serving bowls and platters were full of nothing but comfort foods. There were several kinds of soup and even more types of bread to go with them, two styles of potatoes, various meats and cheeses. The far end of the table was covered with cut fruit and pastries.

"Quite the feast," Emrys said as they took their seats. It was an absurd amount of food for four people. "What's the occasion?"

Wyndham arched an eyebrow. "We did promise you a dinner," he said mildly. "This seemed like the perfect opportunity to make it happen."

"And we wanted to be the first ones to *officially* congratulate you on your engagement, of course," Roger added.

The lingering look he held in Torquil's direction intensified until Torquil seemed to realize something. They blushed and glanced at their lap before they nodded and held their hand up to show the ring, lips pressed together to try and hide their grin. Emrys' magic danced in his chest at the sight.

"Good heavens," Roger gasped. "It's gorgeous."

Emrys' first thought was to make some smart remark about the pity of Roger falling for the second-best Wrenwhistle brother, but he quickly swallowed it down. Instead, he said, "Speaking of gorgeous, you'd best never let Mother near those vases if you want to keep them. I can already hear her subtly asking where you got them with that *face* she gets." He gave his brother a look. "You know the one I'm speaking of."

Wyndham rolled his eyes as he scooped some potatoes onto Roger's plate.

"Envy so thinly veiled with forced curiosity that she just ends up looking sour," he agreed. "Her signature expression."

Emrys laughed as he ladled soup out for Torquil and then himself. "Quite."

The conversation continued in an easy, amiable way as they began to eat. Roger offered some advice on navigating the adventure Emrys and Torquil were about to begin with Mrs. Wrenwhistle while planning their wedding. Torquil had more questions about how their experience had gone with trying to operate the press, which brought about several rounds of laughter. In turn, they all had more questions about Torquil's grandmother and what her sudden reappearance meant for their future.

"Oh, I almost forgot," Roger said after they'd all started on a second helping of the generous meal. "Everyone must have some of the salad." He got up and waved one of the servants away as he reached for the serving bowl himself. Emrys eyed him suspiciously as he began to put some on each plate.

"That's an awfully big smile over a salad," he said. "Is there something special about it?" Upon inspection, it looked rather average. Wyndham groaned into his wine glass and swallowed quickly, setting it down by his plate.

"Do not say it," he warned his husband, but was thoroughly ignored.

"It was made with *love*," Roger beamed. Wyndham pressed his fingers to his forehead as Roger continued. "Wyn and I decided to learn how to make it ourselves while we were on our honeymoon. It's been surprisingly enjoyable. Although, I admit I am still learning to be proficient with the necessary equipment."

Emrys made a valiant effort to contain his reaction, truly. But when he made the mistake of looking at Torquil just as they snorted out a laugh, all hope was lost. The two of them carried on until Emrys' stomach ached and Torquil was wiping tears from their eyes.

Torquil apologized for the both of them, which was the right thing to do, of course, especially considering how embarrassed Roger looked after realizing what he'd said. Emrys could not find it within himself to be sorry, though, because he realized that watching Torquil laugh so hard was another of life's quiet moments. It was a fleeting, inconsequential pause in time, and Emrys hoped for thousands more just like it.

TORQUIL'S TRIBUNE

Greetings, fair folk and handsome humans,

As the year draws to a close, we bid goodbye to several things.

First, we must bid goodbye to the Council for Fae & Human Magical Relations as we know it. This farewell is bittersweet to many. Both Councilmember Iris Wrenwhistle and Councilmember Williams have helmed their sides of the Council for years. However, they are both stepping down to pave the way for the next generation. They have both offered to be available in an advisory capacity if needed, especially as the Council proceeds to bring their numbers back up. Of note, Councilmember Gibbs is also stepping down, and we are thankful for all of his service over the years.

We must also bid goodbye to our esteemed editor, Torquil Pimpernel-Smith, as this will be their final edition of the *Tribune*. We appreciate all of the congratulations and well wishes on the matter of their betrothal to Mr. Emrys Wrenwhistle. Contrary to what many seem to believe, our editor is not stepping down because of this betrothal. This decision was one they have deliberated for months. They wish to focus on their work on the

Council and their social obligations. Taking their place will be Miss Sal Bailey, who has assisted the *Tribune* since its first publication. We are confident she will proceed with a good ear for gossip and a good pen for news. The *Tribune* will keep its name.

With the closing of one year, we greet a new one. And with that, we have a number of items to welcome:

First, as all of London now knows, Mr. Emrys Wrenwhistle and Councilmember Pimpernel-Smith are to be married. Many anticipate their union to be the wedding of the Season. The Wrenwhistle family has announced that a spring date is being decided.

Mrs. Pimpernel returned to London just in time for the Christmas holiday and reunited with her grandchild. We are sure everyone is pleased by the happy reunion.

The Council will be very busy as they fill their recently vacated positions on top of launching their new rubrics. In addition to these tasks, they have announced an intention to better understand the blending of multiple magic systems, as seen at the Wrenwhistle-Barnes wedding, as well as fae-human magic. More information will be forthcoming on what these studies will entail.

With several weddings on the horizon, as well as some promising-looking couples, we do not expect the rest of the Season to be at all quiet. Thank you for remaining our loyal readers and we wish you all a happy New Year.

Your esteemed editor,
Torquil Pimpernel-Smith

EPILOGUE
TORQUIL

"Emrys, do please pay attention," Mrs. Wrenwhistle said. "We have a great deal to go over. Now, do you prefer ivory or cream for your invitations?"

Emrys pulled Torquil closer where they were nestled beside him on the sofa. "I cannot see the difference," he said.

She sighed and turned to Leonora. "I wish one of my children would be less difficult when it comes to wedding planning."

Leonora chuckled and took the two invitation samples. "It is so very hard to focus when one is in love, my dear."

Torquil was relieved she'd joined them for the wedding planning. They weren't sure they'd have been able to handle all of Mrs. Wrenwhistle's newly acquired respect for them otherwise.

Mrs. Wrenwhistle seemed to debate whether or not to argue the point. Instead, she held up what appeared to be an endless list. "I suppose we can decide on invitations later. Now, for the cake, I have a baker in mind who did a marvelous job for Wynnie's wedding. I will write to him to visit with some samples."

"There's no need," Emrys said. "We'd like ginger cake."

She blinked at her son. "Emrys, you really ought to sample them before you decide."

He frowned. "We'd like ginger cake," he repeated stubbornly.

Torquil decided to take pity on her. They reached up to hold the hand that was wrapped around their shoulders and smiled. "He knows ginger cake is my favorite."

Leonora's expression softened. Mrs. Wrenwhistle seemed relieved by the explanation, although it was evident that she was confused as to how Emrys knew this with such confidence. She bent over her list and wrote a note. "Are you sure you wouldn't like a sample of some others?"

"Quite sure," Emrys said.

She returned to her list. "Now, for flowers, I have a number of florists I like to use." She gave her son a beady expression. "Do you have a preferred flower as well?"

"Not that I'm aware of," Emrys said, glancing at Torquil.

Torquil beamed at Mrs. Wrenwhistle, relieved to have an olive branch to offer. "We'd be pleased to see whatever florists you have in mind."

She relaxed and made another note. "Now, for the wedding spell. You don't need to decide anything yet, but it would be helpful if you start—"

"We're going to do a fire spell," Emrys said.

Everyone turned to look at him and Torquil fought the smile threatening to take over.

"A fire spell?" Mrs. Wrenwhistle said. "Are you sure? That's not the safest opt—"

"Torquil casts very good fire spells," Emrys said in a dogged tone.

Leonora patted Mrs. Wrenwhistle's shoulder. "I'm sure we can find a way to make it safe."

"I can do other spells too, you know," Torquil whispered to Emrys.

"But I like watching you do the fire spell," he whispered back. He frowned suddenly. "Unless you'd prefer—"

Torquil squeezed his hand. "I'm happy to do whatever you'd like."

Emrys grinned and slid a finger over Torquil's jaw. "That's a promising statement."

Torquil laughed. "Have I ever been reluctant to do anything you wished?"

"The opera, skating, dinner parties—"

"All right, all right," they said hastily. "I thought we were discussing more enjoyable activities. And you know perfectly well I had good reason."

Emrys kissed them in response.

Mrs. Wrenwhistle tsked. "Could you two please focus on the task at hand? Wynnie and Roger weren't this distracted."

Torquil forebore explaining that Wyndham and Roger were not actually in love yet during the wedding planning. They didn't think anyone else knew that.

They apologized and attempted to pay better attention.

"Do you have any ideas for clothing you'd like to have made? We could put you two in matching outfits, or coordinating ones? You could do what Wynnie did and pick each other's—"

"Torquil looks very good in dark colors," Emrys said matter-of-factly. Torquil glanced up at him, suspecting that he was very proud of having so much knowledge.

Mrs. Wrenwhistle rubbed the bridge of her nose. "This is a spring wedding, Emrys. We cannot possibly have dark clothing for a spring wedding!"

"Why not?"

"Because it isn't done!"

"What colors are we permitted then?"

As she began to list a huge variety of colors, shades, and patterns, Torquil attempted to stifle the yawn that escaped them.

Emrys' attention whipped around instantly. "Are you too tired?" he asked, his hold on their shoulders tightening.

"Only a little. Nothing to worry about."

"I'm sorry, Mother. I think I'd better take Torquil to go lie down now."

"Emrys!" his mother wailed. "You cannot possibly mean to leave now? We've barely started."

"Torquil is still recovering," he said, pulling them to their feet. "They need to rest. I'll take them up to my room and we can discuss this matter more after dinner."

Torquil blushed, but couldn't deny they were pleased.

Leonora chuckled again. "Ah, well that kind of rest has been known to be particularly effective."

Emrys looked smug as he led Torquil out of the room and up the stairs. Torquil barely had time to look around when they were tugged into a room and pressed against the door after it closed. Emrys leaned into their space and kissed them gently.

"I feel a little guilty," Torquil admitted. "Your mother was so excited and we've cut all of her fun short."

Emrys rolled his eyes as he began undressing them. "Nonsense. We're merely extending her fun. So if you think about it, I was doing her a kindness."

"Very magnanimous of you."

Emrys gave them his baffled grin as he freed them of their cravat, waistcoat, and shirt, before steering them toward the bed. Torquil took advantage of the opportunity to look around the room they'd spent so long imagining.

In some ways, it was even grander than expected. A handful of potted plants sunned in the window. There was a large oil painting over the fireplace of a young boy and his horse that looked frighteningly like Emrys. Upon second glance, it *was* Emrys. They would have to tease him about that later.

Despite the splendor, Torquil decided that the room suited him perfectly. It was still welcoming and warm, if not a little disheveled in the places that nobody cared to look too closely, and felt distinctly like the man it belonged to. The bed was enormous, covered with more pillows of various sizes than they had ever seen in one place. There were layers of thick blankets, topped appropriately with a fashionable coverlet, upon which they promptly climbed onto their knees and began returning the favor of undressing him.

"Your bed is quite nice," they said.

"I cannot properly express how relieved I am that we'll never have to sleep in that creaky old thing of yours ever again."

"Yes. Instead of me sharing my bed with you, now you shall have to share yours with me."

"I don't know," Emrys said in a mock pensive tone as his cravat slid from his neck with a soft *fwip*. "As my mother has so kindly pointed out *multiple* times, you now outrank me when it comes to social status. Perhaps I ought to be moving in with you."

Torquil rolled their eyes. "Don't be silly. I wouldn't have the slightest idea what to do if I were head of the household. You've been brought up to it."

"Well, I suppose I can take the responsibility," Emrys said, his smile teasing. He slid his waistcoat off as soon as Torquil finished unbuttoning it. "Provided you allow me to really take care of you."

"I suppose you'll have to show me how you intend to do that before I agree." Torquil eased Emrys' shirt out of his trousers slowly, looking up at him through their eyelashes so that he would have no doubt as to their meaning.

Emrys' grin widened and he tugged the shirt off completely.

Torquil turned their attention to Emrys' trouser buttons. "Now on the subject of wedding clothes, do you think your mother would mind if I told her that I would prefer you to wear those riding breeches? They're quite the best thing I've ever seen you wear."

Emrys laughed as he slid off his trousers and joined them on the bed, gently pushing them to their back. "I think she might have some concerns."

"Whatever for?"

"They're not particularly formal," he said, kissing their neck.

They hummed thoughtfully. "That's a shame. You still owe me an appearance in them, you know."

"I will wear them as often as you'd like." He paused. "In fact, I ought to buy you some."

"Oh! I have some! My grandmother bought me a whole suit."

Emrys' expression turned gleeful. "Did she indeed? Then I daresay you owe me an appearance as well."

"I hadn't the heart to tell her that I can't ride."

Emrys grinned wickedly as he leaned over them. "I have evidence to the contrary."

Torquil laughed and wrapped their arms around his neck. "Ah, yes. Silly of me to forget."

Emrys closed the distance and kissed them deeply. "Can I still call you my precocious wordsmith, even when you're not writing the *Tribune?*"

"I wish you would. You can call me whatever you like. Besides, Sal and I agreed that I can continue to submit news on an anonymous basis."

"Good," Emrys said warmly. "I wish you didn't have to give it up at all."

They cupped his cheek. "So do I. But the Council will keep me busy. And I have you. That's enough. More than enough, really."

As Emrys resumed kissing their cheek, their neck, their shoulders, Torquil closed their eyes and reached out with their magic. Emrys' magic filled the room, crowding the corners, rippling the curtains, and eddying gently around them both on the bed. Emrys groaned as his magic reacted to Torquil's, becoming more vibrant. It was like a crescendo of music, or the way the sun feels on a perfect summer day.

"I will never get tired of feeling your magic," he said.

"I wish I could do more fae magic without the human spells first," they admitted.

"Don't," he said, pausing to frown at them. "I wouldn't change anything about you, or your magic. It's perfect. You're perfect."

And as Emrys kissed them once more, Torquil settled into Emrys' arms, Emrys' magic, and the love that felt like home, and kissed him back.

The End

&

WANT to find out what happens next? Read Keelan's story in book 3 in *Fae & Human Relations: Shade Spells with Strangers !*

NOTE FROM THE AUTHORS

Greetings, radiant readers,

This story came about when Shannon was exploring nature (her greatest muse) and she was struck with an idea for book 2. It wasn't long before we were off and writing.

We had so much fun building this story together. It allowed us to revisit our beloved world from *Breeze Spells and Bridegrooms* but explore a totally different story, one full of friendship, tenderness, and healing.

We hope you enjoyed Emrys and Torquil's story as much as we enjoyed writing it.

Your winsome writers,
Sarah & Shannon

ACKNOWLEDGMENTS

This book wouldn't be possible without our network of support. Thank you to our alpha readers, Ashley, Alexis, Katie, and LelEe. Thank you to our beta readers, Anna, Sebastian, Tessa, Becca, and Meg. Thank you to our amazing editor, Mackenzie! Thank you to our wonderful proof-reader, Ashley. Thank you to our fantastic narrator, Matt. Thank you to all of our cheerleaders who encouraged us throughout the process, especially John and Ashley.

Cover art: Caras Alexandra
Editor: Mackenzie Walton
Proofreader: Ashley Scout

ALSO BY SARAH WALLACE
& S.O. CALLAHAN

FAE & HUMAN RELATIONS

Breeze Spells and Bridegrooms - Book 1

Shade Spells with Strangers - Book 3

Cleaning Spells Before Courtship - Book 4

Protections Spells for Press Buildings - Free to all of Sarah's newsletter subscribers!

POWELL PRODUCTIONS

When I'm in Your Arms

Together on Parade

ALSO BY SARAH WALLACE

Letters to Half Moon Street

One Good Turn

The Education of Pip

Dear Bartleby

The Spellmaster of Tutting-on-Cress

The Viscount Says Yes

Free to Sarah's newsletter subscribers:

The Glamour Spell of Rose Talbot

ALSO BY S.O. CALLAHAN

Fella Enchanted

Fella Ever After

ABOUT SARAH WALLACE

Sarah Wallace lives in Florida with their cat, more books than she has time to read, a large collection of classic movies, and an apartment full of plants that are surviving against all odds. They only read books that end happily.

ABOUT S.O. CALLAHAN

S.O. Callahan has always been fond of sweet things, namely chocolate and love stories. When she's not writing or reading, she enjoys baking, visiting National Parks and Historic Sites, and traveling with her husband. They live in Chicago and have two very spoiled cats named Ozzy and Beau.

www.ingramcontent.com/pod-product-compliance
Lightning Source LLC
Chambersburg PA
CBHW030551020726
47494CB00005B/1571